THE RED KIMONO

The Red Kimono

JAN MORRILL

The University of Arkansas Press
Fayetteville
2013

ISBN-10: 1-55728-994-8
ISBN-13: 978-1-55728-994-0

17 16 15 14 13   5 4 3 2 1

Designed by Liz Lester

⊖ The paper used in this publication meets the minimum requirements
of the American National Standard for Permanence of Paper for
Printed Library Materials Z39.48-1984.

LIBRARY OF CONGRESS CATALOGING-IN-PUBLICATION DATA

Morrill, Jan, 1958–
The Red Kimono / Jan Morrill.
pages   cm
Includes bibliographical references.
ISBN-13: 978-1-55728-994-0 (casebound : alk. paper)
ISBN-10: 1-55728-994-8
1. Japanese American families—California—Fiction. 2. Japanese Americans—
Evacuation and relocation, 1942–1945—Fiction. 3. World War, 1939–1945—Japanese
Americans—Fiction. 4. World War, 1939–1945—Concentration camps—California—
Fiction. 5. World War, 1939–1945—California—Fiction. I. Title.
PS3613.O75545R43   2013
813'.6—dc23
2012041617

Dedicated to my mother
and the entire Sasaki family,
from whom I learned the meaning of *gaman*.

ACKNOWLEDGMENTS

Certainly without the history of my family, this story might never have been told. My mother, her family, and her family's family were Japanese American internees at Tule Lake, California, Topaz, Utah, and Jerome and Rohwer in Arkansas. From their history came the themes of judgment and isolation.

When my parents married, only thirteen years after the end of World War II, I know my father's family must have expressed concerns that he married a Japanese woman. But upon getting to know my mother, they accepted her with open arms and loved all of us equally. From my father's family came the theme of acceptance without regard to color.

Countless people have helped me on my long and winding path to publication. Without their help and support, this book might not have been written.

First, thank you to Dusty Richards and Velda Brotherton, the tireless mentors who began the Northwest Arkansas Writers Workshop more than twenty-five years ago. What a blessing it was for me when, six years ago, I found the group of writers they lead. Though I've always loved writing, it was on the first night I attended this critique group that I became a serious writer. For most of those six years, the fine writers of the NWA Writers Workshop patiently listened to and critiqued what was to become *The Red Kimono*, five pages each week. Their encouragement and motivation were invaluable to me.

Within that group, I also found a sisterhood—four women who have given me encouragement, critique, and friendship. Writers are a different breed and, although each of us in the Sisterhood of the Traveling Pen is different from the other, our love of writing bonds us. With Linda Apple, Pamela Foster, Patty Stith, and Ruth Weeks by my side, I have never felt alone on this journey.

Thank you to Ned Downie for his insights into growing up in southeast Arkansas and for originally suggesting I submit my manuscript to the University of Arkansas Press, though it took me two years to listen to him. Thanks also to Rosalie Gould, former mayor of McGehee, Arkansas, who graciously shared her incredible knowledge of the internment camps with me. She later donated her priceless collection of documents and artwork that she had let me peruse to the Butler Center for Arkansas Studies in Little Rock.

Two words from author Jodi Thomas changed my writing life: "What if?" From this simple question, dozens of scenes and characters have been born in *The Red Kimono*.

Thank you to my beta readers, Marsha Davis, Paul Stevenson, and Maria Tillman, for sharing critique on the story as a whole. They told me what worked—the scenes that made them laugh and cry. As important and perhaps more difficult, they told me what didn't work. For that honesty, I am very grateful. A very special thank you to Maria White Tillman and her sister, Starlina "Nina" White Reid, who, as neighbors during my childhood, were the inspiration for Jubie Lee Franklin.

A huge thank you to everyone at the University of Arkansas Press. I couldn't have been happier when Lawrence Malley requested a meeting upon receiving my query, and I have thoroughly enjoyed working with Melissa King, Brian King, and everyone involved as we prepared my manuscript for publication. A special thank you to Pamela Hill, whose sharp eyes and focus helped me polish and fine-tune my manuscript.

In everything I do, I save the best for last. So, my biggest thank you goes to my husband, Stephen, for his patience, faith, persistence, and love; for carrying my load for so many years; for listening to my readings time after time after time; for trying to understand why I edited and re-edited and re-edited. I said earlier that writers are a different breed. So are their spouses.

THE RED KIMONO

CHAPTER 1
Sachi

BERKELEY, CALIFORNIA
DECEMBER 7, 1941

Like a broken record, Papa's words played over and over in Sachi's mind.

Remember gaman, Sachi-chan. You must learn to be patient.

But Christmas was still eighteen days away. Be patient? It was like asking a bird not to fly.

She tiptoed into her parents' room and opened the closet door, hoping the squeaking hinges wouldn't tattle on her. Pushing her mother's dresses apart, she searched for presents that might be hidden in the darkness. Anticipation tingled in her hands. Finally, Papa had convinced Mama it would be okay to celebrate Christmas. Sachi giggled to herself, imagining how he must have convinced her.

"Sumiko, I doubt Buddha would have a concern with our family celebrating Christmas the way most Americans do."

Pearl Harbor . . . surprise attack . . . sinking ships . . .

Sachi jolted at the words that came from a scratchy voice that drifted in from the living room radio and grabbed at Mama's dresses to regain her balance. Several fell from their hangers.

Taro is in Pearl Harbor!

Images of her oldest brother, surrounded by explosions, flashed in front of her eyes as she ran downstairs. "Papa! Mama!"

Her parents sat across from each other in front of the radio, so still they reminded Sachi of mannequins she'd seen in department store windows. All that moved was the steam rising from the hot tea on the table next to Papa. His eyes looked strange as he stared at it.

She couldn't even see Mama's eyes. Her hands covered her face.

Words blared from the radio and pounded like a drum against the tension in the room.

"The surprise attack has destroyed a large part of the US Naval Fleet, and the casualties are expected to be in the thousands."

"Papa? Is Taro-nisan okay?"

The lines in Papa's brow softened and his eyes crinkled the way they always did when he smiled. He reached for her, and she ran to him and snuggled into his arms, comforted by the scent of cedar incense on his shirt.

"We have not been able to reach him yet," he said.

Mama rose from her chair and walked to the window, her eyes sad and dark, her lips pressed tight. She straightened and took a deep breath. "Michio. She must practice. Sachiko, please go and practice your dance lessons now. Mrs. Thompson will be here soon."

Sachi slumped in Papa's lap and whined. "Dance lessons? On Sunday?"

"Do not argue," her mother scolded. "Mrs. Thompson was kind enough to let you make up the lesson you missed last week."

Mama turned away, but not soon enough. Sachi could see the look in her eyes, too. Sadness. Anger. Fear. It reminded Sachi of how she felt all those times kids at school called her slant eyes. She had wanted to cry. But there was no way she'd let them see a single tear fall. Not one, single tear.

Papa gave Sachi a squeeze, tugged at her ponytail, then nudged her off his lap. "Do not argue with your mother. Off to practice your dance now."

Stomping out of the living room, she grumbled to herself, quite upset that she couldn't stay and listen to the news about Pearl Harbor.

She trudged up the stairs. At her bedroom doorway, she paused to look at the three dolls on her shelf. Silent and still in red kimonos that shimmered in the light from her window, their black eyes spoke what their lips could not.

> *A porcelain mask*
> *Though inside, a heart beats strong*
> *Even the oak breaks.*

She acknowledged their whispers and shuffled toward the dance room. Mama might as well have banished her to a prison cell.

The scent of incense from the Buddhist altar near the doorway greeted her when she entered. A row of tall windows cast a dance of sunlight and shadows onto the dark wood floor and reflected off mirrors that lined the opposite wall. She had to admit she loved the room. It was practice she didn't like.

She walked to the tall, teak bureau in the corner of the room and opened the doors to flowered kimonos and colorful obis, the belts that were sometimes tied so tightly she could hardly breathe. She touched the cool, smooth silk of each kimono and pulled out her two favorites. Which should she wear? The blue one with yellow monarchs? Or the pink one with white cranes? Mrs. Thompson once said her favorite color was blue, so Sachi dressed in the blue kimono with butterflies.

Her teacher was a pretty *Nisei*—second generation—whose dark eyes sparkled when she smiled. She wore her long, shiny black hair pulled back in a barrette. In June, she'd married a navy captain, just before he had left for Pearl Harbor.

Sachi remembered the afternoon she'd overheard Mama telling Papa she couldn't believe her teacher had married outside her race. "I do not care that she loves him," she'd said. "Love is not everything."

But Sachi liked Capt. Gregory Thompson from the day she first met him, so what difference did it make if he was not Japanese? Besides, the way he and Mrs. Thompson looked at each other reminded her of those pictures in books that ended "happily ever after."

Dressed in her kimono, she stood in front of the mirrored wall and posed like her geisha dolls, mimicking the expressions on their porcelain faces. Perhaps her hair was black like the dolls. Perhaps she had eyes the color and shape of theirs. But no matter how she tried, she could not copy the gentle grace of the dolls.

A leaf rattled against her window, shivering before falling from its branch. Mesmerized, she watched it spin, swirl, dance in the wind, until the doorbell rang and she ran to the front door.

Mama and Mrs. Thompson stood in the hall, holding hands and nodding quietly to each other. She strained to hear their hushed conversation.

"No, I haven't had any news from my husband," Mrs. Thompson whispered. "Have you heard from Taro?"

Mama shook her head.

They embraced, then parted.

Sachi bowed to her teacher. *"Konnichiwa."*

Mrs. Thompson smiled, but Sachi noticed the tear glistening at the corner of her eye.

"*Konnichiwa*, Sachi-chan," her teacher replied. "Are you ready for your lesson?" She wiped her cheek.

"Yes. I just finished practicing, even though today I didn't really want to."

Mama scolded. "Sachi-chan!"

Sachi shrugged her shoulders. "Well, it *is* Sunday, and . . . and, you know, because of the attack. But Mama said I had to make up last week's lesson."

"Your mama is right. You must practice, even if there are times you don't want to practice," Mrs. Thompson said. "Shall we go to the dance room now?"

The lesson began like every other. Her teacher pulled a record from its jacket and placed it on the phonograph; hands so graceful, even as she lifted the needle and placed it on the spinning album. The crackling sound before the music always reminded Sachi of rain pattering against leaves on the ground.

She took her place in front of the mirrored wall. When the music started, she began her dance. Her small hands peeked through long, colorful sleeves that drifted like kites in a breeze as she dipped and rose to the music.

Such a fine dance she performed! In fact, why did she even need to practice? She was sure her teacher would be proud. But Mrs. Thompson wasn't watching. Instead, she stared at the album turning on the phonograph.

Sachi slowed her movements, then stopped. "Mrs. Thompson? Are you okay?"

Her teacher's eyes darted back to Sachi. "Oh, of course. I'm sorry."

"Are you thinking about Captain Thompson?" Sachi hesitated. "Is he also at Pearl Harbor, like Taro-nisan?"

"Yes. He is."

"I am worried, too. I hope they are both okay." Such useless words, but what else could she say?

Mrs. Thompson blinked and smiled, but her lips quivered. "Are you ready to continue dancing?" she asked. Something in her eyes still looked far away.

Wasn't there anything Sachi could do to make it better? Maybe if she danced better than ever before, Mrs. Thompson's sparkle would return. "I will do my best for you today."

"That would make me happy—"

The front door slammed, rattling the windows. Startled, Sachi bolted to the hallway to see what all the noise was about. She rolled her eyes. "It's just Nobu."

Yelling echoed from the kitchen.

"Yeah, I heard about the attack," Nobu shouted, breathless. "You want to know how I found out?"

Papa spoke next, so quietly Sachi couldn't hear all of his words. "Nobu! Calm . . . do not speak . . . mother . . . like that."

But her brother's voice boomed louder. "A bunch of us were shooting baskets at Danny's. Then, his dad comes out and tells us Pearl Harbor's been attacked."

She couldn't remember ever hearing Nobu yell at Mama and Papa like that.

His voice cracked as he continued. "Then, Danny's dad looked at Kazu and me and said, 'You Japs get home now.' Don't you get it? He called us Japs in front of our friends."

"Nobu!" Papa never raised his voice.

Nobu's voice broke again. "How can you two just sit there? And what about Taro? Have you heard from him? He could be dead for all we know."

Mama scolded. "How dare you speak of your brother like that!"

Papa spoke, calm again. "Sumiko. Nobu. Stop. We must be patient. I am sure we will hear news soon."

Nobu pounded up the stairs.

At the top of the stairway, he stopped and glared at Sachi. "What are you looking at?" he asked, his face nearly as red as the varsity letterman jacket he wore. Taro had given it to him for safekeeping before he left for Hawaii. Nobu wore it everywhere, even though Sachi always teased him that it was too big. But something in Nobu's eyes warned it was best not to tease this time.

He wiped his bangs from his eyes. Or maybe it was a tear.

"You okay?" she asked.

"Just leave me alone." He pushed past her and ran into his bedroom. When he slammed the door, the windows rattled again.

CHAPTER 2

Sachi

DECEMBER 8, 1941

Sachi stood in front of the mirror and watched her reflection as she slowly buttoned her sweater. Moving close, she opened her eyes wide. What would they look like if they weren't slanted? Would the world look different through big, round eyes? And what if they were blue? Would she see colors differently?

Mama called from the kitchen. "Sachi-chan, hurry up. You will be late for school."

I don't want to go to school today. I have a stomachache.

Excuses never worked with her mother. She huffed and picked up her books from her desk. "I'm coming. I'm coming." She stomped downstairs to the kitchen, where she found Mama and Papa sitting at the table. The radio in the living room was turned up.

"Morning," she said, pulling a chair from the table. "Where's Nobu?"

Papa turned to the next page in his newspaper. "He already left for school."

"Why is the radio so loud?" Sachi asked.

Folding his paper neatly, Papa placed it next to his tea. "President Roosevelt is going to speak this morning."

Mama's slippers swished as she walked to the stove.

"What is he going to talk about?" Sachi asked, twirling her chopsticks through her fingers.

"We will have to wait and see," Papa said. "Are you ready for school?"

"Yes." She placed her chopsticks beside the bowl Mama placed in front of her. "Papa, can we go to the park after school today?" She cringed, waiting. Like always, Mama would probably answer for Papa.

No park today. Sachi must practice her dance and o-koto lessons.

But her father answered first. "The park? Perhaps. We will see."

"Seems like forever since we've been," she said between bites of rice.

Mama clucked her tongue. "Sachiko, do not speak with your mouth full. And no park today. You must practice your *o-koto* lessons after school."

There they were. The words she had dreaded.

"But Papa said we could." Her retort drew a stern look from her father.

Mama leaned against the counter, arms crossed. "How do you expect to master the o-koto if you do not practice?"

"I know," she grumbled. *Who cares if I don't master the o-koto? Maybe I'd rather master the swing set.*

Mama checked the clock above the stove. "Time to go, Sachiko. Get your coat."

Papa stood. "I have a meeting at the bank this morning, Sumiko. I will take her to school. Hurry and get your coat, Sachi."

She huffed as she put on her coat and stomped to the car. Though happy Papa was taking her instead of Mama, she couldn't help pouting about the way the morning had gone. Why was Mama so grouchy?

They pulled out of the driveway. Maybe Papa would drive slowly past the pretty Christmas trees in the front windows of the houses on Peralta Street. That would cheer her up.

One by one, she judged the tree in the window of each house they passed. Some had ornaments of different colors. Some had all green. Some had all red. She had to admit, none were as pretty as the tree in her window. But even Christmas decorations couldn't make her forget how angry Mama made her sometimes, making her practice, practice, practice.

They stopped at the intersection. Gilman Street was always busy and speeding cars zipped back and forth, replacing the parade of pretty lights and Christmas trees on Peralta. Papa glanced back and forth, waiting to turn left.

"Why does Mama make me practice all the time?" Sachi asked. "All of my friends get to play whenever they want to."

He stopped watching cars and raised an eyebrow at her. "*All* of your friends?"

"Well . . . maybe not all," she whispered.

Not even Papa is on my side.

Papa didn't say a word as he turned onto Gilman. It wasn't unusual for him to be quiet, but this kind of quiet made her stomach feel as tangled up as her hair when Mama combed it. When at last he smiled and patted her knee, all the tangles went away.

"Sachi-chan, practicing your music and dance is your mother's way of making sure you do not forget your Japanese heritage. Remember *gaman,* Sachi-chan. Patience. You will understand when you are older." He turned into the parking lot of Jefferson Elementary.

She looked away and out the window, rolling her eyes. She was tired of trying to be patient.

The school yard was crowded with kids waiting for the bell to ring and she hesitated to get out of the car.

They will all stare at me.

That was just one of the things she hated about fourth grade. She also didn't like homework. Or grumpy Mrs. Nelson. And she especially didn't like the kids who called her slant-eyes.

One day at lunch, a boy in her class had moved to another table, all because she sat next to him. Snickers and whispers had surrounded her like moths around a porch light. She left her tray on the table and ran out of the cafeteria. But those moths flitted and batted around her all the way out.

Even the oak breaks.

She opened the car door.

"Are you not forgetting something?" Papa leaned over and turned his cheek toward her.

Why did he always have to do that? She glanced around to see if anybody was looking, then gave him a quick peck on the cheek—even if he was on Mama's side. "Bye, Papa."

"Bye-bye. Have a good day."

She shrugged. How good a day could it be with all the kids teasing her about being Japanese?

She hugged her satchel and hurried toward the red brick building, wishing to be anywhere but walking past those kids. She hurried through the crowd of stares and whispers. Those darned moths flitted around her again, especially when a boy—probably a sixth-grader—yelled at her.

"Hey, girl! You look just like the enemy."

The enemy? What did he mean by that? Ignore it! Ignore it! All she wanted to do was hide. Where were all the other Japanese girls? Hiding?

When the bell rang, she ran to class. That morning, running had nothing to do with being late and everything to do with being Japanese.

The rest of the day she tried to concentrate. But thinking about looking like the enemy took up so much space in her head, it left no room for learning. She might as well have stayed home.

At last, she watched the minute hand of the classroom clock click to the six, and the last bell of the day rang. Three-thirty at last. She grabbed her satchel and hurried out the door, hoping to get out ahead of everyone else.

Once outside, she searched for Papa's car and found him at the end of the parking lot. Running to the car as fast as she could, she'd quit counting how many times someone called her Jap that day.

"How was your day?" Papa asked.

She wanted to let everything that happened burst out, but how could she tell him without hurting his feelings? She didn't want him to feel like the enemy. So, instead, she mumbled, "Fine."

"Oh?" he replied. "It does not sound like your day was fine. Is everything okay?"

She leaned her head against the door. "Yes, Papa. It's just that I hate math."

He smiled, and they were quiet the rest of the way home.

When Papa pulled into the driveway, she said, "I wish you didn't have to go back to work today." She wasn't in the mood to hear Mama tell her to practice again.

"I'll be back in about an hour," he replied. "Perhaps we can take a quick walk to the park then."

"Really?" She kissed him on the cheek, smiled, and rushed inside. With her whole day being ruined by that sixth-grader, she was especially excited about going to the park.

"Mama, I'm home," she called, tossing her books onto the kitchen table.

"Go upstairs and change your clothes. Then, please start your practice," Mama called from the living room.

Okay. Okay. Okay!

She knelt beside the long wooden harp on the floor of the dance room. Gently plucking its strings, she tried to mimic the music playing on the record album. Her fingers began to throb, but Mama said she needed to toughen them up. But today she didn't feel like it. She lifted the needle and turned off the phonograph.

Maybe listening to different music would help. She turned on the radio and heard a saxophone blaring "In the Mood." She giggled. How would *that* sound on the o-koto?

As the trombones entered the arrangement, a voice broke in:

We now interrupt our regular programming to repeat in its entirety, the speech made earlier today by President Roosevelt to the Congress.

"December 7th, 1941—a date which will live in infamy—the United States of America was suddenly and deliberately attacked by naval and air forces of the Empire of Japan . . . "

The words the boy yelled at school echoed in her head again.

Hey girl! You look like the enemy!

She ran to the mirrors on the wall and forced herself to look at her reflection. She touched her black hair. Stared at her slanted eyes.

The Japanese attacked the United States.

I do look like the enemy.

She couldn't stand to look anymore and ran back to her o-koto.

" . . . I ask that the Congress declare that since the unprovoked and dastardly attack by Japan on Sunday, December 7th, 1941, a state of war has existed between the United States and the Japanese Empire."

As her eyes began to burn, she watched the strings of her instrument blur. A tear fell onto the o-koto.

The wood floor in the hall creaked with the flip-flop of Papa's *zoris*. He stopped in the doorway. "Sachi-chan, I've been thinking. Perhaps we should not go to the park today," he said softly.

She rose from her knees. "Because the Japanese attacked Pearl Harbor?"

Papa looked into her eyes. "Why are you crying?"

"I heard the President . . . on the radio." She wiped her nose. "Why did we do it, Papa? Now, President Roosevelt says the United States is at war with the Japanese. And what about Taro-nisan? Was he one of the ones who attacked Pearl Harbor?"

Her father's eyes widened. "What? *We* did not attack Pearl Harbor."

"But . . . today a boy told me . . . I look like . . . the enemy. Are we the enemy?" she asked.

He shook his head. "Sachi-chan—"

"You said Mama wants me to remember my Japanese heritage. And the kids at school tease me. Today they called me the enemy."

He sighed. "Your heritage is Japanese, but you are American. It does not matter who you look like. *We* did not attack Pearl Harbor, the Japanese did—those who live in Japan. Do you understand the difference?"

She thought about how different she felt when she was with her Caucasian friends. They had dolls to play with. She did not. She took dance and o-koto lessons. They did not. She prayed at a Buddhist altar. They had no altars in their homes.

Papa held her face in his hands. "It is very important—especially now—that you remember we are Americans."

"But I *feel* Japanese. I *feel* different from my American friends."

"Every person in America is different. This is a land of immigrants—people from all over the world, all mixed together in one country."

"What are immigrants?"

He pulled his wallet from his back pocket. "I have a picture to show you," he said, opening the worn leather. "This is Mama, the day I first saw her."

"Why is she standing by that ship?"

"She had just arrived in the United States from Hiroshima, Japan. It was 1920. The year before, I had finished college and came to America to live with my older brother, your Uncle Hisao." Papa smiled. "After a year of courting Mama by mail, I was very happy to see her at last." He brushed a strand of hair from Sachi's face. "So, you see, your mama and I are immigrants. We emigrated—came from Japan. But you and your brothers were born here. You are citizens."

"So, I am an American?"

"Yes."

"And Taro-nisan didn't attack Pearl Harbor?"

"No! And you must never ask that question again. Taro is working in the sugar cane fields in Hawaii. He would not attack Pearl Harbor. He is an *American*."

Something still didn't make sense. "Papa, if Taro—if we—didn't do anything wrong, why can't we go to the park?"

"Perhaps later. Let us wait and see." He stared at the altar, where cedar-scented smoke drifted into the air, then disappeared.

CHAPTER 3

Nobu

DECEMBER 12, 1941

The clang of the school bell echoed in the emptying halls of Berkeley High School. Nobu couldn't put off going to class any longer. Hissing whispers hushed when he entered homeroom, but his classmates' stares followed him to his seat.

He gritted his teeth, trying to heed Papa's words. *Do not cause trouble. Nothing to draw attention.*

Papa had even used *that* word again after the Feds confiscated Japanese customers' accounts and he lost his job at the bank.

Gaman. One can endure more than one thinks.

Angry thoughts scattered feverishly, resistant to being controlled by his father's sentiments. How could Papa not get mad about being fired? Ready to explode, his heart raced, face flushed. But this wasn't the time or the place.

When he tossed his books onto his desk, the loud clap silenced murmurs that breathed again, like a beast that refused to die. Before sitting, he nodded at Kazu, who sat in the desk behind his. Did his friend feel as angry?

Chalk screeched as Mr. Bailey scribbled math problems on the blackboard. He wore the same thing he always did—a white shirt and brown cardigan. The only part of his teacher-uniform that ever changed was his bow tie, and on this day, he wore a black one.

After covering the board with a jumbled mess of algebra problems, he turned to the class. "Good morning, students," he said, opening his roll book. "Sarah Andrews," he called.

"Here."

Nobu and Kazu snuck notes back and forth to each other, while Mr. Bailey continued roll call.

Kazu: *Joe and Terrence are coming over to shoot some baskets after school. You coming?*

Nobu: *Why'd you ask Joe? He's a troublemaker.*

Kazu: *Best guard on the team.*

Nobu: *That's if he can manage to stay on the team without getting kicked off. Okay. Guess I'll be there.*

"Nobu Kimura?"

"Here."

Bailey scanned the room over his wire-rimmed reading glasses. "Nobu Kimura?"

"I'm here!" What was the deal with calling his name twice? Didn't Bailey hear the first time? Or was it his way of drawing attention to a Jap?

Bailey continued through the list, ending with Steve White, then announced, "And now, class, please stand and join me in saying the Pledge of Allegiance."

Books slapped shut and chairs scooted as everyone stood and faced the flag hanging at the front of the class.

Nobu put his hand over his heart. "I pledge allegiance, to the flag..." They were words he'd always recited mindlessly, until a phrase caught in his throat. "... one nation ..."

One nation? Yeah, right.

He couldn't help notice Kazu's silence when the rest of the class said the words, "with liberty and justice for all."

The end of the day couldn't come soon enough. When the last bell rang, Nobu rushed down the crowded hall toward doors to the outside. The passage was a gauntlet of words that punched like fists.

"Hey, Nobu. Japs aren't the only ones who can carry out an unprovoked and dastardly attack. Better watch out!"

Another snickered and said, "Yeah. Watch out, all right. The President has declared war. That means open season on Japs."

The taunts were suffocating. He had to get out—had to get away from the bumping and pushing.

"Hey," someone yelled from the crowded hall. "Isn't your brother at Pearl Harbor?"

Nobu turned to find the voice. Dozens were gawking, but he couldn't tell who had spoken.

"Just think," the same voice called again. "One day Taro Kimura is our star player on the ball team, the next day he's a Jap attacking Pearl Harbor. Maybe you should think twice about wearing your traitor brother's letterman jacket."

Someone grabbed him. The last straw. He turned around, fist clenched, ready to belt the jerk who called Taro a traitor.

"Hey, hey. It's just me," said Kazu, holding up his hands in defense. "Come on. Let's get out of here."

"Yeah. Let's."

Joe and Terrence were sitting on the porch steps when Nobu and Kazu arrived to shoot baskets.

"What took you guys so long?" Joe asked, rising from the top step.

"Yeah, yeah. We're here now." Kazu said. "I'm just going to put my books in the house. Be right out."

"Hurry it up," Terrence said, dribbling to the driveway. "I got to take my sister to choir practice in an hour." He tossed the ball through the hoop.

The screen door slammed and Kazu ran out to join the others on the driveway court. "Okay. Me and Terrence will take on you two," he said, grabbing the ball from Terrence.

It felt good to shoot baskets, even if Kazu and Terrence *were* twelve points ahead.

Terrence grabbed the ball from Nobu. "Too bad you white boys can't play basketball."

Nobu wasn't quite sure how to respond to Terrence's joking around. White boys? Is that how Terrence saw Nobu and Kazu? It seemed they'd been called yellow plenty lately.

Terrence shot a basket, then left the driveway court. "Sorry, man. That's all for me. My momma'll bust my butt if I'm late getting my sister. See you guys tomorrow." He ran off, bouncing the ball down the sidewalk.

Kazu, Joe, and Nobu had started shooting baskets again when two black sedans pulled up to the curb. Four men piled out of each and slammed the doors.

A man in a long tweed coat approached. "This the Sasaki house?"

"Yes, sir," said Kazu.

Nobu moved closer to his friend.

"We have a warrant to inspect this house for contraband."

"Contraband? What do you mean, contraband?"

The man ignored the question and signaled his cohorts to follow.

Kazu ran ahead to the front door. "Mom, Pop! There are some men here to see you."

Nobu couldn't believe it. What the hell kind of contraband would a Buddhist minister have? He hurried into the house after Kazu and the men. Straining to see around the barricade of tall men in hats, he found Kazu standing next to his mother and father in the middle of the small, tidy living room. They watched helplessly while several of the men opened drawers and closets, tearing through the Sasakis' personal belongings like dogs through trash. One of the thugs slammed a drawer so hard a crystal vase wobbled on its shelf. Kazu lunged for it, but his mother pulled him back. It shattered on the floor.

Reverend Sasaki addressed the man in the long tweed coat—the one who appeared to be The Boss. "What are you looking for? Perhaps I can help you."

Seeing Kazu's father try to appease the men made Nobu sick to his stomach. He imagined Papa acting in such a conciliatory way to such disrespect and had to force the thought from his mind.

A man wearing black-rimmed glasses answered. "We're looking for radios, cameras. Correspondence from Japan. You know, contraband."

Mrs. Sasaki spoke up. "But we have already turned everything in to the authorities, as requested." Her hand crinkled her pleated skirt.

"Lady, you'd be surprised at what we find in the households of Japanese who say they have 'already turned everything in.'"

The Boss fired off questions. "Have you participated in any mass gatherings of Japanese?"

"Only at the Buddhist temple during our services. I am a minister."

He jotted notes between more questions. "How many of you gather at those meetings?"

Reverend Sasaki thought for a moment. "Oh, I would say maybe a hundred."

Boss grunted and mumbled to the man standing next to him. "A hundred, huh? I'd call that a mass gathering."

A knot tightened inside Nobu. Papa was involved with the Japanese

American Citizens League. Did that mean these men would be paying his family a visit?

Someone called from the hallway. "I found a box of letters up in this bedroom closet."

Mrs. Sasaki's eyes filled with fear. "Those are only letters from my mother." She grabbed her husband's arm, her eyes large with tears.

Reverend Sasaki patted her hand. "Please, sir. They are personal letters. That is all."

Boss lit a cigarette. "Sorry. It's correspondence from Japan," he said, smoke billowing from his mouth. "Like I said, contraband." He dumped the letters out of the box, and they showered down into a large canvas bag. "We'll have to confiscate them."

Kazu rushed toward the green bag and tried to catch the letters as they fell. "You can't do that! These are personal. They mean nothing to—"

"Kazu!" Reverend Sasaki grabbed his son's arm.

Boss nodded to his gang. A short, skinny man heaved the canvas bag and tossed it over his shoulder. The rest followed him out to the car. All except for Boss.

"Mr. Sasaki," he said. "You're going to have to come with us."

"I beg your pardon? Why?" Reverend Sasaki asked.

"We have reason to believe you've been holding secret meetings, thus the warrant. Now, you've confirmed it, and we found correspondence from Japan to boot. Please gather some toiletries and a change of clothes and come with me."

Mrs. Sasaki's voice trembled as questions poured from her mouth. "But where will you take him? When will he be back? Can we go with him?"

"Your questions will be answered later. And no, you may not accompany him."

Reverend Sasaki took his wife's arm, and they walked down the hall to their bedroom. A few minutes later he returned alone, carrying a small suitcase.

Boss took the suitcase and put it down on the hooked rug, among littered pieces of the Sasakis' life. He pulled handcuffs from his back pocket.

"That won't be necessary," Kazu's father whispered.

Boss's reply was cold. "Procedure."

Reverend Sasaki's shoulders slumped. He cast his eyes to the ground. "May I place my coat over the cuffs? You know, the neighbors."

"Yeah, yeah. I guess."

"Son," Reverend Sasaki whispered, "please take care of your mother."

"Sure, Pop."

Before Kazu's father left the house, he drew a breath so deep it broadened his chest and pulled back his shoulders. His head rose in a way that made him look taller.

Reverend Sasaki had it, too. *Gaman.*

Nobu stood with Kazu at the front door, watching until the two cars drove out of sight.

He wanted to say something to his friend, wished there were some way to make things better. But only two words emerged from a fog of emotions. "I'm sorry."

Kazu didn't look at him. He instead fixed his gaze on where the cars had been. "You should go now. I'd better check on my mom." He stared at the mess the men had left behind, then shuffled to his mother's bedroom.

Nobu stayed for a moment, half-tempted to return things to their proper places. Opened boxes were strewn around the closets. Linens had been pulled from drawers and tossed around the dining room. The Sasakis' lives. Tossed about and torn apart in only a few moments.

Kazu's house felt like a stranger's. Disordered. Cold. Maybe the house could be returned to the way it had been before, but the home would never be the same.

Whimpers from the bedroom broke the eerie silence.

CHAPTER 4

Sachi

DECEMBER 23, 1941

Leaves swirling around
Fall to the ground and lie in
Eternal slumber

Sachi sat in front of the Christmas tree and studied the package wrapped in silver paper, mesmerized by the lights of the tree reflecting off of it. If Mama thought she had hidden it, she was wrong. Sachi had found it covered up by other colorful packages the very day her mother placed it there. And she knew by the shape of the box, it was a doll like her friend Kate's!

Papa walked into the living room. "Sachi-chan, do you want to walk to the park with me?"

She jumped up. Finally! After two weeks of begging Papa to take her to the park. "Now?"

"Yes, now. Get your coat."

She ran to the hallway closet and grabbed her coat and scarf.

He called from the front door, "We're leaving now, Sumiko. See you soon."

A gust of cold wind struck Sachi's face as she stepped outside, and she pulled her scarf over her nose. At the edge of the yard, she turned to say goodbye. Mama stood in the doorway, wringing a dish towel until it was as tight as her face.

"See you in a little while," Sachi said, then caught up to Papa. She took his hand, so warm wrapped around hers. But the cold stung her cheeks and made her eyes water.

Wispy clouds floated across the gray sky like the incense smoke that had drifted from their altar, while leaves skipped across manicured yards of white stucco houses, racing to stay ahead of Sachi.

She tugged at her father's arm. "Look, Papa. The swirling leaves. Over there."

"They are dancing for us," he replied.

She let go of his hand and spun around and around. She stopped, dizzy, and smiled. "I don't mind this kind of dancing."

As the world stopped spinning, she noticed a car slow down as it passed. The driver stared at them.

Papa took her hand. "Let's go."

She skipped to keep up and wondered why Papa was walking so fast.

When they arrived at the park, Sachi ran ahead to the swing set. Empty seats swayed in the wind like unruly ghosts. She grabbed one and sat in it, then pushed her feet against the ground. Back and forth. Back and forth. *Too slow!* She wanted to swing higher and faster.

"Papa, come push me!"

Obliging, he walked to Sachi, grabbed the swing, and pushed.

"Higher, Papa! Higher!" Her ponytail flew up, and her stomach tickled. She felt Papa's hand on her back, pushing. Higher and higher.

He grabbed the chains on either side of her and slowed her. "We should go now," he said.

"Just a little longer," she pleaded. She jumped from the swing and ran to the slide before he could say no, then climbed the ladder to the top and waved. Sliding down, cold metal stung the back of her legs, but she jumped up and ran to the ladder again, trying to beat Papa's next call to leave. As she climbed each step, she waved at the paper boy who rode by on his bicycle, and laughed at the little dog who tried to keep up.

She wasn't going to wait for permission before climbing the ladder again. "Just one more time, Papa." Perched at the top, she turned to wave.

Papa was not alone. Three boys surrounded him, pushing and hitting as he tried to protect himself.

Panic surged through her and she almost lost her balance. She grabbed the slide rail.

Why are they hitting him?

She screamed. "Stop! Papa!"

But the boys kept bullying, yelling ugly things like the kids at school.

The fat boy with brown hair threw Papa to the ground like a rag doll, kicked him in the stomach, then tossed his cigarette at Papa.

Papa's gaze found Sachi. He drew his finger to his mouth. *Shhh.*

The tallest boy, his blond hair greased back, spat at Papa. "Enemy Jap!" He kicked her father in the face.

Sachi squeezed her eyes shut.

The two Caucasian—*hakujin*—boys stepped aside, and a colored boy—*kokujin*—walked to where her father lay. *Kokujin* leaned over to say something to Papa and stood over him for a minute.

Maybe he was going to stop.

No!

He plunged his foot into Papa's stomach. The other two boys patted *Kokujin* on the back, laughing.

How could they laugh? Once, she kicked a dog because it was chasing her. But even with a dog, when it yelped and ran away, she didn't laugh.

Her father was moaning, but Sachi couldn't understand what he was saying. She watched, confused, her heart beating hard like it wanted to crawl through her tightening throat. Every part of her body urged her to slide down, run to help Papa. But he told her to be quiet. Still, how could she sit and watch them hurt him? Tears burned her eyes but turned cold on her cheeks. She couldn't breathe.

Cars drove past. Someone must have seen what was happening. Why didn't they stop to help?

The boys kept kicking, chanting, "Dirty Jap!"

Papa covered his head with his hands and curled his body.

She could no longer obey. It didn't matter that Papa told her to stay and be quiet. Didn't matter that there were three boys bigger than she was. She'd kick. She'd bite. She'd scratch. Anything to help Papa. At last, she pushed herself down the slide. Her scream erupted. "Stop it! Stop!"

As she ran toward them, the colored boy looked at her. *Hazel eyes.*

He turned to the other two. Was he trying to pull them away? It didn't matter. They kept kicking and yelling. Over and over and over.

The colored boy with hazel eyes ran away.

Papa's body uncurled, motionless.

She ran harder than she'd ever run before, but couldn't get there fast enough.

"That'll teach you a lesson," said the blond. Cigarette smoke puffed from his mouth. "Now get on back to Japan and tell your enemy brothers to leave us alone." He kicked Papa again.

Leave him alone leave him alone please leave him alone. The words pounded in Sachi's head even faster than she ran.

The boys stepped away and slapped each other on the back, the way Nobu's teammates did when they'd won a game.

Almost there. Almost there. They turned and glared at her—the big, blond bully, cigarette hanging from his mouth, and the fat, ugly one with stringy, brown hair and freckles all over his face.

Someone was screaming. She turned to see through a blur of tears. He was running from across the street. Nobu!

"What have you done?" her brother cried. "Joe? Terrence? How could you do this to my father?"

The colored boy looked back as he ran, stopped for a moment, then took off again, stumbling in his haste. The two *hakujin* boys dashed away, like cockroaches at the flick of a light.

Sachi dropped to Papa's side before Nobu reached them. She held his head in her lap and wiped the blood from his face. "Papa, wake up. Papa!"

CHAPTER 5

Terrence

BERKELEY, CALIFORNIA
DECEMBER 23, 1941

Early that day, signs of morning stirred Terrence from sleep. Sunlight through the blinds. The smell of bacon. Coffee. Momma humming in the kitchen. He yawned and stretched his arms over his head, feeling his body wake. He smiled, remembering the dream he'd had about that cute girl in biology.

Momma's slippers swished down the hall. "Time to get up," she called. "Y'all come eat breakfast, then we gonna go and get us a Christmas tree."

The door hinges creaked as Momma poked her head inside his

room, her pink curlers sticking out all over her hair. "Morning, son. Do me a favor and get your sisters up. I got to finish cooking."

Momma sure couldn't wait to get a Christmas tree. She'd been talking about it forever, and now it was only two days left 'til Christmas. He guessed they'd waited long enough, but he couldn't get excited. It wasn't gonna be any fun without Daddy home. And there hadn't been any news from him since the Japs attacked Pearl Harbor.

Momma kept reminding them, several times a day, matter fact. "You got to have faith." She said God would look out for Daddy and bring him home safe, especially with the whole congregation of St. Paul's AME Church praying for him.

He figured Momma reminding him that God would watch over Daddy was just one way of her comforting herself. No matter. Couldn't hurt none to think the way Momma thought.

Any. Couldn't hurt any.

How many times had Momma told him she'd have none of his talking like she did?

"I was born and raised in Mississippi," she always said, waving her finger at him. "You was born and raised here in California. Maybe I ain't got no education, but you educated."

Momma might not know the right way to talk, but she darn well knew the wrong way. He'd lost count of all the times she'd waved that finger at him, "You ain't gonna make nothing outta yourself if you don't learn to speak right."

Momma would never say it, but Terrence was pretty sure she wanted him to "get educated" so he wouldn't have to join the military the way Daddy did. No way could she handle worrying about both her men.

He'd seen pictures of what was left of Pearl Harbor after those Jap cowards attacked, but blinked them away and tried to think of something else.

Like the Christmas tree. It was just one of the ways Momma tried to keep their lives normal, as if keeping things normal would make Daddy walk through the front door.

He groaned and stretched again. Dang. Wasn't he supposed to get to sleep-in over Christmas break? He dragged himself out of bed and pulled on a T-shirt and jeans, then shuffled to the bathroom. "Missy. Patty. Get up," he called.

"Just let us sleep a little longer," Patty mumbled, rubbing her eyes.

"Nope. Momma said it was time to get up."

Little Missy sat up with a sleepy grin. "We gonna get a tree today?"

He smiled at his baby sister. "Only if you two get yourselves out of that bed. I'm gonna wash up. You two best be up by the time I get back," he said, closing the door.

He stretched in front of the bathroom mirror and groaned to chase away his own sleepiness. A few splashes of cold water might do the trick. He patted his chin with a towel then rubbed his fingers over it. He could get away without shaving.

He thought about that girl in biology class again—about that afternoon, just before Christmas break, when she'd flirted with him as she passed in the hall. There she was, smiling and winking, all coy.

"Sure are some pretty hazel eyes you got there, Terrence," she'd said.

He leaned over the sink and looked into the mirror, flashed a cocky wink at his reflection, then rolled his eyes.

Chicken shit.

Okay. That was it. He'd work up the nerve to ask her out after Christmas break if it was the last thing he did.

"You two up?" he called from the bathroom. "I'm on my way in, and you best be up when I get there, else I got cold water to splash on you." That was how Daddy always got him out of bed.

Squeals and giggles burst from their room. "Okay, okay! We're up!"

"Momma's got breakfast ready. Hurry on now."

Their places were set around the maple table. Steam rose from a mound of scrambled eggs at the center. Terrence could smell the biscuits and bacon that sat on either side. His stomach growled.

Momma was sitting at the table behind her morning paper.

He touched Daddy's empty chair before pulling out his own. "Any news from Daddy yet?"

"No, baby. 'Spect it'll come any time though." She rolled up the newspaper and tossed it in the trash. "They most likely still tryin' to get everthing cleaned up."

Patty dragged herself into the kitchen. It seemed like she got taller and skinnier every day. Her voice still squeaky with sleep, she complained, "I thought we got to sleep late over Christmas break."

"You wanna get us a tree today, don't you?" Momma asked.

"Yes ma'am. Just not so early."

Finally, Missy skipped in, beaming with her usual morning cheer. "Hi, Momma."

"Morning, Baby Girl," Momma said and kissed Missy's cheek. She tugged at one of her pigtails before scooping scrambled eggs onto her plate, then clasped Missy's hand on one side, Patty's on the other. Terrence joined hands, too, and everybody bowed their heads.

"Dear Lord," Momma began to pray, "Humble our hearts and make us truly thankful for these and all thy blessings. And please bring Daddy home safe, too." She opened her eyes and put her napkin on her lap. "Hurry up and eat now. After we get the tree, we got the rest of the day to decorate."

A damp breeze blew in with the fog off San Francisco Bay, thickening the scent of pine in the tree lot. Patty and Missy played hide-and-seek through the rows of trees, while Terrence dawdled behind his mother, rolling his eyes every time she touched and sniffed a tree. How in the heck did Daddy keep his patience every Christmas, watching her go up and down every single aisle looking for *just* the right one? What difference did it make if it was tall or short, fat or skinny? A tree was a tree.

Finally, she stopped beside a six-foot spruce. "This here look like a good one. What do ya think, son?"

Looks like every other tree to me.

"It's perfect, Momma," he said, barely giving it a glance. All he wanted to do was get home and get the darn thing decorated so he could go shoot baskets with his friends. He reached through the prickly needles and lifted it out for Momma to see.

"Boy, you just like your daddy." She chuckled as she dug in her purse for her wallet.

Just like Daddy? Maybe in past years, Terrence had been so busy chasing around the rows with Patty and Missy that he hadn't seen his father rolling his eyes, huffing and puffing, getting annoyed with Momma for spending all that time picking the perfect tree. At any rate, it made him feel kinda good inside for Momma to compare him to Daddy.

"Come on, girls," she called. "We found us a tree. Let's go home and put lights and ornaments on."

Missy and Patty serenaded all the way home. "Jingle bells, jingle bells . . ." Over and over. Way too many times.

He shook his head. "Come on, you two. Don't you know any other songs?"

It wouldn't matter anyway. He just wasn't in the mood, even with a tree tied to the top of the car, Christmas carols, and colored lights showing through windows everywhere. It'd be a fine scene—if only Daddy was home.

Momma turned into the driveway. "Wonder why Brother Harold's sitting on our porch swing? And who's that man . . . in the uniform?" Her voice faded to a whisper.

Patty and Missy stopped singing.

No.

The whole world came to a stop. The talking. The movement. The breathing. Something buzzed in his ear and clutched Terrence's heart tight. Wouldn't let go. It might never let go.

No.

Momma's hands clutched the steering wheel. She whispered real slow. "You kids . . . go on in the house now. I be there in a minute."

Terrence lifted Missy out of the car and took Patty's hand. No matter how bad he didn't want to know, he knew.

Let's just back up, Momma. Get back in the car. Get back to the Christmas tree lot. I promise I won't complain about looking for the perfect tree. Won't never complain about having to get up early. Just please. No way. No way do we want none of what Brother Harold has to tell us.

Terrence nodded at Brother Harold as he shuffled past. But he couldn't—wouldn't—look him in the eye.

Brother Harold touched him on the shoulder with his large, warm hand. It sent shivers all over, tensed every part of his body. Somewhere, deep inside his head, he heard, "No. No. No."

Once inside the house, Terrence put Missy down and shut the front door. "You two go on and play now," he said.

Missy ran off to her room, but Patty stared at her brother, her eyes looking bigger than he'd ever seen them. "I don't want to play. Why is Brother Harold here? Is it Dad—"

Don't you say it!

"I said go on now Patty. I wanna talk to Momma when she comes in."

He pressed his ear to the door, wanting to hear, yet so desperately not wanting to hear. His heart begged for a way—any way—to stop time, to go back in time. He struggled to rationalize Brother Harold's visit.

There could be a hundred other reasons why Brother Harold would be here with a navy man. Maybe he needs Momma's help with a special sermon for veterans. Maybe someone else's Daddy got killed and he wants Momma to help him tell the family.

But his head pounded with the hopeless truth that refused to be ignored.

Not with the sad, sorry look in their eyes. Daddy's dead. I know it. I feel it. No, no, no. Don't think that, else it'll come true! Daddy, Daddy. Don't let it be about Dad—

Momma's long moan sliced through the thick wood door like a dull knife—the saddest sound he'd ever heard in his life. He bit his lip hard, and clutched the knob. On his side of the door, he could pretend for just a little while longer that Daddy was still alive. Once he opened it, Daddy was gone and his world would change forever. He squeezed his eyes shut, let the tears fall, then wiped them away with his sleeve.

Gotta be brave for Momma.

When he opened the door, he found Brother Harold holding Momma, limp in his arms as she sobbed. She clutched a crumpled piece of paper. Terrence took it from her and helped Brother Harold walk her to the porch swing.

"Momma," he whispered, wiping the tears from her face.

"He's gone, Terrence. Your daddy's gone."

He read the paper he'd taken from her hand. A telegram:

> THE NAVY DEPARTMENT DEEPLY REGRETS TO INFORM YOU THAT YOUR HUSBAND, JOHN TERRENCE HARRIS, COOK THIRD CLASS USN, WAS KILLED IN ACTION IN THE PERFORMANCE OF HIS DUTY AND IN THE SERVICE OF HIS COUNTRY. THE DEPARTMENT EXTENDS TO YOU ITS SINCEREST SYMPATHY IN YOUR GREAT LOSS.

It was true.

The words shuddered through his body. Sucked everything out of him. Left him emptier than he'd ever felt. Monster waves of sadness, rage, and revenge filled him up. Flooded him. He couldn't breathe.

The Japs killed my daddy!

Brother Harold placed his hand on Terrence's shoulder. "I pray God will comfort you," he said.

Terrence jolted up and glared at Brother Harold.

Pray for comfort? Yeah. Hell of a lot of good praying did for Daddy!

Shuddering, he fought hard to keep from punching the man in the face. He snarled. "Brother, I ain't never gonna feel comfort again."

Momma wailed again. He couldn't let her see him this way. He had to get away.

Go! Go! Go!

"I gotta leave for a little bit, Momma. I'm sorry." He kissed her cheek and ran from the porch.

Gotta get away.

His head buzzed. He struggled for memories of his father, but they swirled like crazy in his mind. He chased after those memories. Tried to grab them, hold them. Couldn't reach them.

The world around him faded to a gray blur. Nothing out there. Nothing inside. His heart was cold, but he burned like fire.

He ran somewhere. Anywhere. Nowhere.

Got no place to escape.

"Hey, Terrence."

"Hey man, wait up."

Familiar voices. He turned to find them. Tried to ignore them. Joe from his basketball team. And Ray. Trouble.

Joe came up and put his arm on his shoulder. Smelled like cigarettes.

Terrence pulled away. They were like mosquitoes whining in his ear. Buzzing. Bothering. "Get away from me, man."

The other voice. Ray. "Hey! What's going on? You in a hurry to get somewhere?"

Terrence stared straight ahead. Swatted them out of the way. Didn't want them around. "Leave me alone."

"Aw, come on," said Joe. "What's eating you?" He shoved a pack of cigarettes in Terrence's face. "Want a smoke?"

"Hell no."

Joe tucked the cigarettes back in his pocket. "Damn, Tee. You're in some kind of shitty mood." He shrugged his shoulders. "But if you don't wanna talk about it, me and Ray'll leave you alone. Come on, Ray. Let's get outta here."

"Wait a minute," Ray said, his snake eyes studying Terrence.

"There's something ticking in that brain of yours, and it's itching to get out. I can see it in your eyes. Come on, man. Spill it."

"Shit! Why can't you leave me the hell alone?" Terrence's throat tightened. His heart beat harder. Faster. Everything swirled around like crazy.

"Terrence! Watch out!" Joe grabbed him.

A horrible screech. *Honk!*

A car. Only inches away. The man behind the wheel yelled at Terrence. "You stupid kid! Watch where you're going."

Terrence glared at him and pounded his fists on the hood.

The driver honked again.

Joe pulled Terrence out of the way.

The car accelerated. Its tires squealed and burned as it sped away.

That's what Terrence wanted to do. Get away. *Speed* away. It was like Daddy's death was driving him, and anger was accelerating his engine so hot and fast he was gonna crash if he didn't do something to slow it down.

"You okay?" Joe asked.

Terrence snarled and pulled at his hair. "Okay. You wanna know what's wrong? Think you can handle it?" He looked up at the gray sky.

You ain't up there, are you, God?

He wiped his face on his sleeve. "Just found out my daddy's dead. That's what's wrong. DEAD! He ain't never coming home. Got it? Never." He poked Joe in the chest. "The goddamn Japs killed him at Pearl Harbor." He fought to hold back burning tears.

Don't you dare cry in front of these two.

"Ah, man. You shittin' me?" Joe took a last drag on his cigarette before tossing it on the ground and smudging it with his foot. He licked his thin lips and spit out a fleck of tobacco.

The world buzzed again. Terrence walked faster. Joe and Ray kept talking at him, he didn't—couldn't—pay attention to anything they were saying. Until . . .

"We're gonna go Jap hunting," Ray said. His eyes were flashing wild. "Gotta get back at one for killing your daddy." He marched off in a determined stride.

Joe jogged to keep up. "You coming, Tee?"

Terrence watched shriveled leaves skip after them, unable to move, unable to breathe. *Get a Jap?* His heart pounded hard through his body, and finally, through clenched fists. He began to breathe again, deep and hard. Yeah. Maybe. Just thinking about getting a Jap made him feel a little better. Just rough one up a little. Teach him a lesson is all.

He called after Joe and Ray. "Hey! Wait up."

They hid behind a bush at the edge of the park and watched the Japanese man sitting on the bench. Nobody else around except for a paper boy riding on his bike. A dog chased behind him, yipping and barking.

"Hey," Ray whispered. "You two ready?"

Joe rubbed his nose. "Yeah, I guess. Looks like an easy enough target."

Terrence felt a chill on the back of his neck and pulled his collar up. A memory busted into his mind. Two summers ago, he and Daddy had been waiting in a long line at the hardware store. It was hot, and he'd been swatting at a mosquito buzzing around his ear.

When they finally reached the counter, the clerk slammed the cash drawer shut and said, "You know, last week a Negro man robbed this store." He squinted and stared at Daddy like he was already behind bars. "Looked kind of like you. 'Course, you all look alike."

Daddy smiled and placed a hammer and nails on the counter. "Well, it wasn't me."

"Sorry. This register's closed. I'm not selling to a Negro who might be the man who robbed me. Matter of fact, you better get before I call the cops."

Daddy nodded and left the hammer and nails. "Let's go, Terrence."

Terrence had wanted to hit something. Sweat trickled down his forehead. "You're not gonna let him get away with that, are you?"

Daddy was quiet until they got in the car. He shut the door and said, "Son, it ain't my problem if the man's just plain stupid. And if I react to it, I be just as stupid. 'Sides, with that kind of folk ever where, I'd wear myself out." He chuckled. "We'll get the hammer and nails somewheres else."

Yeah, Daddy. Look where not reacting got you. Dead!

His fevered anger had even boiled over onto memories of Daddy.

He stared at the Japanese man sitting alone on the bench, his hands folded on his lap. Yeah, an easy target.

Still, maybe beating up a Jap was, as Daddy put it, plain stupid. But hell, what was he supposed to do? He had to do something.

"Hey, Terrence. You chickening out on us?" Ray asked. "We're doing this for you, y'know."

The Japs killed Daddy. He couldn't get that out of his head and it fanned his emotions like a bellows, pumping him with hatred, revenge, until he was ready to explode. No. Wondering what Daddy would think wasn't helping him at all. Besides, it didn't matter anymore what Daddy thought. He was gone. Dead.

"Let's go," he said.

He clenched his fists, keen to make contact with the skin of a Jap. His vision narrowed in on the man sitting on the bench. Nothing else mattered. Only the Jap.

The man stood up and faced them with questioning eyes.

Ray snickered. "You a Jap?"

"I am Japanese. Is there a problem? What do you want?"

Joe poked him in the chest. "We wanna get us a Jap."

Ray grabbed the man's coat and threw him to the ground, then kicked him once.

Now! Now! Do it for Daddy!

Everything. Everyone. All blurred together.

Kicking.

Yelling.

Spitting.

The Jap. Weakened prey. Fuel for the pack's rabid attack.

Minutes passed. Or was it hours?

Didn't know. Didn't care.

He gasped for breath. Stared at the man lying on the ground, motionless.

Was he alive? Yeah. He was breathing.

Terrence was hovering at the edge of a cliff. So very dizzy. Yet, he couldn't make himself step away from the edge.

Anger. Sadness. Rage. Emptiness. Every emotion—violent and swirling inside—pushed, pushed, until . . .

He lifted his foot. Held it for a split second. Plunged it hard into the man.

He'd gone over the edge.

He felt the sickening crush of ribs giving way to the heel of his shoe. Sour tingled on the back of his tongue. He shook all over.

He leaned over the man and gritted his teeth. Bitterness overflowed. "You. Japs. Killed. My father."

The man stared up at him with swollen, dark eyes. "I am sorry for your loss. But . . . I . . . am not . . . a Jap."

Terrence panted. Fast. Shallow. Bile rose in his throat. A million thoughts raged in his head.

Daddy didn't rob that store and this man's not the Jap who killed my Daddy you all look alike we all look alike.

"Stop it! Stop!" The cry came from the playground.

Terrence blinked hard and looked around. He was cold again. The winter wind chilled through his sweat-soaked clothes. Ray and Joe were laughing. Slapping each other on the back. The man from the bench was on the ground. Moaning. Too loud. Blood. Red blood. On the man's face. On the ground. On Terrence's shoe.

"Stop! Leave him alone!"

Where did the cry come from? The swings? No. He turned to see a little girl coming off the slide. A Japanese girl.

"Stop! Please, stop!" she cried, running toward them.

He grabbed at Ray and Joe. "Okay! Okay! That's enough. Let's get outta here!"

But Ray kept kicking the man. His head. His stomach. He'd gone wild, frenzy in his eyes.

"That'll teach you and your people a lesson," Joe said, patting Ray on the back.

Terrence pleaded again. "Come on! We gotta go! You're gonna kill him!" He ran away when the little girl approached.

"Papa!"

That's her daddy.

He looked back and caught a glimpse of the girl's tear-filled eyes. A split-second. Forever.

He ran faster, harder; trying to escape what he'd done, knowing he never would.

Ray and Joe followed at last.

Someone yelled from the sidewalk behind them. "What have you done?"

Terrence stopped running and turned back again. *Nobu?*

His friend's voice haunted. "Why would you do this to my father?" *Nobu's father?*

The world buzzed and turned gray again.

Daddy was dead, and the only thing left were his words, ringing in his head: "just plain stupid."

He turned the corner for home. Did he feel better now? Hell, no. *God help me. God forgive me. Hell, there ain't no God. No God.*

CHAPTER 6

Sachi

DECEMBER 23, 1941

The sounds in the emergency waiting room were the worst. Sachi could close her eyes to escape the sights, but she couldn't block out the whimpers of the little boy who sat across from her, holding his bloodied arm. Or the baby wrapped in the blue blanket who cried as the nervous mother bounced him in her arms, whispering, "Shh, shh, shh." Gurneys with new patients startled Sachi each time they came crashing through the doors.

Papa moaned while Mama held her *o-juzu* beads and softly chanted a prayer to Buddha. Sachi liked the pretty crystal beads. But her favorite part of Mama's bracelet was the tiny Buddha etched inside the large center bead.

Nobu couldn't sit still and paced the floor, back and forth, running his fingers through his hair at every turn. Maybe Mama should let him hold her beads.

The second hand on the clock above the check-in desk moved slowly around the white dial. Sachi calculated how many times it had made its journey around the dial since they'd arrived. Seven fifteen. That would be about 117 times.

What was taking so long? Couldn't the doctors and nurses see that

Papa needed help? Nobu must have asked, "How much longer?" a dozen times already.

Finally, a nurse peeked from behind a door and called Papa's name. "Michio Kimura?"

Mama and Nobu lifted Papa from his seat and walked him to the door. Sachi wrapped her finger around one of his belt loops and followed behind.

The nurse took Papa's arm and started to enter the examination room. "Please, wait here."

Mama clung to him. "But I would like to stay—"

"Please," interrupted the nurse, "have a seat in the waiting room."

When the door began to close, Sachi let go of his belt loop. She returned to sit with Mama, Nobu, and all of the other sick people who had to wait in the hard chairs that lined the dingy, green walls.

Mama moved the circle of beads through her fingers, making a clicking noise that was somehow soothing to listen to. Nobu stared ahead, trance-like and still, except for his left foot rapidly tapping the floor.

Sachi watched a roach skittle across the yellowed floor, then went back to watching the second hand, passing the time by creating rhymes with the numbers on the clock. *One, two, three. Look at me. Four, five, six. Do this trick. Seven, eight, nine. Papa will be fine . . .*

A lump caught in her throat and tears burned her eyes. She laid her head on Mama's lap and listened to the clicking of the beads.

"Sachi-chan, wake up." Mama shook Sachi's shoulders. "It's time to go see Papa."

Where am I?

Crying echoed in the room. Ringing phones. The clacking wheels of passing gurneys. Her eyes focused again on the clock. Nine thirty-five. It hadn't been just a bad dream.

They followed a nurse down a long hallway where a light flickered and buzzed. The nurse's starched, white uniform looked like it might crack if she sat down. Her nylon stockings swished, and her white shoes squeaked on the shiny floor. Sachi wondered why nurses wore those funny-looking hats.

They stopped in front of Papa's room.

"Visiting hours are over, but you may have a few minutes," the nurse said. "Then you'll need to leave and return in the morning."

"Can't one of us stay with my father?" Nobu asked.

The nurse raised an eyebrow and pursed her lips, clearly irritated by his question. "Your father needs his rest, and so does Mr. Ihara in the bed next to him. You may have ten minutes, then I'll have to ask you to leave. Like I said, visiting hours are over."

Sachi could have sworn the nurse turned up her nose when she walked away, kind of like older girls at school who thought they were better than everyone else.

When she followed Mama and Nobu into Papa's room, her heart beat so hard it hurt. She hid behind her mother, afraid to see what her father looked like. The man in the bed next to Papa was Japanese, too. He looked like a ghost and made wheezing noises that made Sachi feel like she couldn't breathe.

Mama walked to one side of Papa's bed and Nobu to the other. Sachi stood alone at the foot of it. Her head throbbed when she saw his bandaged head. His blackened and swollen eyes. A fat, bloodied lip. Tubes everywhere. The fluorescent light above cast a blue-white light that gave his skin a strange color she didn't like.

"Papa," Sachi said, her voice quivering.

Mama touched his hand and whispered something that Sachi couldn't hear.

Nobu wiped his eyes with his sleeve.

A man walked into the room. His head was shiny bald, and his eyes were huge behind his thick glasses. A white moustache rested above his slight smile.

Sachi read the badge on his white coat. Dr. Theodore Evans, MD, Neurology.

Mama rose from her chair and greeted him, bowing slightly.

"Mrs. Kimura?"

"*Hai* . . . yes," she said, bowing again.

He extended his hand. "I'm Dr. Evans. I'm very sorry about what happened to your husband."

Mama looked at Nobu. "Please take your sister out of the room for a few minutes so I can talk to the doctor." She moved her o-juzu beads even faster through her fingers.

Nobu took Sachi's hand and pulled her out of the room.

"What do you think the doctor will say to Mama?" Sachi asked.

Her brother brushed his bangs away from his eyes, then put his hands in his pockets. "I don't know. We'll have to wait and see."

After pacing up and down the dim hall for several minutes, they returned to the room. Dr. Evans smiled and leaned over to talk to Sachi. "Your father will need plenty of rest tonight. Maybe you should rest, too."

Sachi smiled to be polite, but couldn't take her eyes off Papa.

"I'll see you tomorrow," Dr. Evans said before leaving the room.

For a few minutes, everyone watched Papa in silence.

The nurse came into the room like a cold wind. "It's time to leave now."

Nobu touched Mama's arm. "We should go."

Mama removed her o-juzu beads from her wrist and wrapped them around Papa's as she softly chanted another prayer.

Sachi rested her hand on his foot—the only part of his body she wasn't afraid of hurting.

"You rest now," Mama whispered.

Sachi kept patting his foot as Mama pulled her away. "We'll see you tomorrow, Papa."

"Please don't arrive before nine o'clock tomorrow morning," the nurse ordered. "And the little girl will need to stay in the waiting area. No one under twelve is allowed in the rooms."

The words were like a door slamming shut. She looked up at her mother. "I can't come in to see Papa in the morning?"

Mama clutched Sachi's hand and pleaded with the nurse. "Please. My daughter won't be any trouble."

The nurse's gaze shifted away. "I'm sorry. Those are the rules. We don't want Mr. Ihara disturbed. She'll have to stay in the waiting area."

Sachi didn't like this nurse at all. Didn't like the way she looked down over her upturned nose, like she was better than Mama. Didn't like the way she was so bossy when she spoke to them. It made Sachi want to scream and cry at the same time.

When Mama pulled her away from Papa's bed, Sachi held on to the image of her father, even if she didn't like the way he looked under that strange, blue light. Mr. Ihara's wheezing followed her out of the room.

After a long and quiet drive from the hospital, they pulled into the driveway. Sachi walked in the front door to silence so huge it pressed against her. She passed the Christmas tree—unlit, gloomy, and dark—and decided it was the saddest tree she had ever seen. Maybe turning the lights on would help. She plugged them in and watched the colors glitter on the tinsel. It didn't help much.

Mama called from the kitchen. "Time for bed, Sachiko."

Sachi gazed at the tree, in a trance. Was it really only that morning she had stood there, looking at presents? It seemed like days ago. Really, like another lifetime, when Papa asked her if she wanted to go to the park.

"Did you hear me?" Mama called again.

"Yes, Mama." She walked up the stairs, wondering if she would ever return to that life.

In the darkness of her room, all of the sights and sounds of the park flashed in front of her. She squeezed her eyes shut to block them out, but the scene played over and over. The boys kicking, calling Papa a Jap. Cigarettes tossed on him. His body, curled on the ground. The colored boy with hazel eyes.

Shadows of leaves danced on her ceiling like fairies in the moonlight. She made three wishes: that Papa would be all right, that it had all been only a dream, and that they'd never be called Japs again.

After a time her body grew heavy. Then light. Floating, drifting into sleep, a dream.

She stood in her front yard, and followed Papa's stare to a sign where words were scribbled.

Dirty Jap! Go Home!

Patches of color were tossed all around the yard. She walked onto the brown grass, bent to see, to touch. Silk. No! Ripped and scattered, pieces of her kimonos—pinks, purples, yellows, and blues—were bright against the dead grass.

Then she saw the tiny body parts. Her geisha dolls! Broken. Scattered. Delicate white hands still clinging to broken fans. Their porcelain faces, cracked and dirtied by the muddy soil.

She turned to find Papa. But he was gone.

CHAPTER 7

Terrence

DECEMBER 23, 1941

The doorbell rang. Terrence's heart stopped. He turned on his lamp and checked the clock on the nightstand. Ten thirty-five.

Momma called from the front door.

He knew who it was. He'd felt hunted all day. Even if he didn't see the hunters chasing him, he knew they'd find him. No place to hide. Should he run? Crawl out the window? How could he do this to Momma? And on the same day she found out Daddy was dead.

"Terrence! I said come here!"

Shuddering at the sound of fear and anger in her voice, he turned off the light and shuffled out of his room. "Yes'm?"

Momma stood by the sofa, straight and rigid, except for hands that twisted a handkerchief. The gold cross she'd worn since he could remember caught the lamp light and shone against her dark skin.

Two cops hovered over her. A tall, skinny one took notes while the second cop watched Terrence walk into the living room. He must have been the leader of the two—his uniform was perfectly creased. All business.

Momma's voice broke as she asked, "Where'd you go this afternoon after you left here, son?"

The clock on the wall *tick-tocked* and he wished he could just listen to it for a while longer. What was he supposed to say to her?

"Terrence, I'm talking to you."

"Nowhere, Momma. Just walking." He hated lying to her, but not as much as telling her the truth.

The beanpole cop continued to take notes.

"I'm Lieutenant Jackson," the creased cop said. "We've spoken to a witness . . . a Nobu Kimura? Son of the man who was beaten up at the park?"

Terrence's eyes flashed wide open, but he caught himself. Crossing his arms, he stared at the floor.

The cop continued. "Yeah, he gave us three names. We've already picked up your friends Joe Grant and Ray Morrison earlier. They said it was your idea. Now, care to change your story any?"

Momma wiped her eyes with her handkerchief. "Terrence? You wasn't there, was you? Tell them where you went."

He couldn't stand the hope in her voice, trust that he'd been somewhere else, not where the cops were accusing him of being. He broke down. "I'm sorry, Momma."

With reddened eyes, she searched his face, looking ten years older than she had a second before. Her lips quivered. "What'd you do, son?"

"I . . . we . . . Ray, Joe, and me. But it wasn't my idea! They . . . we beat up a man at the park. I'm sorry. I tried to stop them, but they wouldn't listen to me, Momma." He searched her eyes for forgiveness, even a tiny bit. But she covered them with her kerchief.

"Why, Terrence? Why'd you go and do a thing like that?" She rubbed her cross.

"'Cause the Japs killed Daddy, Momma. I had to do something. So I got back at a Jap—"

Her eyes widened and she gawked at him like he was a stranger in her house. "What you say?"

"A Japanese man. I needed to get back at a Japanese man. For Daddy." It sounded so stupid now. He felt his heart pounding in his neck, his temples. "But like I said, when I realized what we were doing, I tried to stop them."

"For your *daddy*? No, no. I don't believe this." She wouldn't look at him and held her stomach like she was going to be sick.

Lieutenant Jackson drew his handcuffs from his belt and grabbed Terrence's hands. The cold metal stung his wrists.

"Boy, you didn't do nothing but shame your daddy tonight," Momma cried.

He wasn't sure what hurt more—Momma's words, or getting handcuffed in front of Momma in their own house.

"We're going to have to take you in, son," Boss Cop said.

Son? The word punched him in the gut. *I ain't your son. Only one man called me son.* His throat clutched so tight it pressed down on his heart. Daddy would never call him "son" again. He wanted to lash out at the cop. But he knew to stay quiet. Daddy had told him before, "You don't never talk back to no police. You understand? You do whatever they tell you to do."

"You're under arrest for the attempted murder of Michio Kimura."

Attempted murder? "What do you mean, murder? I didn't kill no one," Terrence said, panicked. "Just wanted to rough him up a bit."

"Mr. Kimura is in the hospital. In a coma," Jackson said. "Not sure if he'll make it through the night."

"Oh, dear God," Momma cried.

Jackson grabbed his arm and pushed him toward the door.

When Terrence turned to say goodbye to Momma, he caught the twinkle of lights on the tree they'd bought that morning and shook his head. Still trying to keep things normal. Momma and the girls must've decorated that tree while Terrence was out beating that man. Neither act brought Daddy home.

Just that morning. A lifetime ago.

A dozen handmade ornaments dangled from the branches. Shapes cut from red and green paper were clustered at Missy's height. Near the top hung a single glittered ornament, cut in the shape of an angel.

He recognized Patty's writing. "For Daddy."

CHAPTER 8

Sachi

DECEMBER 24, 1941

Sachi sat at the kitchen table, looking out the window at fog that blanketed the neighborhood. Blurry dots of Christmas lights on the house across the street blinked through the grayness. It was not merry like Christmas Eve should be.

Nobu walked in. "Hurry up, Sachi. Visiting hours start in thirty minutes."

She pushed her bowl of rice and eggs away. "I'm not hungry anyway," she said and scooted from the table.

He picked up her dish and put it in the sink. "We're leaving in five minutes. Mama's upstairs getting dressed."

"I'm almost ready," she said, then ran upstairs to her bedroom. She called for Mama. No answer.

She called again. "Mama!"

She found her mother in the dance room, kneeling in front of the altar. Her hands were pressed together and wrapped by o-juzu beads. Incense drifted from the wooden box where a small bowl of rice and an orange had been placed—an offering to Buddha. Mama bowed several times.

Sachi listened to Mama's whispered prayer. Though she couldn't hear all of the words, she did hear "Papa" and "Taro" repeated over and over. Twice she heard Nobu's name, and once her own. What prayers did she say for them?

Mama's head remained bowed, and she did not acknowledge Sachi.

In silence Sachi watched, until at last, Mama placed a hand on the table to pull herself up.

"What is it, Sachiko?"

She held out a handful of books. "Can I bring these to the hospital today?"

"Yes. But not too many—maybe three or four." Mama walked out of the room.

Sachi followed, still trying to talk to her mother. "Look at this picture I drew for Papa." She held it up for her mother to see. "It's a picture of our Christmas tree . . . to hang by his bed."

But Mama didn't turn to look. "Nobu," she called, removing her coat from a hanger, "are you ready to go?"

"Yes, Mama," he replied. "I'll start the car."

Sachi placed the picture inside one of her books, guessing Mama didn't care if she brought it. Papa would like it though.

From the back seat of the car, Sachi watched Christmas decorations on street light poles drift by as they drove along University Avenue. Smiling children looked out windows of cars with suitcases tied on top. Mothers sat in the front seats. Fathers drove. She wondered where they were all going. It didn't matter. Any place was better than the hospital on Christmas Eve.

They walked into the waiting area on Papa's floor, and Mama

pointed to the green vinyl chairs. "Wait here, Sachiko" she said. "One of us will come out in a little while to let you know how Papa is doing."

She plopped down and felt the slap of cold vinyl against her legs. "Wait! Don't forget this," she said, holding her drawing.

Nobu took the picture of the Christmas tree and smiled. "Papa will like this, Sach."

She watched them walk down the hall. The waiting area was empty. One, two, three . . . fifteen chairs in the room, and nobody to keep her company.

Swish, swish. Swish, swish. A patient shuffled down the hall. Maybe he would stop to talk to her. But he passed, and when she saw the open back of his gown, she closed her eyes and held her hand to her mouth so the poor man wouldn't hear her laugh.

This place was quieter than the emergency room the night before. Too quiet. Only an occasional cough or moan from patients in the rooms broke the ringing in Sachi's ears.

She opened one of her books, but couldn't concentrate to read. She hated silence. In hushed moments, horrible images of her father's beating haunted her. Flipping the pages, she hummed "Santa Claus Is Coming to Town."

After what seemed like forever, Nobu returned and sat next to her. His face held no expression, but his eyes were red and puffy.

"What, Nobu? Was Papa awake? Is he okay?" She longed for good news, but feared it would be bad.

"No, Sachi. He hasn't woken up since we brought him here last night."

She felt the urge to cry, but wanted to be strong like her brother. "Maybe he just needs more rest. Did you give him my picture?"

"Yes. He'll see it as soon as he wakes up." Nobu took a deep breath and patted her hand. "I better get back in there. Sorry you can't come in, too."

"It's not fair." She could no longer hold her tears. "He's my papa, too."

Nobu hugged her; so like Papa's hug. For the first time since she held Papa in the park, her tears rushed forth like crashing waves between deep, panting breaths.

"It's okay, Sach," Nobu said, stroking her hair.

Her usual soft voice teetered on the edge of a scream. "How can you say 'it's okay'? Why did those boys hurt Papa? He wasn't bothering them. And what about that mean nurse? Why does she look at us the way she does? Just like the way kids at school look at me."

Nobu slumped into the chair. "I don't know, Sach. I wish I did."

He held her for several minutes. The beat of his heart comforted her.

Straightening, he asked, "You know what?"

"What?"

"I've been keeping an eye on that nurse behind the desk. She's so absorbed in reading charts, she's not paying attention."

Sachi's eyes widened.

"Let's sneak you in. No one will know."

"Really?"

"But only for a few minutes, okay? Promise you won't get upset when it's time to leave?

"Promise. A few minutes will be better than nothing."

"Okay, let's go. Be very quiet, and walk quickly."

She tiptoed behind her brother, trying not to giggle, yet at the same time scared about what might happen if the nurse caught them. Would she lock Sachi in a dark closet? Make her wait outside in the cold? No. She was sure she could out run those squeaky white shoes.

Besides, seeing Papa was worth any trouble she'd get into. Maybe he'd wake up for her.

She turned the corner into his room. The sight of him was like a kick in the stomach. He'd looked bad last night. But now in the light of day, his swollen eyes looked like raw meat. His cheeks were black and blue. Blood had seeped through the bandages on his head. And he was wheezing like Mr. Ihara.

"Papa," she whispered, then walked to the front of the bed. She wanted to hug him, but was afraid to tangle in the tubes that seemed to be connected to every part of his body. Instead, she placed her hand on his fingers sticking out from his cast. Did they move when she touched him?

"I drew a picture of our Christmas tree for you." She held her breath. If she was very quiet, she might hear his response.

Nothing.

"If you wake up, you can come home to have Christmas with us."

She smiled, but tears threatened to spill over the brave mask she wore for her father. *This is Christmas Eve. Tomorrow is Christmas. No, Papa will not be home.*

Nobu touched her shoulder. "We better get back to the waiting area before someone sees you."

"Just a few more minutes?"

"Sachi, remember? You promised you wouldn't argue. Maybe I can sneak you in again later."

She kissed her finger and placed it on her father's cheek. "Bye for now. I'll see you later."

Though Sachi felt her heart being tugged to stay, she crept behind Nobu back to the waiting room.

"I'll come back and check on you soon," Nobu whispered, then turned to leave.

"Nobu?" she called. "Thanks for sneaking me in to see him."

He returned two more times to sneak her in. Still, Papa slept.

When they returned home that evening, trees glittered through the front windows on Peralta Street. But the Kimura house stood in darkness.

It didn't matter. It didn't feel like Christmas Eve anyway. How she'd looked forward to celebrating Christmas like all of her friends. Now, Papa wouldn't even be there. There'd be no last-minute rush to wrap presents. No aroma of cakes or cookies or ham cooking for Christmas dinner. And Papa wouldn't read *The Night Before Christmas* like he had promised.

Lying in the quiet darkness of her room, she tried to think about the gifts she'd open in the morning—about what Santa Claus might bring in the night. But the silence brought only thoughts of Papa's beating. She wanted to sleep, to escape everything that had happened in the last few days. But she was afraid. Afraid of the dreams that would come again in the silent night.

Moonlight coming through her window cast a soft, blue light on the porcelain faces of her geisha dolls. They seemed to move in the light and shadows, and their black eyes stared at Sachi, so like Papa's eyes when they had stared into nothingness at the park.

She threw off her covers and ran to her shelf. Then, she turned the dolls to face the wall.

CHAPTER 9
Sachi

DECEMBER 25, 1941

Christmas morning. Quiet. Was she the first to wake?

What did Santa bring? Did I get my doll?

Then she remembered Papa.

She shut her eyes again, so tight, as though that might make it all a bad dream. But when she opened them, it all became real again.

The shrill ring of the telephone interrupted the silence. Mama rushed past Sachi's room, tying her robe.

Sachi jumped out of bed to follow.

"Hello?" Mama twisted the phone cord around her finger. "Taro!" Her eyes widened and a smile lit her face. "Yes, merry Christmas to you, too."

She rushed to Mama's side to speak to her oldest brother.

"No, there hasn't been any change in Papa's condition. We'll be going to the hospital again this morning."

Sachi tugged on Mama's robe. "I want to talk to him," she whispered.

Mama shushed Sachi with her hand. "What did you say?" she asked. "You joined the Hawaiian Guard?" Her eyes rounded with worry. "Taro. Why did you do that? We need you here at home."

Sachi's heart pounded faster with each passing second. She had so much she wanted to say. "Can I talk now?" She tugged again.

Mama shook her head. "Yes, I understand. I will let Papa know. Yes. You have a merry Christmas, too. Goodbye."

When Mama returned the phone to its hook, a door slammed on everything Sachi had wanted to tell Taro. The picture she'd drawn for Papa. Nobu sneaking her into Papa's room. The mean nurse. "Why didn't you let me talk to him?"

"It is very expensive to call from Hawaii. Your brother asked me to say 'Merry Christmas' to you, Nobu, and Papa."

"He's joined the Hawaiian Guard? What's that?"

"It's like the army. He said lots of Japanese American boys are enlisting." Mama walked downstairs.

Sachi felt sad all over again. Papa in the hospital. Taro joining the army instead of coming home. No presents to open.

She followed her mother into the kitchen. She needed to ask a question, but hesitated. Still, she had to know. "Mama?"

Mama turned from the stove. "Yes? What is it now, Sachi-chan?"

"When do you think we might open our presents?" She felt selfish for asking, but she'd been waiting for days and days to celebrate a real Christmas.

Mama clucked her tongue and shook her head. "Sachiko, Sachiko. How can you even ask me such a thing . . . with Papa in the hospital and Taro joining—"

Nobu ambled into the kitchen. "Merry Christmas, you two." He pulled out a chair and winked at Sachi, then said, "Why don't we see how things go at the hospital today? Then, we'll see about opening presents tonight."

When they arrived at the hospital, Sachi knew the routine and plopped into a green chair in the waiting area. A tiny tree with colored lights twinkled from a table in the corner.

Before leaving the waiting area, Nobu whispered, "I'll come back for you as soon as the coast is clear."

Sachi smiled at her brother, then opened a book she'd brought. She'd only read a couple of pages when a cheery voice broke the silence.

"Well, good morning and merry Christmas to you!"

The deep, cheerful voice surprised her. But she was even more astounded when she looked up to see Santa Claus standing in front of her. Santa Claus? In the waiting area of the hospital? How could that be?

"Are you really Santa?" she asked.

"Mr. S. Claus himself," he said, kneeling to greet her. "What's your name?"

"Sachiko Kimura."

"And why are you here on this Christmas morning, Sachiko Kimura?"

"We're visiting my papa. Well, my brother and mother are visiting my papa. I have to wait out here."

"Now that doesn't seem quite fair, does it?" He put his hand into the large bag he carried. "Maybe this will make you feel better."

"A doll? Thank you, Santa! It's just what I've been wanting."

"I have another surprise I think you'll like even better." He rose and extended his gloved hand to her. "Come with me."

She hesitated. "Mama told me to stay in the waiting area."

"It's okay. Come on."

What could be wrong with going with Santa Claus? She gave him her hand and followed him down the hall.

As they neared Papa's room, a nurse approached. "Excuse me, the child must stay in the waiting area."

Santa held up a hand to the nurse and said, "Merry Christmas, Nurse Sherman."

She looked at him, rolled her eyes, and continued walking.

At the entrance to Papa's room, Santa kneeled to speak to Sachi. "How do you like this surprise?"

"You're right, Santa. It's the best."

"I'll stand guard outside while you go in."

She smiled at him, then went in and heard Mama talking to Papa. *Is he awake?*

Disappointment filled her again when she saw her father. Eyes still swollen shut. Head still bandaged. Tubes still connected everywhere.

Mr. Ihara was still asleep, too. Did he ever wake up? Did anyone ever come to see him?

Mama leaned over Papa as she spoke. "Taro called to say merry Christmas this morning, Michio-san. He's doing well and sends his love to you." She straightened and looked to Nobu before continuing.

Nobu nodded.

"Michio-san, Taro has joined the Hawaiian Guard. I am not happy with his decision. But after what happened to you, he believes he must do this to prove he is a good American."

Still, Papa did not wake.

Mama looked at Sachi, standing at the foot of the bed. "Sachi-chan, what are you doing here?"

She smiled. "You will not believe it, but Santa Claus brought me."

"What?"

"Yes, and he's standing guard outside the room."

Nobu went to see what she was talking about. Mama followed.

Sachi watched for their expression when they met Santa.

Mama smiled, yet her eyes filled with tears. She bowed to the man in the red suit and held her hand out to his. "Thank you, Doc—" She glanced at Sachi and then again at Santa. "Thank you, Mr. Claus. You couldn't have given my daughter a nicer gift."

"It was my pleasure, Mrs. Kimura." He smiled at Sachi. "I suppose we should go back to the waiting area, before Nurse Sherman catches us again."

"But I want to give Papa a hug first," she said, and ran to his bedside. "Merry Christmas, Papa," she whispered. "I wish you could come home with us today."

She took Santa's hand and walked with him back to the empty waiting area.

CHAPTER 10

Sachi

CHRISTMAS NIGHT, 1941

Sachi scooted her peas around her plate and watched them roll into each other like marbles. Nothing tasted good. Not the pork, not the peas. Not even the rice. Even worse, Papa's chair was empty.

Mama hadn't eaten much off her plate either, and even Nobu, who usually asked for seconds and thirds, played with his food—stacking peas on top of his rice, only occasionally putting one in his mouth.

Sachi really wasn't hungry. She laid her chopsticks on her plate and said, "I ate three more bites. Can we open presents now?"

"I suppose that's the best you will do tonight. You and Nobu help me clear the dishes, then we'll open them."

Sachi leapt out of her chair and carried her dishes into the kitchen.

"I'll wash, you dry," Nobu said.

She picked up a dish towel and waited for him to hand her a dish. "What do you want for Christmas, Nobu?"

He was quiet as he held his hands under the running water. Sachi caught a glimpse of his dreamy gaze reflected in the window over the sink.

"The bubbles are going to spill over," she said.

He grinned at her and handed her a dish. "I knew that."

"Were you thinking about what you want for Christmas?"

"It's nothing you'd be interested in. You want dolls and crayons."

"What's wrong with that? Come on. Just tell me."

"For Taro to come home. For Papa to be okay. For there to be no war. And to be treated like everyone else."

He was right. After that, dolls and crayons felt silly. "Of course . . . I want those things, too," she said softly.

Nobu gave her another dish to dry.

Mama called from the living room. "Are you two ready to open presents?"

"Be there in a minute," Nobu replied. "Come on, Sach. We'll finish these later."

When they entered the living room, Mama was sitting on the couch next to the tree. Its tinsel shimmered with color; presents overflowed on the floor around it.

But Papa wasn't sitting next to Mama. And he wouldn't be bouncing around the room, taking pictures like he always did at birthdays and weddings. No Papa to hug after she opened the gift she'd most wanted.

"I think you will want to open this one first," Mama said, handing her daughter the big, silver package she'd had her eye on.

A flitter of excitement sparked a smile. "Thank you, Mama," she said.

"Papa helped me choose it for you."

Sachi ran her fingers under the creases on each end of the box and removed the tape.

"Come on, hurry up!" Nobu said. "You're unwrapping like a girl."

She giggled and ripped at the silver paper, then tossed it to the side. Her eyes widened. "It's exactly the doll I wanted!" She removed the doll and held it close. "I already have her name picked out—Sally." She hugged her mother. "Thank you, Mama."

"Be sure to thank Papa when you see him tomorrow," Mama said. "Nobu, will you get the camera and take a picture of your sister and her doll for Papa?"

When Nobu returned to the living room with the camera around his neck, Mama's eyes filled with tears. "You look more like your father every day."

Sachi noticed it, too, and missed Papa even more as her brother stood in front of her.

"Smile," he said softly, then snapped the picture.

Sachi watched the Christmas lights twinkle around the dark spots left by the camera's flash and remembered the presents she had for her mother and brother.

"This is for you," she said, handing Mama a box wrapped in red. "And this is for you." She gave Nobu a flat package wrapped in blue. "I bought them with my birthday money."

"How thoughtful of you, Sachi-chan," Mama said.

Nobu stared at the blue package. "I didn't know we were giving each other presents. I don't have anything for you."

"Oh, it's just something small I found. Thought you'd like it," she said. "Just open it."

"Let Mama open hers first," he replied.

Sachi sat on the couch next to her mother. "Go ahead and open it." She leaned close to watch. "And don't open it like a girl."

A whisper of a laugh cheered the room.

Mama did open it like a girl and placed the red wrapping paper neatly beside her. "It is beautiful."

Sachi beamed. "It's stationery for you to write letters to Taro-nisan. I painted little kimonos on each one."

"It's the nicest thing you could have given me, Sachi-chan. "I'll write him a letter tonight before I go to bed."

"Your turn, Nobu." Sachi quivered with anticipation.

Her brother ripped the paper off the small package. "Wow. A leather book with a lock on it. But it's blank," he said, grinning.

"Silly," Sachi said and grabbed it from Nobu. "See? It's a journal for you to write in. The key is inside. You can write whatever you want, and when you lock it, nobody can read it. I have one, too."

Nobu hugged her. "I guess I have lots to write about these days. Thanks, Sach."

Rising from the couch, Mama clutched her gift. "It's been a long day. We should get to bed so we can get an early start to the hospital in the morning."

Sachi followed, holding her doll. "You coming, Nobu?"

He flipped through the blank pages of the journal. "In a minute. I'm going to make a journal entry."

The phone rang early the next morning. Sachi woke with her arm over her new doll and listened for Mama to answer. She strained to hear the conversation.

"Yes. I understand. Thank you, Nurse Sherman. We will be there as soon as possible."

Mama hurried up the stairs and called, "Nobu! Sachiko! Get up and get dressed. We must get to the hospital quickly."

Nobu came out of his room. "What's wrong?"

"Nurse Sherman wouldn't give me any details. She just said we needed to hurry."

He peeked into Sachi's room. "Get up. You need to hurry. It's Papa." He slammed her door, then hurried to his room, and slammed his.

The tone of their voices left her heart racing and her stomach queasy. Something was wrong. She jumped out of bed, hurried to her closet, and picked the blue jumper and the white sweater with little yellow flower buttons. Papa had told her once how pretty she looked in it.

She dressed in less than two minutes. Brushed her hair. Stuffed her pajamas under her pillow. Pulled the covers over her bed. Grabbed her doll. Dashed into the bathroom to brush her teeth.

"Sachiko, are you ready?" Mama called.

"Almost," she replied between the toothpaste and toothbrush.

Nobu rushed past the bathroom, buttoning his shirt. "Hurry up, Sach."

She spat and rinsed her mouth. Glanced in the mirror as she wiped her face.

It's Papa. Hurry.

It was a quiet ride to the hospital. Sachi rode in the back seat and watched the raindrops shimmy across the car window, as if racing to the edge.

CHAPTER 11

Sachi

DECEMBER 26, 1941

Everything at the hospital looked gray and moved in a strange, slow motion: nurses walking in and out of patients' rooms, the second hand on the clock in the hall.

Sachi held her mother's hand tighter as they approached the waiting area.

Please don't leave me here. Not today.

But Mama pulled Sachi with her toward Papa's room.

Hurry.

Nurse Sherman met them at the entrance to Papa's room. "He's gone," she said, her face expressionless.

Sachi peered around her white-stocking legs to try to see inside the room. Papa's bed was empty. And so was Mr. Ihara's. "Where did you take my father?" she demanded.

"Sachiko," Mama scolded. Yet she, too, watched Nurse Sherman, waiting for an answer. "What do you mean he is gone?"

"Well, I don't know if I should tell you." Nurse Sherman started to walk away.

"Please," Mama cried. "You must tell us what happened."

"Well, I suppose so. You see, some government men came. Said they were FBI. They didn't tell me what they were doing, just flashed a couple of badges and said they were taking your husband and Mr. Ihara into custody. But I did overhear one of them say your husband was . . . an alien enemy." There was that snooty look again. Sachi could almost swear Nurse Sherman was trying not to smile as she continued. "Anyway, they said the men were being taken to a . . . what was it now . . . a Justice Department camp."

Nobu rubbed his forehead. "But my father was in no condition to leave the hospital."

"I'm sorry," the nurse replied. "It was out of my hands. Now, if you'll excuse me, I have work to do." She walked away, shaking her head.

Mama gasped. Her eyes filled with tears. "What are we supposed to do? How do we know where they took him?"

"It's out of my hands," Nurse Sherman repeated, not looking back.

Hurt overflowed and had to be released. Sachi called to the nurse, "Why didn't you call us sooner? Maybe we could have stopped them. We did not get to say goodbye!"

The nurse kept walking.

"Look at me! I was only nice to you because I thought you'd take care of my father. But now . . . now he's gone and—"

Nobu grabbed her and put his arm around her. "Sachiko, shh, shh."

She felt the warmth of Nobu's hand when he touched her cheek and wiped the tears away. Papa wiped her tears the very same way. The morning she'd fallen off her bike. When she'd found a butterfly she caught, dead in the jar. The afternoon she'd come home from school crying because some kids had teased her.

Trance-like, Mama moved her o-juzu beads through her fingers and chanted prayers to Buddha. She whispered as she walked away. "There is nothing left to be done here now. Let us go home."

CHAPTER 12

Nobu

DECEMBER 26, 1941

They've taken Papa away.

How is it that the government can come without warning to take an injured man, a man who has committed no crime, to a "Justice Department" camp? Where is the justice in that?

There are no words to describe my anger, my emptiness. Last night he was here. Now he is gone. Last night, as Mama, Sachi, and I opened Christmas gifts, there should have been five of us, but there were only three.

As we celebrated, Papa was being taken away by strangers. Was he even aware of what was happening? Did he wonder why we were not there to protect him?

So why did we celebrate? We told ourselves it was what Papa would want. First, we watched Sachi open the package that held her doll. For a little while, her smile made me forget all that had happened.

Sachi gave Mama some stationery that she'd painted kimonos on. She said it was so Mama would have something pretty for her letters to Taro-nisan. She gave me this journal where I am writing now. I felt bad that I had no gift for her.

How could we know that Papa would be taken the next morning?

Last night when I took pictures with his camera, Mama said I looked like him. When she said that, something inside me yelled "No!" Something in her words almost swallowed me, as if they would chase away Papa's spirit. Now, when I look in the mirror, all I see is Papa.

I thought Joe and Terrence were my friends. I still don't understand how they could beat up my father. Are we Japanese hated so much?

And if they could forget we are friends, why can't I, too, forget? Why did I hesitate to tell the police what happened at the park, like I was "ratting" on my friends? And why would I give a second thought to letting them sit in a jail cell over Christmas?

Papa was like a shelter against the cold wind of hate that swirls around us. Now he's gone and I shiver inside. Who will be our shelter now? Taro is gone. Will it be up to me? How can I be strong for Mama and Sachi?

CHAPTER 13

Nobu

JANUARY 2, 1942

Nobu picked up a towel and folded it. "I'm sure we'll find him, Mama. Maybe now that the holidays are over we can talk to someone who can actually give us some information."

Mama didn't look up, but kept folding laundry, as if the repetitive movement of picking up and folding, picking up and folding, was a meditation. She'd been too quiet in the days following Papa's "abduction," and Nobu couldn't decide if it was strength or stress that caused her silence. Was she thinking of ways to find him, to get him back? Or was she doing whatever she could to survive the adversity?

"Mama?"

At last she looked up, as if she'd just realized his presence.

He searched the pile for a matching sock to the one he held. "I'll call Representative Gearhart's office on Monday. Maybe he can give me some information. Or, at least tell me who else I can call."

Mama nodded her head. *"Hai."* Then, she went back to folding laundry.

The doorbell rang.

Sachi ran past the living room and into the foyer. "I'll get it."

Nobu wondered who it would be on a Friday morning. They weren't expecting anyone. "I'll go see who it is," he said, tossing the mismatched sock on the sofa.

He turned the corner into the entry hall. Sachi stood in the open doorway and turned to Nobu when he approached. "I was just telling this man I'd better get someone else to sign for this," she said.

Nobu's stomach sank. Western Union never brought good news.

His hand shook as he signed for the telegram. Even the delivery man's expression showed that he knew it was likely not good news. He nodded, backed away, then turned to leave.

Nobu shut the door.

Sachi stared up at him. "What is it?"

What could he say to her?

Stop it. Stop it. Sure, it's probably bad news, but it doesn't have to be the worst news.

"Nobu?" Sachi's eyes were wide with anticipation.

"It's a telegram for Mama. Go back to what you were doing. It doesn't concern you." He didn't mean to sound heartless, but if it was bad news . . . the worst news . . . he was *not* ready to tell his little sister.

Mama called from the living room. "Who is it, Nobu?"

His heart stopped then pounded hard. "Go on, Sach. I'll take this in to Mama."

"Oh, okay," she said and returned to her bedroom.

Nobu tore open the telegram. It was addressed to Mama, but he needed to read it first, in case it was the worst news.

In an instant, everything was sucked out of Nobu, and he fell against the closed door. He couldn't make himself read the rest, but couldn't stop himself either.

> TO INFORM YOU THAT YOUR HUSBAND, MICHIO KIMURA, DIED EN ROUTE TO THE DETENTION CAMP IN SANTE FE, NEW MEXICO. THE DEPARTMENT EXTENDS TO YOU ITS SYMPATHY FOR YOUR LOSS.

"Nobu? What is it?" Mama stood in the entryway.

He snapped erect and crumpled the telegram, as though he could hide what he knew Mama had already seen.

"What is in your hand?" she asked, walking toward him.

"Mama . . . Mama." He struggled to keep the tears that burned his eyes from falling. Words scattered around in his head as he tried to grasp the right ones. But there were no right words.

"Papa is dead." He handed her the telegram.

She glared at Nobu and shook her head, as if she thought he'd played an awful joke. But as she read the telegram, her lips, her hands began to tremble, until her whole body quaked and she began to fall.

As Nobu grabbed her, she screamed, "No! No! Michio-san!" and her body melted to the floor.

Sachi came running from her room. "What's wrong? What's wrong with Mama?" She knelt beside Nobu and Mama.

Nobu put his arm around Sachi, too. As she searched his eyes for answers, he thought his heart would burst with pain and a sudden flood of loneliness overwhelmed him. He had to care for Mama and Sachi, somehow make it all better for them. Papa was dead. Who was there for him?

"Nobu?" Sachi waited.

Nobu. Nobu. Nobu. Never before had he so hated the sound of his name.

Papa's voice echoed in his ear. *Gaman, son. Gaman.*

He took a deep breath and pulled his little sister and mother closer to him. "Sach, we just got a telegram and . . . and it said . . . that Papa . . . he died. Papa died."

Sachi's eyes widened with the weight of her tears. She shook her head as if trying to chase away a monster that frightened her.

Nobu wrapped his arms around Sachi as she buried her head in his shirt. He pressed her head into his chest, muffling her cries. "It'll be okay, Sach." Why did he say that? Why? It wasn't going to be okay. How could it ever be okay? What were they going to do without Papa? And even if he could make it okay for Mama and Sachi, it would never be okay for him.

Taro. When would they tell Taro? Why wasn't Taro here? *He* should be the man of the house now. Nobu did not want to be the man of the house.

Mama gave Nobu and Sachi a quick hug, kissed Sachi on her head, then stood up and smoothed her hair, then her skirt. The pain that had contorted her face only a moment before had been covered by a mask of resolve. She turned and walked toward the kitchen. "We must plan your father's funeral."

That night, when the unsettling silence had settled into a quiet that was normal in the house at that time of night, Nobu removed his journal from under his pillow.

January 2, 1942

Papa didn't deserve to die en route to a detention center where he didn't deserve to be. A Justice Department camp. But justice for who? Certainly not for us.

My father always told me not to cause trouble. Keep your nose clean. Behave. Lately, he'd begun telling me not to do anything that might seem un-American. Shikata ga nai. Nothing can be done about it, he used to always say. Gaman. Be patient. This will pass one day.

He lived his life like that. Pleasant. Patient. Polite.

Look where it got him.

CHAPTER 14

Nobu

JANUARY 5, 1942

January 5, 1942

Today we returned to school after Christmas holiday. I have to admit, it was a welcome break from the sadness that has filled our home since we found out that Papa died. Everything there reminds me of him, and though I know Mama tries to be strong, she can't hide the faraway look in her eyes.

At least Sachi and I have school to escape to. I wonder what Mama did today while we were gone? Could this house have felt any emptier than it does when we're here?

We spend a lot of time in our own rooms now. A few days ago, I peeked in on Sachi while she played in her room with the doll that Mama and Papa got her for Christmas. She was on her bed reading a book, the doll in her lap. I sat next to her and noticed all of her Geisha dolls had been turned to face the wall.

When I asked why, she was quiet for a minute, then said, "They remind me of Papa."

I wish Taro was here. I don't want to be strong for everyone. He is the first born and should be here. There is nobody to be strong for me.

I still don't understand how Taro thinks joining the guard is the "honorable thing" to do. Mama calls it his sense of giri—duty. But why should we have a sense of duty to a government who stole Papa out of the hospital, called him an alien enemy, probably caused his death? And what about those who call us Japs? Why should we be honorable when we see signs on stores that tell us we're not welcome?

Taro should return home and fulfill his role as the oldest son. That would be the honorable thing to do.

A few of my friends came up to me to say they'd heard about Papa and that they were sorry. I could tell by the looks in their eyes, they didn't know what else to say. Mostly I heard whispers as I walked past classmates and teachers.

They'd glance at me, then quickly look down, probably hoping I hadn't noticed. But I heard their whispers—that Terrence and Joe were in jail for killing a Jap. That it was my father.

Happy New Year. I heard those words many times today from students passing each other in the hallway as they made their way to classes. Nobody said those words to me. A month ago, I thought this would be a good year. I'd graduate from high school. Go off to college.

Now? Papa is dead. I hear Sachi crying at night. Mama is distant. Taro is in Hawaii. I am the accidental man of the house.

Happy New Year? Not for me.

CHAPTER 15

Terrence

JANUARY 5, 1942

Jailhouse sounds jerked Terrence out of a deep sleep. Keys clanked. The cell door squealed as it opened.

A gravelly voice followed. "You got visitors, kid. Get up and get dressed."

Terrence pulled himself up and sat on the edge of the cot, rubbing his eyes.

"Come on, boy. I haven't got all day."

He pulled on prison-issued pants and slippers and followed the guard to the visiting area.

A gray room. No windows. No pictures. Only a table and four chairs. Momma sat in one chair. Though she smiled, her eyes were puffy and red. Next to her, a man Terrence had never seen before. She stood and kissed Terrence on the cheek.

"Hi, Momma," he said and stared at the stranger.

"Son, this here is Mr. Edward Blake, the attorney who be handling your case." She started crying.

"What's wrong, Momma?"

She covered her eyes with her handkerchief and turned away from him.

Edward Blake's steel-blue eyes studied Terrence through round, wire-rimmed glasses that looked like they held the weight of a single bushy red eyebrow. His full, red moustache—practically the size of a squirrel's tail—moved up and down with words spoken in a Southern drawl.

Blake extended his hand. "Mr. Harris—"

"Call me Terrence," he said, surprised at the strength in the attorney's handshake. He watched Momma, wondering why she was crying all of a sudden. "Momma, what is it?"

Blake touched Momma on the shoulder, then took his glasses off and began to wipe them. "Terrence, I'm afraid we've got some bad news."

Now what? Daddy was dead. Terrence was in jail for beating up a man. What news could be worse than that? Then, he knew. And he felt like someone hit him so hard in the stomach everything was gonna come up. He stared at Mr. Blake, waiting for him to say what he already knew.

"We learned yesterday that Mr. Kimura died. The prosecutor is going for a murder charge."

Momma cried out, then blotted her eyes with her handkerchief.

Terrence's knees weakened and he fell into a chair. Sure, he already knew what Mr. Blake was going to say, but hearing the words . . . a cold sweat broke all over him and his brain overflowed with thoughts until it was so full words began to flood out of his mouth. "Dead? I thought he was in the hospital. He *can't* be dead. Hell, I didn't mean to kill nobody, Momma. Oh, my God, I killed Nobu's father? We were just roughing him up some. I didn't mean to kill him."

"I believe you," Blake said, popping open his worn briefcase. "Now, take a deep breath. We've got to get to work on your case." He stared at Terrence for a moment. "You okay now?"

Terrence nodded.

Blake opened a file folder, then licked his finger and flipped through its pages. "I've read the police report." Running his hand back and forth along a paragraph, he continued. "Found some extenuating circumstances I think will help your case . . ." He looked over his glasses. "With the right attorney. That's why I contacted your mother."

Terrence wiped his forehead with his shirt sleeve, then narrowed his eyes, and considered what Blake was saying. Why would a white man want to represent a colored kid? What was he up to? Trying to cheat Momma out of money or something? Maybe make a name for himself?

Blake pulled out a chair and opened a notebook. "Tell me what happened that day at the park."

Terrence sat across from the attorney and stared him full in the eyes. There was a part of him that was grateful to have a lawyer defending him, especially now that Mr. Kimura was dead. But there was another part of him that just couldn't understand why a stranger—a white stranger—would want to defend him. "No sir. You go first. Why'd you decide to take my case? What's in it for you?"

Momma stood in the corner and crossed her arms. She cleared her throat and gave her son one of those glances that needed no words.

Even Blake caught her unspoken scolding. "It's okay, Mrs. Harris. A valid question." He straightened, slapped his knees, and gazed at the ceiling, then cleared his throat. "When I was a young man—I'd just started my law practice in Berkeley—I received a telegram from my mother, asking me to come home to Arkansas. Said she had something important to tell me. Well, I knew she didn't have much money. And for her to send a telegram, and with my pa off fighting in the First War, well, I had a bad feeling." He stood and started pacing. "So I wired Ma that I'd take the next train home. She met me at the station, and when I saw the look on her face, it confirmed my fears. Pa was dead. Killed by the Germans." He turned around and looked at Terrence. "I still remember the anger—no, the rage I felt. Thought I might go crazy for a bit."

Hearing those words, seeing Blake's piercing eyes, Terrence's heart raced. Rage. Yeah, that's just what he'd felt the day he learned the Japs killed Daddy.

"I couldn't imagine not ever seeing Pa again. Couldn't imagine Ma living alone."

Terrence understood the distant look in Blake's eyes. Sorrow. Loss.

Anger returned to the attorney's face. He continued, his voice hoarse. "I hated the Germans. Hated them! I wanted to go over there and kill every one 'em. But when we found out Pa was dead, the blasted war had just ended. There'd be no revenge." He took a handkerchief from his pants pocket and wiped his forehead.

JAN MORRILL

Terrence pressed his hands to his eyes to stop the burn of tears. He could tell Mr. Blake still felt it. Did this mean the anger would never end? "How'd you get over it?"

Blake wiped his glasses. "The night of Pa's funeral, my ma told me something I've never forgotten. Countries may go to war, but that doesn't mean that there needs to be a war between people."

Between countries, not people. Was that why he didn't feel better after beating up a Japanese man? Matter fact, he felt worse. Now, he had sorrow *and* guilt. It was like swallowing bad medicine every time he remembered seeing the little girl's eyes. Hearing her cries.

"I don't think you ever really get over the death of a loved one," Blake said. "But with time, you learn to live with it. I still remember how I felt, so I understand a little about what happened the day you found out about your daddy." He sat again. "And now you know why I wanted to take your case. That, and I'm a good attorney." He chuckled. "We've got a lot of work to do before your trial begins. Now, are you ready to tell me your side of the story?"

CHAPTER 16

Sachi

APRIL 1, 1942

A stare needs no words
You are different. Go away.
A slap needs no hand.

Sachi held her doll close and rang the doorbell. She heard shoes tapping on hardwood floors on the other side of the door. While she waited, she admired purple and yellow pansies that bloomed and overflowed from garden boxes lining the porch rails. Maybe Mama would plant some flowers with her now that spring was here. Like Papa used to do.

The door opened, and Kate's mother stood behind the screen.

Sachi looked up at the very tall woman. "Can Kate play?"

"Why, hello, Sachi." She opened the door and called for her daughter. "Katie, Sachi is here to play with you."

Sachi sensed that Mrs. Cook was looking at her—like she wanted to say something. She still got that awkward feeling from people, even three months after Papa died.

Finally, Kate's mother put her hand on Sachi's shoulder. "How are you and your family doing, Sachi? I've been meaning to call your mother, but I've been so busy lately."

The knot in her stomach and the lump in her throat returned, like unwelcome guests—surprising and prickly. "We're fine, Mrs. Cook. Thank you for asking." It had become her standard reply.

Mrs. Cook smiled nervously. "That's good, dear. Katie, did you hear me?"

Kate replied from the back of the house. "Coming, Mommy."

"Have a seat in the living room, Sachi. I'll make a snack for the two of you."

Sachi watched Mrs. Cook walk out of the room. She had such pretty blonde hair, and she was so much taller than Mama.

"Hi, Sachi," Kate said, skipping into the living room. She plopped onto the couch next to Sachi. "Oh, good. You brought baby Sally with you. Come on. Let's go to my room. You and me and Sally and Susie can play house."

There must have been a hundred dolls sitting on shelves in Kate's room, overflowing out of the toy box and lying on the bed. Baby dolls, porcelain dolls that looked like they were from the olden days, rag dolls. But no geisha dolls.

"Sit here," Kate said, pointing to the center of the yellow carpet, where doll clothes lay scattered all around.

She sat next to Kate, and they chatted as they fed their babies, changed diapers, swapped clothes, and put pink ribbons in the dolls' hair. Just like grown-up ladies.

"Do you think Susie looks like me?" Kate asked, wrapping her doll in a pink blanket.

Sachi considered the question. Yes, the doll had blonde hair like Kate's. Blue eyes. "I suppose she does."

"Sorry, but I really don't think Sally and you look much alike. Couldn't you find a doll that looks like you?"

The words stung. She looked down at Sally, lying between her crossed legs. Brown hair, blue eyes. Pinkish skin. No, they didn't look alike at all.

Silly old doll.

Mrs. Cook called from the kitchen. "Girls, I've got snacks for you on the table."

Kate jumped up, holding Susie in her arms. "Come on," she said, walking out of her room. "Mommy made some peanut butter cookies yesterday. Bet that's what she put on the table. That and some grape Kool-Aid, I hope."

Sachi left her doll on the floor, and followed Kate to the kitchen. She picked up a cookie from the plate in the center of the table and sat across from her friend. Taking a bite, she watched Mrs. Cook washing dishes at the sink. Kate put her cup down and Sachi giggled at the purple moustache above Kate's lip.

The scene was so unlike how things looked at her house. When she thought about how different she always felt, her mouth went dry, and the cookie tasted like sandpaper. She didn't want to be rude, so she quietly hid the cookie in her jumper pocket.

"Mama, I'm home," Sachi called. She found her mother sitting at the kitchen table, sorting through a pile of mail.

"Did you have a good time at Kate's?" Mama asked, skimming along the edge of an envelope with a bamboo letter opener.

"I guess so. Mrs. Cook made cookies for us. She asked how you were doing and said she's been meaning to call." She placed her doll on the table. "We played dolls, too."

Mama studied her daughter. "And was that fun?"

"Kind of. But—"

Mama opened a few more envelopes between glances at Sachi. "But what?"

Mama wouldn't understand, and she sure wouldn't want to hear that sometimes Sachi wished she had blonde hair and round blue eyes. "Nothing, Mama. I'm going to go play in my room for a while."

Mama stacked the mail and rose from her chair. "Sachi-chan, you haven't practiced your dance today, and you have lessons tomorrow. Go practice, then we will take a walk to the grocery store."

Now she was sure her mother wouldn't understand. All she did was push her to learn the Japanese ways. Papa wanted her to be an American, to fit in. American food. American music. American dolls. Just like everyone else.

She passed through the living room on her way to practice and saw Papa's reading chair in the corner. Sunlight shone in through the blinds in stripes on the chair's brown leather. She saw him sitting there, with his reading glasses resting on his nose and his arms held out for her to join him. She remembered rushing to his lap.

She curled into the chair. But without Papa's arms around her, it was too big and too empty, even cold. She closed her eyes and buried her nose into the leather—breathed deeply to find the scent of him. It was hardly there anymore. Would her memories of Papa fade the same way?

In the dance room, she watched the clock, tracking every minute of the hour Mama said she had to practice. At the sixty-first minute, she called, "Mama, I'm finished. Can we go to the grocery store now?"

"Yes," Mama replied from her bedroom. "Get your jacket and we will go."

The sky was clear and blue, and the sun warmed Sachi between brushes of cool sea breezes that blew in from the bay. Spring bloomed all around. Red tulips, purple pansies, yellow daffodils, emerald lawns. Perfectly-groomed houses bordered both sides of the street, like finely-dressed boys and girls lining the walls of a dance room.

When they turned on to Gilman Street, traffic sounds replaced bird songs. The street hummed with passing cars and an occasional honking horn at a stop light. Spring, summer, fall, or winter—not much changed about this busy street.

But that afternoon, something was different. White sheets of paper hung off street lights and utility poles, flapping in the wind as though calling everyone's attention. Store windows were plastered with them, too. People slowed to read the words, forming small crowds everywhere.

Mama took Sachi's hand and pulled her over to where several Japanese had gathered. Some scratched notes on small pieces of paper they held with hands that trembled as they wrote.

Sachi stood on her toes to try to read the words, but the grown-ups were too tall. She jumped up and caught a glimpse of the bold letters at the top of the notice: INSTRUCTIONS TO ALL PERSONS OF JAPANESE ANCESTRY:

Mama searched her purse and pulled out a pen and a piece of paper. Sachi was able to read some of what her mother wrote:

All Japanese persons, both alien and non-alien, will be evacuated from the above designated area by 12:00 o'clock noon Tuesday, April 7, 1942 . . . Responsible member of each family . . . must report to Civil Control Station . . . between 8:00 a.m. and 5:00 p.m. Thursday, April 2, 1942 . . . the size and number of packages is limited to that which can be carried by the individual or family group . . . Go to the Civil Control Station . . . to receive further instructions.

Whispers hissed through the crowd. Some people shook their heads and walked away. Mama returned the pen and paper to her purse and took Sachi's hand.

"What did the sign say?" she asked. Maybe Mama's answer would take away the bad feeling that made her stomach hurt. She put her other hand in her pocket and felt the crumbled cookie from Kate's house.

Mama walked faster, and Sachi noticed she held her head higher than usual. Those who were lucky enough not to be of Japanese ancestry stared when they passed.

"Mama, why are they staring at us?"

"Do not concern yourself. We will do our grocery shopping on another day."

CHAPTER 17

Nobu

APRIL 1, 1942

April 1, 1942

When Mama came home this afternoon, I knew something was wrong. She looked frightened, and I could tell Sachi had been crying.

She told me about the notices that were posted everywhere. Notices that we are to be evacuated by April 7. Evacuated from our own homes? How can they do this? They say it's for our own protection. Bullshit! It's because they are afraid of us! Afraid we are spies for the Japanese. They thought Papa was a spy!

Mama and Papa raised us to be proud of our heritage. Now we are ashamed, even try to hide it. No matter how much I want to fit in—to look and act like the other Americans, I wear my Japanese ancestry like a mask I can't remove. There is no place to hide.

We have done nothing wrong, yet they will gather us and lock us up. Hell, I might as well be Terrence, locked up in that jail cell. We're no better than prisoners. No better than the bastard who killed my father.

Mama wants me to go to the Civil Control Station tomorrow. I don't want to go. I don't want to hear an American give me orders about where we must go, when we must leave our home, even what we can bring with us. I AM an American!

Mama says this is how we must show our loyalty. Where is the loyalty to us?

But I'll go, no matter how much I don't want to. It's my duty as man of the house. I'm tired of it. But just like being Japanese, there's nothing I can do to change it.

He slammed the journal shut and threw his pen across the room.

CHAPTER 18

Sachi

APRIL 1, 1942

The large suitcase lay open in the middle of her bedroom floor, and Sachi watched Mama neatly arrange sweaters, pajamas, socks, and underwear.

But Mama wouldn't know which books to pack, so Sachi ran to her bookshelf and skimmed her finger over the titles, choosing her favorites. It was not an easy choice. Each of them had taken her to imaginary places she had grown to love.

Finally, she made her reluctant decision. "These need to go, too," she said, laying the books next to Mama.

Mama looked at the stack. "You cannot take all of those. The notice said we can only bring what we can carry. Books are too heavy. You may choose two of your favorites."

"Two? I had a hard enough time choosing ten."

"Please, do not argue with me. We all have to make sacrifices. Please choose two."

She carried the books to her bed and tossed them onto the pink chenille spread. How could she choose between castles or farms? Princesses or pirates? Witches or fairy godmothers?

"Mama, why must we sacrifice? Why do we have to leave our home? All of our favorite things?" She hesitated. Anger strangled her confusion, until it swelled—grew bigger and bigger, until, like a balloon, it burst. "Papa said we are Americans! But do other Americans have to make sacrifices? No! Well, I don't want to make sacrifices either!" The words spilled from her mouth like marbles, scattered so quickly she knew she'd never get them back.

Like a ghost, Papa had returned and slapped Mama with his words. Her eyes reflected shock, dismay, hopelessness, anger. For a tiny moment, it was all right there in the glare Mama blasted toward her. But as quickly as it had fired in her eyes, flushed in her cheeks, it disappeared. She tilted her head down, closed her dark, tired eyes, folded her hands, and straightened her back. In silence, she rose from the floor and walked to the bedroom door.

Without looking at Sachi, she calmly let her own words escape. "You may choose two books . . . and one doll." Then, she walked out and closed the bedroom door.

The next day strangers came to the house, ringing the doorbell early in the morning. Sachi had never seen any of them before, yet Mama let them in. Caucasians. Americans who didn't have to choose which books to pack, which doll to bring. In walked tall men in overcoats and fedoras, following prissy women with white-gloved hands that touched everything. They opened cabinet doors to look at the dishes. Flipped through pages of books on the bookshelf. Talked about whether or not the pattern on the couch would match their decor.

"How much for the set of dishes?" a lady with red hair asked.

"Two dollars for the whole set," Mama said.

The redhead took her wallet out of her patent-leather purse. But the bald man with her told her to put it away. "Seventy-five cents," he said.

Mama touched a dinner plate. "They are from Japan."

He stared at her. "Precisely. That's why they're not worth two dollars. Like I said, seventy-five cents."

"Very well," she said, avoiding his eyes when he handed her the coins.

"Hi, Sach."

Sachi was surprised to see Kate and her mother standing in the kitchen.

"Hi, Kate. What are you doing here?"

"My mom wanted to come over to talk about a few things with your mom."

Mama walked toward them, putting the coins in her purse. "Hello, Mrs. Cook. Kate. How are you?"

"Fine, thank you," Mrs. Cook replied. "We wanted to come by to see if there's anything we can do to help."

"*Arigato*. Thank you." Mama bowed slightly. "But I'm afraid there is not much you can do."

"Would you girls like a snack?" Mama asked. "I have some *omanju* if you'd like."

Kate looked at Sachi, her nose crinkled. "O-man-gee? What's that?"

Sachi leaned over and whispered, "They're sweet bean cakes. All kinds of pretty colors. I think you'll like them."

"Yes, please, Mrs. Kimura," said Kate.

Sachi smiled, excited to have her friend try the Japanese treat.

Mrs. Cook stood by the counter while Mama placed the pastel-colored desserts on a white plate. "Mrs. Kimura . . ."

"Please, call me Sumiko." She smiled. "Or Sue, if that's easier."

"If you'll call me Nancy," replied Kate's mother.

Mama nodded.

"Anyway," Mrs. Cook continued, speaking softly, "I'm so sorry about what's happening to you and your family . . . to all of the Japanese. I can't imagine what I'd do in your place."

"*Shikata ga nai*. We do what we must do."

"How can we help? Anything we can hold for you while you're gone?"

Mama looked at Sachi. Moving closer to Mrs. Cook, she whispered. "The notices say we can only take what we can carry," she said. "We will sell most of our belongings, but some things . . . are very difficult to part with. Like Sachi's doll collection."

"What about my dolls?" Sachi asked.

Mama's words spilled quickly. "My mother gave them to me when I was a little girl, and when Sachi was born, I gave them to her."

"Mama? What about my dolls?"

Mrs. Cook touched Mama's hand. "Of course we'll take care of them until you return."

Sachi rose from her seat. "You're going to give my dolls to them?"

"We cannot take them with us," Mama said, her voice shaking. "I do not want to sell them. It is the only thing we can do."

Mrs. Cook walked out of the kitchen, signaling Kate to follow.

Mama pulled out a chair. "Kate and her mother were very kind to offer. You know they will take good care of them until we get back." She wiped tears from Sachi's cheeks.

"But it's not fair."

"No. Life is not fair. But we must endure it."

Kate and Mrs. Cook returned to the kitchen.

"I'll take good care of your geisha dolls" said Kate, placing her baby doll on the table. "And . . . you can have Susie. I have lots of dolls."

It was like sunlight peeked through the dark clouds of the last few days. She was letting her keep Susie!

The two women carried each of the glass-cased geishas to the car and put them on the back seat. Mama placed blankets between each, as though tucking them in for a long night's sleep. She bowed to Kate's mother. "Thank you, Nancy."

Sachi held Kate's baby doll in one arm, and her own doll with the other. When the Cooks' car pulled away, she wasn't sure if the tears she blinked away were happy tears or sad ones.

Mama took her hand and they walked up the front porch steps, back to the hard reality of the pack of strangers picking through their belongings.

Sachi wanted to escape the whispers and decided Papa's chair would be a good place to hide. But she found an old man sitting there, head tilted to one side, cheek smashed against his hand. Loud snores rumbled in and out of his fat lips.

That's Papa's chair. "Get out of my papa's chair!"

Everyone—strangers with blond hair, brown hair, red hair, blue eyes, green eyes—stopped what they were doing and turned to look at her. The old man woke with a look of surprise.

Mama and Nobu ran into the room.

"Please accept my apologies for my daughter's behavior," Mama said to the man, bowing as she spoke, pulling Sachi behind her.

He rubbed his thick, nicotine-stained fingers over the arms of the chair. "Pretty comfy. What do you want for it?"

Mama's eyebrows pressed together above sad eyes.

Mama can't sell that chair. If that man took it, he'd be taking with it memories of Papa.

"Ten dollars, please," Mama replied.

Ten dollars? For the chair where I fell asleep while Papa read to me in the afternoons?

"No, Mama! You can't sell it," she cried.

Mama paled and looked at Nobu. "Please take your sister outside."

He placed his arm over Sachi's shoulder and led her away.

The man's voice haunted her ears again. "I'll give you eleven. Give your girl a dollar for some candy or something. Maybe that'll make her stop crying."

He reached into his pants pocket and pulled out a wallet that bulged at its seams. "Can your boy help me load it in my truck?"

Mama took the money from the man. "Of course."

Mama was letting him take Papa's chair—the chair Sachi would have kept forever—if only they didn't have to leave in three days with only what they could carry.

"Sachiko, come with me, please." Mama led her to the dance room, closing the door behind her. She lit a stick of incense and knelt in front of the altar. "Sachiko," she said, pointing to the mat next to her.

Sachi's prayers hadn't done any good lately, so what was the use? She'd prayed Papa would get better. Prayed the kids at school would quit calling her names. None of her prayers had been answered. Still, to appease her mother, she bowed her head and closed her eyes.

In the silence of her make-believe prayer, she heard the old man's truck engine start. It rumbled quieter and quieter as it drove away with Papa's chair, until she could hear it no more.

CHAPTER 19
Nobu

APRIL 2, 1942

Nobu needed a place to hide. He walked into his bedroom, slammed the door, and stood in the middle of the darkness, holding his breath as he tried to cast away the anger he felt. Nothing took away his rage. It danced around him, hot and wild as the flames he'd just watched in his backyard.

Sweat beaded on his forehead, dripping off his bangs. His shirt, damp from perspiration, felt cold against his back. But his face still burned.

How could Mama burn all of their pictures, her letters from *Ojiisan* and *Obaasan,* Mama's own parents, that she'd managed to keep hidden from the government men? Did she really believe tossing the mementos of their past into the fire would change who they were today?

The bluish glow from a street light shone through the window blinds. He held his hand under the lines of light, turning it over and looking at the stripes across his skin. If only he were a different color . . .

He pulled the chain on his desk lamp. When the light blinked on the stripes vanished, returning his skin to the color of a Japanese man again.

A small stack of books lay on the corner of his desk—books he planned to take with him when they were relocated. The damn government called it an evacuation. For your own protection, they said. The books were all that remained on his desk. The pictures he'd had there— Mama and Papa before they were married, his grandparents in front of their home in Hiroshima—all of it was gone. Burned.

He pulled his journal from the bottom of the stack and opened it. The desk lamp cast a circle of light onto a blank page.

Hands trembling, he began to write.

April 2, 1942

Today, I reported to the Civil Control Station as head of my family. I stood in line, looking at the other Japanese and wondering if they, too, would spend their last few days here selling their belongings and trying to find friends who might store property for them.

After hours of waiting, I finally sat in front of the desk of a hakujin—*a damn Caucasian—so busy processing paperwork, he barely looked up.*

He asked our name, how many in our family. Didn't even look at me as he jotted down the information.

He gave me several tags and told me to attach them to each family member and to each piece of baggage. Then he reminded me that we could only bring what we could carry.

"Next," he said. Then he stamped our papers and added them to the pile.

I looked at the tags. A small blank space for our name, then in large, bold letters, "Family No. 13754." To the right of our family number were instructions: Report ready to travel on Tuesday, April 7 at 8:00 a.m.

So Family No. 13754 replaces our family name on our ID tags. The same tags we will put on our suitcases. To the hakujins, *we are little more than baggage.*

I've just watched Mama burn our family pictures, old letters—anything of our Japanese heritage.

Earlier tonight, I was reading in my room, trying to forget what's been going on in the last few days: The Civil Control Station and the idiot behind the desk who wouldn't even look at me. Selling our belongings—practically giving them away. I hated having strangers—leeches—in our house. Handling our personal belongings and arguing with Mama about what they were willing to pay. I hated seeing all that Mama and Papa had accumulated over the years, in the hands of greedy people; so anxious to steal from us for their homes, yet they wouldn't even look us in the eyes!

Then, I smelled something burning and went downstairs to see what it was. An orange light flickered through the kitchen window. I ran out the back door. In the center of the backyard, Mama's face glowed above a fire that burned in a steel drum. She stared into the flames, and I saw light reflecting in the tears that fell down her cheeks.

When I called to her, she wiped her face. I asked her what she was doing. "Nothing, Nobu. Go back inside."

But I didn't listen, instead, walked over to her. I noticed scraps of paper scattered around the drum. Torn pictures with brown, curled edges. Pieces of letters lined by black ash.

I couldn't believe it. Even pictures of Papa!

I crawled on the ground, trying to gather the charred scraps. They burned my hands. "Mama? Why are you burning these?"

"We must destroy anything that might make someone believe we are loyal to Japan," she said, staring into the blaze.

No, no, no! I cried inside, but bit my lip so Mama wouldn't see.

I got up from the ground, holding a charred photo in my hand.

"Toss it in the fire, Nobu," she said softly.

I told her I couldn't do it.

"It's for our protection. You must."

I looked at the scrap and realized I couldn't make anything of it—could no longer recognize that piece of our lives. So I threw it into fire. The heat grew hotter and hotter until it burned my skin. But I couldn't make myself move away.

When the orange glow dimmed, I told Mama we should go inside. She still held a picture in her hand.

"What is it, Mama?"

She didn't answer, but held it up to look at it, then tossed it into the fire.

Now our house is empty of everything we held dear. All that remains are our suitcases—only what we can carry.

Tuesday we must report for relocation. Where will we carry those suitcases tagged Family No. 13754?

He closed the journal and turned off the light.

CHAPTER 20

Terrence

APRIL 3, 1942

The courtroom hummed with whispers about the three boys sitting at the front of the room. Every once in a while, bits of conversation jumped out and bit Terrence.

"I think the colored one did it."

"Doesn't really matter who did it. The Jap had it coming."

A sour taste burned on the back of Terrence's tongue, and he wasn't sure what made him sicker—sitting next to Joe and Ray or the whispers. Then he figured he didn't have to decide. The whispering people? Joe and Ray? They all thought the same way: The Jap had it coming.

Heck, he'd felt it, too, that day in the park. At least until he saw that little Japanese girl running toward them and he realized the man huddled on the ground was her daddy.

Blake touched his shoulder. "Doing okay?"

Terrence shrugged, trying to be cool. But inside, he thanked God that at least Mr. Blake believed him.

Joe stared in Terrence's direction, eyes squinted and hateful.

The court clerk came through a door at the right. "All stand for the Honorable Judge Anderson."

When the judge entered, the sound of shuffling feet and the moan of chairs scooting across the floor echoed in the room and drowned out the whispers.

"You may be seated," Judge Anderson said, opening a file before he sat in a big leather chair. He turned each page, seeming unaware of the hundred eyes on him.

Terrence watched. Waited. His pulse pounded in his temples like his brain was about to explode. What kind of man was this judge, the man that would decide his future? He sure hoped the judge wouldn't see him the same way as he saw Joe and Ray. 'Cause no way was he like those two. No way.

The man in the black robe looked too young to be a judge. Buzzed-short brown hair. Thin lips. Stiff demeanor. Looked more like a drill sergeant than a judge. The man was just a little too stiff-looking, and it gave Terrence an uncomfortable tickle way down in his gut.

More whispers churned in the courtroom, then silence. Then more whispers. Back and forth, like the pant of an invisible demon. Ceiling fans whirred with an irritating click. Hell, it was like a clock ticking his life away.

Finally, the judge spoke. "Joseph Brian Grant. Raymond Dean Morrison. John Terrence Harris Jr. You have each been charged with first-degree murder." He took off his glasses and looked at the boys. "How do you plead?"

Joe's attorney stood first, scratching his head as he spoke. "Not guilty, your honor."

"Not guilty, your honor," followed Ray's attorney.

Blake took a breath to speak next.

Terrence held his.

"Your honor, we would like to move for a separate trial for Terrence Harris, based on extenuating circumstances that set the facts of his case apart from Mr. Grant's and Mr. Morrison's." He held up a file. "May I approach the bench?"

"You may," replied Judge Anderson.

Blake signaled for Terrence to follow.

The judge was even scarier up close, staring down at them like he was God on Judgment Day. He removed his glasses and folded his hands. "Continue, Mr. Blake."

Blake laid the thick file in front of the judge. Terrence knew it held his report cards, Honor Society certificates, and letters commending his community service. It also contained his father's naval service record, and the most important document—the one that made Terrence's story different: the crinkled telegram that informed the Harris family of Daddy's death at Pearl Harbor.

Terrence studied Judge Anderson's face as he reviewed each document in the file. Only the sound of shuffling paper broke the room's silence.

He looked at Blake and Terrence again. "Is there anything you'd like to add?"

"Your honor," Blake placed his hands on the bench, "most significant is the fact that Terrence and his family received that telegram the day of the beating. A terrible mix of circumstances led to the unfortunate beating and death of Mr. Kimura—Terrence's emotional state after being notified of his father's death at Pearl Harbor, and running into Mr. Grant and Mr. Morrison, two boys with previous records who were intent on getting into trouble even before my client came along. As you will note in the file, prior to this event my client had no criminal record. His grades are excellent. Neither can be said about the other two defendants."

Judge Anderson returned the file to Blake.

"Your honor, it is for these reasons that we request a separate trial for Terrence Harris. The circumstances differ so greatly from the other two boys, we believe it is warranted."

In the silence between the request and Judge Anderson's decision, something clutched at Terrence's throat, squeezing until he felt his heart beat in every part of his body. His knees shook and he needed to sit again. He closed his eyes, thoughts whipping through his head.

Don't lump me in with those other two. I'm not like them. I'm not like them.

The judge's face went stiff again. "Please return to your seats."

As Terrence followed Blake to their seats in front of the courtroom, Momma's glance gave him silent support.

It's gonna be okay, son.

But the ice-cold glares of his co-defendants screamed at him. *What're you up to, nigger? You gonna betray us? You'll be sorry if you do.*

The whispers grew louder too, like snakes hissing all around him.

"Mr. Blake," Judge Anderson began, "Mr. Harris, in further consideration of your request, this court will recess until next Monday morning at nine o'clock." He pounded the gavel. "Court is adjourned."

Gasps whipped through the room like a blast of wind. The bailiff took a set of handcuffs off his belt and approached Terrence. With each step the big uniformed man took, he felt a familiar darkness.

The bailiff threw the handcuffs over Terrence's wrists. *Click.* The cold hard metal on his skin held him—shamed him. A prisoner. But no more a prisoner than he'd become of feelings he had carried since that day at the park.

"Traitor!" Ray shouted.

"Order!" yelled Judge Anderson. "I'll not have such outbursts. Order in this court."

The room quieted, all but the hissing sounds.

CHAPTER 21

Sachi

APRIL 7, 1942

My house is empty
But memories will remain
Echoes in my heart.

It was almost time to go. Sachi listened to Mama's heels tapping on the floor as she rushed around the house for a final check before they'd leave for good.

Tap, tap, tap, tap. Silence.

What did Mama think about as she walked into the kitchen? The living room? The bedrooms?

Tap, tap, tap, tap. Silence.

Sachi wandered around, too, drifting from empty room to empty room, trying to gather memories to hold. Each footstep echoed on the hardwood floor, and she, too, stopped walking to remember: getting mad at Taro because he kept winning at jacks, watching Papa build a fire in the fireplace. Even practicing her dreaded dance lessons in front of the mirror was a good memory now.

The government might be able to limit the number of suitcases they could carry, but they couldn't make her leave her memories behind.

Hollow echoes swallowed her. She paced around her bedroom, running her hands along the pink walls. *Tap, tap, tap, tap*—like the heartbeat of her home. When they left, the heartbeat would stop.

Mama called from the hallway. "It is time to go."

Time to go? Time to *go*? Her heart ached. She didn't want to leave her room. Her house.

Mama called again. "Did you hear me? It's time to go."

Nobu peeked into her bedroom. "Come on, Sach. It'll be okay," he said, leading her out.

When Mama closed the door behind them, Sachi squeezed her eyes and thought of all the times she'd heard that door shut before. The fall mornings when she left for school. The evenings when Papa arrived home from work. The afternoons she returned from playing and Mama told her not to slam the door. Mama wouldn't have to worry. She'd never slam it again.

Nobu was quiet as he drove, and his hands kneaded the steering wheel like clay.

Sachi sat alone in the back seat, suitcases piled so high around her she had to struggle to see out the window. She watched the morning fog roll off the hills surrounding San Francisco Bay. Where did fog disappear to during the day, before returning to the hills again at sunset?

Her family would disappear, too. Would they ever return?

"Turn here, Nobu," Mama said.

When they rounded the corner onto Van Ness, Sachi couldn't believe the line of people—so long it stretched around the block. The last time she saw so many Japanese together was at Papa's funeral. They stood still and quiet, their solemn faces hidden between hats and pulled-up collars of gray and brown overcoats. Piles of bags and stacks of suitcases cluttered the sidewalk beside the line. Some of the women whispered to each other, their children huddled close by. Strange that these children didn't run, didn't chase, didn't giggle.

Nobu drove up and down the street, searching for a place to park. After a couple of passes, he said, "I'll let you out at the end of the line, then I'll go to find parking."

Mama got out and opened the back door for Sachi, while Nobu unloaded all but three suitcases and carried them to the curb.

A car honked, and Mama hurried to the sidewalk. "Get those two, Sachi, and stay close to me." When she reached the end of the line, she placed Sachi between the wall of the building and herself.

Sachi could hardly see daylight and felt suffocated by the forest of grown-ups in drab coats. She faced the wall and found green paint chipping off in places, revealing patches of white plaster. One patch looked like an ice cream cone. That one might look like California, if she could just pick off one tiny piece of green. Moving close to the wall so Mama wouldn't see, she flicked a piece of paint to make the white plaster look more like her home state.

JAN MORRILL

The long blast of a car horn startled her, and she peeked around Mama's coat to see a black sedan creeping past the line. The driver rolled down the window, and she heard a familiar song drift from the car. "Pardon me, boy. Is this the Chattanooga Choo-choo?"

But the driver's voice drowned out the music. "About time you people go back to where you belong."

Nobody responded. Most didn't even look at him. *Look straight ahead. Do not cause trouble.*

Nobu ran from across the street. "I left the key under the floor mat," he told Mama. "I hope Mr. Cook can find it okay."

Sachi thought about her dolls, probably displayed now on Kate's bedroom shelf. "The Cooks are keeping the car for us, too?"

"Yes," Mama said, pulling at her gloves. "At least we will have a car when we return."

Nobu shuffled his feet, looking fidgety. "This line hasn't moved at all. Why did we have to come so early?"

Something tickled Sachi's stomach when she saw Mama's lips press so tightly the pink turned pale. She shot a warning look at her brother. *Papa is not here, and you are the man of the house now. You better behave yourself!* Mama wasn't in the mood to deal with his attitude this morning.

"I wanted to beat the crowd," Mama replied, barely above a whisper.

"The crowd, huh? Guess we didn't do that," he said, looking ahead, then behind. "Just how many Japanese do you suppose they're rounding up, anyway?"

Sachi glared at him. Why was he being so mean? She tried to get him to stop, kicking his foot to get his attention, even as she wondered, too. How many Japanese could there be and what were they going to do with all of them?

At last the line moved, slowly, like a huge caterpillar. Each dull coat inched forward, and murmurs drifted through the once-quiet line. Children whined and cried and their mamas said, "Shhh!"

Inside, the room smelled like cigarettes, and Sachi saw smoke rising from ashtrays on eight gray metal desks lined up against a yellowed wall on the far side of the room. Signs with the alphabet hung above each one. Every once in a while an official-looking Caucasian sitting behind the desk took a long drag and blew smoke into the air.

Her family approached the desk that was beneath the sign that read Last Names Beginning with *I-K*.

The woman who sat there seemed nice enough. She smiled as she asked questions: How many in your family? How many suitcases did you bring? Do you have property to store? Do you have your immunization records? She stamped forms so hard Sachi blinked each time she pounded. First the ink pad. *Bang!* Then the piece of paper with Family No. 13754 on it. *Bang!*

Mrs. Lady-Behind-the-Desk made sure all of their tags were in place before pointing to the rear of the crowded room. "Please go out that back door and wait for the bus that will take you to the temporary assembly center at Tanforan."

"You mean the racetrack?" Mama asked.

"Yes. You'll stay there until it's been decided where you'll be moved next." Now the lady didn't sound so nice. "Please, move on to the waiting area so I can process the next family."

"Process?" asked Nobu. "You mean like cattle?"

Mama moved close to him and tugged on his jacket. "Shh! Let's go!"

Process. The word hadn't bothered Sachi so much. She was already thinking about what it would be like living at a racetrack. She loved horses, and maybe they would let her ride one. This might be an adventure after all.

They sat on their suitcases in the crowded parking lot and waited, surrounded by the smell of diesel and the rumble of idling buses. Sachi watched the monsters swallow the lines of Japanese, one by one. Then, bellies full, each pulled out of the parking lot and disappeared around the corner.

Which one would swallow her family?

She'd never ridden on a bus before and wasn't sure if the tickle in her stomach was nerves or excitement. All she knew was her hand was getting numb from Mama holding it so tight.

Forever. That's how long they'd been sitting on those suitcases. Sachi looked around at the hundreds of people and wondered how many of their backsides were as sore as hers.

Then she noticed. So many women, sitting in little mini-forts stacked with what was left of their belongings. With stern eyes and pointed fingers, they told their children to sit still, and they would obey, for a little while. But if Sachi watched long enough, she would notice pulses of energy escape in bursts, before their mamas would again point their fingers and snap at the suitcase where they should sit still. She knew how that felt.

But where were all the men? Why would so many families be missing their papas, too?

"Family number 13754?" A voice called from across the parking lot.

Mama looked down at the tag that hung from her coat. Sachi looked at hers, too.

"That's us," Nobu said, rising from the suitcase. "That must be our bus."

Sachi followed her brother, wishing she had a free hand to hold onto his jacket. But Mama held one hand, and in Sachi's other was a suitcase that was way too heavy. They walked by men in khaki uniforms, so tall they blocked the sun and cast long, dark shadows. Though curious, she was afraid to look at their rifles for too long. Some of the men seemed to sneer at her as she passed by, and it made her heart beat hard, as if trying to break free from something that clutched it as tightly as Mama grasped her hand.

When they reached the folded doors at the front of the bus, the rumble of the engine vibrated inside her, and the diesel smell made her queasy feeling worse. The first step into the bus was so high she could hardly lift her leg to reach it. When she did, the suitcase she carried made it hard to pull herself up.

As if he read her mind, Nobu turned around and whispered, "You sit next to Mama. I'll sit behind you."

He could be grouchy sometimes, and it made her mad, especially when he was mean to Mama. But every once in a while, he did something that made her think he was the best brother in the world.

He grabbed her suitcase and placed it above a row of empty seats. "Sachi, you sit there, next to the window." Next he took his mother's luggage. "Mama, you sit here next to Sachi."

Mama plopped down in the aisle seat and exhaled. She stared ahead, the look in her eyes sad and very far away.

Sachi laid her head against Mama's arm. Though she'd meant to comfort her mother, for a tiny moment, she felt a familiar calm of her own when she caught the scent of cedar in Papa's coat that Mama wore. She closed her eyes and inhaled, trying to hold on to Papa's scent. She missed how he would have put his arm around her and pulled her toward him. And as fast as it had come, the comfort was gone, quick as the hummingbird she'd seen near the porch when they left that morning.

The bus doors closed with a loud hiss and Sachi stood to see the front of the bus. A man in a khaki uniform sat in the driver's seat. He shuffled around, flipping a switch here and a lever there.

Mama tugged on Sachi's coat. "Sit down."

"I think we're getting ready to go," Sachi whispered. The knot in her stomach began to throb again.

The engine rumbled louder. When the bus jerked forward, Mama grabbed the seat in front of her. Her eyes widened.

The look frightened Sachi, but she placed her hand on Mama's arm. "It'll be okay," she said, trying to reassure her mother. As the bus pulled out of the parking lot, she watched the people standing in line get smaller and smaller. Her heart became heavy with a longing to hear someone say those words to her.

It'll be okay.

CHAPTER 22

Nobu

APRIL 7, 1942

Nobu exhaled, his heart still beating hard after seating Mama and Sachi and getting their bags loaded. He had been afraid he wouldn't find room for everything. Shoving and pushing at one point, he'd even elbowed a man to get him to move his suitcase so he could squeeze the last one onto the shelf above them.

All morning, anxiety and uncertainty had been unwanted companions. He'd been swept along in a river of lost Japanese who rushed to wherever directed, until the river dumped him in the seat on the bus. Now, as it rumbled past a line of armed guards and onto the street, the current had slowed, and he sat in strained silence with dozens of other

Japanese that drifted down the same stream, wondering where it would ultimately take them.

He watched Mama and Sachi in the row ahead of him. Mama faced ahead, with no traceable movement, while Sachi rested against Mama's arm.

It had been a long day, and it wasn't even noon yet, so the humming vibration of the engine and the rocking motion of the bus lulled him into sleepiness. But there was no place for him to rest his head.

He reached into his coat and pulled out his journal.

April 7, 1942

I'm sitting on a bus headed for Tanforan Race Track. Imagine. A race track will be our home for who knows how long. Nagare no tabi. A stream's journey. I have no control over where it will take me.

I ask myself, "How can they do this to us?" Then I ask myself, "How can we let them do this to us?" Aren't we American citizens? Don't we have rights?

Mama and Sachi are sitting in front of me. Mama stares straight ahead. Sachi is asleep, worn out from getting up so early this morning.

Strange, that I want to protect them, yet at the same time, feel burdened by them. Especially by Mama. By her Issei generation. First generation. Their rules. Their pride. Their loyalty to a country that won't even allow them to become citizens!

If it weren't for Mama, I would speak up to these people who came into our homes, looking for things to confiscate—contraband they called it! Who were they to tell us we couldn't go out at night in our own country—the place where we were born! We complied with all of their rules, and still, they made us sell everything, move out of our houses. Now they are sending us to Tanforan, to remove us from a place they now call a military zone. Hell, it was no military zone. It was our home.

But to save face for Mama, for the family, for the entire race, I keep my mouth shut. We must do nothing to impede the war effort, Mama says. So we comply with the laws against the Japanese, even those who are Americans themselves.

Saving face. It has always meant that we are proud and must maintain our dignity. But instead, I feel ashamed. We have allowed ourselves to be treated like a herd of animals, directed by men with rifles. To show we are loyal Americans, we have become less than human, and we hide our faces.

Okay, I am afraid, but not of the Caucasians—the hakujins! No, I am afraid of myself. How long can I swallow my dignity to appear dignified? How long can I comply with Mama's wishes to accept the way we are treated?

Like the noise of this bus, it all rumbles inside me. And it's taking me to Tanforan Racetrack. How long can I keep it inside? How long?

CHAPTER 23

Sachi

APRIL 8, 1942

Murmuring. It soothed her like a lullaby. The scent of cedar beside her. But why did her arms hurt? A loud hiss. Where was she? Her body jerked forward and she opened her eyes. The light—too bright.

An unfamiliar voice: "Ladies and gentlemen, welcome to Tanforan."

She rubbed her eyes and looked around. They had arrived. But she was too sleepy to wake yet. She closed her eyes again and leaned against her mother's arm. *Just a little while longer.*

Mama shook her. "Wake up. It's time to get off the bus."

"But I'm so tired. I don't want to wake up yet," she whined. "Can't I sleep a little bit longer?"

Nobu mussed her hair. "Come on, Sach. Listen to Mama. Here, take your suitcase."

As the bus rocked back and forth with the movement of everyone trying to get their bags at once, a man boarded the bus. "Ladies and gentlemen. Please. Please! Be seated. There has been a change of plans. Please remain in your seats until you are notified further."

Nobu threw his suitcase onto his seat. "What the—"

But Sachi was happy they didn't have to get off the bus yet. At least she could go back to sleep for a while.

How long had she been sleeping when another loud voice woke her?

"Please remain seated. You will not be staying. This bus will be going on to Santa Anita Assembly Center."

The stuffy bus exploded with complaints and questions. Several men raised their hands, trying to get the attention of the speaker.

"I'm sorry. No time to take questions. You should arrive at Santa Anita by midnight."

The sky turned pink, then purple and black. Sachi's stomach growled as she stared out the bus window. Funny how signs and houses on the ground passed by so quickly, yet the stars in the sky hardly seemed to move at all. Everything was boring. Nothing to do. And she was hungry. When would they get there? She closed her eyes and fell asleep again.

The bus stopped and the sudden silence woke her. She looked outside the window, wondering where they were. Was it Santa Anita? It was dark outside. The only light came from guard towers and inside the buildings. An armed guard walked toward the bus. When he boarded, she decided they must have arrived.

"Attention, please," he called from the front. "Please proceed to the building on the left for your apartment assignments and orientation packets."

Nobu hissed. "Yeah, right. Apartment assignments. This *is* a horse track, right?"

Mama stood and turned around. "Nobu!"

The line of people getting off the bus moved faster than the one getting on. Sachi could understand why everyone seemed to be in such a rush. They probably had to use the bathroom as badly as she did.

She followed Mama and stepped down the bus's big steps. Outside, she breathed in fresh air while being swept along in a line that moved so quickly she feared she'd be run over.

They were surrounded by more uniformed men with guns and once again, she began to talk to herself. She'd been doing a lot of that lately.

Would they really shoot us? Sure they would. Why else would they carry guns? And what about that wire fence around the whole area? Not just any wire fence, either. Did you see the sharp-looking points sticking out every few inches? Do they think we'll try to escape? They must. But escape from what?

Questions popped into her head faster than she could come up with answers. It reminded her of how she felt when she watched a scary movie, always afraid of what would come next. Only, this wasn't a movie.

Find something good.

Horse stalls! How could she forget about the horses? With the size of this place there had to be at least a hundred of them. She giggled. *Don't be so silly. That fence is for the horses, not the Japanese!*

The line came to a stop outside a building where the sign read "Administration." She was tired of being in lines. Start, stop. Pick up your suitcases, put them down. What's around the corner? What are they going to tell us to do next? All she wanted to know was where they would live next.

Then she could look for the horses.

Nobu dropped his suitcases onto the ground near the administration building. "Mama, you and Sachi wait out here. I'll go inside."

Mama sat on her suitcase. "Sit down, Sachiko. Rest."

She reluctantly complied with her mother's request. All she could do from her suitcase seat was watch people, which she really didn't want to do, because it made her think of things she didn't want to think about. In the dim light cast from the administration building, all the adults' faces had a kind of sadness she hadn't seen before, at least not on so many of them at once. Lost. Misplaced. Yes, that's what it was, they looked misplaced. Still, if she looked deep into their eyes, she recognized pride—trapped there, and hardly noticeable once her gaze panned out to the rest of their sad faces.

She had seen that look before. On Papa's face the day he was fired from the bank.

And in his eyes, when those boys called him names that day in the park.

She studied the faces again. Japanese faces. *But they are Americans.* So why were they all sitting on suitcases, surrounded by men who carried guns? Fenced in by prickly wire that she knew in her heart was not for the horses.

It still caught her by surprise sometimes, when a hunger for comfort drew her to look for Papa. The path to his arms had been well-worn— the only path she'd known. When he was alive, somehow he always made her believe everything would be okay.

She rested her head on her knees and watched her tears fall to the dirt. Each droplet made a tiny mud ball that disappeared into the ground next to her dusty, patent-leather shoes.

"Ready to go?" Nobu waved a piece of paper in the air and held a flashlight in his other hand. "I have a map that will take us to our . . . apartment."

Sachi wiped her face and looked up.

He picked up his suitcases. "Follow me."

They walked past rows and rows of horse stalls. Sachi slowed between each pair of buildings, trying to catch a glimpse of a horse that might peek out its head in the ricochet of Nobu's flashlight. Nothing. But hay was scattered all over the place. Surely there must be horses somewhere.

After what seemed like a long walk from the administration building, Nobu turned left down a row of stalls. He shined a light on the map, then up at the stall numbers, stopping in front of one. "This is it," he said, opening the door and walking inside. He pulled on a string that hung from a light on the ceiling.

Sachi glanced up at Mama. "A horse stall? I thought they said 'apartment.' If we're going to live here, where will the horses live?"

CHAPTER 24

Nobu

APRIL 8, 1942

Nobu ran out—past Mama and Sachi, down the row of horse-stall barracks.

Mama called after him. "Nobu! Where are you going?"

He didn't stop, but yelled back to his mother and sister. "I don't know. I'm sorry. I'll be back later."

He had to get away. Run. Run away from that smelly stall. From the look in Mama's eyes.

He collapsed behind one of the buildings and watched other families tentatively approach their new homes as he held his flashlight and wrote in his journal. They stood at the doorways and stared before walking inside. He listened to whimpers that drifted between the rows, and wondered if one of those cries came from his own mother. Guilt tensed in his shoulders as he held the flashlight to write in his journal.

April 8, 1942 (continued)

Santa Anita! Horse stalls. All three of us will live in a horse stall that is smaller than my bedroom at home.

Each blindfolded step we are led on this path, I think it can't get any worse. But with every step, it does.

They call them apartments, but they have given us goddamn horse stalls to live in. The smell! Stains of horse piss and shit in the dirt floors. It's dark—only one bulb hangs in the center. And bed? Ha! The mattresses are wool blankets, sewn together and stuffed with hay.

Four shelves nailed up on one wall. Is that enough for us to place our belongings, such that they are?

And what about all the knotholes, where you can see into the stall next door . . . and they can see into ours.

They tell us it is temporary, but they can't—or won't—say how long we'll be here.

What will they do with us next? I wonder who asks that question more . . . the Caucasians who make the plans, or the Japanese who must follow them?

CHAPTER 25

Terrence

APRIL 12, 1942

Sunday. Pot roast for supper. About this time, Missy and Patty would be jabbering at each other across the table like nobody else in the world existed. And afterwards, Terrence would wish he'd done his homework on Saturday, 'cause he sure wasn't gonna feel like doing it after pot roast.

He opened his eyes, and Sunday at home disappeared. Now it was Sunday in a cell of four dirty walls, scarred by a thousand hands with nothing better to do. The stench of body odor and piss. Hacking coughs made him shudder like nails on a chalkboard.

A tiny window near the ceiling shed dim light into the cell. Must be cloudy outside.

"Hey, you. Time to get up. Lunch." The guard opened a slot in the door and waited for Terrence to take the tray.

He took it, more grateful for the break from boredom than for the lousy food. Peanut butter sandwich. Some kind of soup. Lukewarm, like usual. Sure didn't match up to the supper he'd been thinking about. Maybe Momma would bring him something when she came to visit later. Didn't matter. He wasn't very hungry anyways, what with the queasiness stirred up by all this wondering about what might happen in court tomorrow. He set the tray aside and leaned his head against the wall.

Maybe he deserved to be punished—spend the rest of his days in jail. He'd helped take a man's life, after all.

But he also figured he deserved a second chance. He knew he'd made a mistake. A big one. One he'd regret for the rest of his life. Judge *had* to see it. Had to see that he wasn't a bad kid. Jail or no jail, he'd pay for what he did for the rest of his life.

Damn! He had to stop thinking about it. It was driving him crazy. Like a pendulum, swinging back and forth. Swinging forward—the judge had to see he wasn't like Ray and Joe, that he'd made a mistake he was sorry for. Swinging back—the judge wouldn't see it, and he'd go to jail for the rest of his life. All for a mistake that didn't do anything to take away the loss of his daddy. The pendulum cut.

He took a bite from the sandwich. Rancid. Dry and sticky in his mouth. A sip of soup to wash it down. Yeah, cold all right.

A prisoner across the hall threw his soup cup out of his cell. It clanked against the hard floor. "This stuff is shit," he yelled. "Why don't you heat it up!"

Sympathetic voices echoed through the jail.

He wondered about Nobu and his little sister. So often he heard her in the darkness of night, when her cries surrounded him like a whole other prison. He'd overheard two guards talking the other day, something about rounding up all the Japs.

Rounding them up for what? What's that all about?

He thought about his high school baseball team—the Yellowjackets. In their junior year, he and Nobu had played for the division championship. Bottom of the ninth. Yellowjackets–4, Indians–3. Indian runners on first and third. Terrence played on second base and Nobu played on first. One out. Full count—three balls, two strikes. The pitcher threw a hard slider. The batter swung. It was a grounder straight to Terrence on second base. He dove for it. Grabbed it. Tagged the kid running to second. Threw the ball to Nobu on first. He caught it. Batter out! A double play and they'd won! Man, they'd won the division championship.

The crowd in the stands went crazy. Nobu ran to Terrence, pumping his arms in victory, while the Yellowjacket band blasted the school's fight song. The rest of the team rushed out of the dugout toward the two team members who had saved the day. Terrence smiled. That day, everyone cheered in the stands. Skin color hadn't mattered none.

"You got a visitor." With the guard's words he came crashing back to his cell.

Momma stood behind the guard as he fiddled with the lock, and hunkered down as if she was looking to hide from the yelling and whooping. Terrence knew she didn't like being in there. He'd even told her not to come. But there was no way she was going to listen to his nonsense.

"Don't be silly, boy. 'Course I'm gonna come see you. You my baby boy," she'd said.

He had shuddered. "Momma. Shhh! You can't be saying those kinda things in this place."

She walked into the small cell, wearing her flowered church dress and smelling like lilacs. She held a brown bag, one hand on top, the other below for support.

"How you doing, son?"

"Doing okay, Momma. Just a little worried about what the judge'll say tomorrow."

"I know. But remember what I told you. We got to leave it in God's hands." She gave him the bag. "Here you go. Maybe this'll help take your mind off your troubles."

The brown paper rustled when he opened it, and the smell of pot roast burst forth. He inhaled. "Ah, Momma. How'd you know?"

"Your favorite, right? Mommas just know these things."

"I didn't think I was hungry," he said, pushing his peanut butter sandwich away. "But all of a sudden, I'm starving."

"Well, dig in."

He pulled out a large covered bowl. "You want some?"

"No. It's all yours. I already ate with Missy and Patty."

"How're they doing? Never thought I'd say it, but I miss those two."

"They good. Missing you, too. Patty won her fifth-grade spelling bee this past week. We pretty proud about that."

Steam rose from a large chunk of meat on his fork before he put it in his mouth. His stomach growled in anticipation. He chewed the tender meat, and gravy—seasoned just right—spread over his tongue.

Momma watched him, a pleased look on her face.

He rubbed his stomach. "Mmm-mmm. That was so good."

"Glad you liked it, son."

An awkward silence followed. Terrence avoided his mother's eyes, gazing instead at the scribbles scratched into the wall. Stick tallies of days gone by. Stick figures making out with "Larry loves Lucille" carved below it. He'd stared at the scratches a million times before—nothing else to do in this cell.

"What you thinking about, son?"

How'd she always know when he had something on his mind? He stared at his empty bowl, stalling.

"Talk to your momma," she said.

"I heard a couple of guards talking the other day." He still hesitated. Maybe he didn't really want to know the answer. Or maybe he didn't want to raise the subject with Momma. She had enough on her mind. Whatever it was, something kept the words locked inside.

"What was they talking about?"

He inhaled deep. "Something about . . . rounding up all the Japanese. You heard anything about that?"

She looked away.

"Momma?"

"It's true, Terrence."

"Why? And what's happened to the Kimura family?"

"Official word is that it's for they own protection. But the talk 'round town is that they afraid them Japanese are gonna spy on us. You know, after Pearl Harbor."

"And the Kimura family?"

She touched her necklace and moved the gold cross back and forth along its chain. "Now I'm not sure about this . . . but . . . I heard they been moved to one of them assembly center places. Tanforan Racetrack, I think. Anyways, I drove by they house and it's empty."

The pot roast felt heavy in his gut. His head hurt, full of churning thoughts. Nobu. His family. Sent away because they're Japanese. Just like that day with Daddy in the hardware store. Denied service 'cause Daddy was the same color as the man that robbed the store.

And he'd beat up Mr. Kimura 'cause he looked like the Japs that killed Daddy. Hell, that made him no better than the rest of them.

CHAPTER 26

Sachi

APRIL 12, 1942

Sachi was the first to wake. Mama slept next to her, breathing in, then out, in a slow rhythm. There were times she wished she had her own bed again. Like when Mama whispered to Papa and Taro in the middle of the night.

Danna. Husband.

And she kept whispering something in Japanese to Taro, but Sachi didn't understand much Japanese. The whispers pulled her away from dreams of tea parties with her dolls at her house in Berkeley and back to the cold, dark stall.

Nobu was still sleeping, too. His snoring practically rattled the walls.

She liked being the first to wake. In those first quiet moments, she could look around and pretend the walls were painted white and the floors changed from dirt to gleaming wood. Dirt floors. Why did Mama waste her time sweeping them each morning?

Pulling the blanket over her arms, she wasn't sure what was worse—shivery goose bumps from the chilly air or prickly ones from the itchy blanket. Nobu had patched most of the stall's holes with mud or tin can lids, but now in the early morning, the sun bolted through cracks and holes he'd missed, leaving bright lines and dots on the dark floor and letting in the brisk morning air. But she liked to watch dust drift and float in the shafts of sunlight that came into the dark room. In the right light, even dust could sparkle.

She shook her blanket to stir more flecks into the air. Something about the way it whirled around reminded her of practicing her dance lessons with Mrs. Thompson. She didn't think she'd ever miss those lessons, but here at the assembly center nobody ever danced, and it often made her regret that she used to hate her lessons.

When Mama turned over and sighed, Sachi wished she hadn't shaken her blanket. She wasn't ready for her mother to wake up. Her imaginary world would disappear and she'd have to face the barren room and look at Mama's and Nobu's glum faces.

She didn't like being ungrateful. In the last few days, they had done what they could to make the stall a home, but she still missed their real home. The smell of Mama's cooking, the sound of her shoes on the wood floor, Nobu slamming the front door. She missed her bed, her toys, her books. The list went on and on. Now all she smelled was horse poo and hay that made her nose itch all the time. And she was tired of hearing the mumbles from surrounding stalls. She wondered what kinds of things they heard from her family. She tried to be quiet so she wouldn't bother the neighbors the way they bothered her. Even so, Mama was always telling her "shhh."

Gravel outside crunched with footsteps going by. A few minutes later, more footsteps and muffled voices. People must already be going to breakfast at the mess hall. When would Mama and Nobu wake up? If they didn't get up and get going, they might run out of food before they got there.

Sachi's stomach gurgled. "Mama?"

Mama sat up and stretched her arms above her head. "What is it, Sachi?"

"I'm hungry. Can we go eat now?"

Mama sighed. "Nobu. Wake up. It's time for breakfast."

"Ah, Mama. Can't I sleep just a little longer?"

"No, I want you to take Sachiko to the mess hall. And please bring a tray back for me. I'm going to straighten up in here."

Sachi looked around. Mama had already cleaned up before they went to bed last night. She never wanted to leave the dark room. "Why don't you want to come with us, Mama?"

"I'll just eat here when you get back." She got out of bed and shuffled over to Nobu's bed and shook him. "Nobu. Please. Get dressed and take Sachi for breakfast."

He shooed her away. "Okay, okay. Why do I always have to take her? You're her mother." He stopped and took a deep breath.

She glared at him for a second, fury and pain carved on her face. Then, she closed her eyes and turned away.

Sachi walked to the front door and peeked out one of the cracks in the wood, looking for some place, any place, to escape from the tension. Did the same conversations take place behind those other doors, between other people who never used to talk to each other like that before?

Nobu came to her and touched her shoulder, ran his warm hand over the length of her long hair. "Better get dressed, Sach. Breakfast will be gone if we don't hurry."

"Okay." She opened the cardboard box that held her clothes. As she dressed behind the curtain, she heard Nobu whisper. "Sorry, Mama."

Sometimes Sachi didn't know why she looked forward to breakfast. All they ever had was oatmeal or cold cereal, plus some boring kind of fruit like an apple or banana. It was never bacon or eggs or pancakes. That day, it was oatmeal, and by the time they got there it had gone cold, and as usual, they'd run out of sugar. She scooted lumpy glops around her bowl, as though moving them enough would make the entire glop go away.

Maybe she looked forward to going to the mess hall just to get out of the dark, stinky room, filled more with sadness than light. The grown-ups sitting around the metal tables in the dining hall didn't seem much more cheerful than Mama, but at least every once in a while she'd notice a smile escape a stoic face. A time or two, she caught a couple of ladies covering their mouths, stifling giggles that seemed out of place. It seemed fine to Sachi, though, like standing in front of a fire on a cold night.

And at least the kids still cajoled and laughed, though it was quickly followed by taps on knees or, "shhh!"

"Hi."

Sachi looked up from her cold oatmeal to see a boy standing next to her table.

"I'm Sam. What's your name?"

She wasn't sure why, but it surprised her for a boy to come up and introduce himself. But, she returned his smile and replied, "Sachi." It occurred to her Sam may have meant to meet her brother instead. She put her hand of Nobu's shoulder. "And this is my brother, Nobu."

Nobu nodded as he peeled a banana.

She studied Sam. He was kind of cute. Maybe a year or so older than she, so probably too young for him to be interested in meeting Nobu. He must have been smiling at *her*. She liked his smile, too.

"I have an older brother, too—Ken," he said. "And I have an older sister. Her name is Mariko. We live in the third row."

"Really? So do we. Where did you live . . . before?" She scooted closer to Nobu and patted the bench next to her. "Have a seat."

"We lived in Los Angeles. You?"

"Berkeley."

"Berkeley? You came a long way. I haven't seen you before. When did you get here?"

Sachi stirred her oatmeal slowly. "We've only been here for a few days."

Sam sat next to her. "It's been two weeks for us. Don't worry. You'll get used to it. So what does your father do?"

The question, always unexpected, was like a punch to her stomach. She put her spoon down.

Nobu dropped the banana peel into his bowl. "Our father is dead. Come on, Sach. Let's go. Mama must be hungry by now." He picked up the extra bowl of oatmeal.

Sam stood and nodded to Sachi and Nobu. "Oh. I'm so sorry."

"No, it's okay," Sachi said. "You didn't know."

Nobu called as he walked away. "Come on, I said. Let's go."

"Sorry. I have to go now. It was nice to meet you. Maybe we—" There was so much she wanted to say. "We live in the fourth stall from the end." It sounded so strange to say it. *We live in the fourth stall.*

Sam laughed. "Ha! You live in a stall? Why, I thought only horses lived in stalls." He whinnied as he galloped by. "I live in the stall in the middle," he said, and turned to wave.

Sachi giggled and called to her funny, new friend. "Maybe I'll see you later today."

CHAPTER 27

Terrence

APRIL 13, 1942

Terrence looked up at the blue light coming through the cell window. Long night. Too many goddamn thoughts kept him tossing and turning.

He was supposed to appear in front of Judge Anderson at nine o'clock. Edward Blake said he'd come by around seven thirty to brief him on what would happen in court. About how he should behave. Hell. First they locked him up, now they were telling him how to behave. Sure wasn't how he wanted to be living his life about now.

He figured he had several minutes before the guard came to get him for a shower. A lot of waiting and wondering in the last few months, and he was afraid of more of it. If he went to prison, he'd always be waiting —waiting to get out. He thought about the conversation he'd had with Momma the other night.

She'd brought a fresh shirt and tie for him to wear in court, and had filled him in on her conversations with Mr. Blake.

Hanging the shirt over a chair, she asked, "How you doing today?"

Her greeting was always the same. And always, he tried to think of something to say other than the truth.

I'm doing shitty, Momma. Get me outta this place. I'm going crazy.

So he always lied. "I'm okay, Momma."

"Been talking to Mr. Blake about his ideas for your trial. He say he gonna go over all that with you." She paced around the table, dragging her hand along its top.

"What'd he say, Momma?"

"He say . . . he say if the judge grants you a separate trial, he gonna advise you to enter . . . a guilty plea. Manslaughter."

"What? Guilty? To manslaughter? But—"

"It's 'cause with a plea, there won't be no jury. He afraid . . . he afraid—"

"What Momma? What's he afraid of?"

"He afraid 'cause you colored, you might not get a fair trial with a jury. You seen all them signs outside? He say he knows this judge—went to the same college—and he think the judge will go easy with your sentence 'cause of the circumstances of Daddy's death. And 'cause you wasn't thinking right after you found out. Like maybe you didn't know right from wrong. And you ain't never had a criminal record before, unlike those other two boys."

"I don't know Momma. What if he's wrong?"

"Shower time." The guard's voice startled Terrence.

God, he hated showers at the jail. After almost four months of showers there, he hoped he'd never see another yellow-green tile again.

The water barely trickled and was never hot enough. He tried to keep from touching the slimy tiles. No privacy. That's why he always took a shower at the end of the row. Least then there'd only be a naked body on one side of him. He shuddered. Sure hated looking at those naked bodies. Even worse was having those naked bodies looking at him.

A fat, white guy walked in—white except for the blue-green tattoos all over his body. He'd heard rumors about him. Peachie, they called him, 'cause he was from Georgia. His real name was probably Francis or something. Anyway, Terrence knew he was a real troublemaker when Peachie took the shower next to him. Eleven empty shower heads and he had to take the one right next to Terrence.

He figured he'd try to lighten Peachie up a bit. "How's it going?"

But fat white boy wasn't having anything to do with lightening up. "That's my shower you're standing under."

Terrence turned his back and rolled his eyes. Sure didn't want any trouble before showing up in court. Peachie's hot breath on the back of Terrence's neck gave him goose bumps.

"I'm talking to you, nigger."

Nausea rolled in Terrence's stomach and adrenaline pumped through him, tensing every muscle. He turned and got up in the tattooed man's ugly face. "What do you want? Huh? Tell me what you want. You want this shower? Here. Take it." His heart pounded invincibility through his veins with every word he spoke.

Peachie's eyes grew larger, madder, until Terrence thought they might pop out of his head.

But he couldn't stop himself. "There's eleven other places empty. But you want this one? Okay. Take it, then leave me the fuck alone."

He was two showers down when Peachie grabbed his arm and held it tight. "I think we're gonna make this a segregated shower. That means you're gonna wait for me to finish mine before you can take yours. Whites shower first. Coloreds shower last. You got that, nigger?"

Terrence ripped his arm from the grip. Peachie's fingernails left bloody trails on his wet skin. Terrence's opposite fist came around like it had a mind of its own, itching to make contact with that big, ugly face.

"Hey! You two break it up!" The guard's hand clutched a club.

Terrence moved back and pulled his fist behind his back. *Don't cause trouble today.*

"Get over here, Harris. Back to your cell you go," the guard said, grabbing Terrence. Cuffing him, he called to Peachie's guard. "Hey, Kelley! Get in here and take your guy back to his cell."

Nasty jeers and raucous cheers followed him down the hall. It all depended on the color of the howling inmate. He took deep breaths, trying to calm himself.

"You best hope that lawyer of yours figures out a way to get you outta here," the guard said. "Guess you know by now you've gone and made the wrong person mad. He's got a lot of friends in this place."

"Hey, man. I didn't do nothing. I was just minding my own business, taking a shower."

The guard sneered. "Don't you know by now, it doesn't matter what you did or didn't do? You're colored. He's white. That's the only thing that matters. Inside this jail and outside in the real world. Better get used to that or you're gonna have a real hard time."

Deep down, he'd known all along that's how it was, but he'd been able to pretend it wasn't so. Yeah, the white kids at school treated him a little different. He might have played on the same baseball and basketball teams as them, but how often did one of his white friends ask him over to one of their houses?

He returned to his cell and held his bed sheet against his arm, watching red spots ooze onto white before closing his eyes, trying to clear his mind. He inhaled deep to settle down before seeing Mr. Blake.

When it looked like the bleeding had stopped, he carefully pulled the clean, ironed shirt over his arm. Staring at each button, he moved from the tail of the shirt to the collar and wondered whether to tell Blake about what happened.

It was only a short drive from the jail to the courthouse. The front window was down and a cool breeze reached Terrence in the back seat. Smelled like the ocean. He stared at things he'd always taken for granted before. Seagulls fighting over scraps on the sidewalk. Music drifting in from the car at the stoplight. The guy on the corner, taking a drag off his cigarette while he watched pretty girls walk by, their skirts swishing back and forth. He didn't get the chance to be outside much, and now he felt sick just thinking about spending the rest of his life locked up in a smelly cell.

An hour before, Terrence had wanted to be out of his cell and in the courtroom. But once he arrived at the courthouse, he wasn't so sure that jail cell was a bad place to be. What made him think today would be any different from other days at this place?

He walked handcuffed through a crowd of shouting gawkers. They glared at him; the colored boy who killed the Jap. Some waved signs and shouted as the guards hustled him through the crowd.

"You'll get what a Negro deserves."

"Good riddance to the Jap."

What bothered him more—the clowns who thought he should be punished because he was colored, or the ones who thought Mr. Kimura deserved to die because he was a Jap? Hell, there were probably jerks out there who had a hard time figuring out which side to be on; they didn't like any color but white. A pit settled in his stomach. What kind of people would be sitting on the jury that would judge him?

Maybe Mr. Blake was right. Take the manslaughter plea.

He walked in and found Momma sitting in the front row. She smiled as he passed, her eyes glistening.

Mr. Blake was already seated at the defendant's table. "You ready for this?" he asked.

"I guess. Don't have much choice, do I?"

"Sure you've got a choice. But I think you'll be taking a big risk to go with a jury trial." Blake jotted notes on a tablet. "The judge'll come in soon. We'll find out if he'll grant us a separate trial, then we'll make our plea."

Our plea? My plea.

He hated the thought of admitting to manslaughter, even if it was true. As long as he kept the confession to himself, it didn't seem so real. It was kind of like standing behind a big, closed door. Massive and dead-bolted, it protected him from something unknown and scary that stood behind it. Long as he didn't admit it, the door was closed, and he was hidden, safe.

But Momma said they had to trust Mr. Blake. And mostly, he did.

She rubbed his back and he turned to her. "You look good, son." But her eyes widened.

He followed her gaze to where she stared at his shirt, where the scratches had bled onto white. *Damn!* It was the last thing she needed to see.

Her voice rose, and a dozen faces turned to look at her. "Son! What's that blood on your arm?"

He folded his arms over the blood stain. "Nothing, Momma. Don't worry about it."

"What you mean 'nothing?' Look like something to me. Who did this to you? And why?"

Now, Mr. Blake stared, too. "Terrence, what happened?"

"I . . . I just scratched—"

The bailiff's voice interrupted. "All rise for the Honorable Judge Anderson."

Terrence's heart jumped and he spun around, grateful he didn't have to explain, at least not yet. He watched the judge enter the room and tried to read his expression. Poker-faced, he held Terrence's file—his life—in his right hand. His mouth went dry and his tongue swelled so it was hard to swallow.

"Please, be seated," Judge Anderson said and looked up at Terrence. "Mr. Blake. Mr. Harris." He glanced at the prosecutor. "Mr. Foster." Then, he began to flip through the papers in the folder. "I have reviewed the documents you presented and see reasonable cause to accept your motion for a separate trial from Mr. Grant and Mr. Morrison." He removed his glasses and watched Terrence. "I understand Mr. Harris wishes to make a plea. Mr. Foster, will you please review the factual basis for this plea?"

Foster stood. "On December 23, 1941, in Alameda County, California,

Mr. Terrence Harris did knowingly participate in the killing of a human being . . ."

Terrence felt dizzy.

Did knowingly participate in the killing of a human being. But no! He *didn't* know he would kill Mr. Kimura. His mind drifted, trying to run away from what was being said.

The judge spoke again. "Mr. Harris, is that a true and accurate statement of what happened, and of the crime to which you are admitting?"

Blake nudged Terrence and whispered, "You need to answer the judge."

Strength drained from Terrence's legs. His knees trembled. He leaned against the table and stared at veins that bulged from his hands.

Say it! No, don't—there'll be no turning back! Say it!

He took a deep breath. "Yes, your honor."

"And Mr. Harris, do you understand that by pleading guilty to manslaughter, under California law that it is a second-degree felony punishable by up to fifteen years in state prison, regardless of whether the act may have been intentional or not?"

"Yessir."

Judge Anderson closed the file. "Mr. Foster, do you have a recommendation as to sentencing in this case?"

"Yes, your honor. Pursuant to negotiations with Mr. Blake in this matter, the state of California recommends that the court impose a sentence of ten years of incarceration with the California Secretary of Corrections, with Mr. Harris to serve twenty-four months of the sentence here at the county jail, with the remainder suspended pending successful completion of standard probation."

Amidst the gasps in the courtroom, he recognized Momma's muffled cry.

"Mr. Blake, do you have anything to add?" asked Judge Anderson.

"No, your honor, I believe the court is fully-apprised of the pertinent facts and circumstances concerning Mr. Harris's crime and you have seen the extent of his regret and remorse. We request the court accept Mr. Foster's recommendation, and assure the court that it is in the best interests of the people of the state of California."

Terrence wanted to turn around and tell Momma he'd be okay. But he was frozen. Ashamed that Momma had to hear him plead guilty.

Afraid of all the people staring at his back, probably thinking he deserved a longer sentence.

Judge Anderson spoke again. "Very well. Mr. Harris, you have pled guilty to manslaughter, a second-degree felony. Therefore, it is the judgment of this court that you be committed to the custody of the California Department of Corrections for a period of ten years. Eight years of the sentence shall be suspended upon the completion of twenty-four months incarceration in the county jail, and successful completion of two years of probation. It is so ordered."

It was done. He had pled guilty to manslaughter. The big, locked door that had protected him was open.

CHAPTER 28

Sachi

MAY 2, 1942

Sachi sat at the edge of the bed and pretended to read a book. But it was only a place to hide while she watched her mother get dressed for breakfast.

Finally, Mama had agreed to go out. Since arriving at Santa Anita, she had refused to leave the stall they lived in, and Sachi couldn't understand why. She had never been shy before. At home in Berkeley, she went out all the time: to the grocery store, parent meetings at school, afternoon tea with friends. But at Santa Anita, she hardly ever left, even to go to the mess hall.

Mama stared into the tiny mirror that hung on the wall and brushed her long hair. She pulled it into a ponytail before wrapping it in a bun and poking hairpins all around. How pretty she had always been. But as Sachi studied Mama's face, she noticed it had changed. Now, her mother looked tired and pale. Beneath her once smiling eyes were dark circles that left Sachi feeling unsettled. Something wasn't right. Mama didn't act like Mama. She used to fix meals and serve her family at the table.

Now Nobu brought meals from the mess hall. She used to keep the house in order. These days, it was up to Sachi.

Maybe Mama missed Papa as much as she did. Maybe even more.

She watched Mama pat the dark circles under her eyes, then run her fingers over her cheekbones, too prominent now that she'd lost so much weight. Her black, silken hair that Sachi loved to run her fingers through had begun to show signs of gray that streaked from her creased forehead.

But on this day, Sachi shooed away thoughts that left her uneasy. For the first time, Mama said she would go to breakfast. Maybe it meant the return of the mother she'd missed since leaving their home.

Mama turned from the mirror and took a deep breath. "I'm almost ready."

"Me, too," Sachi said, smiling. "Nobu, are you ready?"

He answered from behind the curtain. "You two go on. I'm going to the showers first. I'll meet you there."

Sachi put her book down and scooted off the bed. She wiggled Nobu's curtain and whispered. "Can I come in?"

"Yeah, what is it?"

She tiptoed into the corner of the apartment that Nobu called his bedroom and closed the curtain behind her. Leaning over his bed, she whispered, "This is the first time Mama is going to breakfast with us. You can take a shower later."

"Ah, come on, Sach." He rolled over and faced the wall. "I'm sick of waiting in those lines at the shower. I'm going during breakfast when there won't be so many people waiting."

Frustration threatened to chase her appetite away. This might be the start of Mama getting back to normal, and it felt as fragile as a dandelion puff, held between an inhale and exhale.

Dandelion puffs. Fairy balls. How many times had she closed her eyes to make a wish before blowing on the puffs, then watching the tiny fairies fly away to make it come true?

"Sachi, no!" Papa had scolded when she found them on their lawn in Berkeley. He told her each of her little "fairies" would grow into a weed.

You mean grow in to a new wish to make. So she always made sure Papa wasn't looking before she made her wish.

Blowing dandelions used to work. But lately, none of her wishes came true.

No way would she let Nobu ruin Mama's morning. She leaned in close and whispered. "I mean it. You need to come with us. Please."

He sat up and huffed. "You can be a real nag, you know?"

She grinned, pleased with herself. "Good. Now hurry up and get dressed," she said, then returned to Mama. Closing the curtain, she reported, "Nobu said he'd be out in a minute."

Sachi stepped out of the dark apartment into the sunlight and squinted against its brightness. A cloud of dust hovered over the path as they walked to the mess hall, but above, the sky was brilliant blue, cloudless. Mama held her purse close and walked just behind.

A man jogged by and turned to greet them as he passed. *"Ohayogozaimasu,"* he said. "A good morning, *neh?"*

Mama smiled and nodded. *"Hai."*

Sachi couldn't wait to show Mama the flowers that some of the residents had planted. She especially liked two of the gardens—purple and yellow pansies in one, bright red begonias in the other. Maybe she'd let Sachi plant flowers, too. As far back as she could remember, she'd looked forward to spring, time to plant seeds with Papa. He'd help her water them, and weeks later, when the first colorful blooms appeared, they celebrated together.

"See the pretty flowers," Sachi asked her mother. "I like the purple ones best. Which do you like?"

"The purple ones are nice."

"Don't they brighten the doorway? Do you think we could plant some in front of our door?"

"Perhaps," Mama said. "We shall see."

They passed horse stall after horse stall, until several rows down, they passed the showers. Nobu punched Sachi's arm.

"Ouch!" She rubbed where he'd hit her. "Why did you do that?"

"You see there?" he asked, pointing. "Two people in line. That's all. Two people!"

"Children!"

Unaffected by the scolding, Sachi smiled. The old Mama was back.

Dozens of people stood outside the mess hall. Another long line.

Maybe Nobu was right. So many waited in lines to eat. To take showers. To buy supplies. Even to go to the bathroom. Lines, lines everywhere. Waiting, waiting, waiting.

But today, she didn't care if Nobu had to stand and wait. He needed to be there for Mama. She whiffed the air. Even oatmeal smelled good in the fresh air and sunshine, so why would her grouchy brother complain? The week before, they'd waited in the rain, and she'd shivered so hard it didn't matter what scents came from the kitchen. It could have been brussels sprouts for all she cared. She only wanted to get inside where it was warm and dry.

"Hi, Sachi!"

Her heart leaped at the sound of Sam's voice. When she saw him approach with his parents, she checked the yellow ribbon in her hair and moistened her lips. Then, she skipped over to meet them.

"Hi, Sam!" Excitement bubbled inside. She ran back to the line and touched Mama's hand. Finally, Sam would get to meet Mama. "This is my mother, Sumiko Kimura. Mama, this is my friend, Sam, and his parents, Mr. and Mrs. Uchida." She had the urge to giggle and felt the warmth of a blush across her cheeks. What a good morning—Mama was having breakfast at the cafeteria *and* meeting Sam and his parents. She hoped Mama would like Sam as much as she did.

"*Ohayogozaimasu.*" Mama bowed to the Uchida family. "Sachi has told me about you, Sam."

"Mr. Uchida owned a butchery in Los Angeles," Sachi said, beaming. "Sam says he wants to be a butcher someday, too."

Mama's lips pursed and her body stiffened. "How nice." She turned toward the mess hall door. "This line moves slowly, does it not?"

A prickly silence placed a barricade in the narrow space between them.

Mr. and Mrs. Uchida stared at the ground.

Sachi's stomach hurt. What had just happened?

Sam shrugged his shoulders at Sachi.

Nobu stepped in. Resting an arm on Sachi's shoulder, he offered his hand in greeting to Mr. and Mrs. Uchida. "I'm Sachi's brother, Nobu. It's nice to meet you."

Mr. Uchida shook his hand. "Hello, Nobu. Have you met our son, Ken? He's about your age."

"Not yet, but Sam told us about him."

Mr. Uchida nodded toward the showers. "He said he'd join us for breakfast after his shower."

"I had thought about doing that myself." Nobu tugged Sachi's ponytail. "Not this morning, though. But I do look forward to meeting him."

Only when Nobu nudged her did Sachi realize the line had finally started to move. She tried to shake a bad feeling that gnawed at her, but it was as stubborn to shoo away as the stinging horseflies that lingered around the race track.

Something very strange had just happened between Mama and the Uchidas. And the light, skipping feeling she felt earlier had turned to a heavy pit in her stomach.

After Mama's unfriendly greeting, Sachi wasn't sure if Sam would meet her at their secret hiding place. Still, she leaned against the school building, hidden in the shade of the storage shed, and waited. Surely he wouldn't hold her mother's behavior against her. After all, they'd played together almost every day since meeting weeks before, and now Sachi considered Sam her best friend. And she was pretty sure he had a crush on her.

She'd never had a Japanese best friend before, and hadn't realized how much she missed it. She knew she was different from all her Caucasian friends, but in the past, had told herself to ignore the feeling. Now here was Sam, the same as Sachi—a Japanese American—not quite Japanese, not quite American. Always treated just a little bit different by Caucasian friends. And then there were the kids at school who teased about her looks, her name, her parents.

She had to admit, fitting in was something she liked about being at Santa Anita. She bit her lip, hating that she could like anything about being locked in a place away from their home. Nobu walked around with a scowl on his face all the time. Even worse, the camp made Mama quiet and sad every day.

But for once, I belong.

Her stomach twitched. Then, glancing around the shed, she giggled to herself. Of course nobody heard her thoughts. For the first time in her life, she didn't hunker as she walked through a crowd, afraid of what others thought when she passed by. Here, there were no girls with blond or brown or red hair for her to envy. And at Santa Anita, it was okay that her name was Sachi Kimura and not Sally Smith.

Sachi left the shade of the secret hiding place and ambled away, certain that Sam wasn't coming. Anger boiled inside. It was all Mama's fault. Now what was there to do? Where would she go? The last place she wanted to be was back with her mother, where she'd probably blow up at her. That hadn't happened since they still lived in Berkeley, where Mama would send her to her room. Here, she had no room of her own, so what would Mama do?

She walked up and down the rows of stalls. What did the other families do behind those doors? What were the homes they left like? These were the same old questions she always wondered, and she was bored with them.

There wasn't much else to do but to go back to her stall.

She walked into the apartment, where Mama lay on the bed flipping through the pages of a magazine. How would she avoid talking to her?

"Where's Nobu?" Sachi hoped the question wouldn't lead to any discussion of what had happened earlier. Besides, maybe she'd go find her brother instead of being stuck in that room with Mama.

Mama laid the magazine on her stomach. "I have no idea. I cannot keep up with you children. He just said he was going out."

Sachi sat on the bed and stared at the single painting they brought from home, cherry blossoms in Tokyo. It had seemed so full of springtime when it hung on the wall in the living room. But in this dark room, it only served as a reminder of what was outside of the camp and it made the room even drearier.

"Why so quiet, Sachi-chan?"

She rolled her eyes and shrugged her shoulders. "Don't know."

Mama sat up and put her hand on Sachi's shoulder.

She pulled away so swiftly, the magazine fell to the floor.

"Sachiko!"

There was no place to escape in the small, dark room. Mama stood too close, gave no space. Sachi felt it coming—in her rapid heartbeat, her quickening breath, her desire to scream—her anger was ready to erupt.

She glared at her mother. "Why did you treat Sam and his family like that? You were nice at first, and I was happy that you finally got to meet them." Her eyes began to burn with tears. She turned from Mama so she wouldn't see, but couldn't control the tremor in her voice. "Then something happened, I don't know what it was, but you became rude. I wanted you to be friends, like Sam and me." She couldn't control her tears. "I don't understand you sometimes, Mama." She ran to Nobu's room and pulled the curtain shut.

Mama had better not follow. She needed to be alone. Besides, she wasn't so sure she was ready to hear Mama's reason for her behavior. Somehow, she had a feeling learning why might be one of those awful times when there'd be no going back to before. Maybe not knowing was better, so why did she bring it up anyway? And now, Mama had seen her cry.

But it was quiet now. So quiet she could hear muffled conversations from next door. Maybe they heard her blow up. It would serve Mama right. Maybe she'd even lose face at the thought a neighbor overheard their argument.

Looking around Nobu's room, she wondered. What secret things did he keep? She didn't often have the chance to snoop around when he wasn't there. Well, it wasn't really snooping, just curiosity. She wouldn't bother anything, and if she put it back the way she'd found it, he'd never know. So what would be the harm?

Her heart pounded hard as she wondered where to look first, and a merry wave of mischievousness swept over her, a welcome distraction from her anger. She pinched the corner of his pillow and lifted it quietly, gently. Nothing there. She tiptoed to the corner of his room, where his tennis shoes rested on top of an assortment of books. Boring books and smelly shoes that she didn't want to touch. Surely there was something more interesting somewhere.

She returned to the bed and plopped onto the mattress. Didn't all older brothers have something snoop-worthy for their little sisters to find? Ah, under the mattress! She knelt on the floor and lifted it. Hay dust escaped and made her nose tickle, threatening a sneeze. She closed her eyes and pinched her nose hard. If a sneeze escaped, Mama would come into the room, and her spell of naughtiness would be broken.

There it was. The most valuable find of all—Nobu's journal. Oh, to read his thoughts. It couldn't be so bad, he was her brother, after all.

She felt very naughty, but very excited and knew to make a mental note of the journal's position before slowly, silently pulling it from under the mattress. She held it and ran her fingers along its binding as she battled the angel and devil inside. The angel: *How would you feel if Nobu read your private thoughts? Thoughts about your crush on Sam? About how cute you think he is?* The devil: *But Nobu is so quiet sometimes. Wouldn't it be good for you to know what he is thinking?*

Yes. It would be good.

She gently opened it, holding it close to her chest so Mama wouldn't hear the binding crack.

"Sachiko, come in here, please."

The sound of Mama's voice startled Sachi and she almost dropped the journal. Did Mama know what she was doing? She took a deep breath.

"Okay, Mama," she replied, though she still didn't want to talk to her mother. She closed the journal and returned it to its hiding place. Before she rose to her feet, she checked it one more time, shifted it the littlest bit to make sure Nobu wouldn't be able to tell. As she opened the curtain to return to Mama, she felt a curiosity bigger and hungrier than it had been before she'd entered Nobu's room only moments before. She'd have to find another chance to read that journal.

She took a deep breath. "Yes, Mama?"

"I want to try to explain what happened this morning. Sit down, please."

She sat on the bed. By the look on Mama's face, she wasn't going to like the conversation.

"Sachi, have you ever heard the word *eta* before?"

"No, what does it mean?"

"*Eta* means social outcast. In Japan, any occupation that has to do with death—undertakers, leather workers, butchers . . ." Mama looked away from Sachi.

"Butchers? What are you saying, Mama?" Sachi's voice rose with each word she spoke.

Mama continued, still not looking at Sachi. " . . . they were considered ungodly. Unclean. Outcast."

"So are you saying Sam's father is *eta*? Outcast?"

"Yes. And Sam said he wants to be a butcher like his father."

"Then what are you telling me?" Sachi asked the question, but wasn't sure she wanted to hear the answer.

"You should not associate with them, or you will lose face." Mama stared squarely into Sachi's eyes. "You will bring dishonor to our family."

Sachi stood, crossed her arms and leaned toward her mother. "I will bring dishonor to my family by playing with Sam?"

"Yes, I'm afraid that's right. It's tradition, Sachi-chan."

Sachi would explode if she stayed. She ran for the outside, but before leaving, turned to speak again. "I don't care about tradition! I don't care about losing face or family honor! All I know is Sam is the best friend I've ever had." She ran from the stall, a place she hated even more than before.

How could Mama judge a man—his whole family—by his occupation? She wiped her tears on the sleeve of her blouse.

Her own mother was no better than those who'd made Sachi cry when they called her a Jap.

CHAPTER 29

Nobu

JUNE 19, 1942

Nobu sat in the shade of the administration building, trying to escape the sun, trying to hide from too many people. He tossed pebbles at a fence post, unable to quit thinking about the graduation ceremony he'd missed at Berkeley High School.

He pulled his journal from his shirt and began to write.

June 19, 1942

I should have graduated with the Berkeley High School Class of 1942 last week and keep imagining what it would have been like to be there. The parade of my classmates in their crimson and gold gowns while the band played "Pomp and Circumstance." Watching our proud parents gawk as they searched the procession for their graduate. Maybe it shouldn't matter, Papa wouldn't have been there anyway. But it was stolen away from me! Only a month and a half to go, and they sent me here. I missed the parties, the celebration. The prom! I missed talking about where we'd go to college.

Sure. They put together a small ceremony for all the graduating seniors at Santa Anita, but hell, what the fuck did that mean to any of us? We'd been here less than two months. Few of us even knew each other.

So now I'm a high school graduate. I should be getting ready for UC-Berkeley. And I would be if I weren't in this godforsaken assembly center, this prison!

Will I ever go to college now? And if not, what about my future? What kind of shit job can I hope to get without a college degree? Hell, even with a college education, I'm a Jap. With the way things are today, who's going to hire a Jap? Guess it doesn't matter if I have an education anyway.

He tucked his journal inside his shirt. Now what? Boredom swelled with every breath he took. There was nothing to do in this place. He picked up a large rock and felt its coolness against his palm, until his jittery restlessness erupted and he threw it at the fence that locked him inside the miserable camp. Missed.

He hung his head between his knees until the shade wandered away and left the sun to beat on his neck.

The rumble of a bus engine signaled more Japanese being delivered. He watched, though it was nothing new. Buses arrived every day with new evacuees. Only difference was that in recent weeks, rather than leaving right away, they waited to be loaded with Japanese families being transferred to a more permanent relocation center. His family's time could come at anytime. Then he could be bored someplace else.

He watched lost-looking souls shuffle off the bus and recognized the look in their eyes, a search for answers to questions that pounded in their heads from the start of their journey: Where are they taking us? When will we return? What have we done to deserve this?

A few were close to his age. He tried to interpret the looks in their eyes. Not so resigned but anger raged in some of their stares, anger he knew. They didn't belong in this place. Didn't do anything to deserve being treated this way. They were American citizens.

The sun's reflection burned his eyes. He stood and dusted off. Time to get back to pick Sachi up for lunch. But a familiar face caught his eye. He moved closer and held his hand to block the sun's glare.

Kazu?

He yelled. "Kazu?"

The kid looked up and around, searching for who had called his name.

For the first time since arriving at Santa Anita, happiness burst inside and he waved with all his might. "Kazu! Over here!" The words caught in his throat and the urge to cry surprised him. He swallowed hard.

Kazu's eyes widened. "Nobu? Is that you?"

He ran over to Kazu and took a suitcase from him. "Oh my God. I don't believe it. How are you? How is your mother?" He had a thousand questions, a thousand things he wanted to say.

Kazu nodded toward the bus. "Mother is here, too. Over there."

"And your father?" Nobu asked, not sure he wanted to hear the answer.

"Pop is still at a camp in New Mexico. Still don't know when we'll see him again. We get letters every once in a while, but so much of it is blacked out, we don't really know what's going on. Hey, don't bring it up in front of my mother, okay?"

"Hello, Mrs. Sasaki," Nobu said when she approached.

Mrs. Sasaki studied his face for a moment before she spoke. "Nobu? Oh, my! How are you? How is your family?"

"My mother and Sachi are fine, but we haven't heard from Taro since we've been here."

"Ah," she said. "Perhaps no news is good news, *neh?*"

"Keep moving. Keep moving," called a young guard, swinging his arms forward. "Proceed to the administration building for further instructions."

"You'll get directions to your new living quarters there," said Nobu. "Don't expect much. I'll warn you now. They're not much more than swept-out horse stalls."

Mrs. Sasaki clutched her bags tighter and looked up at her son.

The urge to soften his words struck Nobu in the gut. "A little bit of mother's touch adds a lot though." He could kick himself.

Kazu took one of his mother's suitcases. "Guess we better keep moving."

"We're in Row 3, the fourth stall on the right. When you're finished, come by and I'll treat you to lunch at the mess hall." Nobu flashed a sly smile at his friend.

"Okay, we'll see you in a bit."

He jogged back to his apartment to tell Sachi and Mama the good news, still not believing it. Kazu. Here. Maybe now they could start a baseball team. And he'd have someone to talk to. Someone who understood his anger.

He found Mama sweeping the dirt floor. Sachi was reading a book on the bed.

"Great news," he announced.

"What is it, Nobu? You have not smiled like that since we arrived."

"You'll never believe who just got off the bus. Take a guess."

"I have no idea. Just tell me."

Sachi leaped up and began to recite a list of names. "Uh, let's see, was it Mr. Sato from the grocery store? No? How about Mrs. Thompson? That would be so nice if it was Mrs. Thompson. Then I could take my dance lessons again."

"No, no, and no," he said. "Okay. You'll never guess, so I'll tell you. It was Kazu. Kazu and his mother."

"How nice for you to have a friend here now," Mama said. Her voice softened. "But I suppose I should not wish being here on anyone."

"Thanks, Mama." He went to his bed and drew the curtain, the door to his "room." The mattress hay crackled as he laid his journal beside him and began to write. For the first time since Sachi had given him the journal, he recorded good news.

CHAPTER 30

Terrence

JULY 14, 1942

Terrence traced the line he'd marked on the wall that morning. One line. One day. He knew without counting how many had passed so far; thought about it every hour of every day. Ninety-two since the judge sentenced him, drawn on the dingy wall next to his cot. How the hell was he going to make it another 638 days?

He stared at the ceiling, recalling the morning the judge had handed down the sentence that put him in prison for two years. Dozens of restless spectators watched and waited for him to punish the nigger. He guessed most figured a colored boy was a lower life form than a Jap. Or, maybe they were just hungry for whatever scrap was dangled in front of them.

Manslaughter. Mr. Blake said he was lucky to get off with two years plus probation, but he couldn't help the anger that ripped at his gut every time he lay down on that cot and counted the lines on the wall.

The place was a hellhole. That scuffle in the shower hadn't been the last time Peachie harassed Terrence. Matter of fact, things had gotten worse. And the deadbeat guards didn't do anything to stop it. Peachie had friends, too. He rubbed the scars on his arm left by Peachie's fingernails.

He thought about Daddy. Here in the cell, sometimes he could almost pretend his father was still alive in the world outside, doing what he always did. Just waiting for Terrence to get out so he could help with the chores. He pictured Daddy in the driveway, fixing Patty's bike. Pushing Missy on the swing in the backyard. He smiled, remembering the way Daddy used to sneak up behind Momma while she was doing the dishes after supper. But the best memories were those of Daddy cheering at his ball games.

He'd have told Terrence how to handle Peachie. He'd had to deal with that kind of folk plenty of times in his life, even though he said things were a whole lot better in California than they were in Mississippi when him and Momma were growing up.

Must've been pretty bad in Mississippi, if it was worse than in California.

Terrence kept thinking about the Saturday when Daddy took him to a steak house to celebrate the team's big win. He smelled smoked hickory as soon as he walked in, and his mouth watered just thinking about tasting a juicy piece of meat.

They had waited at the hostess desk for a long time. Terrence figured maybe they were busy. Some of the white folks sitting at white-clothed tables began to stare and whisper. Made his stomach queasy, his neck hot. But Daddy stood straight and tall. Look like he didn't have a care in the world.

When the hostess finally approached them, Terrence noticed her red lipstick had smudged onto her teeth. She looked real nervous, fidgeting and twisting a pen in her hands.

She stopped behind a podium that held a reservation book. "May I help you?"

"Yes," replied Daddy. "Table for two, please."

She tucked a white-blonde curl behind her ear and flipped a few pages of the book. "Do you have a reservation?"

"No, sorry, ma'am. We sure don't." Daddy smiled and looked around. "But look like you got plenty a empty tables."

Her eyes shifted and she flipped pages back and forth. "Then, I'm afraid we can't accommodate you."

"But . . . you got empty tables," Daddy said, still polite.

She rolled her eyes. "Would you excuse me for a moment?"

"Yes ma'am."

The hostess picked up the reservation book and walked toward the kitchen, fast as her skinny high heels would carry her. She pushed through the double-swinging doors like a wide receiver headed to the goal post. The patrons' stares followed until she disappeared, then darted back to Daddy and Terrence. The whispering got louder than the sound of silverware clanking against dishes.

Something inside Terrence rumbled, and it wasn't his stomach anymore. He wanted to yell at the unwanted audience, maybe even turn over a table or two, especially where those puckered-up old biddies with their flowered hats and uppity stares sat.

What the hell are you looking at?

He needed to get in their faces and change their snooty expressions, get them to show a little respect. Even if it *was* only 'cause they were afraid.

How the hell could Daddy just stand there, looking so calm? Terrence was boiling inside. But somehow he knew he best settle down.

"What's going on, Daddy?"

"Just be patient, son."

Finally, a tall, thin man in a black suit walked up to them. "Is there a problem?"

"No sir, we just want a table for two."

The man huffed. "Follow me."

Daddy winked. "Let's have us a steak, son."

They followed the man through the restaurant. As they walked by each table, backs stiffened and gazes turned away. Yeah, they were staring all right, even though they tried to look like they weren't.

They passed the biddy with daisies on her hat. Terrence fought the urge to get in her face, though he couldn't resist having a little fun. "Fine piece of meat you got there, ma'am," he said, winking. He didn't think a white person could get whiter, but she sure did.

Daddy tapped him on the shoulder and pushed him along.

The skinny-man-in-the-black-suit led them to the back of the restaurant. There weren't any windows and it was dark, except for candles on a few of the tables.

"This'll do just fine," Daddy said. "I 'preciate it."

The jerk had purposely seated them away from the rest of the patrons.

"I don't get it, Daddy," he said, placing the white cloth napkin on his lap. "Why do you put up with being treated like that?"

Daddy opened his menu. "Like I told you before, they treating us like that only 'cause we a different color. They don't know the first thing about who I am on the inside. So it's got nothing to do with me. It's they problem." He moved the menu closer to the candlelight. "Don't do no good to fight it no how. You know when I was a boy in Mississippi, some colored folks fought against it and it didn't do no good. Matter fact, I know of a couple stories where they was beat or even killed. Ain't worth it, son."

Sometimes Terrence didn't understand his daddy's logic. But he sure missed it anyway. He fluffed up his pillow and watched a spider in the corner above his cot. Back and forth it wove, building its web. What prey might drift into its lair?

If he tried real hard, maybe he could keep memories of Daddy long enough to get to sleep. Maybe he could even convince himself this was all a bad dream, and he'd wake up in the morning to find Daddy in the kitchen at home, smooching up behind Momma while she tried to cook breakfast.

But every night, as he waited for sleep to take him away from the four walls of the cell, inmates shouting ugly words instead of goodnight shattered the flimsy hold he had on his make-believe world. The return to reality was cold and hard, filled with emptiness so big it sucked the breath out of him. Then, he'd lie awake and stare again at the marks on the wall, wondering if there'd be room for the 730 lines he'd mark before waking from his nightmare and leaving for good.

Yeah, one day he'd be free. But dream or no dream, he'd never again wake to find Daddy at home.

"Hey, Harris." Waking to the guard's raspy voice was even worse than the sharp clang of the cursed alarm clock next to his bed at home. "You got a visitor. Says he's your attorney."

What time was it, anyway? And why was Mr. Blake coming to see him now? He smoothed his hair and waited by the door for the guard to lock handcuffs on his wrists.

In the visitors' room, Blake sat behind a stack of books on the table. When Terrence walked in, he looked up over his reading glasses. "Morning," he said, standing to greet him.

Terrence looked up at the clock on the opposite wall. Seven thirty. "Mr. Blake, what are you doing here? Everything okay?"

"Fine. Just fine. I wanted to stop by before going to the office this morning. How are you doing?"

"I get bored. Nothing to do but stare at the walls. Other than that, guess I'm as good as can be expected."

"You guess?"

"Yessir. It's just . . . I'm getting some harassing . . . but I'm dealing—" He stopped himself and held his breath.

Blake removed his glasses. "Who's harassing you?"

"It's nothing. Don't worry about it. And don't tell Momma."

"I can speak to the warden, you know."

"I said don't worry about it. Please."

Blake stared him down for several seconds. "You'll tell me if it gets too bad?"

"Yeah. Just don't say anything to Momma. I've given her enough to worry about as it is." He pulled out a chair and sat across from Blake. "What are all those books for?"

Blake took one from the top of the pile, a worn edition of *America Past and Present: History of a People and Nation,* and pushed it toward Terrence.

"What's that for?"

"It'll give you something to do. You said you're bored, right? Read it. Study it."

"Ah, come on, Mr. Blake. I don't wanna read a dumb history book. That's one *good* thing about being in this place. No school and no Momma to hassle me about getting an education. Besides. History's boring, too."

Blake sat back and folded his arms over his big belly. "It's good your Momma hassled you about getting educated. You made good grades in school before all this happened. She's right. You don't see it now but those grades—your education—it's your ticket away from where your life is headed."

Terrence slouched in his chair and rolled his eyes. "You right about one thing, Mr. Blake. I sure don't see it now."

"You will. One day you'll look back on all this. And when you do, you can either be proud, or you can have regrets. Know what I mean?"

Terrence shrugged. "Maybe."

"You can either get yourself educated while you're in here, or you can sit around and be bored. But then, that'd be a big waste of a lot of good time. You know, there's a good chance you can still go to college. Get a degree. Make something of yourself. Make a difference in this world."

Terrence opened the book and turned the pages, not really looking at any of them.

"I'll work with you, if you study. Prove yourself, and I'll send you to college."

What the . . .? He stopped flipping pages, frozen between disbelief and mistrust. *Send me to college?* Why in the world would Blake do that? For a black kid he doesn't even know? A kid convicted of manslaughter? What did this guy want anyway?

Terrence slammed the book shut. "Why, Mr. Blake? Why would you do this for me?"

CHAPTER 31

Nobu

SEPTEMBER 20, 1942

Nobu gripped the bat and studied Kazu's face as he wound up for the pitch. His eyes always gave away how the ball would leave his hands. A twitch of his right eye, he'd throw a curve ball. Left eye, you could expect a fastball. Nobu had learned to interpret his friend's facial expressions over the years, and though they shared many secrets, this one he kept to himself.

There it was. A tiny blink of his right eye, just before Kazu threw the pitch. Nobu swung and made contact with the ball, then tossed the bat behind him. It clunked and bounced on the ground as he tore away, headed for first base. Long, hard strides. He glanced to the outfield, where the ball whizzed past Kazu on the pitcher's mound. An outfielder grabbed it and threw it to the infield.

Run! Run!

Nobu touched first base, ran past it.

Safe!

God, he loved baseball. Anticipating the pitch. Running for base. Seeing the girls at the edge of the field jump up and down, giggling, and clapping their hands. Especially the girl in the dark green skirt. Moments like those, he could just about forget he was surrounded by barbed wire.

But as his heartbeat settled, he watched his teammate at bat.

"Strike one."

The cry of a hawk drew his gaze up to where it circled in the sky, far above the barbed wire, beyond the boundaries of Santa Anita.

"Strike two!"

Nobu mumbled. "Come on, man. Open your eyes and hit the ball!"

"Strike three! You're out."

Damn! Nobu kicked dirt up and headed infield. He watched Kazu and his teammates run to the bench, arms waving in victory. Five to four. So close this time!

He flipped Kazu's hat off. "Good game."

Kazu grabbed his hat from the dusty ground and slapped it against his jeans. "Better luck next time."

"Hey," Nobu said, flagging Kazu in closer.

"What?"

He grabbed Kazu's jacket and pulled him even closer. "See that girl over there? The one in the green skirt?"

"Yeah, what about her?"

"I saw her cheering when I made the run to first base. You know her?"

Kazu flashed a sly grin and shoved Nobu. "Got a crush on her? Yeah. I know her. What's it to you?"

"Just give me her name."

"Yuki. Her name is Yuki Kobayashi."

"Thanks." Nobu grabbed his duffle. "Gotta go."

"Hey, you want to meet her?"

"Another time. I have to get Sachi and Mama for dinner."

"Okay. See you tomorrow."

Nobu waved as he left the ball field. "Yeah. Same time, same place."

It was great having Kazu at Santa Anita. Having a friend to talk to made the days tolerable. A friend to do things with—things that would take his mind off his anger. A friend who understood what it was like not to have a father around.

And maybe now he might strike something up with Yuki. Yuki. He liked that name. It suited her, cute and perky. All he had to do was figure out a way to talk to her.

Hot wind whipped through the rows of stalls, stirring up dirt that stung his skin and settled like grit in his eyes. He held his hand over his face to shield from the blowing dust and bright sun.

The flowers Sachi had planted in front of their apartment caught his attention. The red petunias had been so bright, but now in the heat, they'd begun to fade and wilt. He'd water them for her after dinner.

When he walked inside, he rubbed the grit out of his eyes and tried to adjust to the darkness in the room. A blurry silhouette sat on the bed.

He blinked to focus. "Hi, Mama. Are you and Sachi about ready to go to dinner?"

She replied softly, "Sachi is still out playing."

He sat next to her. "Everything okay?"

"Read this," she said and gave him a sheet of paper she held.

He carried it to the lamp in the corner and read out loud. "Notice to family number 13754 . . ." He hesitated to continue reading and glanced at his mother.

"Go on," she said.

He took a deep breath, held it for a moment, then exhaled. "Effective September 25, 1942, members of your immediate family are to report to the administration building for relocation to Rohwer, Arkansas." Resting his head against the wall, he began to bang against the wood planks. That meant leaving his friends. Kazu. His ball team. Yuki. "You mean we have to move again? Why can't they let us stay here?"

Mama shook her head. "We knew this was temporary and that we would have to leave within a few months. We have watched families board the buses every day." She lowered her head into her hands. "But Arkansas?"

Nobu crumpled the notice and threw it on the floor before going to his mother. He struggled to draw strength. Touching her shoulder, he whispered. "It's okay, Mama. At least we'll be together. We did okay here. We'll do okay in Arkansas. Let's go get something to eat."

"I am not hungry. Perhaps later. Please find Sachi and go without me."

"I'll bring something back. You okay?"

"I am fine. Go on now."

It was a relief to leave that room, to leave Mama. He wasn't sure how long he could be in control.

He stepped outside and fought the urge to slam the door. Anger surged inside and he tore away, running fast and hard as if racing to beat something ready to erupt—a scream he didn't want Mama to hear.

Then it escaped, one long cry of frustration that echoed through the camp. Residents in nearby stalls peeked through doors but quickly shut them again when Nobu slowed and shot an angry glare. He darted off, not sure where to go. He didn't want to face Sachi, couldn't be strong for her, too.

The baseball field. He could be alone there.

He dropped into the dugout and caught his breath. Inside, he wanted to cry, but he wouldn't allow it. Boys cried. Men didn't. He wiped his face on his shirt sleeve before taking his journal out of his jeans pocket.

September 20, 1942

We've just learned we are to be moved to another "camp"—no, a prison—in Arkansas. We've been given five days to pack our things. To say our goodbyes.

I'm mad. Again. And I'm tired of feeling like this all the time. It's a monster that's eating me up inside. But I can't help it. Today, after reading the notice, I felt it gnawing in my stomach. The more I tried to hide it, especially from Mama, the madder I became.

What feeds the monster now? Is it that once again, we are not in control of our own lives? That we're being moved to yet another place? And we could be moved again after that? Or, is it that I had just become accustomed to this place? Is it that with Kazu here, it had almost begun to feel like home, and now home, once again, is taken away from us? And what about Yuki? Finally, I see a girl I can't wait to get to know. But what's the use now?

Hell! Words. These are only words, and they don't come close to describing what I feel inside.

Here. Here is my anger!

He plunged his pen over and over onto the page before scribbling a long, black line through what he had written. Not enough! He stabbed the entry with exclamation marks.

A rock hit the bench next to the dugout and bounced off.

Someone screamed, "Goddammit!"

Nobu peered out of the dugout and saw Kazu at the edge of the field, throwing rocks like fast balls at the bench.

"Hey, hold on!" Nobu yelled, rushing out. "You trying to hit me or something?"

Kazu turned away and Nobu saw him breathe deeply.

"Hey," Nobu said. "What's wrong?"

Kazu glared at him. "I'll tell you what's wrong. We're being sent to goddamn Arkansas in five days."

CHAPTER 32

Sachi

SEPTEMBER 20, 1942

Sachi knew Sam had to be around somewhere. But where? There were only so many places to hide, but she'd already searched most of those. Behind the shower house? Under the school room stoop? Where was he?

She kicked up dust as she searched their favorite hiding spots, careful not to get too close to her own family's apartment. After all, she didn't want to get caught playing with Sam after Mama told her not to. It was the dumbest thing she'd ever heard. Can't play with Sam because his father is a butcher? So silly. Sachi had decided to ignore it. And so far, she'd managed to keep their friendship as secret as her crush on Sam.

It was almost dinnertime. Maybe he was hiding at the cafeteria building. He liked to go there and sneak a piece of dessert when nobody was looking. She skipped over and searched the line that had begun to form outside. Not there, either.

Okay. Now hide-and-seek was getting boring, and the hot sun wasn't helping any.

"Sam!" she yelled. "I give up. Come out, come out, wherever you are." She looked around. No Sam, but she did see Nobu and Kazu walking toward her. This wasn't good. If Sam came out, she'd be caught and Nobu would tell on her.

She skipped up to her brother, trying to look like she had not a care in the world. "What are you two doing?" she asked.

Nobu's reply was clipped. "Just finished playing ball."

Why was he in such a bad mood? Did he know she'd been playing with Sam? And Kazu. He was always joking around with her. Why was he so quiet now? "Hi, Kazu," she said.

"Hi."

Something was definitely up. She'd been caught. But how could

Nobu know? Had he been watching them play hide-and-seek? She looked around again.

Whatever you do, Sam, don't come out now.

She couldn't stand the tension. "What's wrong with you two sour-pusses anyway?"

Nobu and Kazu looked at each other. Kazu spoke first. "You tell her. She's your sister. I'm going home." He shook his head as he walked away. "Home. Yeah, right."

She watched Kazu mope. Anxiety pinched harder. She decided it must be something besides being caught with Sam. But not knowing was even worse. "What is it, Nobu?"

At just the wrong time, Sam came running around the corner of the barracks. "Here I am! I was hiding behind the big oak tree. I won—"

Sachi rolled her eyes and gasped, then shook her head at Sam.

Go away!

It was a useless attempt to chase him away. He wouldn't know what her actions meant—she hadn't had the heart to tell him she wasn't allowed to play with him. How could she tell him her mother thought his family was *eta?*

Nobu placed his hand on her shoulder and scooted her along. "We need to go to dinner now."

"Bye, Sachi," Sam said, skipping toward his apartment. "See you tomorrow. Same time, same place."

Sachi turned to wave, resisting her brother's nudge. She gritted her teeth and swallowed hard to push back the lump in her throat. When her sadness was replaced by anger, she was grateful for it. "That was rude. What's the big deal, anyway? And why are you and Kazu in such a bad mood?"

He stopped, grabbed Sachi's chin and drew her to look into his eyes. "Didn't Mama tell you not to play with Sam anymore?"

"Yes, but—"

"No 'but' Sachi! You must listen to Mama." He walked away.

Who did he think he was, Papa? She ran to catch up. "Are you going to tell?"

"Not if you agree that you won't see Sam again."

He might as well have ripped her heart out. Her own brother. "Okay," she replied. "Just don't tell Mama."

"Let's go eat now," he said.

Something else was bothering him, but she was too mad at her mean-old brother to care anymore. They walked in silence, until she realized they were going straight to the cafeteria. "Aren't we going to get Mama first?"

"She's not hungry. We'll bring something back for her."

Now she knew something was wrong. "Nobu! I'm tired of asking. I know something's up. What is it?"

"We're leaving in five days."

"What?" There it was. That feeling. Like someone took a vacuum and started sucking her breath out of her. Memories whipped past. Spending time with Sam. Trying to teach him how to jump rope. Giggling when he dropped the piece of cake he'd tried to sneak out of the mess hall. Wondering what she liked better about Sam, his smile or his eyes. "Are we going home?"

"Home?" He snarled. "Yeah. Right. Heck, no. We're being sent to Arkansas."

"Arkansas? Isn't Arkansas on the other side of the country? Why so far away?" The vacuum whined and drew faster, sucking up memories like they were pieces of dirt on the ground. She imagined the look in Sam's eyes when she told him she was leaving.

Nobu shoved his hands into his pockets and walked faster. "How am I supposed to know? You think we're allowed to ask questions around here or something?"

Sachi wasn't hungry anymore either. "I'm going home," she said, tired of trying to get her brother to talk. She ran, faster and faster, hoping if she ran fast enough, she could escape the tears that chased her.

She arrived at her front door and leaned over to catch her breath. There, pressed into the dusty earth were the flowers she'd planted. Wilted. Brown. She knelt to touch one of the blooms, once bright red but now the color of dried blood, and propped it against the wall. When she let go, the lifeless flower fell again.

Mama opened the door. "Sachi? Why aren't you at dinner?"

"I wasn't hungry."

"Have you been crying?" Mama dabbed her cheeks.

Sachi turned away and wiped her tears with dirty hands. "No."

"I think you have. Did Nobu tell you?"

"Yes, Mama. I can't believe it's already time to leave. I was just making friends—" Her voice quivered and she wrapped her arms around her mother. Finally, she gave up fighting back tears.

"There's Nobu," Mama said.

He ambled toward them, hands still in his pockets.

"You aren't going to dinner either?" Mama asked.

"Nope. Lost my appetite." He took his thumb and rubbed a dirt smudge from Sachi's cheek. "Guess you told Mama you've been playing with Sam?"

Sachi's eyes widened. How could he just blurt it out like that? Brothers could be so stupid sometimes. She wanted to hit him.

Mama glared at her.

Cringing, Sachi backed away.

For what seemed like a very long time, nobody spoke. Then, Mama crossed her arms and said, "No, Sachiko didn't say anything about playing with Sam. She told me she was crying about leaving this place."

Nobu wiped a bead of sweat that trickled near his eyes. "Oh," he said, shrugging at Sachi.

Mama opened the door and waited. "Let's go inside."

Sachi and Nobu faced each other, their eyes communicating what they couldn't say out loud in front of Mama.

How could you, Nobu?

Sorry! I thought you told her already.

"Children. Inside."

Nobu went in first. Sachi followed. She couldn't resist the urge to punch him. "I owe you," she whispered through gritted teeth.

The front door had hardly closed before Mama began to scold. "Nobu, go to your room. Sachi, you sit down here." She pointed to the bed.

She did *not* want to hear this again. She watched Mama pace back and forth and pretended to listen to her rant. Her voice got higher with every word she spoke and her arms flailed about like birds in a hurricane, pointing in the direction of where Sam lived. At Sachi. At herself.

"I told you . . . butcher . . . *eta* . . . never listen." Mama's eyes squinted and the skin on her face reddened.

Then, at last, silence. It was over.

Mama turned away. Her shoulders rose with a deep breath. "What would Papa think of you now?"

Those words, Sachi could not ignore.

CHAPTER 33

Terrence

SEPTEMBER 20, 1942

Terrence stared at the small table in the corner of his cell, where a stack of books beckoned him, nagged him in a weird, silent way that he should be studying. Kinda like Momma used to tell him he should be doing his chores—without saying a single word. Just a look in her eyes.

Boredom weighed on him like a soggy blanket. But reading about history? Doing math problems? Nope, that sure wasn't what he had in mind.

An inmate down the corridor yelled. He'd been calling out for over an hour. "Hey, guard! Ain't it yard time yet?"

Homework. Yeah, right. Who could concentrate in this noisy place anyway?

Thoughts of Nobu and his family crept into his mind, like seeping water from melted ice. No way to stop it. Water was gonna go where it wanted to go. The newspapers Mr. Blake brought him every week were full of articles about the Japanese being sent to camps. Some of the articles said it was because the government didn't want to take a chance the Japs were spies. Others said sending them away was for their own protection. Either way, they'd been sent away against their will.

He shook his head and stared at the four walls surrounding him. Nobu was in a hellhole too. Only it was different for him. He didn't do anything to deserve being there. Neither did his mother or little sister.

Being stuck in that tiny cell gave Terrence plenty of time to think about things. Even things he didn't want to think about. No matter how hard he tried to keep certain thoughts behind a dam, thoughts of that day in the park kept leaking through. Yeah, it'd be easy to keep saying it was all because he found out Daddy was killed at Pearl Harbor. And maybe that was the biggest part of it. But thinking about it day after day had rearranged stuff in his mind, made him ask questions he'd never thought of before.

How much of a role did the color of skin play in Mr. Kimura's death? The color of Terrence's skin. The color of Ray's and Joe's skin. The color of Mr. Kimura's skin.

He was mad all right, that day they'd gotten the telegram. Maybe he did want to get even. But would he have thought of "getting a Jap" on his own, if Ray hadn't put it to him?

He remembered thoughts that had flooded his mind as he ran away from his house that morning, leaving Momma on the porch with Brother Harold. They were painful thoughts that stabbed at the crushing thought that Daddy was dead. Thoughts of Daddy being turned away at store counters. Not being seated in a restaurant. Being told colored folk weren't allowed in that part of a room.

Yeah, America was a country for white men, all right. No place for colored folk. And yet, Daddy served in the white man's navy at Pearl Harbor. Lost his life for it.

He remembered the pang of disgust he felt when Ray first said it. "We're gonna get you a Jap. Get one for your daddy."

Strangest of all, lately Terrence had been asking himself what role the color of his white friends' skin had played that day at the park, watching Mr. Kimura from behind the bushes. Would he have agreed to go along with the beating if Ray and Joe hadn't been white?

Days and days of boredom. Nothing else to do but think. It had forced him to deal with memories that had been hidden in faraway corners of his mind. A tug-of-war with things he might not want to admit. When he'd hid in those bushes at the park, they'd been nothing more than fleeting thoughts, flashing through his mind like lightning.

Can't say no to a white boy. Especially one who calls me "chicken." If I go along, maybe he'll see me not so different from him.

But what kept pounding in his mind was the thought that finally justified it all.

Get a Jap for Daddy.

And with that, all the other reasons were gone, scattering away like creepy bugs back to safe, dark places.

He wished he could explain it all to Nobu. But could he ever make his friend understand? Hell. The way things were going, he'd probably never see him again anyway. Probably just as well.

He paced the floor of his small cell. Where were those guards? The jerk down the way was right. Wasn't it about yard time?

The notebook next to the stack of books caught his attention. He sat on the bed and fanned its blank pages. A letter. Maybe he'd write a letter to Nobu. Maybe he'd send it, maybe not. Couldn't hurt to write it down on paper.

He leaned against his pillow, propped the notebook on his knees, and began to write.

"Yard time!" The guard's words were followed by the sound of shuffling and cheers that echoed down the row.

Terrence stared at pages and pages of words he'd written to Nobu. How long had he been writing, anyway? He'd lost track.

I'm sorry. I didn't know he was your father. I about lost my mind when I got that telegram telling us Daddy was dead. I'll never forgive myself. I'm sorry.

"Hey," the guard's keys jingled at the door, "you going out, or not?"

Terrence closed the notebook and leapt off the bed. 'Course he was going out. Being outside in the yard was the only thing he looked forward to every day. That is, long as he could stay out of the way of Peachie's gang. Why'd they always have it in for him?

He stepped into the long yard, surrounded by chain link and barbed wire, and took a deep breath. Fresh air. Coming out of that building was every bit as sweet smelling as filing back in would be stale. He walked around the yard, scoping out who to talk to. Careful not to make eye contact with the wrong inmate. The whites huddled in a shady corner to the left. They were the ones to avoid. No eye contact. In the far corner on the right, a couple of black inmates gathered around a bench. He walked over to them. Safety in numbers.

"Hey, man."

"What's going on?"

It was the usual bullshit conversation about nothing, until someone tapped his shoulder and whispered in his ear.

"Yeah. What's going on?" He recognized the voice. Peachie. His hot breath, sour with stale coffee and cigarettes, turned Terrence's stomach and sent shivers down his back.

He hunkered, glanced at Peachie, then returned his gaze to the ground. "Not much."

Two other whites lurched behind Peachie. "Not much, huh?"

"Just trying to mind my own business." Terrence gave a quick glance around the yard to check the location of the guards.

Peachie got in his face. "Hey, boy. Look at me when I'm talking to you," he said, spit spraying.

Terrence gagged and wiped his face with his sleeve.

Peachie nudged his pal on his left. "Anyone looking?"

"Nope. Coast is clear."

Grabbing Terrence by the collar, Peachie pulled him so close he could hardly focus on the big, ugly face. He fought to keep his feet on the ground. Struggled to breathe.

One of the black guys in the crowd spoke up. "Hey man, he wasn't bothering nobody. Leave him alone."

Peachie's eyes bulged and he loosened his grip on Terrence. "You wanna be a part of this?"

"Nah. Nah, man."

Terrence felt the grip tighten again.

"You ain't so tough without a guard around, are you, nigger?"

What was he supposed to say to that?

Peachie shook him. "You gonna answer me? I said, are you, nigger?"

The goddamn fat shit. Terrence wanted to shove his knees into Peachie's stinking balls. But he didn't want no trouble neither. He tried to look around. Where were those worthless guards? "Guess not," he said, still struggling for air.

Finally, with a punch to Terrence's gut, Peachie tossed him to the ground and stood over him. The monster blocked the sun with his dark form. He cleared his throat and spit on Terrence. "Nah. I didn't think so. You ain't never gonna be tough. Ain't never gonna be nothing. 'Cause you just a stupid nigger."

The other two inmates laughed with Peachie. "Come on," one of them said. "Let's get outta here before someone sees us."

Terrence lay stone still. Not because he was afraid. Not because he was hurt. He was remembering.

Spit on the dirty Jap.

Sometimes the memory returned like a cold slap in the face, sometimes like a punch in the gut.

Terrence watched clouds drift by like fat, white monsters eating up the sun, while Peachie's words pounded in his head.

'Cause you just a stupid nigger.

CHAPTER 34

Sachi

SEPTEMBER 20, 1942

Suddenly my heart
Shivers when I catch a glimpse
Of Mama's cold glare

The question was like a slap in the face.

Mama wiped her nose with a handkerchief and asked again, "What would Papa think of you now?"

The words pulsed in Sachi's ears. *What-would-Papa-think-what-would-Papa-think-what-would-Papa-think.*

Mama glared at her, and she returned her mother's stare. Like chess players Sachi had seen at the park, she waited for her opponent's next move, while anger, hurt, memories, and loss swirled and expanded inside, threatening to explode.

Mama moved. Turned the lamp on. That was all it took to break Sachi's gaze and light an emotional fuse.

Tears wet her cheeks as her words sputtered. "What . . . would . . . Papa think of me? What would Papa think of me, you ask?"

The fuse spent, she exploded. "How can you ask me that question? What would Papa think? I'll tell you what he'd think. He'd be proud that I do not judge Sam for what his father does. He would not believe in this *eta* baloney."

Nobu threw his curtain back and grabbed Sachi. "Stop it! How dare you talk to Mama like that!"

Mama didn't move. Said nothing.

Sachi tore away from him and darted toward her mother. She tapped Mama's shoulder and asked, "Do you hear me? The real question is, what would Papa think of *you* right now?"

Nobu pulled Sachi away and shook her. "I said, stop!"

She punched Nobu in the stomach. "Leave me alone! You're not Papa, so quit acting like you are. It's all your fault, anyway. If you hadn't told, none of this would have happened."

He held her tighter and she couldn't break from his grasp.

But she continued her fight with Mama. "Answer me! What would he think of you? I'll tell you what. He would say you are no better than the Americans who look down on the Japanese. The same Americans who put us—"

When Mama whipped around, Sachi knew she'd gone too far. Never had she seen that look in her mother's eyes. Was it rage or pain reflected there? She wasn't sure, but wished she could take back some of her words. Rewind them like the motion pictures Papa used to take her to see.

"Come on, Sach," Nobu said, pulling her into his room. He shut the curtain and whispered, "See what you did? I told you to stop."

"See what *you* did," she said, pushing away from him. "If you hadn't said anything about Sam, Mama would never have found out. And how could she say that about Papa?" She threw herself onto Nobu's bed. "Papa would be on my side. I just know it."

He sat next to her. "You know Sach, I don't know what's more important to Mama. Respect, or saving face. She thinks if we don't respect her, we don't love her. And right or wrong, she was raised to believe that if we associate with certain people we will lose face. You know what that means, don't you?"

She propped up on her elbows. "Lose face, lose face, lose face. I'm sick of hearing it. What about the dishonor in judging someone? Treating them differently because of what their father does for a living? That's no better than judging us because we look like the enemy. I don't care what Mama says, and I *don't* care if she loses face. I'm not giving Sam up."

Nobu pressed his hands against his eyes before running his fingers through his hair. "It doesn't matter. Stay friends with Sam. We're leaving for Arkansas in five days anyway."

It wasn't fair. Sachi dropped her head into Nobu's pillow and tried to muffle a cry that shook through her body.

After several minutes, she felt the warmth of her brother's hand on her back. "I think Mama has gone to bed. We should, too. We've got a long day of packing tomorrow." He pulled Sachi up. "Come on, off to bed."

Dragging her feet, she pushed through the curtain into the room where Mama lay silent. Early evening twilight cast a dim light below the front door, and muffled voices from surrounding stalls drifted into their room. She wasn't ready for sleep, and she sure wasn't ready to crawl into bed with Mama. But there was nowhere else to go.

She gently lifted her pillow, hoping not to disturb Mama. She knew her mother wasn't asleep—her breathing did not hold the rhythm she'd grown accustomed to since sharing a bed. What did Mama think about as she lay there? Was she still angry with Sachi? Did she still wonder what Papa would think? No matter. The last thing she wanted was to get Mama started again.

As she slowly pulled her pajamas from under the pillow, her heart pounded so hard she wondered if Mama might hear it. She undressed in the darkening room and laid her clothes on the table next to the bed. In the lonely stillness, she buttoned her pajama shirt. Her fingers trembled as she anticipated the return of Mama's anger.

But there was only quiet. Maybe silence was worse than rage.

She lay down and waited for the sound of Mama's slumber. Long, slow breaths. A gentle snore. Instead, she felt Mama's warm body, tense and unmoving. Inches apart, yet a world away.

Sachi clung to the edge of the bed, sad at the thought that Mama disliked her as much as she disliked Mama.

CHAPTER 35

Nobu

SEPTEMBER 25, 1942

Nobu carried the last of the bags out of the stall. Mama and Sachi had already left, taking what they could carry to the area where they had been told to wait. In less than an hour, all of the families scheduled to be transferred to Arkansas would be loaded onto buses that would take them to the train station.

He walked back into the apartment and looked around once again to make sure they had not forgotten anything. Mama had tried to make the small space feel like home, but nothing she placed in the room, not the pictures on the wall, the dish towels by the large bowl that served as a sink, or the books that had lined their shelves, could take away the lingering stench of manure in the dirt floors. No, it was never like home, just a horse stall in disguise.

He sat for the last time on his hay mattress and took the journal from his shirt pocket.

September 25, 1942

Today we are leaving for Arkansas. I know nothing of Arkansas, except that it is far away from this place—so far that we will be on a train for days. I've never been on a train before. Maybe I'd be excited if it weren't for the reason we're going. Once again, we have no choice in the matter. Once again, Mama cries at night and Sachi is sad to leave her friends.

Though I hate to admit, maybe it's best that Sachi must leave her friend, Sam. Don't get me wrong. I do not agree with Mama that Sam should be judged by his father's profession. I know what it's like to be considered less than equal for something out of my control. Am I less American than the uniformed guard who stands at the gate, only because Japan attacked Pearl Harbor? Is Sam less than Sachi, because his father is a butcher and our father was a banker? We do not have control over such things, yet we are judged because of them.

But Mama has nobody to support her. Sachi is still angry with me for acting like Papa, but I am the man of the house now and must protect the honor of this family, whether I like it or not. Shikata ga nai.

Still, I'm sorry Sachi must leave Sam. I think she has a crush on him. And what about me? I'm damn mad about not getting to know Yuki, too. It would be even harder if we had had the chance to get to know each other like Sachi and Sam did.

At least Kazu is going to Arkansas, too. He and his mother will be on the same train. Imagine. They still don't know when they will be reunited with his father again. I wonder. Now that Kazu is being sent to Arkansas, will his father's letters still find him?

What kind of place is this Arkansas? Where will we live? Another horse stall? Maybe something worse? And how long will we be there before they decide to move us again?

I can only hope that Sachi will soon forget about Sam, and that I'll forget Yuki. Then maybe things will return to normal between Sachi and me.

Nobu slapped the journal shut and left his apartment at Santa Anita for the last time. He picked up the bags and walked down the center of Row 3, past other stalls with suitcases and boxes stacked in front.

When he turned the corner, his stomach sank at the familiar sight of dozens and dozens of men, women, and children sitting and standing around boxes, bags, and luggage.

Buses rumbled outside the gate while armed guards with clipboards shuffled from family to family, making checkmarks as they passed.

He searched the crowd. Where were they? They were supposed to wait by the administration building. He looked at the face of every little girl close to Sachi's age, but no Sachi and no Mama.

At last, Mama called from somewhere behind him. "Nobu!"

He turned to find her voice.

She ran toward him, alone, breathing hard, her skin flushed.

"Where's Sachi?" he asked.

Mama's brows pressed together over eyes filled with worry. "She was sitting right next to me, then she was gone." She grabbed Nobu's shirt. "We must find her! They just called our number to load the bus."

CHAPTER 36

Terrence

SEPTEMBER 25, 1942

You ain't never gonna be nothing, 'cause you just a stupid nigger.
Get a degree. Make something of yourself. Make a difference in this world.
Nothing but a nigger.
Make a difference in this world.

No way could Terrence sleep with the words of Peachie and Mr.

Blake wrestling round and round in his head. He flipped to his side and punched his lumpy pillow. Flopped again and stared at dust that rolled across the floor, like a ghostly mouse running to hide. He pulled the pillow over his ears to shut out noise coming from other cells. But it didn't do anything to stop the clatter in his head.

Okay, he'd admit Momma and Daddy always told him the same thing Mr. Blake had said that day in the visitors' room.

"Son, only way you gonna make something of yourself is to get you an education."

He'd gotten tired of hearing it, even though Momma made sure he couldn't ignore her.

But he could ignore Mr. Blake. That was for damn sure.

Man, he had to get his mind off all that education bullshit back-and-forth or he'd go crazy.

Think of something. Anything. Patty and Missy. Yeah. Momma said she'd bring them on Sunday. Never thought he'd say it, but he sure missed his sisters. How many times had he slammed his bedroom door to keep them from coming in to pester him? Right now, he'd give just about anything to have Patty barge in, even if it was to ask him to fix that old, flat tire on her bike. She was always bugging him about that. He thought about all the times Missy crawled up into his lap, dragging along her favorite picture book. He smiled thinking about that silly book and how he'd grown tired of reading it over and over. Heck, if he had the chance, he'd even read that one to her again.

Some nights, when the guards called "lights out," he'd close his eyes, and he could almost feel her sitting there with him, pointing at the pictures while he read.

He took a lot for granted back then. Jesus. By the time he got out of this place, Missy would be in first grade and wouldn't need anyone to read to her. And Patty? She'd be a teenager. Boys would probably be chasing her all over the place, too.

He sat up and propped the lumpy pillow on his knee before resting his head on it. How could he be so tired, but not be able to sleep? Why couldn't he shut up those voices in his head that kept saying it over and over.

You ain't never gonna be nothing but a nigger.

He took a deep breath, lifted his head, and looked around the cell, searching for a way to escape the ranting going on inside.

There were those books again. Nagging him without saying a word. Only this time they looked different. What were those dark stripes against them? He turned to look at the cell door bars and the light that shined from down the hall. Shadows.

Jail bar shadows.

Ain't never gonna be nothing.

And Mr. Blake's books. On the other side of those shadows.

Make something of yourself.

He closed his eyes, and the voices in his head quieted. Something happened inside him. The battle was over. He wasn't sure if he'd given in or given up. Didn't matter.

He'd finally figured it out. Mr. Blake had planted a seed—get educated. Make something of yourself. And it had been growing inside like a weed. For sure, Terrence had been spending plenty of energy trying to kill it.

He grinned and shook his head. Then there was what Peachie said, the ugly shit he threw at Terrence to put him down. All the while, that shit was just the fertilizer Blake's seedling needed to make it grow even faster, until tonight, it was too big to ignore anymore.

Those books waiting behind those striped shadows? They were the way out.

CHAPTER 37

Sachi

SEPTEMBER 25, 1942

Sachi had to find Sam before Mama and Nobu found her. "Sam!" She called over and over as she searched the crowd of people that milled around like wind-up dolls. "Sam, where are you?"

She caught a glimpse of Mama talking to Nobu and hid behind a man reading a newspaper. Her mouth went dry and a chill ran down the back of her neck. Her heart pounded like it wanted to escape from her body and stay at Santa Anita. Where was he? He knew they were leaving today.

"There you are."

Sam. Her heart fluttered at the sound of his voice. She was surprised by the lump in her throat when she turned to see him smiling at her. She would miss the way he laughed at her silly jokes.

"Sam," she said, biting her lip. "I was afraid I wouldn't find you before we have to leave."

"But I found you." His hand reached for hers. "Come with me."

She didn't think her heart could beat harder than when she thought Mama and Nobu would catch her and take her away, but now it did. Sam had never tried to hold her hand before.

"Let's go to our hiding place," he said.

"But . . ." She didn't want to say it. "I heard them call our number. It's time to get on the bus."

"Just for one minute."

They might never see each other again. The bus—the world that conspired to keep them apart—could wait one minute.

He took her to the shade behind the mess hall. The shade where every day for four months they'd hidden from the world and talked about everything. The place where she'd shared secrets with Sam, every secret except what Mama thought about his father being a butcher. It was here that she learned his favorite food—cheeseburgers. Where she told him about the worst day of her life—when she found out Papa was dead. Where she watched him as he talked, and wondered what he would look like when he grew up. Where she blushed when he called her a "silly girl" for being afraid of a beetle that had scurried over her foot. So many memories she would never forget.

"This place won't be the same without you, Sachi."

She stared at the ground so he wouldn't see her cry. "I wish you were going to Arkansas," she whispered.

"I'll write to you. I promise."

"And I'll write back. Every day."

He leaned over and searched her face. "Are you crying?"

She spun away and wiped her eyes. "No."

"Don't try to deny it, silly girl. I see where your tears fell in the dirt."

With a pouty frown, she hid the smile his "silly girl" prompted and gave him a gentle shove. "So what. I'm sad, okay? Aren't you sad?"

Putting his hands in his pockets, he smiled. "Yeah. But boys don't cry." He turned to the mess hall and began to flick off paint from the peeling wall. "Think they'll ever paint these buildings?"

Sachi moved to his side. "Sam?"

He looked at her as a tear fell to his cheek. "I don't want you to go," he whispered, before pulling her toward him for a hug.

An awkward second passed before she also wrapped her arms around him. She'd never been hugged by a boy before. Well, at least not a boy that wasn't her brother. And this was different. Sam's arms held her on the outside, but on the inside, something warm and wonderful wrapped around her heart.

"Do you think we'll ever see each other again?" she asked.

"I hope—"

"Sachi! We've been looking all over for you!" Nobu's words brought the real world crashing back.

She pushed Sam away.

Nobu grabbed her arm. "Didn't you hear them call us? Come on! It's time to get on the bus."

She resisted Nobu's tug, but knew it was useless. No amount of time would have been enough to say goodbye. As he pulled her away, she turned to wave.

Sam wiped his face with his sleeve.

When they reached the bus, Mama pushed her up the steps. "Hurry and find a seat. All of these people have been waiting for you."

She sat in a window seat and pressed her face against the glass, searching for Sam. There he was, standing under her window.

"Goodbye," she cried.

The engine revved and the bus jerked forward. She turned to watch Sam and listened for his voice through the rumble of the engine, until she could no longer hear him.

In the cloud of dust the bus left behind, she watched him wave and read his lips.

"*Sayonara*, Sachi."

CHAPTER 38

Nobu

SEPTEMBER 27, 1942

The train clacked and swayed through yellow summer heat that beat down from a cloudless blue sky. With windows to the outside world barely cracked open, the air was thick with the smell of too many people who hadn't bathed in two days. Nobu rubbed his forehead. The attempt by some to use perfumes and colognes to mask their odors had given him a headache.

But the sultry, heavy air in the train car was a sedative; the rhythm of the train a lullaby. Many slept. Those still awake fanned themselves with hats, a newspaper, whatever they could get their hands on to move the sticky air.

Nobu listened to Sachi sleep, her gentle purr each time she breathed in and out. He brushed a wisp of damp hair off her forehead and watched tiny beads of sweat trickle off her nose. When she slept, her face was serene, like an angel. Such a change from the wicked glare she sometimes gave him, a reminder that she was still angry he told Mama about Sam. It didn't matter to her that they would have had to leave Santa Anita whether or not Mama found out about Sam. And that wasn't Nobu's fault.

He fanned his face with a ball cap. The heat made everybody a little grouchier, and he felt himself growing more hot and irritable with Sachi's body stretched across his lap. Still, he was grateful for her slumber. She'd cried off and on since leaving Santa Anita two days before, and though he tried to blame it on the miserable conditions on the train, he knew it was because she missed Sam.

He pulled his journal out of his satchel slowly, afraid of waking her. A tiny moan escaped her, and he froze. She rubbed her nose and returned to sleep again. He began to write.

September 27, 1942

Halfway to Arkansas. They told us it would take four days and we've been on this hot train for two. Seems like a week already. I never thought I would come to miss the stall at Santa Anita, but after being crammed in this cramped car for so long, I do.

There are some kids at the back of our car who have been rowdy and scream-ing since we left. Their parents don't do anything to control them—they sleep all the time! But noisy as those brats are, it's Sachi's crying that bothers me most.

She couldn't know how hard it was for me to pull her away from Sam. Seeing her hands reach for him as I dragged her to the bus, I wanted to let her stay for one last hug. But the stares of those who waited told me to hurry. Their impatient faces scolded, "Can't you control your little sister?" And Mama waited by the bus steps, trying to hide her embarrassment with a proud mask. She couldn't hide the loss of face that shone in her eyes and tight lips.

I was torn by what to do. Sachi was torn from Sam.

Sometimes I'm hard on her, but if I don't act hard I will seem weak. It would be easier for me to let her do whatever she wants, but then Mama would have to be the mean one. She has enough to worry about.

Sachi blames me. She used to look up to me, now the only looks I get from her are angry ones.

Kazu and his mother are on another car, somewhere near the back of the train. I've seen him a couple of times when the train stopped to let us get out and stretch. I wonder if he feels the same sense of obligation to his mother? Is it different for him, knowing one day his father will return, than it is for me, knowing Papa is dead? I haven't asked Kazu this question. I don't want to let him know my thoughts.

I wonder what Arkansas will be like. If the countryside we have passed through is any indication, it will be in the middle of nowhere. No big cities since leaving California. Only a lot of empty space. Tiny little towns. Every time we pass through, the guards make us pull down the window shades. Is it because they do not want us to see out? Or is it because they do not want the residents of these towns to see us?

And it's hot. Everywhere, it's hot.

Thinking about it doesn't do any good anyway. I have no choice but to go where the stream takes me. Nagare no tabi.

But Sachi? And my role in this family? Those questions are not so easy to put out of my mind.

He closed the journal and rested his head against the window. The countryside they passed was a blur of desolation, mile after mile of nothing except tumbleweeds that skipped along, hopelessly trying to keep up with the train.

Sachi yawned and stretched. She rubbed her eyes and looked around. "Are we still on this silly train?" she whined.

Nobu fanned her. "Yes, we're still on this silly train."

"But when are we going to get there?"

"We're a little more than halfway there. Two more days."

"Two days?" She kicked the seat in front of her.

Mama turned around. "Sachi! Why are you kicking my seat?"

"She just woke up," Nobu said.

Sachi glared at him. "Sorry, Mama. I forgot you were sitting there."

Mama shook her finger. "It is a good thing I am sitting here, or you would have kicked someone else. Now behave yourself!"

Sachi flopped back against her seat. "I'm hungry. When are we going to eat?"

"They should be passing out sandwiches for dinner in about an hour."

She moaned her high-pitched reply. "No fair!"

Nobu rested his cheek against the warm glass and gazed out the window, choosing to face the misery outside over that of his sister.

Minutes later, he turned to find Sachi still pouting, arms crossed defiantly. He rolled his eyes.

It was going to be a long two days to Arkansas.

CHAPTER 39

Sachi

ROHWER RELOCATION CENTER, ARKANSAS
SEPTEMBER 29, 1942

A far away war
Angry words pelt like bullets
The battle brought home

It seemed like forever that they'd been on that stupid train. Sachi's body hurt, and she was bored, bored, bored. At first, she could get comfortable on the hard seat by changing positions, but after four days, every position hurt. And she was darned tired of sitting next to Nobu. Tired of sandwiches for breakfast, lunch, and dinner. Tired of using the stinky toilets on the train. Tired of seeing armed guards walk up and down the aisle, looking at her like she was doing something wrong. Her head pounded and smelly bodies pressed around her until she couldn't breathe.

She stretched and whined. "When will we get there?"

Nobu huffed and rolled his eyes. "How many times do you have to ask?"

"Children!" Mama glared over her shoulder.

Nobu held a finger to his mouth. "See what you did? Now be quiet. It's the fourth day. We'll get there soon, so quit asking."

"Soon, soon, soon. That's what you always say."

A loud squeal of metal against metal hurt her ears, and her body swayed forward. Brakes! She leaned over her brother to look out the small opening of the window.

Nobu groaned and pushed her. "It's too hot. Get off of me!"

What a grouch. Good thing they'd finally arrived—he was really getting on her nerves.

Farther down the track, she saw a sign above a tiny building that got bigger and bigger as the train moved closer. It didn't look like much more than an old wood shack. And there were soldiers with guns lined up in front. McGehee, Arkansas.

The clacking on the track clicked slower and slower. She held a hand over her eyes to shield the bright sun as she looked out the window to see what kind of place McGehee was. It didn't look like any place she'd ever seen in California. A tiny little town. Not even a town, really, just a few small, shabby buildings on a two-lane gravel road. The old, dusty cars parked in front of the buildings looked like they hadn't been driven in years. She even caught a glimpse of a horse pulling a cart, just before it turned a corner.

As the train slowed, the breeze that came through the window— warm as it was—went stagnant. A buzz of activity swept through the hot and sticky air. Whispers rose to an excited hum. Feet shuffled on the floor. Suitcases banged and knocked as they were pulled from under seats, jerked off racks. Children cried.

"We're here!" Sachi said, jumping out of her seat. "Finally, we can get off this stupid train." She grabbed the doll Kate had given her before she left California.

Nobu pulled two suitcases from under the seat. Mama struggled with a big one from the rack above her.

A soldier walked to the front of the car. "Rohwer! Rohwer Relocation Center! When the train comes to a complete stop, get off and wait beside your car until you are given further instructions."

The man in the khaki uniform clutched his gun tight. No smile, either. Maybe he was ready to get off the train, too.

Everyone piled into the aisle, shoving, pushing. It made her sad to see Japanese people acting that way. She realized she wasn't the only one who thought it was a long ride.

Grabbing Mama's skirt, she felt her way down the steps of the car. She couldn't wait to get outside to breathe fresh air, so tired of smelling stinky people.

Sunlight at last. But no breath of fresh air. It was too hot, like standing over rice when Mama cooked it. No breeze. And what was that strange buzzing that filled the air? *Zoooweee. Zoooweee.* She heard it everywhere. Was it birds? Bugs? Whatever it was made it seem even hotter outside.

Everybody pressed against the train car, its shade the only escape from the sun that beat down.

She looked across a big field of cotton. There it was. Rohwer Relocation Center. Rows and rows of rectangular black buildings, lined up perfectly. Is that where they would live? It looked even uglier than Santa Anita, but some of it looked just the same. Barbed wire all around. Guard towers with soldiers who wore guns over their shoulders.

There were a bunch of people from the town standing around staring at them, just like people in California had stared when they entered Santa Anita. Only these Arkansas people dressed different from Californians. Some wore overalls. Some were barefoot. But strangest of all? Colored people stood together in one cluster and whites stood together in another. But they all stared like they'd never seen Japanese people before.

A large crowd of Japanese people stood behind the barbed wire, some searching, some smiling, some just staring. She'd never seen so many buildings, all lined up like black building blocks behind the Japanese people who waited. Couldn't they have picked a different color? Not very pretty for a house. How many were there, anyway? She started counting.

Before she'd counted the fourteenth barrack, an awful, loud squelch startled her. She covered her ears and looked around and found the same uniformed man that had given instructions on the train, holding some kind of horn in front of his mouth.

"Attention," he called through the horn. "Welcome to Rohwer Relocation Center. Wait by your train car until your number is called." The horn squealed again and he walked to the front of the train.

The sun was hot and the shady area where they waited by the train was shrinking and people pressed together more tightly. Sachi walked over to where Mama sat on her suitcase. "What do you think our new home will be like?"

Mama fanned herself with her hat. "I have no idea, Sachi. We will have to wait and see."

She looked around. "Where's Nobu?"

"He said he was going to look for Kazu."

Nobu had Kazu here. She had nobody. She missed Sam all over again and opened a book he'd given her, even though she'd already read it a hundred times. Reading it didn't help any. But she pretended to read it anyway, hiding behind it to watch the people that watched her.

The Arkansans paced, impatient and restless, never taking their eyes off the Japanese internees. It reminded her of pictures she'd seen of lions stalking prey. She wondered what they would do if the soldiers weren't standing between them. She didn't want to look at them. They scared her. Yet, she couldn't seem to turn away.

"Go on, get on outta here!" one old man dressed in overalls yelled. "We don't want your kind 'round here." She didn't know what was uglier, the scowl on his face or the way he spoke.

She pulled the book over her eyes. What had they done to make him so mad? Her heart pounded so hard her fingers throbbed as they held the book.

She peeked again. Maybe that mean old man would go away.

A movement caught her eye. By the tree near the gate. A colored girl was hiding behind it. She peeked around the trunk, then hid again. She looked a little older than Sachi. Why was she hiding? The girl stared right at her, but pulled behind the tree trunk every time Sachi looked at her.

Slowly, she peered around her hiding place again. Her skin was even darker than the bark.

Sachi lowered the book and put it on her lap.

The colored girl smiled a funny, crooked smile, then waved hello.

CHAPTER 40

Terrence

OCTOBER 1, 1942

"Hey, Harris." Sometimes that weasel guard's voice was like nails on a chalkboard.

Terrence looked up from the history book on his lap. His stomach twisted when he saw the white boy slouched next to the guard.

The kid rubbed his hand back and forth on his crew-cut blond head and glared at Terrence with icy blue eyes.

What was going on? That guard for damn sure wasn't gonna put no white boy in the same cell as a black kid.

"This here's Carter. Your new cell mate." The guard sneered.

What? Did he think he was being funny or something?

A memory from a few years back flashed into his mind. When Momma accidentally splashed dishwater into a pan of hot cooking oil. That oil sizzled and spattered right out of the pan. Burned Momma pretty bad.

Some things just didn't mix.

Terrence tried to act like it wasn't a big deal and pretended to keep reading. But he felt Carter's cold stare on him as he shuffled to the empty bunk above his.

He closed his eyes. Tried to imagine slapping the stupid grin off the guard's face. Tried to ignore Carter.

He opened his eyes and focused on what he'd been reading before the guard thought he'd be funny.

Fourscore and seven years . . .

He struggled to pretend Carter wasn't there. Mr. Blake was coming to test him on the Gettysburg Address that afternoon, and Terrence wanted to prove he'd studied.

. . . a new nation, conceived in liberty . . .

"Hey, boy. What's your name?"

There it was. Boy. A blow to the gut. Impossible to ignore. Now what?

Carter pounded the wall. *Bang. Bang. Bang.* "You hear me? You know my name. Now what's yours?"

"Terrence," he said, his gaze fixed on the Gettysburg Address.

"Terrence?" Carter snickered. "What kinda sissy name is that?"

His heart pumped an explosive brew through his body. The words in front of him blurred. Still, he tried to focus. Concentrate.

. . . dedicated to the proposition that all men are created equal.

"Ter-rence, Ter-rence, Ter-rence," Carter chanted.

Shit. All men are created equal? No way this asshole was equal to anybody, especially Terrence. His head throbbed, and he was ready to explode. But he knew damn well it would only cause trouble.

"Look, man. I got a test this afternoon. Leave me alone, will you?" He gritted his teeth. "How about we finish this conversation later?"

"Oh, you a smart boy, huh? No wonder you got a name like Terrence. Terrence, the smart nigger. 'Sif that's possible."

Boom. Boom. Boom. It wasn't Carter hammering the wall this time. It was Terrence's heart, banging in his neck and head, his fisted hands.

Gotta ignore him. Shut him out.

The mattress squeaked above him and Carter moaned. "You might think you're a smart boy, but guess you ain't smart enough to carry on no conversation with me. Okay. Later, then." Finally, his gurgled breathing turned to a roaring snore.

Snoring rumbled through the jail like rolling thunder, but it didn't bother Terrence near like the piercing glares and bullet words that Carter had fired off moments before.

The hours passed too fast, and queasy nerves rippled through Terrence when the guard came to his cell to tell him Blake was waiting. At least Carter the Creep had slept the rest of the morning, so Terrence had near memorized Lincoln's address. Slapping his book shut, he gathered a few papers.

"Best not mess up on your test, Smart Boy," Carter said, yawning. "And don't forget. We're gonna get to know each other better when you get back. Right?"

Great. Just what he needed to be reminded of. He sneered at Carter and followed the guard to the visitation room.

The guard chuckled. "Sounds like you boys are gonna get along just fine."

When Terrence walked in, Mr. Blake was sitting between a neat stack of books and a pile of newspapers, hands folded on the table. Somehow, the perfection of the scene didn't mesh with Blake's wrinkled shirt and rumpled tie. A blank tablet and pencil had been placed across the table. All very proper.

The guard shut the door, and the click of its lock echoed in the quiet room. A new set of nerves surged as Terrence feared losing everything he'd just studied.

"Afternoon." Blake hitched his pants up when he stood. "Ready for your first exam?"

"Yessir, I guess so. Might've been more prepared though, if I hadn't got a new cell mate this morning. Kind of hard to concentrate, if you know what I mean."

"New cell mate, huh? What's he like?"

"Rather not talk about it now, if you don't mind. I got all this information in my head, and I best let some of it out, else it's gonna disappear. Can I just take the test?"

"Sure. Have a seat." Blake opened a notebook. "I've got a list of questions I'm going to read to you. You write down as much as you know about each. Understand?"

"Yes, sir. I guess so." Terrence panicked, as bits and pieces of information he'd read over the last few days began to leak from his mind, like sugar pouring from a sack a rat chewed up.

Blake tapped his pencil on the table. "Hey. Just do the best you can."

Terrence took a deep breath. "Yessir. Guess I'm ready."

"Okay. First question. Why did Abraham Lincoln write the Gettysburg Address?"

Terrence put his pencil on the blank sheet of paper and waited for the words to come. His mind started to fill up with things Carter said. Flooded his brain so fast, it pushed everything he'd learned to some far-away place he couldn't reach. What was he going to say to Carter when the test was over, when it was "time to get to know each other better?" Carter damn sure didn't have any interest in getting to know a black kid. So what was the deal?

He stared at the point of lead pressed on the blank paper. It hadn't moved. What happened to all that stuff he'd learned about Abraham Lincoln?

Stop it! Forget about that jerk.

"Terrence?"

Mr. Blake's voice ripped him away from thoughts of Carter. He looked up.

"You need me to repeat the question?"

"No . . . uh, yes. That might help," Terrence replied.

Mr. Blake repeated the question slowly.

At last his brain overflowed with facts he'd learned, until his hand couldn't keep up with thoughts that demanded to be put on paper.

. . . these dead shall not have died in vain—that this nation, under God, shall have a new birth of freedom . . .

After several minutes, he dropped his pencil and shook out the cramp in his hand.

"Okay," he said. "Ready for the next one."

An hour later, Terrence had finished answering the five questions

Mr. Blake had asked. Heaviness left his shoulders. He felt good about how he'd done.

Mr. Blake took the pad of paper and flipped the pages, looking over Terrence's answers. "You want to wait here while I grade it?"

"How long will it take? I only have another thirty minutes."

"Maybe twenty. Depends on the quality of your answers." Blake winked. "In the meantime, I brought these newspapers for you to read. Circled a couple of articles you might be interested in."

Terrence read the circled headlines: *Atlanta Constitution,* October 7, 1941, "Jury Charged with Defense of Civil Rights"; *Chicago Daily Tribune,* March 3, 1942, "Lawyers Urged to Stand Guard on Civil Rights"; *St. Louis Post-Dispatch,* August 14, 1942, "Thousands Gather to Demand End to Discrimination in Factories."

"As you can see," Blake said, wiping glasses that never seemed to be clean, "there's a lot going on in the big world out there. People trying to right some of the wrongs being done." He returned his glasses to his nose and turned his attention to Terrence's test. "You know they could use the help of people like you."

There he was planting seeds again. Only this time, maybe the planting season was right. Terrence was hungry to learn. Hungry to get hold of anything he could read about how folks on the outside were working to change things. Right some wrongs, as Mr. Blake had said.

But he still wanted to know why Blake cared about his education. And he for sure didn't get why Blake was interested in civil rights, being a white man and all. He browsed the article in the *Chicago Daily Tribune.* Jury charged with defense of civil rights? Maybe Mr. Blake knew some of the lawyers who were "standing guard" for civil rights. Was that where all this was leading? Planting seeds. Maybe Blake wanted him to become one of those kind of lawyers. Heck. Could he really be a lawyer one day?

"Mr. Blake, why are you . . ."

Blake stopped grading the test and looked across the table at Terrence. "Why what?"

But time was almost up and Terrence decided he wanted to know how he scored more than he wanted answers to his questions. At least for now. The questions would have to wait. "Uh, sorry. It ain't . . . I mean, it *isn't* . . . anything. Do you know how I did yet?"

Mr. Blake continued to peer over his glasses, his bushy eyebrows arched. "Everything okay?"

"Yessir. Just anxious to know how I did." He turned the newspaper page, and tried to keep reading. But curiosity and anxiety caused the words on the page to jiggle around so that he couldn't catch them. Couldn't get what they were trying to tell him.

Blake put his pen on the table. "Very good."

Terrence's heart beat like it'd been jump-started by those two words. He watched, waited for Blake to say more.

Very good.

He remembered being in first grade, running across the front yard, waving his report card in his hand. "Daddy, Daddy, Daddy!" he'd called. "Miss Woods gave me two 'excellents.'"

His father had come through the screen door, smiling big and proud. Made him feel all warm inside seeing his father smile at him like that.

The screen door slammed, and Daddy disappeared.

Mr. Blake took off his glasses and clutched them before scooting the test across the table. "Fine answers, Terrence. I can tell you studied." He smiled, big and proud.

"Did the best I could." Terrence felt silly, sitting there smiling, but heck, he couldn't help it.

Blake cleared his throat. "Okay. On to the next assignment. Read the next three chapters. I'll test you on those in two weeks. Day after tomorrow, let's see how well you're doing with algebra. Any questions?

"No sir. I've been working on the algebra problems, too. Might need a little help later on. We'll see."

Mr. Blake's gaze penetrated. "We still have a few minutes," he said, drumming his fingers on the table. "Anything you want to talk about?"

A few minutes. There was a lot he wanted to talk about. Like why was Blake so interested in him and his education? What'd he care about civil rights? And what should he do about Carter the Creep? Too many questions. And they were all backing up behind a wobbly wall that wasn't gonna hold much longer. But a few minutes? No way he could talk about it in just a few minutes.

Blake's fingers kept drumming. "I can see there are a lot of questions swimming around in that mind of yours. Come on. Pick one. If we don't finish today, we can take it up next time."

Yeah, right. Pick one. Which one? Terrence wanted answers to all of them. He glanced at the clock on the wall, and swore the second hand moved faster than usual. "Better hurry," it told him. "Time's a flying."

"Carter the Creep." The words escaped before Terrence realized what he'd said. But that was the one he figured he'd better talk about first, having to face the kid again in a few minutes and all.

"Carter the Creep?" Mr. Blake asked, half smiling.

"I mean, Carter. My new cell mate. He's gonna give me trouble. I can tell already. Why'd they even put a white boy in my cell?" He shot a quick glance at Blake and shifted his stare to the clock again. Probably shouldn't have said "white boy" in front of Mr. Blake. "Sorry. Anyways, I just know they did it to stir up trouble. Matter fact, the guard even said he wanted to 'mix things up a bit.'"

"So what kind of trouble's he giving you?"

"All kinds. Making fun of my name. Calling me a smart boy—" Should he say it, tell Mr. Blake how bad it really was? That second hand was moving even faster now. "A smart nigger. Said I was 'Terrence, the smart nigger,' just 'cause I was studying for a test. Now how I supposed to study with talk like that going on 'round me?"

"Now how *am* I supposed to study," Mr. Blake corrected.

Terrence rolled his eyes.

Mr. Blake's moustache twitched with a sudden smile. "Sorry. Your momma asked me to watch the way you talk while you're here in prison. Said she worked too hard raising you to talk right to let it all go down the drain here."

"I know, I know," he replied. *Momma.* How was it she could pester him even when she wasn't around?

"Anyway, back to how you're supposed to study with this Carter around. Maybe you should get to know him."

"Huh? Why would I want to get to know that jerk? How I supposed to do that?" He took a deep breath. "How *am* I supposed to do that?"

"Find some common ground between the two of you. What kind of sports does he like? What's his favorite food? You know, that kind of thing. Just because you're black and he's white, doesn't mean you don't have anything in common."

What the hell was he talking about? Common ground. He didn't have nothing in common with that white boy. Except the damn jail cell they shared.

"Terrence?"

He felt kind of sick to his stomach and now his heart was beating a whole lot faster than that second hand was moving. He shouldn't have brought it up. Better calm down. Didn't want to make Mr. Blake mad, else he wouldn't come back to help him with them . . . *those* . . . algebra problems he didn't want to admit he needed help with.

"Appreciate the advice, Mr. Blake. I just don't see as we're gonna have anything in common though."

"Trust me, Terrence. Try to find something you two have in common."

"I don't know what much good it'll do." He heard the jingle of the guard's keys and scooted his chair out. He rose and shuffled to the door. "Guess it's time to go."

"Think about it this way," Mr. Blake said, quietly. "When you beat up Mr. Kimura . . ."

You mean killed Mr. Kimura. The unspoken words were still like a punch in the gut that knocked the breath clean out of him. He stared at the floor.

Blake loosened his tie. " . . . you saw him as a faceless Japanese. It was easier that way, wasn't it?"

Terrence turned to the door. Wasn't nothing he could say.

"Terrence," Blake said, walking toward him, "as much as you hated the Japanese at that moment, would you have done it if you'd known him? If you'd known the two of you had Nobu in common? Your friend? His son?"

CHAPTER 41

Nobu

OCTOBER 15, 1942

Drab. The word kept returning to Nobu's mind. Everywhere he looked. Drab. Black tar paper on the outside of the barracks. Scant brown leaves, shriveled and clinging to tall, bare trees. Gray sky. Brown mud everywhere.

He hopped over puddles and walked around gloppy patches of sludge, an oozy mix of clay and fallen leaves. Funny the things he missed about home, like leaves skipping and clicking along the sidewalk. Now he cringed at the squishing sound from puddles too big to avoid. And when he missed, the way the mud felt and sounded was like the ground would swallow him up. Though he tugged his pant legs up, mud splashed, freckling the blue denim.

He arrived at the mess hall and scanned the room for Kazu. He studied the plates on the table, trying to figure out what was for lunch. It didn't matter. At this point, he'd eat anything.

Kazu waved over the mass of people sitting in rows of tables. Nobu waved back from the food line. A worker plopped a spoonful of meat and gravy onto his plate that didn't look too different from the stuff he'd tried to avoid walking through earlier. Plop. Runny mashed potatoes. What he wouldn't give for some steamed rice.

"Over here," Kazu called. "I saved a place for you."

He took a seat across from his friend. "How is it?"

Kazu chewed and swallowed hard. "Not bad. Not good either. But I've got something that might make it better."

Nobu tore at a piece of meat with his spoon. "When in the hell are they going to get us some forks to eat with?" He picked up the meat with his fingers and took a bite. "So what will make *this* better?"

Kazu pushed his plate away. "Look behind you. In the corner to your left."

Nobu turned to look. "What. I don't see anything."

"Over there. See the third girl at the end table?"

Nobu's eyes widened with surprise. "Yuki? When did she get here?"

"Don't know. I saw her just before you came in. You walked right past her. She smiled at you."

Nobu lost his appetite and dropped his spoon. "I have to talk to her."

Kazu hissed and shook his head. "Too late, man," he said, nodding again toward Yuki.

"Why's that?" Nobu turned to look at her again. His stomach sank when he watched her walk out of the mess hall, escorted by a couple of guys who looked like roosters strutting for attention. He slumped in his chair.

Kazu slapped the table. "Hey, I heard they're looking for some guys to help clear an area of shrubs and trees—*outside* the camp."

"Yeah, so?"

"So you want to help? We're supposed to meet at the front gate at one. I'm going."

"Why would I want to help *them*?"

"Come on. It'll give you a chance to get out of here for an afternoon. Forget about Yuki. Maybe we can see a little of the town."

Nobu stared across the table. The last thing he wanted was to do anything that would help the same people who put him in that camp. But to get out for a while? Get his mind off things? Yuki? Maybe it would be worth it. "I don't know," he said.

Kazu stood and said, "Well, I'm going. If you decide to go, I'll see you at the front gate at one."

Nobu shrugged. "Maybe I'll be there. Maybe not."

"Okay. See you whenever."

Why in the world would Kazu want to help after they arrested his father as a Japanese spy and sent him to another camp? Now what was he supposed to do? He didn't want to help out, but what else was there to do in this dreary place? Sit around and mope?

He left the mess hall and again attempted to dodge the mine field of never-ending mud.

Mine field? He thought of Taro enlisting to fight in the war. He'd probably face real mine fields.

So stop whining about the mud.

That did it. He made up his mind. The least he could do was help out at home. So he *would* meet Kazu to clear shrubs.

He sat on the stoop outside his apartment and untied his laces. Muddy shoes might be okay in the mess hall, but no way would his mother allow them in her house.

"Hi, Mama. You didn't miss much for lunch."

"I wasn't hungry anyway." She swept the floor in such a trance she didn't bother to look at him.

"I still don't know what kind of meat I ate. Where's Sachi?"

"She told me she was going exploring after lunch. Didn't you see her at the mess hall?"

"No. But it was crowded. If she was there, I didn't see her." He pulled his jacket off the hook on the wall. "Kazu told me they're looking for volunteers to clear some land outside the camp. If you don't need me for anything, I guess I'll go help. Maybe I'll get to see some of the town."

She looked at him, eyes wide. "Are you sure, Nobu?"

After plenty of thinking about it, he *was* sure, until she asked that unexpected question. "I guess. Why?"

She resumed sweeping. "It's nothing."

"Mama?"

"Nobu, we have been isolated in these camps for so long, I do not think it is safe outside. *Abunai! Abunai!*"

Dangerous.

She said the words over and over as she swept the broom back and forth.

That was it. Mama's words confirmed his decision. No way did he ever want to become so accustomed to being in camp that he no longer felt safe on the outside. Even if it did mean helping *them* out.

He put his arm around her. "Don't worry. Nothing's going to happen. There will be a group of us out there. I'll be back by dinnertime."

He shut the door quietly, leaving Mama in the dim room, still sweeping a floor that didn't need to be swept. A spitting wind slapped him. He pulled his jacket collar over his ears.

"I knew you'd come," Kazu said, smiling.

"Yeah, yeah. Like you said, it's a chance to get out of this place for a while."

"This way, guys," called a young soldier as he walked toward the front gate. He pointed to a truck outside the camp. "Hop in back. We'll be going just a few miles out."

Nobu climbed into the truck behind Kazu, followed by four other boys. The engine sputtered and spit, and released a pop so loud that one kid lost his balance and fell out of the truck bed. Laughter and wisecracks filled the air, along with a dirty cloud of fumes that hovered, then drifted over the boys. The kid dusted himself off and climbed back in.

The engine revved. The truck jerked, and they were on their way.

Nobu figured the soldier driving the truck aimed for every damn pothole. The boys bounced up and down, and grabbed for anything to hold on to. Every rutty jolt brought mud splashing up to splatter anyone who couldn't dodge it.

"How much longer?" one kid asked, wiping mud off his face with his jacket.

"Who knows," Nobu replied. He cursed himself for agreeing to come.

Kazu, ever the peacemaker, spoke. "He said it would only be a few—"

The brakes slammed. The boys jerked forward and fell over each other like bowling pins.

"—miles," Kazu continued. "Guess we're here."

"Who taught him to drive, anyway?" Nobu asked.

The soldier hopped out of the truck. "Everybody out! And grab a tool, too." He lit a cigarette while the boys climbed out.

Cold, thick mud oozed into Nobu's shoes, soaked into his socks. His feet had been chilled already, but now they were numb. He lifted a foot, heavy with mud.

"Okay, men," the soldier yelled, "see that big oak over there?"

They nodded.

The soldier pointed in the opposite direction. "And see that creek over there?"

"Yes, sir."

"From that oak, to where this road curves, to that creek. That's the area you need to get cleared. Y'all should have all the tools you need. I'm taking the truck back to camp. Someone will be back to pick you up before dark. Questions?"

The boys shook their heads and mumbled, "No, sir."

Was he really leaving them alone, unguarded? Maybe this wouldn't be so bad after all. It had been months since Nobu had been anywhere that he wasn't being watched.

"Now y'all get to work," the soldier said, before climbing into the truck.

Nobu watched the truck disappear in front of the puff of exhaust it left behind.

The boys stared at each other in a gaping silence.

Finally, Nobu spoke. "Really?"

One by one, cautious grins replaced nervous stares. Then, one kid's chuckle seemed to give notice to the rest of the group that it was okay, and uncorked laughter burst from the others.

Kazu slapped Nobu on the back. "Can you believe it? He left us alone?"

The kid who had fallen out of the truck asked, "Aren't they afraid we'll run off?"

"Yeah, right," Nobu replied. "Where would we go? We're out here in the middle of nowhere, USA. And besides, in these parts, we stick out like sore thumbs." He walked away from the group. "Guess we'd better get started. I'll work over there."

He plunged his shovel into the dirt near a scraggy-looking bush. The ground was harder than the soft mud suggested, and the unexpected force of dense earth shuddered through his arms. Maybe he'd hit a root. He jerked the shovel and lifted a heavy mound of mud and hard soil; he scooped it to the side and leaned against the handle, looking around. Damn. Must be hundreds of these old shrubs. Thoughts of Yuki walking out of the mess hall with those two guys came to mind, and he jammed the shovel back into the hard mud.

At the oak tree boundary, two of the boys moved back and forth against a trunk with a cross-cut saw. Nobu looked around at the forest of trees and huffed. One thing was for sure—this wasn't something they were going to get done in one afternoon.

An odd energy vibrated inside him as he fought to remove the shrub. He'd almost forgotten what it felt like to be free, unwatched. No, this work was not what he wanted to be doing, especially since it was helping *them* out. But it was almost worth it, to feel this way again.

Several yards away, Kazu wrestled with another shrub.

"Hey, how's it going?" Nobu called.

Kazu gave a thumbs-up, barely breaking the rhythm of his pickax.

"Well, what do we have here?" The gravelly voice was accompanied by the squish-squash of approaching footsteps.

Nobu's sudden rapid heartbeat signaled danger. That voice didn't belong to any of the internees. That was a local. He could tell by the accent. Nobu's hands clutched the shovel handle as he recalled a night when he was a child. He'd had a bad dream. Didn't remember what it was about. But a strange noise in his room had wakened him, and he'd listened, trying to figure out what it was. Should he open his eyes to see it? Or keep them closed; pretend he didn't hear it? Maybe it would go away then.

But this was a real nightmare. And when he finally turned, he saw four men with shotguns. He shut his eyes and opened them again. This bad dream wasn't going away.

The man with the gravelly voice faced Nobu, while his three buddies held their guns in the direction of the other boys.

"What you boys doing here?" A cigarette butt dangled from the corner of his mouth.

"We're from the camp down that way. We were ordered to clear this area," Nobu replied. He took a quick glance around at the other boys. All were aware of the locals now. Some stood with their hands in the air.

"That right?" The man laughed. "Hear that boys? They been ordered to clear this land."

The men chuckled. The one wearing overalls hacked and spit.

The man with the gravelly voice, apparently the leader, spoke again. "Well, I don't believe you. They wouldn't go and leave a bunch of Japs unguarded." He scratched his head. "Boys, I think we got us some escapees."

"Even better," said a man who wore a bright orange ball cap, "maybe we got us some Jap paratrooper spies!"

The man in overalls hacked again. "Yeah, spies!"

What were these men thinking? Spies? Paratroopers? What did they think the boys were doing in the middle of that field with picks, shovels and saws? Preparing to attack?

"Wait a minute," Nobu said. "We aren't spies. We're Americans. Like I said, we're from that camp a few miles down the road. Go ask. The guards will tell you."

The leader poked his shotgun at Nobu. "Shut up! I know when something don't smell right. Ain't no need to go check with some guard 'bout what's going on here."

"You tell 'im, Howard," one of his buddies said, eyes and gun still aimed at three of the boys.

A cocky grin swiped across Howard's face. "Heh, heh. Pretty funny, ain't it fellas? We come out here to hunt some deer, and what do we catch us instead? Japs." He stared at Nobu with a cutting glare. "You don't get it, do you? A Jap's a Jap. It don't matter if you're spies, escapees, or even workers from that camp down yonder. It's our duty as law-abiding citizens—red-blooded Americans—to take the enemy in."

"What? You can't be serious!" Nobu tossed his shovel to the ground.

Howard lunged his gun at Nobu. "I said, 'shut-up!'"

Nobu tried to back away, but mud had hardened around one of his shoes, and he lost his balance. He fell into the cold mud, twisting his ankle before his foot dislodged from his shoe.

"Get up!" shouted Howard. "Boys, gather up the others. We're taking them into town."

Nobu got up and wiped his hands on his pant legs, staying focused on the gun Howard had pointed at him. How could this be happening? He was American. He had rights, too. When he stood, pain pierced through his ankle.

Howard pushed him toward the other internees. "This way."

"I don't think I can walk," Nobu said.

"The hell you can't. Don't you be playing no games with me."

"No. Really. I think I twisted it or broke it when I fell."

"Don't matter. You're walking anyway." Howard signaled to one of his buddies. "James Earl! Send one of your boys over here to help this pain-in-the-ass Jap walk."

Kazu ran over.

"Hey, you!" Howard sneered at Kazu. "Your pal here says he needs some help walking."

"You okay?" Kazu asked.

Nobu put his arm over his friend's shoulder. "I twisted—"

"You two keep your mouths shut. Now git." Howard shoved Kazu.

The group started down the road. Nobu assumed they were headed toward Rohwer. Two men walked on each side of the boys, guns positioned as though they expected an escape attempt at any moment.

Nobu's ankle swelled and throbbed with each hobble. But his heart throbbed too, hard and fast; so full of anger he thought it might burst through his chest. The men and their shotguns marched the boys down the road like they were trophies or something. "You'll be sorry," he mumbled.

"Quiet, Nobu," Kazu whispered.

"Oh, grow some balls," he replied.

A fiery sunset cast long shadows onto the road. Mama expected him home before supper. He imagined her peeking from behind the curtain at the setting sun, knowing he should be home. Sachi would make Mama worry more, asking why he wasn't home every fifteen minutes.

He should have listened to her warning. But no, he didn't want to listen to her lately—or to anyone for that matter. He was the man of the family now. Nobody should tell him what to do. He knew best. Yeah, right.

They stopped and huddled in shadows that blended together as the blue-gray sky turned to black. The sun deserted them, sending a cold wind in its place. Its frigid fingers searched Nobu's body for warmth, and stole what it found.

Howard lit a cigarette. "James Earl, you go on into town and bring back the sheriff. We'll wait here."

As Nobu recalled Mama's warning—*abunai*—he wasn't sure what it was that shuddered through him, the cold wind or fear.

CHAPTER 42

Sachi

OCTOBER 15, 1942

Stones stacked, one by one
One day, two days, three days pass
Each a new surprise

Sachi walked out of the latrine, wiping her wet hands on her dress. She hated the public bathrooms more than anything else in the camp. Strange, the things she took for granted in her old life. Like privacy in the bathroom. Some of the women in camp covered their faces in the latrine, as if that would give them the privacy they needed.

She was bored already and it wasn't even lunch time. Maybe she could go to the front gate, find that colored girl who had been hiding behind the tree when she'd arrived. Sachi had come to the entrance gate several times since arriving at Rohwer, looking for any sign of her. There was nothing else to do. It seemed like all she did was try to miss the mud puddles, but with little success. And the yucky mud was everywhere. Every night, Mama had to take her shoes from the porch step to clean the mud off, even though Sachi tried to tell her it was just a waste of time. They'd be dirty again the next day.

But Mama ignored her and cleaned them anyway.

Sachi had met a couple of girls her age, but they were boring. Besides, she still missed Sam an awful lot. It was so much more fun running around with him, looking for new adventures. And that had given them plenty of secrets to keep. The only secrets her new friends wanted to share were about each other.

So where was the colored girl who had waved to her? She had never had a Negro friend before. What did Negroes like to do anyway? Did they have dolls? Maybe they had some kind of toy she'd never seen before.

She watched the soldier in the guard tower pace back and forth and wondered what it felt like to watch everyone from so high up. Did the Japanese look like little ants on the ground? How many steps were on that ladder to the top? Back and forth he walked.

He must be as bored as I am.

The soldier didn't look much older than Nobu, and maybe even younger than Taro. He stopped and looked down at her.

Her heart skipped a beat. Maybe she wasn't supposed to be so close to the gate.

"What's your name?" he called.

Had she done something wrong? Guilt turned to fear, but she knew she had to answer. "Sachi."

He waved. "Hello, Sachi. I'm Private Collins."

She returned his wave and wondered if he could see her hand trembling from the tower.

"I've seen you at the gate a few times now. Are you waiting for someone?"

"No, not really," she said.

"Then why do you keep coming back?"

She didn't want to tell him about looking for the colored girl.

"Well?" he asked again. "Come on, you can tell me."

This was very strange. Why would a soldier talk to her? It had to mean trouble.

"I have a little sister about your age, back home in Utah. Come on. Maybe I can help."

Sam would have thought this was an adventure. She decided to answer him, though her voice trembled. "Well, when we arrived . . . there was a girl . . . hiding behind that tree."

"Yeah? Was she colored?"

Sachi's eyes widened, and she nodded, "How did you know that?"

"'Cause she's been on the other side of that gate almost every day. I figured she was looking for someone, too."

"Really?"

"The two of you are just missing each other. You've been coming in the morning before lunch, and she's been coming after lunch. I asked her name, too. It's Jubie Lee. Pretty, huh?"

Sachi couldn't believe the girl had been looking for her, too. For the first time since she'd arrived at Rohwer, she was excited about something.

Private Collins leaned over the rail, like he had a secret to tell from way up in the tower. "Bet if you wait by the fence over there by that tree, you two might finally meet up again."

But she couldn't wait. Nobu would be looking for her in the mess hall for lunch.

An adventure!

Who cares. Nobu would get over it. He'd probably be busy eating with Kazu anyway. He hardly ever had time for her anymore.

"Okay," she called. "I'll wait over there for Jubie Lee." She skipped along the barbed fence, running her fingers along the wire, careful to lift over each prickly point.

She stopped suddenly and turned, then skipped back to the entrance gate. "Private Collins?"

He pivoted. "Yeah?"

"Thanks for letting me know about Jubie Lee."

"My pleasure," he said, smiling. "Let me know how your meeting goes."

It seemed she'd been waiting for a very long time and her growling stomach told her it was almost time for lunch. But, in perhaps another hour or so, she would finally meet Jubie Lee. So, what could she do for an hour? If she didn't think of something, it would seem like forever.

She sat against a fence post near the tree and looked over her right shoulder. Cotton fields. Colored people moved slowly down the rows, bent over and pulling white bolls off prickly brown stems; she wondered if any of them might be Jubie Lee's mama and papa.

Behind the cotton field was a forest so dense she couldn't see past it. What was beyond those tall, thick trees?

She looked to the left. Black barracks. Most of them were still empty, but the train arrived every day, full of more Japanese to fill the six rooms in each rectangular building. Mama told her as soon as there were enough school-age kids in the camp, they'd start holding classes. At the rate they were arriving, it wouldn't be long. Better have some fun while she could.

Sitting against that fence post was getting dull, dull, dull. What would Sam do? What kind of adventure could she have sitting there waiting? She couldn't think of anything.

A butterfly flitted and danced around her, before landing on her knee. Blue. So blue, it caught her breath. Even the sky paled next to it. She reached to touch it—slowly, slowly. How would the color blue feel? Closer and closer she moved, until her finger brushed its velvety wing, but only for the tiniest instant. The blue fairy shivered and bound from her knee. Its sudden flight startled Sachi, and she whipped her finger away. But she smiled when she saw the bright blue dust on the tip of her finger.

Papa's garden at home had lots of butterflies. Orange, yellow. But none as pretty as the blue one.

She hadn't thought of Papa's garden in a long time. His flowers were the prettiest on the block, the pink peonies, especially. And his rock garden. Though not as colorful as the flower garden, he tended it as often. She loved the rocks as much as the flowers, after he'd told her stories about each stack.

Under the big, red maple tree they would sit, and he would tell her how he had carefully stacked each rock on top of another. If he was troubled by what people said to him, or about the events in the world, it calmed him to build the towers. He'd told her that finding just the right stone to place on top of another was like meditation. It forced him to concentrate—to steady his hand.

"Try it, Sachi-chan."

Still hearing his words, she leaned her head against the fence post and closed her eyes, remembering the calm in his voice, then remembering her frustration when the tower tumbled after only the third rock.

"Concentrate," he said, placing his hand over hers. "Put everything else out of your mind. Focus only on balancing the rock in your hand then, place it on top of the other. Do not linger too long there." When he let go, she had tried again.

There! It had balanced. And she had stacked another. Then another, until she had seven rocks. And a clear, calm mind.

A flutter whispered in her ears, and she opened her eyes. The butterfly had returned, perhaps to keep her company while she waited for Jubie Lee.

Maybe Jubie Lee wouldn't come. And if she did, would she even want to talk to a Japanese girl? What would they talk about? Maybe she would only come to stare. And to tease.

Papa's words returned. *Try it, Sachi-chan.*

But she wasn't in his garden anymore. Would stacking rocks calm her fears, even in this internment camp?

She reached for a stone. Round and flat, it felt cool in her hand. She looked around for others like it and placed them in her pocket. Where could she stack them?

The butterfly sunned itself near the post where she'd been leaning, moving its blue wings. Up. Down. Up. Down. How the sunlight made the blue on its wings glitter! But as she moved closer to see the brilliant blue, it flew away. She touched the ground where it had been. Flat. It was a perfect place for her to stack her rocks.

Steadying her hand, she placed one stone on top of another, concentrating. Balancing. Waiting until just the right moment to release it and reach for another.

Papa was right. Every thought left her mind, and her world consisted only of the rocks. She stared at it, grinning. Five. Maybe just one more. She scanned the ground and found a tiny one for the top of the tower. Slow. Steady. She hovered her hand over the five rocks.

"Sachi?"

The voice startled her, and she jerked her hand away from its task.

The voice called from the gate. "Over here."

Finally, there she was. Now that Sachi could see more than Jubie Lee's head peeking around the tree, she was taller and skinnier than she had imagined. Jubie Lee wore jeans and a T-shirt, and Sachi might have thought she was a boy if it weren't for the blue ribbons in her pigtails.

"You Sachi?" Jubie Lee asked. "That guard up there, Private Collins.

He told me your name was Sachi." She put her hands in her jeans pockets and walked along the outside of the barbed wire.

"Yes, I'm Sachi. And you must be Jubie Lee. He told me your name, too." She giggled.

"Yeah, but they call me Jubie for short."

Silence followed, and Sachi shuffled her feet in the dirt.

Jubie spoke again. "What you doing with them rocks, anyways?"

Sachi tossed the small stone to the ground. "Nothing. Just passing the time until you came."

"Look to me like you was doing something. Concentrating mighty hard and all." Jubie picked up the stone. "Can I try?"

Sachi smiled. "Sure, I guess."

Jubie plopped down on the other side of the fence post and held the pebble over the stack of five rocks. Her tongue swirled around her lips and her eyes stared wide, not blinking once.

"Okay," Sachi whispered. "Concentrate."

Jubie dropped her hand and rolled her eyes. She took a deep breath. "Just how you expect me to concentrate when you talking to me?"

"Oh. Sorry. It's just . . . that's what my papa always used to tell me to do."

"Aw, it ain't nothing. I just didn't want to knock over that nice pile of rocks you been working so hard to stack." She put her hands in her pockets again. "Anyways, you said your papa *used* to tell you that?" Jubie bit her lip. "Why he don't tell you that no more?"

Sachi didn't want to answer, couldn't answer. Why did she still feel queasy and get a lump in her throat at the mere mention of Papa? Of course she knew he was dead. But every time someone brought him up, it was like he was alive for an instant before dying all over again.

Jubie leaned against the fence post. She moved her foot back and forth in the dust on the ground. Her big toe stuck out of a hole in her shoe. "Ain't he here with you?"

Sachi was going to have to say something, because it didn't look like Jubie was going to give up. She brushed her hair out of her face. "No, he's not here. He . . . died."

Jubie's eyes widened for an instant, before she looked at the ground.

Why so quiet all of a sudden? Sachi had just finished telling her that Papa was dead, and that's all she got? Silence?

"Did you hear me?" Sachi asked.

"Yeah, I heard," Jubie whispered. "I heard you real good."

Silence again.

Jubie leaned her head on the post. "My daddy's gone, too. Been gone almost a year now. It happened just after Thanksgiving."

Jubie's words made Sachi dizzy. She had to sit, too, and rested on the camp-side of the same post Jubie leaned on. "Papa died after some boys beat him up."

"Why'd they beat him up?"

"Because he was Japanese. They wanted to get back at him for attacking Pearl Harbor. But he didn't attack Pearl Harbor." Sachi picked at splinters on the post. "How did your daddy die?"

Soft whimpers filled Sachi's ears. It was worse than any silence. "Jubie? What is it?"

"Just when I think I done put that awful image outta my head, someone goes and says something that bring it all back again." She hugged her knees close and buried her head. "I can't never seem to forget what I saw."

Sachi could tell by the way Jubie cried, it was something terrible. She was afraid to ask, but knew she had to. "What did you see?"

Jubie took a deep breath. "That night." Her voice trembled. "Ma had just tucked me in bed . . . when I heard some yelling outside. She came to my bedroom door and told me to stay put. Then I heard the front door slam." She was quiet again.

Sachi waited for her to finish.

"My heart was beating fast. I tried putting my head under the pillow to shut out the awful noise. But it didn't shut out Ma's scream." She sobbed and took deep breaths over and over.

Sachi reached through the fence to touch Jubie. "It'll be okay." Dumb words. She knew how Jubie felt. It would never be okay.

"Then . . . I couldn't wait no more. I had to see what was going on. Figured knowing would be better than wondering. So I ran to the front window and hid behind the curtain. Peeked around it to see outside."

Sachi was afraid to hear what Jubie saw. She was sick to her stomach and her face got hot, then cold.

"Daddy was laying on the ground next to a tree. Ma was leaning over him and shaking him, screaming for someone to help him. But a couple of white men just stood there watching and by the time I run outside, they was running away. Daddy was just staring up at Ma, but it was like he wasn't really seeing her. Now when I go to bed, I still see his eyes. No matter if I put my head under my pillow, I still see his eyes. Won't it never go away?"

Again, Sachi had nothing to say. She looked up at the sky, searching for words that might make Jubie feel better. But she knew those words didn't exist. She remembered her own father's eyes.

Then, the butterfly—the beautiful, blue fairy—danced at the edge of her vision. She watched it land on the rocks she had stacked earlier.

"Maybe it will never go away, but Papa taught me how to take my mind off things that bother me."

Jubie wiped her tears with her sleeve. "Yeah?"

"That stack of rocks I made? The one you were going to put the little stone on top of?"

"Uh-huh. What, it got some sorta magic or something?"

"Yes, you could say that, sort of like magic." Sachi watched the butterfly move its wings up and down. "Remember when I told you to concentrate?"

"Yeah, but I couldn't 'cause you was talking to me."

"Right. Well, what Papa always used to tell me was to concentrate *and* put everything out of your mind. Don't think about anything except balancing that next rock."

Jubie snickered.

"Trust me. I've tried it. It works." Sachi looked around. "Where is that rock you had?"

"Right here," Jubie said, opening her hand.

"Come on. Try. Put it on my stack of rocks. Right where that butterfly is."

The butterfly left its perch.

"Just remember. Put everything out of your head, so all you're thinking about is balancing that one rock."

Jubie dangled the stone over the five rocks.

Sachi held her breath. Wisps of hair tickled her face in the breeze, but she dared not move.

The stones clicked softly. Jubie let go . . . waited for a second . . . moved . . . her hand.

The rock stilled, stayed.

Jubie smiled. "Your papa was right. It worked."

CHAPTER 43

Nobu

OCTOBER 15, 1942

Something made Nobu shiver. Maybe it was because the streets were deserted, though he caught people peering from hidden places. He zipped his jacket and crossed his arms.

Gravel crackled and Nobu wondered what in the world was going to happen to them now. Headlights approached. An army jeep.

His pulse quickened. Who would ever think he'd be happy to see an army jeep?

It came to a quick stop beside the group of men. Dust swirled up around the headlights. An officer approached from the passenger side, and the soldier who had left them earlier in the day hunkered behind the wheel.

"This all of them, Private?" the officer asked.

"Yes, Captain McCutcheon, sir," answered the private from the jeep.

Captain McCutcheon held a flashlight on the faces of the locals. "What do you gentlemen think you're doing?"

The one in the orange ball cap answered. "Well, uh, we was—"

Howard elbowed his way toward the officer. "Sir," he said, smiling, "we believe we got us some Japanese spies." He waved the gun at the boys. "We was just keeping an eye on 'em 'til the sheriff gets here."

The officer moved closer to Howard, got in his face. "These boys aren't Japanese spies. They were on work detail from the internment camp." He turned toward the jeep and scowled at the soldier. "Unfortunately, someone didn't follow orders. But these boys haven't done anything wrong."

The captain herded the rescued hostages toward the jeep. "Get in, boys. We're going home."

As Nobu climbed in, the private whispered, "Sure sorry about the mess I got y'all into."

"Hush up, Private!" the captain ordered. "And you can bet you and me are gonna have words when we get back to camp."

The engine chugged to a start and exhaust surrounded them as the private backed up to turn around. The headlight beam shone thick in the dust, then crossed over the locals they were leaving behind in stunned silence.

The ride back to camp was quiet, a comfortable silence. Nobu closed his eyes and leaned his head against the seat. What would he say to Mama? Strange, how returning to the camp he'd hated that morning, now felt like returning home. But he couldn't help wondering if they had really just been rescued, or were they plundered treasure?

When the jeep pulled up to the front gate, the private left it idling.

"You boys go on to your barracks now," the captain said. "I guess you've had enough excitement for one day."

Nobu got out and looked up to see an armed guard in the tower. He shook his head. What difference did it make who held a gun on him, a bunch of stupid locals or a uniformed guard? He walked into camp, his path lit by headlight beams.

"Hey, wait up!" Kazu called.

Nobu slowed but didn't stop.

"That was a close one, huh?" Kazu asked.

"Yeah. I should have never agreed to come help today."

The jeep's headlight beams flashed along the fence line as it backed up. Nobu turned to watch it drive away, but something caught his attention, something beside one of the fence posts. He walked toward it.

"Where are you going?" asked Kazu.

Nobu didn't reply, too focused on what he saw. He moved closer, knelt. A stack of rocks. Like what Papa used to make. The very sight of it brought him unexpected comfort and peace, as he recalled what Papa used to say about stacking the rocks.

"What is it, Nobu?"

Kazu was a good friend, but sometimes he got on Nobu's nerves—always in the way. "Just a stack of rocks. Why don't you go home? I'll see you at breakfast in the morning."

"You sure? You okay?"

Nobu glared at his friend. "I'm fine! I just want to be alone for a while."

Kazu threw his hands up. "Okay, okay. I can take a hint," he mumbled and walked away.

Nobu studied the stack of stones and wondered who put it there. He was embarrassed to admit it—even to himself—but it was like a message from Papa. A way to calm him after the day he'd had.

Put everything out of your head, and focus only on balancing the rock on the others.

In his contests with Papa to see who could stack the tallest, he'd focused on calming his thoughts many times. Maybe it would work now.

He searched for a flat stone, smaller than the rest of the stack. The selection was sparse, and he paced in the dim light from the guard shack, looking for just the right one. There it was, just on the outside of the barbed wire. He stretched his arm to reach it. Grabbed it.

Taking a deep breath, he let his hand hover over the top rock and put all thoughts out of his head, except balance. Balance.

He steadied his hand.

Lowered it.

Felt the stone touch the stack.

Let go.

Carefully, carefully, pulled his hand away.

"Hey! You there!" Someone called and flashed a light beam in Nobu's eyes.

He jerked his hand to shield his eyes from the bright light, and brushed against the stack. The stones tumbled to the ground.

"I asked you a question. What are you doing there?"

Nobu stared at the scattered rocks, speechless. His heart pounded as he tried to find an answer the *hakujin* army guard would understand. Finding peace by stacking rocks? No Caucasian army guard—no Caucasian—could ever understand.

"You gonna answer me?"

"I . . . I . . . I'm sorry. It's been a long day." He had the urge to put his hands in the air. "I was just trying to spend some time by myself before going home to my family."

"What's that in your hand?" The guard motioned with his gun.

"It's a rock," Nobu said, tossing it on the ground.

Just a stupid rock.

"Well, it's past curfew, so you'd better get home now." The guard waved his flashlight in the direction of the barracks.

Bowing his head slightly, Nobu walked in the direction of his apartment.

When he entered the tiny room, Mama rose from a chair in the dimly lit corner. "Nobu! Where have you been?" She twisted at a dishtowel in her hand.

Sachi looked up from the book she was reading, her eyes, too, wide with worry.

"Sorry I'm late, Mama." He felt bad that Mama and Sachi had been so worried but was not in the mood to face their questions either.

Mama's voice shrilled. "Sorry you're late? You've been gone all day with no word. You said you'd be home by dinner." She slapped the table where a plate of food waited. "Now it's ice cold. Sachi and I have been all over this camp asking about you. So do not tell me you are sorry you are late." She clutched the towel as she walked toward him, her angry, watery eyes glaring. "I told you not to go out. *Abunai, abunai!*"

"I know Mama. Dangerous! You don't have to tell me again." He struggled to hold his temper.

"Where have you been? What were you doing?"

Should he tell her the truth? How much should he say? Would she worry more or less if he told her everything? He sat on Sachi's bed and ran his hands through his hair. "Mama, just give me a minute. Please?"

Sachi sat up and touched his shoulder. "Don't be mad. We were worried about you," she whispered.

He smiled. Feeling the burn of tears, he covered his face with his hands and rubbed his eyes.

Mama wasn't going to give up. "Well? Nobu?"

He stared at the lamp in the corner, waiting for the right words to come. "There was a misunderstanding while we were out clearing brush."

"A misunderstanding? What do you mean, misunderstanding?"

"The guard that took us out there left us. It felt great to be trusted, to be free, Mama. But then, some local hunters came up to us. They thought we were . . ."—he took a deep breath—"Japanese spies."

"Japanese spies?" Mama began to cry. "Oh, *abunai*. I told you, *abunai!* What did they do? Did they hurt you?"

"No. We're all fine."

"How did you get home?"

"A captain from the camp came and got us. Brought us back to camp. I guess that private who was supposed to guard us is in trouble tonight."

"And I guess you won't be going outside of camp anymore, right?" Mama wore her I-told-you-so face.

Of course he would go outside the camp again, given the opportunity. But he wasn't going to argue with Mama about it tonight. He headed to his curtained corner. "*Nagare no tabi*, Mama. We cannot control our destiny."

His corner of the small room gave him comfort and escape. It was tiny, barely enough for his cot, but it was his. No Mama, no Sachi. No guards, no locals. He stuck his hand under the mattress and felt around until he touched the smooth binding of his journal.

He opened it on his lap and began to write.

October 15, 1942

Today I was taken for a Japanese spy. Me, an American. I've never even been to Japan. But I look like one of them. Hell, I'm reminded of that every day. But being taken prisoner at gunpoint? It was a hard slap of reality.

But I did feel freedom for a time today, when the guard who took us outside of camp for work detail left us alone. What a huge feeling freedom was, not to be watched because of what we look like. I didn't care that we were put there to work—didn't even care that the work would help the same people who took us from our homes. We were free.

Until the hunters found us. We were the treasure their egos searched for— Japanese spies! Paratroopers, they called us. Booty for them to bring into town to show off.

I've never been so scared in my life. Sure, the guards around this place have guns, but they don't point them at us. These men pointed, cocked, even shoved them at us, and I think they believed if they shot one of us, they'd be heroes all the more.

It all made me wonder about fear and hate. Does America fear us because they hate us, or do they hate us because they fear us?

CHAPTER 44

Terrence

NOVEMBER 1, 1942

Mr. Blake's question kept coming back to haunt Terrence. Yeah, the Japs killed his father, and he never thought he could hate like he'd hated that day he found out. Still, if he'd known that man he beat up—killed—in the park that day was Nobu's father, would he still have hated him?

No.

So maybe Blake was right. It was a lot harder to hate someone when you knew something about them. Had something in common.

You could say he'd tried to get to know something about Carter, sort of. They were hardly friendly to each other, but somehow in the last month, they'd settled in on their territories in the cramped cell and pretty much kept to themselves. Didn't hurt none that they both disliked the guards enough that neither would give the weasels something to hoot and holler over.

But in the cautious few words they did exchange, he'd learned a few things. He knew Carter graduated from high school. That was more than Terrence could say. And Carter grew up without a daddy. Not Terrence. Didn't have that in common neither. Terrence's daddy had always been around.

Though Carter didn't mention it, the week before Terrence had learned Carter had a sister when a guard announced his mother and sister were waiting in the visiting area. A sister. Now there was something they had in common.

But when Terrence asked about the visit, Carter ignored him. Walked straight to the toilet, undid his pants, and pissed. Only when he zipped his pants back up, did he mumble, "That ain't none of your business."

So they'd gone another week, talking to each other only when they had to. Sure, it was better than the day Carter first arrived and said all those hateful things. But Terrence still had a knot in his stomach from the tense quiet. The kind when you know there's things that gotta be said. But those things don't get said—just keep building up behind a wall of silence that gets taller and thicker. You know one day it's gonna explode from everything built up, but still nobody says a word. And more bricks keep getting added.

It wasn't helping that they'd been in lockdown since two trouble-makers fought in the yard. When other inmates got in on the action, the guards ran waving their clubs to break it up. Terrence and Carter just stood and watched, but everybody suffered for the brawl. Lockdown. No yard time. They even had to eat their meals in the cell.

So if he couldn't figure out a way to talk to Carter, there'd be no one to talk to. That made the silence even worse.

Damn. He'd been staring at the same old algebra problem on that page for over an hour. Couldn't make sense of it. His mind was too full of wondering when that brick wall was gonna come tumbling down and what it was gonna take to set it off.

It was time. Time to see if Mr. Blake was right about finding common ground. Way past time.

He scribbled out the hundredth math calculation he'd attempted then blurted, "I got two sisters." He inhaled deep to slow his pounding heart. *Okay, that's a start. Now keep going.* "Patty. She's eleven going on sixteen."

"Hey, man," Carter said, "what do I care about your dumbass colored family?"

Terrence's fist clenched. *Stay calm.* He scooted his chair out and put his feet on the table. Let out a long, slow breath. "Then, there's my little Missy, she's three. She loves to sit on my lap and listen to stories."

"Man, are you deaf?"

Terrence fought to keep his voice steady. "What about your sister? What's she like?" He wove the pencil through his trembling fingers.

"I told you, my family ain't none of your business." Carter flipped over on his bunk and faced the wall. "Now leave me alone."

Time to push harder. "Guess your white-ass family ain't worth talking about then."

Carter bolted up. If his eyes could've shot bullets, Terence would be on the floor bleeding.

He fought the urge to up the aggression—shoot back. He grinned and forced a laugh as he folded his arms. "Aw, come on man. I'm just kidding around with you. Don't be telling me you like this silent treatment we been giving each other no more than me."

Carter turned his angry eyes toward the pillow he clutched.

Rocking his chair back and forth on its back legs, Terrence continued. "What's it gonna hurt to tell me about your sister? I told you about mine." *Don't stare at him. No eye contact.* He watched the pencil weaving through his fingers. *Come on, man. Talk to me.*

Carter threw his pillow.

It hit Terrence and he lost his balance. He and his chair fell to the floor.

Carter burst into laughter. Laughed so hard he fell back on his bunk, holding his belly. "Sorry, man. I couldn't resist," he said, wiping tears from his cheeks.

Terrence picked up the chair and sat again, holding the pillow in his lap. "Yeah, that's okay, 'cause now I got me two pillows."

Carter sat up, alarm on his face. "Gimme back my—"

Terrence laughed. "Gotcha!" He threw the pillow back at Carter.

The sound of silverware clanking against dishes rattled toward the cell. "Supper time," called the guard. "You boys are lucky. Tonight, round 2 of Lucille's Meat Loaf Surprise."

"Great," said Terrence. "Round 1 was bad enough." He figured Lucille's Meat Loaf Surprise was a mixture of all the leftovers scraped from everyone's plate the night before.

Carter jumped from his bunk and pulled out the other chair. "Hey, smarty-pants, you gonna clear off your mess so we can eat?"

That was about the most civil thing Carter had said. Least he didn't call him a smart-ass nigger this time.

"Why you in such a hurry for Lucille's Meat Loaf Surprise?" Terrence shoved papers in his books and stacked them on the floor. "You like it or something?"

"No way, man. But lunch was so awful I'm about to starve to death."

One guard carried in a tray with two plates and dropped it on the table. Another blocked the doorway. "Enjoy, boys."

Terrence stared at the lump of dried, brown mystery meat and the shriveled peas with cubes of orange carrots next to it. He poked his fork in the yellowish glop of mashed potatoes and it stood straight up on its own. What he wouldn't give for one of Momma's home-cooked meals. He'd never complain about having to eat her turnip greens again. Least they were fresh and hot.

Carter stared at his plate. "Don't even know what bite to take first." He tore at the meat with his fork. "I'd give just about anything for some of Ma's cooking."

"Just what I was thinking." Terrence smiled. Maybe Carter wouldn't talk about his sister, but he'd found another thing they had in common. They both missed their mothers' cooking.

He took a bite of potato. Man, it was cold. Needed salt, too. "So what do you miss most about your ma's cooking?"

Carter sneered as he chewed a piece of meat. "Aw, come on, man. Why do you wanna talk about my family so bad?" He spit the mushy clump out and put his fork down, plopped against the back of his chair and closed his eyes. "Fried chicken. I miss her fried chicken."

Terrence's tongue tingled with the taste of it. "Oh, yeah. My momma's fried chicken sure is something to miss, too. But I gotta say I miss her pot roast the most. Shoot. In here I even miss the oatmeal she used to make me eat every morning, and that stuff used to make me gag."

"Man, Jenny hates oatmeal. Wasn't nothing Ma could do to get her to eat it."

Jenny. Must be his sister. Terrence hid a smile that swelled from inside. Didn't want to scare Carter off. "Heck. I don't know anyone who likes oatmeal. Patty and Missy like Momma's pancakes for breakfast best. Me? Give me ham and scrambled eggs."

CHAPTER 45

Sachi

THANKSGIVING DAY, 1942

Thanksgiving blessings
Elusive as butterflies
Each one a treasure

Sachi stared at the ceiling, feeling her body wake with a good, sleepy stretch and yawn. She listened to the patter of light rain outside and imagined Fred Astaire and Ginger Rogers dancing on the rooftop, like they did in the movies. The pitter-patter took her back to California, where she woke to the irregular cadence of drops falling from the elm tree in her backyard to the roof above her bed. Drip. Drip-drip.

But in camp, other noises accompanied the sound of the rain—Nobu's snores rumbling like thunder from behind his curtain, and the sound of plop, plop, plop from the bucket Mama placed by the door to catch water from the leaky roof. Nobu had tried to patch the holes with tin can lids, but somehow water always found a way to drip, drip, drip.

Mama lay still and quiet next to her, but Sachi knew she wasn't asleep. Every once in a while, she heard her sniffle, cluck her tongue. What was Mama thinking about? The rain? Papa? Thanksgiving Day?

Sachi remained still and pretended she was asleep, too, listening to the sounds of the world waking; wind howled between the rows of barracks, rain whooshed against her window.

How would the residents of Rohwer celebrate Thanksgiving? Many of them were Buddhist. But Papa always said Buddhist or not, there was always plenty to be thankful for. So they had celebrated with the American customs: turkey, stuffing, sweet potatoes, and pumpkin pie.

She remembered her last Thanksgiving morning—the sounds and smells that drifted into her bedroom from the kitchen. Utensils clanked against pans, drawers and cabinets slammed, as Papa and Mama worked together to prepare the turkey. She had giggled about the way they whispered to each other so they wouldn't wake their children. But all that clanking and banging could wake the neighbors next door!

And oh, the scents of that morning. Hot turkey broth mixed with stuffing. Pumpkin pies baking in the oven. Wood burning in the fireplace. But that morning at Rohwer, the holiday aromas were only imaginary. She breathed in, yet no matter how deeply she inhaled, there was nothing of Thanksgiving in the air, only the smell of wet dirt, wood, and tar paper.

She closed her eyes and tears began to burn. The first Thanksgiving without Papa.

Mama turned toward the wall.

She must be thinking about Papa, too. Sachi wanted to move closer to Mama's warm body and wrap her arms around her for comfort. But she was afraid they'd both start to cry. No, not on Thanksgiving. Papa wouldn't want that.

She felt like she was bobbing up and down in an ocean of happy memories that made her sad to remember. Acknowledging the emptiness she and Mama shared would surely pull her under.

"What are you thankful for, Sachi-chan?" Papa had asked her that last year, as she watched him carve the turkey.

"Turkey!" she'd answered, sneaking a piece and putting it in her mouth.

Her tongue tingled with the memory of its taste.

Papa had frowned. "No more turkey until you give me a real list."

Then, she'd recited her list to him: "Well, I'm thankful for you, Papa. And Mama, Taro, and Nobu. My friends, a bed to sleep in." She looked up and thought some more, before sneaking another piece of turkey. "And, of course, food to eat." She grinned.

Everything was different now. True, she still had most of what she was thankful for that Thanksgiving, but she was missing what she'd named first on her list. Papa. Still, she knew he would want her to focus on what she had, not on what she didn't have.

Her friends. How thankful she was for Jubie. So different from any other friend she had known before. Funny, sassy, silly, adventurous. And best of all, mischievous!

What a daring surprise they'd planned for the day—a homemade meal, right in Sachi's very own apartment. The mess hall was probably serving turkey, but where was the fun in waiting in line while a lukewarm lump of gravy was plopped onto meat and potatoes? Besides, she doubted Mama would think the day was special enough to go to the mess hall. She'd probably stay in the apartment like she did every other day.

What a surprise it would be for Mama when Jubie, her mother, and Auntie Bess showed up at the door with turkey, stuffing, mashed potatoes, and sweet potato pie.

Two days before, she and Jubie had sat by the creek, planning the event. "Sweet potato pie?" Sachi had asked Jubie. "I've never heard of such a thing."

"Tastes like pumpkin. 'Spect you'll like it, 'specially the way Auntie Bess adds extra nutmeg. Know what else?" Excitement sparkled from Jubie's eyes. "I'm gonna ask her to bring you some of her special recipe pickled okra. Betcha never had that."

Sachi crinkled her nose. "Pickled okra? What in the world is pickled okra? Doesn't sound very tasty, but I guess I'll give it a try. Hey! Bet you've never had rice for Thanksgiving, either. That will be my contribution —I'll make a pot of rice. Deal?"

Jubie held her hand out to shake on it. "Deal."

The sun had begun to set, and a cold wind rattled red and gold leaves that still clung to their branches. Some whirled down to rest with those scattered on the ground.

Sachi stood and shut her eyes. She began to twirl, round and round. Round and round. Remembering.

Papa, see? I dance like the leaves.

As long as her eyes remained closed, she could almost make herself believe he was right next to her, watching and smiling.

"It's kinda like snow falling, ain't it?" Jubie had asked.

Her words had broken the spell.

When Sachi opened her eyes Papa disappeared. She collapsed to the ground and stared up at the falling leaves. "Snow? I wouldn't know. I've only seen pictures."

Jubie stopped spinning and sat beside her, breathless. "Huh? You ain't never seen real snow? I thought ever body saw snow."

"Nope. It doesn't snow where I lived in California."

"Girl, you in for a treat, then. Nothing prettier than a blanket of fresh snow. Why, it might even dress up that ugly, old camp of yours."

"Yeah, speaking of that ugly, old camp, I guess I'd better get home," Sachi said.

The pink dusk turned to red as Jubie walked with Sachi back to the camp. When Jubie turned to leave, she smiled. "We gonna have a good time in just two days! See you tomorrow, 'kay?"

Those two days had flown by, and Thanksgiving had finally arrived. Sachi got out of bed, moving the covers off gently, careful not to wake Mama. She checked the clock on the table across the room. Ten minutes after eight. Jubie and her family would arrive with the food in three hours. She had figured it would be best for Jubie to arrive around eleven, before it was time for lunch at the mess hall. That way, everyone would still be home for the surprise.

She couldn't wait! She opened the drawer for something to wear.

"What are you doing, Sachi-chan?" Mama asked as she sat in bed.

"Just trying to decide what to wear today. Happy Thanksgiving, Mama."

Mama hung her feet over the bed, and felt around for her slippers. "Oh. It is Thanksgiving."

How could Mama not remember it was Thanksgiving? A pesky lump in her throat threatened her attempt to smile, and she wiped a tear on her shirtsleeve. Then, her stomach tickled. Maybe it wasn't such a good idea to surprise Mama with Thanksgiving dinner. After all, Mama had not even met Jubie yet, much less her family.

She pulled a blue jumper from the drawer and found a white print blouse to match. "Do you think this is okay?" she asked.

Mama shuffled to the wood stove and poured hot water into a teacup. "Wear what you would like, Sachi-chan."

Nobu flung his curtain open. He stretched his arms over his head and groaned. "Morning."

"Happy Thanksgiving, Nobu!" Surely he'd be excited.

Mama handed him a cup of tea. He blew off the steam and tested it with a loud slurp. "Thanksgiving, huh? Oh, boy. We sure do have a lot to be thankful for, huh? Like our first holiday in camp. Yeah, it should be a great day."

Sachi forced a smile. "I think so. We'll see."

He put his tea on the table and pulled out a chair. "Think they'll have turkey in the mess hall today?"

"Who knows," replied Mama. "I'll just have something to eat here."

Nobu frowned. "Oh, come on, Mama. It's Thanksgiving. You have to come with us to eat today."

Sachi held her breath. How would she keep them from going to the mess hall before Jubie arrived with the turkey?

Mama bent over to pick up the last piece of wood, and tossed it onto the last embers in the stove. "Thanksgiving in camp? What is there to celebrate? What is there to be thank—"

Sachi interrupted. "Papa said there's always something to be thankful for."

Mama's glare felt like a slap across her face.

Nobu broke the hard silence. "Right. I'm thankful for a good, hot cup of tea this morning." He pushed his chair back and stood. "Looks like we're out of wood. I think Kazu and I will go out and get some more." He disappeared behind his curtain again.

She watched her brother's make-believe wall sway back and forth until it stilled and wished for her own barrier, a place to hide from the look in her mother's eyes.

CHAPTER 46

Nobu

THANKSGIVING DAY, 1942

"I'll be back in time to take you to the mess hall for lunch," Nobu said as he buttoned his jacket.

"Be sure to get back before eleven, so we can leave early," said Sachi. "It'll probably be pretty crowded today, with everyone looking forward to turkey."

"Don't worry, I'll be back in plenty of time." He shut the door behind him and hurried down the steps. Every time he left Mama in that dark room, it felt like an escape. He knew she was unhappy; she still missed Papa. But heck, it was the same for him, yet he didn't spend all his time locked up in that dark room.

And what about the way she took it out on Sachi? He wasn't happy about being in camp for Thanksgiving either, but why let their sour attitudes spoil it for his little sister? What could he say to Mama to change her? Nothing.

Skimming close to the barracks to block wind that whipped through the row, he jogged to Block 20 to find Kazu. He landed in one puddle as he tried to miss another. Water splashed up, soaking cold into his pant leg.

He was sick of scavenging for wood, even if it did mean the guards would let them out into the forest to pick up limbs and cut small trees. Anyway, now that the wood piles in camp had been picked clean, what were they going to do? Let everyone freeze to death? Besides, it was a good excuse to escape from Mama and Sachi. It wouldn't be so bad with Kazu along.

He knocked on Kazu's door. Mrs. Sasaki peeked from behind the yellow-flowered curtain. She smiled and nodded at Nobu, then opened the door. An aroma of sweet potatoes wafted from behind her. Happy memories filled him like turkey and stuffing at the holiday meal, but in an instant, the fullness of those memories was replaced by hunger. This Thanksgiving would not compare to those he remembered so fondly.

"Ah, Nobu," she said, her dark eyes crinkling in a smile. "Happy Thanksgiving."

How he admired Kazu's mother, that she could give him such a warm greeting on a day of thanks, though still separated from her husband. How could she be so forgiving? Even he hadn't overcome the anger he'd felt that day the government men took Reverend Sasaki from his home in California.

He couldn't help compare her to Mama. Why couldn't his mother pick herself up like Kazu's mother had? Get on with her life? The answer hit him like a gust of cold wind and he scolded himself. Reverend Sasaki was alive. Mrs. Sasaki could hope to see him again one day. Papa was dead. No such hope for Mama.

"Nobu? Would you like to come inside?"

"Thank you, Mrs. Sasaki. Happy Thanksgiving to you, too. Is Kazu home?"

"Yes. He is helping me prepare our Thanksgiving meal. Come in. Please." She opened the door wider and stepped aside.

"Hi, Nobu." Kazu was wiping his hands on a dish towel. "What's going on?"

"I'm going out to get some wood. Want to come?" He noticed firewood, neatly stacked against the wall.

"No. Did that yesterday. Besides, I told my mom I'd help her with dinner today. She's invited a few friends over. Hey, what's your family got planned?"

Nobu bent over to sniff the sweet potatoes and tried to think of a way to dress up his reply. "I told Mama and Sachi I'd be back in time to pick them up for the festivities at lunch. Sachi's pretty excited." He was embarrassed his family had nothing better planned for the day.

"Well, if you get the chance, stop by. Everyone's bringing something, so we'll have plenty."

"Yeah, thanks. I'll let Mama know. Guess I'd better get going if I'm going to get back in time for lunch." He gave a slight bow to Kazu's mother. "Nice to see you, Mrs. Sasaki. Have a happy Thanksgiving."

She nodded and smiled. "You too, Nobu. Please give my best to your mother and sister."

What was it about leaving Kazu and his mother that left him feeling lonelier, emptier? You'd think the warmth in the room would bring him comfort, and it did while he was there. But as soon as he walked out, the wind felt colder, howled louder. He pulled up his collar and put his hands in his pockets, wishing he hadn't volunteered to gather wood.

He stopped by the guard shack at the gate to sign out.

"Where are you going on Thanksgiving Day?" asked the young soldier. The tag stenciled on his shirt read "Collins."

Nobu looked up from the book he signed, surprised by the soldier's friendly tone. "Have to get some wood before my mother and sister freeze to death," he said, half-joking.

"You're not the only one. There've been about a dozen people leave camp today to find wood. Maybe we'll get some delivered to camp before long."

Nobu struggled to keep his sarcasm in check. "Yeah, maybe."

The soldier grinned. "Anyway, be sure to get back in time for the Thanksgiving meal at lunchtime."

"Don't worry. I've been reminded plenty by my little sister. See you."
Collins waved. "Yep. Happy Thanksgiving."

Something about walking outside the gates made him feel strange. One minute he felt free, a part of the huge world outside camp. And the next minute, he was afraid of that very same world. *Unguarded.* The word gave him two completely different sensations. Freedom and apprehension. What would happen to the Japanese when they finally left camp for good and there were no guards to protect them from the world outside?

A gust of wind shoved him toward the forest. Leaves raced ahead of him.

Run. Run. Follow us away from this place.

He entered the woods—a quiet place a world away from camp. When his feet touched the sun-mottled ground, the moaning wind turned to whispers through the boughs of the trees. Holding his breath, he stopped to listen. He listened to the sound of leaves and twigs crackling beneath his feet. Then, he stopped again to listen to the wind.

Crackle.

What was that? He turned in the direction of the sound. Someone else was in the forest. But who? Where? Trees with scraggly branches reached toward the sky, skeleton arms, and he couldn't help thinking about the hunters who had taken him prisoner the month before.

Maybe it was only the leaves, rustling on the ground.

He searched the ground for kindling, but the area near the edge had been well-picked of usable branches. He'd have to walk further into the canopy to find anything worth burning.

Crackle, crackle.

His heart skipped a beat. Someone was definitely there with him.

Not another hunter!

"Who's there?" he called.

Silence.

Turning in a slow circle, he watched for movement. "I know you're there. You might as well come out."

Something whipped behind a tree trunk.

"Okay, I see you there. Come on out."

The hidden intruder inched from behind the tree.

Yuki?

He wiped his loafer on the back of his pant leg and smoothed his hair back.

"I'm so sorry," she said, staring at the ground. "I was gathering wood for my family, and heard your footsteps. I wasn't sure who you might be, so I hid." A faint smile curved between cheeks rosied by the cold. "Then, when I saw it was you, I was too embarrassed to come out."

Nobu walked toward her.

Her gaze moved from the ground to his face, then darted to the ground again. She shuffled her oxfords in the leaves and smiled bigger.

"You're Yuki, right?"

Her head tilted and a tiny gasp escaped her smile. "How do you know my name?"

That was dumb. Now she'd know he'd been interested in her. "Uh, my friend, Kazu, knows you. He told me your name when we were all at Santa Anita together."

"You were at Santa Anita, too?"

Damn. He was sure Kazu told him she'd stared at him that day in the mess hall. Had he made it up? His knees felt weak. "Yes. But we've been here at Rohwer since September. When did you get here?"

"We've been here since October. It's very different from California, isn't it?"

"Very," he said, reluctantly taking his gaze from her and staring up at the tall trees. *But it will be a lot better with you here.* He wiped his hand on his jeans pocket before extending it toward her. "My name is Nobu. Nobu Kimura."

She bowed slightly and gave him her hand.

At her touch, something warm surged through his body—the feel of her soft hand in his. He squeezed, a reflex.

A soft giggle—a purr—escaped her playful smile. "Nice to officially meet you, Nobu-san."

The lilt in her voice made his heart race. He let go of her hand, crossed his arms and studied her, until he realized he was staring. Then, he tore his gaze away to find something else to look at.

How strange she made him feel. One minute, like the strongest man in the world. The next, a weak and vulnerable boy.

"What are you doing in the woods by yourself?" he asked. Was that too protective? Or worse, possessive? "I mean, I don't know if it's safe around here. A few weeks ago, I ran into some local hunters. They thought I was a Japanese spy."

Her eyes widened. "A spy?"

"Yeah," he replied, puffing his chest.

She stepped toward the deeper woods, scanning the ground. "Well, my father has the flu, so he's too sick to gather wood." She glanced at Nobu with flirty eyes. "And I don't have a big, strong brother to do the man's work. Mother said she was cold, so that left me to gather some wood." She knelt to pick up a stick and placed it in the large bag she carried.

He reached for it, touching her shoulder. So delicate, he wanted to linger there. "Here, let me carry that for you."

"Thank you, Nobu."

The farther they walked into the forest, the more alone with her he felt, and the stronger his urge to be close to her. To smell her skin, her hair.

The wind brushed his face. He wanted to feel her touch.

Stop thinking those things. You've only just met her.

An uncomfortable silence walked with them, like an unwanted chaperone. Struggling to hold back such strong and true feelings, he couldn't think of anything else to say.

Yuki spoke. "Do you have any brothers or sisters?"

At last, a safe topic. "I have an older brother, Taro. He's with the 100th Infantry Battalion. Then, there's Sachi, my little sister."

"You're lucky. I often wish I had a brother or sister. It's hard being the only child. Especially in camp. Mother and Father have very high expectations." She pulled at her sweater and folded her arms across her chest.

"Are you cold?" He tossed the bag to the ground and removed his jacket.

"Just a little."

He placed his coat over her shoulders and wanted to leave his arm to rest there. But he thought better of it, and knelt to pick up another branch. "Yuki, anytime you need help with something a brother might do, let me know."

She stopped and turned to him, bowing slightly. "Thank you, Nobu-san. Then, you will be like a brother to me?"

A tingly, uncertain feeling struck him in the gut. Was that mischief sparkling in her eyes? "Well . . . ,"—he laughed, a little too goofy, a little too loud—"maybe not your brother."

She touched his arm as she placed a handful of twigs in the bag. "I was teasing, silly."

They walked and talked, shared laughter and a few moments of awkward silence. Nobu moved close to her, then away again, like an accordion, unable to find just the right note.

When, the bag was full, crammed with branches and twigs, he wondered how much time had passed. All he knew was it had flown too quickly.

"I should probably get home before my parents begin to worry," Yuki said.

Panic set in. When would he see her again? Should he ask her to Thanksgiving lunch? No, too soon for that. When they turned in the direction of the camp, he wasn't sure what pulsed faster—his pounding heart or the rampant thoughts in his head. When? *Think!*

They walked from the woods, into the bright light of day. She was even prettier in the sunlight, where her black hair glistened and the blush in her cheeks brightened. He tried not to stare. His hands sweated again.

"Thank you for helping me gather wood," she said.

There! The excuse to see her again. "I'll help you again tomorrow."

She laughed. "I don't think we'll use all of this today. But maybe in a day or two?"

"Sure. Any time. Would you like me to check with you day after tomorrow?"

"That would be nice. We live in Block 20, three doors down from Kazu."

Jealousy prickled at him. How'd Kazu get so lucky?

When they arrived at the gate, Private Collins greeted them with a broad smile. "Hello, Yuki. How'd it go, collecting wood?" His blue eyes lingered on her too long.

Now jealousy stung. Interrupting their interlude, Nobu showed the bag of wood to Collins. "We gathered all of this together. In a day or so, I'll help her gather more."

She's mine.

Collins smiled at Nobu. "That's good of you, man." He pushed a clipboard toward them. "You two want to sign back in?"

Nobu kept his eye on Collins as Yuki signed first. He signed next, and the two walked through the gate together. He thought about putting his arm over her shoulder—show that guy Collins she was his. But he didn't want to startle her. He casually moved closer to her instead.

"You two have a nice Thanksgiving," Collins called.

Yuki turned around and waved. "You, too, Private Collins."

Obliged, Nobu waved, without turning. "Yeah. You, too."

Yuki reached to take the bag from Nobu. "I can take that now."

"No, it's heavy. I'll carry it to your apartment for you."

He felt out of control. His lingering jealousy was so consuming it left room only for the misery of leaving her.

Gusts of wind whipped around them as they strolled through the rows of barracks.

"Oh!" she cried.

Her skirt blew up over her knees, briefly exposing her thighs. The most beautiful patch of skin he'd ever seen.

When she clutched the pleats of her skirt and pushed it back down, Nobu's jacket fell from her shoulders. Her cheeks blushed bright red when she knelt to pick it up. "I'm so sorry," she said, returning the jacket with one hand and holding her skirt with the other. "I can wash it for you."

He took the jacket. "It's okay." He smiled, but inside chided himself for his thoughts. A dirty jacket had certainly been worth the view of her lovely legs.

"Here we are," she said, facing him.

He searched her eyes for any sign of the same disappointment he felt at parting.

"Shall I take the bag now?" she asked.

Such a pretty smile.

He took the strap from his shoulder and gently placed it over hers. "You sure you don't want me to carry it inside for you?"

At once, her smile disappeared. Her eyes flashed. "No, I'll do it." She touched his arm. "But thank you."

"You're welcome." A magnet to her metal, he couldn't tear himself away.

Watch it. You're making a fool of yourself.

Stepping away, she whispered, "I'd better go in now."

"Right. I'll see you in a few days, then. Bye for now, Yuki-san." He watched her go inside and shut the door.

He shook his jacket before putting it on, and grinned at the memory of what he'd seen when it fell from Yuki's shoulders. On second thought, maybe he'd leave a little dirt on the jacket as a reminder.

He headed in the direction of home, but stopped in his tracks. Damn! What was he thinking? He had no wood of his own. Mama would be full of questions. For that matter, so would Sachi.

Desperate for a solution, his mind raced with possible answers: He'd stayed to help Kazu with their Thanksgiving dinner. Maybe he had stopped by the mess hall to see what was for lunch. Neither of those stupid answers would satisfy Mama.

He had to find wood. Somewhere.

He jogged through row after row, frantically searching for anything that would burn. Time was running out. People were already walking to the mess hall for lunch.

A few stoops had wood piles neatly stacked beside them. He could "borrow" some—nobody would notice one or two missing pieces. But he couldn't bring himself to steal from his neighbors, even to cover up his own lovesick foolishness.

There. The answer to his problem. Next to the administration building, a mountain of scrap lumber was piled near stacked two-by-fours used to build new barracks. Who would miss a few scraps?

Casually strolling by, he peeked through the windows of the building. Vacated for the holiday. One more quick glance around for anyone who might see. No one in sight, so he quickly gathered all he could shove inside his jacket. At least it would last the day.

He scurried home, feeling like a thief, sneaky and wicked. But this was survival. Damn government had no problem keeping the camp stocked with lumber for barracks for new internees. Why couldn't they keep the place stocked with wood to keep the internees warm?

As he put his hand on the doorknob of their apartment, the door flew open.

Sachi stood on the other side, eyes flaring. "It's about time you got home. Where have you been?"

CHAPTER 47

Terrence

THANKSGIVING DAY, 1942

Archy the Cockroach was back. From his bunk, Terrence watched the shiny, brown bug scurry into the cell from around the corner, clearly on a mission. Back at home he'd have leaped from his bed, grabbed a shoe, and smashed the critter to death. Back then, he'd even wondered why God put them on this earth.

Funny how circumstances could change the way you thought about things. Ever since Mr. Blake had given him that copy of Don Marquis's *archy and mehitabel*, Terrence had changed his thinking about cockroaches—matter fact, he kinda liked this one. Sure, he'd snickered when Mr. Blake explained that Archy had been a poet in another life and that in his present form, it was difficult for him to continue his literary pursuits. The poor reincarnated creepy-crawly had a real challenge trying to type. Had to dive head first onto each key to type a letter. Since he couldn't hit both the shift and letter keys to type a capital letter, his postings were all written in lowercase. No punctuation either.

Blake didn't fool Terrence none. Nope. He'd figured the old guy out. Introducing Archy had been his way of getting Terrence to practice grammar—by correcting the mistakes of Archy the Cockroach.

He wouldn't admit his secret fondness for Archy to anyone, not even to Momma. But the roach had become kinda like a pet. Terrence would watch for him to come home to the cell, and every once in a while, he'd feed him table scraps, like he used to with his dog, Jake, back home.

Terrence watched Archy zip back outside the bars and out of sight. He'd only stayed a few minutes. Must've gotten bored in the cell. Terrence could understand that. The fact that he had a pet cockroach spoke volumes about how bored he was. Too bad Terrence couldn't come and go as he pleased, too. Sneak out unnoticed. Take a trip outside, even. Might not be so bad being a cockroach. Least he wouldn't be stuck in that cell. 'Course, he'd have to watch out for the folks coming around with shoes in their hands.

Terrence looked up to see Carter's feet swing over the top bunk. They hung there for a minute, then the bed creaked, and Carter groaned. "This mattress ain't worth shit."

"Good morning to you, too," Terrence replied. "Oh, and happy Thanksgiving."

Carter pushed off the top bunk and landed with a grunt. "Oh, yeah. Thanksgiving." He stretched his hands to the ceiling, then scratched his crotch. "Your family coming for a visit today?"

"'Course. Yours?" Maybe he'd finally get to meet the mystery family. Carter still hadn't let on much about them. All that did was make Terrence more curious.

Carter ran his fingers through his blond hair. "My ma said she might come . . . if she feels up to it."

"She sick or something?"

Carter stretched his arms up on the bars and pressed against the cell door. He stared out and hissed. "Shit. Only when she's had too much to drink the night before."

The new information tongue-tied Terrence. What do you say about someone's drunk mother? "Uh, maybe she'll be here . . . since it's a holiday and all."

"Yeah, we'll see. What time's your family coming?"

"Momma said she'd be here with Patty and Missy sometime this morning. Your sister coming? What'd you say her name was?"

Carter stared at him, half studying, half glaring. "Her name's Jenny."

Time was passing even slower than usual. Terrence pushed his notebook away and tossed his pencil on top of it. He rubbed his dry eyes then stretched his arms over his head. He'd had enough—even correcting Archy's mistakes had gotten dull. Heck, it wasn't like there was anything else to do. Some days he thought he'd go crazy sitting in that cell, especially with a kid who didn't have nothing to say. Sure never thought he'd be thankful for homework, but he praised God that Mr. Blake kept bringing him stuff to study. Anyways, he figured homework was like killing two birds with one stone—gave him something to keep him from getting more bored than he would've been, and if he was lucky, it got him closer to getting his high school diploma.

"Hey, Salt and Pepper," said a guard. He shoved a key into the lock and jiggled. "What do you know? You both got visitors."

Terrence stepped out first, not sure if he was more excited about seeing his family, or getting a glimpse of Carter's.

Carter followed, holding his hands toward the guard for cuffing.

As they walked to the visitors' area, Terrence leaned toward Carter. "Now I hate to say 'I told you so' but didn't I tell you your momma would come, this being a holiday?"

Carter snickered and shook his head. "Yeah. Don't know if her coming's good or bad, though."

Terrence had never seen the room so crowded with people. The air buzzed with voices. Hissed with whispers. Babies cried and kids pounded on the windows that divided the prisoners from their families. Every once in a while, the sounds of whimpering mommas or wives drifted above the mingling noises.

One of the guards jerked Terrence's arm, and the quartet stopped at one of the tables. When Carter pulled out a chair, Terrence's glance darted to the woman who sat behind the window.

He'd never seen a woman look so tired and sickly before—especially someone's momma. Mommas were supposed to look like they could take care of their kids, but not this one. No, she looked like she was the one who needed taking care of. She might've made an effort to clean up some. Her stringy, blonde hair was pulled into a messy ponytail, but half of it had already come undone. She watched Carter with gray eyes, bloodshot and sunken. And with such dark circles around them, he wondered if someone had punched her. Or, maybe those black rings were a permanent frame for eyes that reflected a hard-lived life. Seeing her sucked the energy right out of him.

He started to turn away when a girl sitting half-behind the woman peeked around. A younger, prettier version of her momma, she looked to be a little older than Patty. All he knew was, her blue eyes lit up when she saw Carter.

Carter sat down and looked up at Terrence, then nodded toward his momma and sister. "My ma and sister, Jenny."

Terrence smiled and waved.

The guard pushed him toward another table.

"See you back at the cell," he said to Carter, then walked a few steps down. He heard a familiar squeal.

"Ooh, Momma! There he is, there's Terrence!" Missy exclaimed, clapping her hands.

Patty leaned against Momma, all dressed up in her Thanksgiving finery, and smiling her pretty smile.

Momma stood. "Hey, baby. Happy Thanksgiving. I sure do wish I coulda brought you some food, but they told us we couldn't bring nothing from the outside today."

"That's okay, Momma. They gonna feed us some turkey in the cafeteria later on." He smiled, shaking his head. "Sure won't be as good as yours though."

"Whatcha gonna have for dessert, Tee?" Missy asked.

He wished he could hold his baby sister on his lap. Would she be too big once he got out? "Oh, probably some rat cobbler with vanilla ice cream. Maybe some nice, hot cockroach chip cookies."

"Eeewww," she cried.

Patty covered her mouth with her hand and giggled.

Momma grinned. "Now son, you be nice to your little sister. You know how much she been looking forward to seeing you?"

He leaned forward. "We gonna have pumpkin pie. Just like you!"

"How's your studies coming along?" Momma asked.

"Okay, I guess. Mr. Blake said he'd come by tomorrow. It gets pretty boring sitting around doing homework so much of the day, but guess I ain't . . . I don't have anything better to do."

"What's your roommate like?" Patty asked.

Innocent Patty. Carter would get a chuckle out of being called his roommate. He glanced down the aisle and wondered how Carter was doing with his family. What kind of conversation does a momma recovering from a drunken binge have with her son? What was his sister like? Quiet and shy like Patty? Or silly and mischievous like Missy?

Patty knocked on the table. "Tee? What are you thinking about? Did you hear me?"

"Oh, yeah. My roommate. He's cool."

Momma straightened in her chair. "What do 'cool' mean?"

He slumped and stared down at his cuffed hands, not keen to talk about Carter to Momma, especially with his sisters around. The more he told them about all the stuff Mr. Blake had said about getting to know someone, about fear driving hate, the more they'd ask. Just wasn't the right time to be bringing all that up. Stealing a glance back at Momma, he hoped something might sidetrack her away from the subject.

No such luck. Her stare was insistent, kinda like a headache that wouldn't go away.

"Son, what do 'cool' mean?"

Shit. "Oh, you know, Momma." How could he tell her just enough to satisfy her, without bringing on a bunch of questions? "He's okay. Been kind of hard to get to know but we deal with each other just fine. I know he got a momma and a sis—"

A loud crash came from Carter's direction. Terrence jumped up from his seat.

Missy hid behind Mama and Patty grabbed her hand.

Carter was standing and yelling, his chair flat on the floor. "When are you ever gonna understand, Ma. I had to do it!"

The guards grabbed him and pulled him toward the door.

But he kept yelling at his momma. "Maybe if you hadn't of just sat around drunk all the time . . ." The door slammed, and his words muffled as he was shoved down the hall. "And maybe if you hadn't of ignored what was happening to Jenny right in front of your damn eyes, I wouldn't of *had* to . . ."

Quiet held the room like a clutched fist, until slowly, whispers, scooting chairs, and at last, the full hum of activity returned. Carter had gone back to his cell, and the people in the room had gone on with their lives.

But not Terrence. He stared at the door. Felt Momma's stare on him.

Carter had plenty of secrets yet to be discovered.

CHAPTER 48

Sachi

THANKSGIVING DAY, 1942

Relieved and angry at once, Sachi scolded Nobu, "I thought you'd never get back."

She had been pacing the floor for almost half an hour, worried he wouldn't return before Jubie and her family arrived with the food. If he didn't get there before Jubie, he'd miss their big surprise. Not to mention she'd need his moral support if Mama got angry.

The way Mama had been acting lately, who knew how she might react to Jubie's family arriving with Thanksgiving dinner.

Nobu rolled his eyes and walked inside, holding his bulging jacket.

"What do you have in there?" she asked, poking him.

He scowled and pulled away. "It's just wood for the fire. Now leave me alone. Don't you have something better to do than to bug me?" He knelt beside the stove and pulled the pieces of scrap lumber from his jacket.

She leaned over his shoulder. "What kind of wood is that?"

Her question drew Mama's attention. "Where did you get that?"

"It's just scrap lumber. Garbage. Nobody's going to use it, so I figured we might as well burn it."

"Nobu! You know what they said about taking any of the building supplies. What if—"

Someone knocked at the door.

Mama gasped. "See? They have come after you!"

Sachi peeked out the curtain, then skipped to the door. "No, it's okay, Mama." She smiled and nodded. "It's a surprise! My friends have brought Thanksgiving dinner."

"Oh, Sachiko," Mama said, rushing to the mirror. She hastily smoothed her hair into place.

Sachi opened the door. Sunlight shone into the room from behind three figures making the forms of Jubie, her mother, and Auntie Bess even darker.

Nervous excitement swelled inside as Sachi rose up on her toes. "Come in. Come in," she said, swinging her arm toward the inside. She watched for Mama's reaction, her smile quivering. "Mama, this is my friend, Jubie Lee, her mama, Mrs. Franklin, and her Auntie Bess." Her hand trembled as she pointed to each. "Jubie and I planned this surprise."

There, at last. A tiny smile. Better than nothing. Mama bowed slightly, wiping her hands on her dress. "How do you do?" Her voice was too cool. Too calm. "I am Mrs. Kimura, and this is my son, Nobu."

Nobu was kneeling on the floor, a piece of wood in-hand, his mouth agape.

Everyone froze in a tense silence. Cold air blew leaves through the open door. Sachi caught a whiff of the food they carried, and for a tiny moment it comforted her.

Finally, Nobu stood and walked toward them. "Please, come in. Let me take that for you," he said, taking a large pot from Jubie's mother. "Sachi, close the door."

She obeyed her brother, then looked to Jubie for reassurance. They shrugged at each other.

Mama scurried around, trying to make room for all of the food. "I am so sorry I am not better prepared." She shot a dart of anger at Sachi. "But nobody told me you were coming."

Auntie Bess set her pan on the table. "Don't you worry yourself none, Mrs. Kimura. Our girls have been so excited planning this surprise for you." She chuckled and put her arm around Jubie. "They just precious little angels for thinking of something so nice."

Sachi lifted the lid from one of the pans. Steam rose, and she inhaled. Turkey gravy. "Oh, Mrs. Franklin, Auntie Bess. Everything smells so good." She waved the scents in Mama's direction. Maybe the aroma would cheer her up. "Don't you think so, Mama?"

She didn't look at Sachi, but replied. "It is very nice."

You could never say Mama wasn't polite. So courteous, so gracious. So cold. Why couldn't she be thankful for friends willing to share home cooking? Even Nobu looked uncomfortable. Worse, she could tell by the strange silence and crossed arms, it was making Jubie and her family uncomfortable, too. Everybody stared at anything, as long as they didn't have to look at each other.

Auntie Bess slapped her hands together. "Okay. We got us some turkey and some stuffing." Her round body waddled around the table as she lifted lids from the pots and pans. She pulled a jar from the bag Jubie had carried in. "And let's see here. Some pickled okra. That's special from Jubie, just for you, sugar." A wink for Sachi. Then, with great fanfare, she lifted a pie pan and removed the cover. "And last, but surely not least, we got us some sweet potato pie!"

Jubie whispered to Sachi. "Don't you got something, too?"

Sachi's eyes widened. "Oh, yes. And I made rice. Jubie said she has never had rice for Thanksgiving before." She picked up a dish towel, and lifted a pot from the wood stove. "It doesn't smell nearly as good as what you brought, though."

Nobu leaned against the wall. Arms folded across his chest, he rolled his eyes.

She dropped the pan on the stove. This was all a mistake. Nothing would pull Mama and Nobu out of their sour moods.

Auntie Bess pulled Sachi into her warm, soft body. She smelled like roses and Sachi wanted to linger in her embrace.

"Sugar baby, your rice smells mighty fine to me," she said, pulling her tighter. Then she let go and clapped her hands again. "Reckon we best eat 'fore it all gets cold."

Mrs. Franklin spoke. "Mrs. Kimura, you got some plates?"

"Of course." She reached onto a shelf for a stack of dishes. "Nobu, would you get the cups and silverware?"

Sachi raised her hand. "I can help, too."

Mama set the dishes on the table. "No, Sachi. You have done enough. Just entertain your guests."

Your guests? But they're our guests.

Sachi turned away when she felt tears welling.

There wasn't much she could hide from Jubie. Her friend wiggled her finger, an invitation to stand next to her.

She pulled Sachi behind Auntie Bess's gigantic flowered skirt. "You okay?"

Sachi shrugged. "We shouldn't have planned this surprise. I can tell Mama's not happy about it."

"Yeah, I can see that, too." Jubie flashed a sassy smile and put her hands on her skinny hips. "But oh, like she woulda been happier just sittin' here by herself today?"

"I don't know. Maybe."

"No. She'd just been mopin' around, remembering all them other Thankgivings when she had herself some good food and good friends." She put her arm around Sachi's shoulder. "All you done was try to bring her some of them good friends and good food. You done the right thing."

Sachi smiled. "*We* did the right thing. I couldn't have done it without you and your family."

"Look like we ready to eat," said Auntie Bess, turning toward the girls. "You two hungry?"

"Yes ma'am!" replied Jubie.

With all the good smells that filled the room, Sachi knew she should be hungry. But every time she began to feel hunger pangs, the look in Mama's eyes scared them away and left a sick feeling instead. She sure was in trouble. Later.

Mama glanced around, wringing her hands. "I must apologize again. I do not have enough chairs for everyone."

"Jubie and I can sit on the floor. There's plenty of room, right over there in that corner." Besides, the corner was out of the line of Mama's glare.

Mrs. Franklin took Mama's hands in hers. "Don't you fret none about it. Believe you me, we been to plenty of family gatherings where we all stood around and ate."

Jubie filled her plate first. Sachi picked a little of this, a little of that, just to be polite.

"Ain't you gonna eat no more than that? I thought you couldn't wait for Thankgiving. Said you was gonna fill-up with turkey and stuffing," Jubie declared.

Sachi watched Jubie eat and whispered, "I just know I'm in trouble. I wanted your mama and my mama to get to know each other. But I can tell by the look in Mama's eyes—she's not happy about this surprise."

"Maybe it wasn't the right time." Jubie bit her drumstick. "Tell you what. I'll save you some of this food for you to eat when you feel more like it, 'kay?"

If nothing else went right today, at least Sachi had Jubie to be thankful for.

A knock at the door startled her. She put her plate on the floor and gawked at Jubie. "Now what?" She tried to reassure Mama. "Don't worry. It's not another surprise. Want me to get it?"

"I'll get it," said Nobu and made his way through the crowded room to answer the door. Adrenaline surged when he saw the badge on the man's shirt. *Internal police.* "Can I help you?" Nobu asked. Still holding the plate in his hand, he stepped outside.

The man attempted to peer around him. "Someone reported seeing a boy about your age taking some scrap wood from the administration building," he said. "We're just asking around. You know anything about that?"

Mama made her way to the door. "What is it?" she asked.

"It's nothing, Mama. Go back inside." He shut the door.

Sachi scooted toward the door and strained to hear the conversation outside. All she could hear was Nobu saying, "Sorry." Then, something about work detail. What if they took him away? Then she'd have to face Mama alone after Jubie left.

Mama sat in a chair across the room and stared at the door, her food growing cold on the plate she held on her lap.

Sachi wanted this day to be over, even wanted Jubie and her family to go home so the embarrassing silence would end. But another part of her wanted them to stay. As long as she had guests, she wouldn't get in trouble. Mama would never unleash her anger or talk about losing face in front of them. Then again, maybe Mama's silent, cold stare was worse than her angry words.

Nobu came back inside and tossed his plate on the table, causing some of his food to spill.

Mama went to him and whispered something.

Sachi tried to read her lips.

"Is everything okay?" she seemed to say.

He didn't hide his frustrated reply. "Do you mind if we discuss this later?" He stormed to the chair he'd been sitting in before the soldier came to the door.

Sachi's stomach turned queasy at the sight of her brother sitting in that chair, arms crossed and leg bouncing nervously. She closed her eyes.

Go away, world.

"Mmm-mmm. That sure was some good food," Auntie Bess said, rising from her seat. "Sure is too bad we gotta be going. Jubie and me promised to take a sweet potato pie over to the preacher's for dessert."

Jubie raised an eyebrow and shrugged at Sachi.

Auntie Bess cleared her throat. "Don't you remember, sugar? I guess it's been a couple weeks ago now, we was standing in front of the church. I told Preacher we'd bring it by, share some dessert with him and his family for Thanksgiving."

Jubie took one last bite of her drumstick before standing. "Oh, yeah. How could I forget?"

Mrs. Franklin smiled at Mama. "Why don't you keep this food? We got plenty at home."

"No, thank you," Mama said. "We have no place to store it. Please take it with you."

Auntie Bess began to match lids with pots and pans. "All right then. We gonna take the food, but we gonna leave that sweet potato pie for y'all to enjoy later." She winked again at Sachi. "This little one say she ain't never had no sweet potato pie. Ain't that right, sugar?"

Sachi set her plate on the table, pretty certain she wouldn't be getting dessert that night. She thanked Auntie Bess anyway.

Jubie, her mother, and Auntie Bess each picked up the items they'd carried in and made their way to the door.

Mrs. Franklin turned to Mama. "Thank you kindly for having us in your home today. Maybe sometime you and me could have coffee together."

Mama bowed, and in her cool, proper manner, replied, "Thank you, but I drink tea. And thank you for bringing Thanksgiving dinner."

"Guess I'll see you tomorrow?" Jubie asked.

Sachi had a feeling her scolding would include being grounded. She shrugged. "I hope so."

Auntie Bess bent to kiss Sachi on the cheek. "Happy Thanksgiving, sugar. We'll see you soon, 'kay?"

Sachi could tell by the look in Auntie's eyes—she knew the kind of trouble Sachi was in.

Auntie Bess looked at Mama. "Such a sweet idea our girls had, bringing us all together on this day of thanks." She stared upward, shaking her hands in prayer. "Lord, so much to be thankful for—even in these trying times, if you keep your eyes open." She smiled warmly before walking out the door with Jubie and Mrs. Franklin.

All the Thanksgiving spirit whooshed out the door with them. She turned from the closed door, dreading the look in Mama's eyes.

Mama glared at her. Rigid, her eyes expressed a kind of anger Sachi had never seen before. Her words came slow. Deliberate.

"Do you remember the color of the boy who killed your papa?"

CHAPTER 49

Nobu

THANKSGIVING DAY, 1942

Nobu had to admit—Sachi had really done it this time. When she opened the door to that colored family, he'd thought the same thing Mama had asked.

Do you remember the color of the boy who killed your papa?

Hearing it out loud, he realized how unreasonable, how irrational the thought—to hold the color of their skin against them. They'd carried a Thanksgiving meal to share. They didn't even know Terrence Harris.

Poor Sachi. Standing alone in front of the door with confusion in her eyes and hurt written all over her body—slumped shoulders, eyes that could not face her own mother. How could Mama relate Papa's memory to such a question?

But he'd asked the question, too. He just hadn't spoken it out loud.

There was only hardness and anger in Mama's face. No sympathy or appreciation at all for what Sachi had tried to do—bring a little happiness into the dark apartment, if only for a while.

He couldn't—wouldn't—be caught in the middle of this one. He understood them both and would not choose sides. Besides, he had problems of his own to deal with.

He went to his room and pulled the curtain shut. Taking his journal from under his mattress, he flung himself onto the bed and watched the curtain sway as he gathered his thoughts.

Thanksgiving Day, 1942

How could a day be so good, yet so bad? Thanksgiving used to start with good smells and the busy activity of preparing for the holiday. But in camp, it started as any other day, much to the chagrin of Sachi. I saw from the start that she wanted the day to be special. Unfortunately, I did not know what she had planned, otherwise I would have stopped her.

This morning, I had to get out—had to leave the tension already brewing between Mama and Sachi. So, I used needing firewood as my chance to leave. I figured Kazu and I could spend part of the day together gathering kindling to take our minds off of what Thanksgiving used to be, what it couldn't be in camp.

No such luck. He'd already promised to help his mother prepare their holiday meal. When I entered their home, the warmth and the smell of sweet potatoes might have made me believe we were no longer in camp, except for the sparseness of our surroundings. But Kazu and his mother seemed able to ignore that, seemed to have the ability to focus on what they did have. I wished it could be the same for me. For Mama.

There was nothing left for me to do but gather firewood, which meant going outside of the camp and into the woods.

That's where the best part of my day happened.

I couldn't believe it when I found Yuki gathering wood too. Okay, now there was something to be thankful for—the prettiest girl in camp, gathering wood in the same forest as me!

I've never felt the way I did when I was with her, like there was a strange energy between us—something that vibrated faster the closer I got to her. One minute, I wanted to touch her, hold her, the next, I backed away, unable to think of anything to say. I imagined what her body beneath her clothes looked like, imagined touching her soft skin. Then I scolded myself for those thoughts.

But the worst feeling was the jealousy! An awful feeling, wondering if other guys have the same thoughts of her.

When it was time to go, I hated leaving her, but at least I could look forward to seeing her again in a few days. I told her I'd help her gather wood again.

That was all before I came up with the brilliant idea to take some scrap lumber to burn. Stupid me, in all my lovesick wonder, forgot to get my own wood. I was desperate—saw no harm in taking a little scrap lumber. But someone saw me, and the internal police tracked me down, right in the middle of Sachi's big surprise. As if the situation wasn't already tense enough.

I tried to tell him they were just scraps, that I didn't see a problem with using it.

He jotted a few notes, told me that regulations posted last week said nothing was to be taken from construction sites by internees, and that I'd have to report to the administration building in the morning for assignment to work detail for the next four weeks.

Great! That means I won't be able to help Yuki gather wood day after tomorrow. Now how will I see her?

Back to Sachi's surprise. Yeah, to be ten years old again. She didn't let the fact we're in this miserable camp stop her from planning a Thanksgiving celebration. Like always, she looked for what's good in the world instead of focusing on what's wrong with it.

Still, when her colored friends walked through our door, all I could see was Terrence. All I could feel was the hatred I have for him and everyone who wears the color of his skin.

But unlike Mama, I didn't say it.

Nobu closed his journal, no longer able to ignore the conversation on the other side of his curtain. He'd never heard emotion like that from his sister.

"How could you, Mama?" Sachi cried. "Don't you see?" She heaved deep breaths between sobs.

Nobu held his breath, waiting for her next words. The room was silent, except for her crying. Even the murmured conversation of the people in the rooms on either side of their apartment had stopped.

Sachi's voice softened. "First you did it with Sam, and now with Jubie. Don't you see, Mama? If you hold the color of their skin against Jubie and her family . . . if you hate them because they're the same color as Terrence . . . then you're no better than the people who put us here, the ones who hate us because we're the same color as the Japanese who bombed Pearl Harbor."

CHAPTER 50
Sachi

DECEMBER 23, 1942

One year slowly passed
Fog blanketed memories
Hide me from the light

Wind rattled the window. It crept into the tiny room like an intruder and brushed its icy fingers across Sachi's face. She'd never been so cold, and shivered, even through her coat.

But remembering the day stung more than the cold. She wanted to ignore the anniversary and had even taken the calendar off the wall and hidden it under Mama's stack of magazines.

It hadn't helped. The date refused to be forgotten.

One year ago those boys beat up Papa at the park. For three hundred sixty-five days she had missed Papa and wished she could share each one of those days' events with him before going to sleep at night. She still saw him everywhere.

And lately, a new thought had begun banging in her mind, refusing to be dismissed. It poked its ugly finger at her when she least expected. Like now.

She blinked her eyes to shake it away and decided to go see what Jubie was doing. But first she had to get by Mama.

"Mama, can I go to visit my friend Haruko?" she asked.

Mama looked up from the book she was reading. "I suppose so. Say hello to her mother for me."

She didn't like lying to her mother. But ever since the fight they'd had about Jubie, she figured it was easier to tell Mama she was going to play with somebody else. But the Japanese girls in camp didn't know how to do the jitterbug like Jubie, who'd been teaching Sachi all the strange moves. Images flashed through her mind and she didn't know what was funnier: watching Jubie dance like a Japanese girl, or seeing Jubie hold her tummy from laughing so hard as Sachi tried to dance like a colored girl.

"Remember your scarf," Mama called, as Sachi opened the door.

"I have it. Bye, Mama," she replied and wrapped the scarf around her face, leaving only her eyes showing.

She skipped past a row of barracks under construction, where men hustled around the bare frames of long buildings like ants at a picnic. She wondered if Nobu was working there and stopped to see.

He'd been awfully mad about having to be on work detail after getting caught with the scrap lumber. But what was the big deal? He'd have volunteered to help, even if he hadn't been forced to.

She knew exactly why he was so upset, after sneaking a peek at his journal a few days before. What a thrill it was, doing something she knew she shouldn't be doing. What power she felt, snooping on what Nobu wrote without anyone knowing.

Shame on me.

But she couldn't resist. What else was there to do when she was alone and so bored?

Now that she knew all about Yuki, it was hard not to tease Nobu. Of course, then he would know she had read his journal. A real dilemma.

Her brother was in love. The thought of it made her giggle, though she had to admit she felt sorry he'd had to work over the last four weeks. All he really wanted to do was spend time with his secret crush.

She could see why he liked Yuki. She was one of the prettiest girls in camp. Sachi had seen her talking to Private Collins a couple of times, and the way *he* acted around her, he must have thought she was awfully cute, too. Why did boys act so goofy whenever there was a pretty girl around?

She found Nobu leaning over two saw horses, cutting a piece of lumber in two. "Hi, Nobu," she called.

He stopped and turned around. "Hi, Sach. What's up?"

His question caught her off guard. She couldn't tell him what she was really doing; she'd have to lie to him, too, because he would surely side with Mama about playing with a colored girl. "I'm on my way to Haruko's," she replied.

At least she should keep her lies straight.

He waved his hand. "Have fun."

"I will. Bye." She walked away, hoping her brother wouldn't watch her for too long. The turn down Haruko's row was coming up, and she wouldn't be turning. No, she'd go straight to the gate to sign out. Then, on to Jubie's.

What if . . .

There it was again—that nagging feeling that kept sneaking into her thoughts. It bothered her anytime things got too quiet.

She started to skip again and strained to hold the fading sounds of construction in her ears. Anything to avoid the quiet that invited the troubling thought.

Yuki was standing at the gate entrance again, chatting with Private Collins. She smiled and twirled her hair around her finger as she spoke. The private wore one of those silly grins and leaned across the counter like he wanted to get closer to Yuki.

He was okay as far as guards go, but watching him stare at Yuki made her feel sorry for Nobu. She knew from his journal that Nobu thought of Yuki every minute of every day. And here she was flirting with Private Collins.

Unfortunately, there wasn't much she could do about it. She wasn't supposed to know anything about Yuki. Still, maybe she could break up their little interlude by hanging around and talking about dumb things until they got bored. According to Nobu, Sachi was good at talking about dumb things.

Skipping up to the gate, she spoke in her friendliest tone. "Hi, Private Collins. What are you doing?"

Yuki stepped back. The private straightened.

"Looks like you're pretty busy," Sachi continued. "I've been busy today, too."

"Oh?" he replied.

It wasn't lost on Sachi that he didn't ask what she'd been doing. She stood on her tiptoes to sign out. "Don't you want to know what I've been up to?"

He crossed his arms. "I guess."

She extended her hand to Yuki. "By the way, I'm Sachiko. I live here with my mother and my brother . . . NO-BU."

Yuki's gaze flashed toward Private Collins for the tiniest second, then she smiled at Sachi. "Nice to meet you, Sachiko. My name is Yuki."

Sachi nodded and continued. "So, where was I? Oh, yes. First, I had to help Mama fold the laundry. *That* was boring." She looked up at Yuki. "That's a pretty scarf you have on. And you sure do smell good."

The private raised his eyebrow.

Yuki smiled. "Why, thank you."

A deep breath and Sachi continued. "Anyway, so on with my story. Let's see . . . I helped Mama fold laundry. Oh! Then she asked me to sweep the floor, which I did. But that was boring, too. So, I pretended to be Cinderella. Remember how the evil stepmother and stepsisters always picked on her? Made her do all the chores? Well, that helped a little, pretending I was Cinderella, but pretty soon, even that got dull, dull, dull."

Yuki shrugged. The private rolled his eyes.

"So with the laundry folded and the floor swept, I figured there wasn't much more Mama could ask me to do. Right?"

Yuki replied politely, "Right."

The private stifled a yawn.

"Wrong!" Sachi said, slamming her hand on the counter. "Then, Mama handed me a dust rag and asked me to help her dust the shelves. Not that we have many shelves to dust, but still. It was the principle. I do have other things to do, you know. Want to know what?"

Yuki fiddled with her scarf. "I would love to hear what else you have to do, but I'd better be going. Who knows, my mother may very well have a list of things for me to do."

The private flashed a look of alarmed protest, but Yuki held her finger to her mouth and shook her head.

"You two continue without me," Yuki said, a slight giggle in her voice.

"Bye, bye," called Sachi. She watched Private Collins watch Yuki walk away, then leaned toward him as if to tell him a secret. "She's pretty, but I've seen prettier."

"That so," he grumbled.

"Well, I'd better be going now. Like I said, I have other things to do."

She heard Private Collins cluck his tongue as she left the gate. Nobu owed her.

The chill in the air numbed her cheeks. When she arrived at Jubie's door, she looked forward to the warmth inside. Her hand tingled with cold when she pulled it out of her pocket and knocked.

Jubie's mother answered. "Hello, Sachi."

"Hi, Mrs. Franklin. Is Jubie home?

"No, she gone to choir practice with Auntie Bess. She be back in a couple hours."

Sachi shoulders slumped. What was she going to do for the next few hours? "Okay. Will you tell her I came by?"

"Sure will. Say hi to your mama for me, would ya?"

"Yes ma'am. Bye for now." Sachi turned to leave, wishing she *could* tell Mama that Mrs. Franklin said hi.

The door clicked shut behind her. She didn't want to be by herself. She felt a little irritated that Jubie wasn't home. But there had been no way for Jubie to know what day this was.

Everything was still and quiet, as if the cold air had frozen the world. She hated the quiet, especially today.

What if . . .

There it was again, ramming its way into her consciousness. Unease rippled inside, and she searched for a distraction, a place to hide. But the street was empty. Quiet.

She started running, as if she could escape the thought. But it was too strong this time. There was nothing to drive it away. It burst into her mind, full force. She stopped. Breathless. Overcome.

If I hadn't begged Papa to take me to the park, he might still be alive.

Tears burned her eyes. It was *her* fault. She covered her face with her hands, hoping darkness would hide her from the bitter realization.

Mama had warned them that it wasn't a good idea to go to the park that day. Papa had probably agreed, but with Sachi begging day after day, he'd finally given in and ignored Mama's warning.

It was her fault.

If she hadn't dragged Papa there, if she had left when Papa said it was time to go, those boys wouldn't have found him. If Mama and Nobu blamed those boys, surely they blamed her, too.

I'm sorry, Papa.

Something cold tingled on the top of her head, trickled down her collar. Goose bumps? No. It was colder. It prickled on her hands, too. She took them from her face and opened her eyes.

White flakes drifted all around her. They landed on her eyelashes, her nose, her tongue.

She stared at the flakes that landed on her jacket, lifted her arm to her eyes to see better. Tiny, tiny crystals, shaped like the ones she cut from paper, each different from the others, but all clinging together.

Falling, falling.

Softly.

Gracefully.

Unbelievably quiet.

Snow! Her first snow.

CHAPTER 51

Terrence

DECEMBER 23, 1942

Another long night. But then, Terrence didn't know why it should be different from any other. Soon as it got quiet, things would start jumbling around in his mind, popping up as dreams that haunted him. Dreams of Daddy's final minutes. What had his father been thinking about in those minutes? Was he in pain for long, or did he go quick? Then, just as he got those nagging thoughts out of his head, he'd dream about Mr. Kimura. Had it really been one year since his family got that telegram? It seemed like so much longer. It seemed like only yesterday.

It'd been a year since that day in the park, too. Over and over again, he saw flashes of the fear in Nobu's father's eyes as he lay helpless on the ground, wincing with every kick. What did *he* think about in his last minutes? Same thing as Daddy?

He hated the quiet.

He got to wondering what *he'd* think about if he was ever dying. Momma. Daddy. Patty and Missy. He'd think about how he loved them and hoped they'd always know it. He'd wish he could tell them just one more time.

Sometimes his dreams would all melt together into one, and it'd be like he was watching Daddy and Mr. Kimura die right next to each other. Pretty soon, their bodies would disappear, and all that was left was the things they felt when they took their last breaths.

He was sick to his stomach all over again, thinking about killing Mr. Kimura. In those final minutes, when they thought their final thoughts, it didn't matter what color Mr. Kimura's skin was, or what color Daddy's skin was.

Daddy's last thought. Mr. Kimura's last thought. They were probably just the same.

Strange how that realization brought him a little peace, like light shining down in a deep, dark hole. A hole that sometimes pulled him down, down, down.

Maybe it was peace, or maybe exhaustion. Maybe just plain surrender. But finally, he felt himself sink into sleep.

Too soon, morning light blared through the window. A rude awakening, too, like Momma shaking him awake when he didn't want to get up yet. He wanted to sleep some more. But with the sun came noises of the prison coming to life.

Loud yawning. Guys yelling about being hungry. Toilets flushing. No more sleep for him.

One more day, one more mark on the wall. He took a pencil from under his pillow and pressed hard. Still 476 days to go. Felt like it had already been ten years. Long as it seemed, he reminded himself every day: He'd be out someday, but never, never would Nobu have his daddy back.

Outside, he would have been counting down the days to finishing his freshman year in college—instead of inside, where he was counting the days to freedom. Least he was still learning things, thanks to Mr. Blake. All his tests had been going well, and now that he and Carter were getting along better, studying with a cell mate wasn't so bad.

Heck. Those guards were probably good and pissed that they weren't getting the action they'd hoped for when they put a white boy in the cell with a black one. Salt and Pepper. Come to think, it was a stupid nickname, being as salt and pepper go together just fine. Matter fact, one don't go so good without the other. Yeah, him and Carter had shown those jerks. The more the two talked, the more Terrence learned they had things in common. He'd even got to liking Carter.

The turning point had been Thanksgiving Day, when Terrence had come back to the cell after visiting with his family. Carter was lying on his bunk, back to the wall, after the blowup with his mother. Terrence felt like he was walking on glass—didn't really know what to say. He just knew he better say something, and fast. Carter's face was all snarled up and the veins on his neck were bulging out. He'd surely explode as soon as Terrence said something. Didn't matter though. Least Terrence might get to know more about that mysterious sister of Carter's.

He remembered taking a deep breath, trying to figure out what to say. So he'd joked with Carter. "Man, you and that family of yours sure know how to break up a good, old Thanksgiving gathering. When you started yelling at your momma, I thought I'd choke on my turkey!"

Carter's eyes bugged out as he shot back his response. "What're you talking about? You didn't have no turkey in your mouth!"

"Yeah, and it for dang sure wasn't no good, old Thanksgiving gathering, neither. Come on. Lighten up," he said, shoving at Carter. "What went on out there, anyways? Why'd you yell at your momma on Thanksgiving Day? What could've been so bad?"

Terrence could tell by the look in Carter's eyes, there was plenty he needed to talk about. But whether he *would* talk was another story. He leaned against the opposite wall and watched Carter.

Carter bit at the corner of his lip. When he finally started talking, his words came slow. Quiet. It took awhile to come out, but Terrence still remembered the exact words of what Carter needed to get out, the only thing he'd said that really mattered in the jumbled words he'd spoken.

"I killed my daddy 'cause I was tired of hearing Jenny cry when he snuck into her room at night."

He killed his own father?

At first the confession sent shivers down Terrence's spine. Daddy flashed in his mind—a memory of him sitting in his big chair, Patty and Missy on each knee and snuggled into his chest as he read to them. He got queasy thinking about what Carter had said: "Pa did things to Jenny." He shut his eyes and tried to make the image go away.

No way could Terrence imagine Daddy ever doing something bad to his little girls. Yeah, he could imagine wanting to kill anyone who ever laid a hand on them. Sure as hell couldn't stand to hear them cry. But his own Daddy?

"But why'd you yell at your Momma?" Terrence had asked.

"'Cause she still can't get it through her thick, drunk head why I did it. She kept trying to tell me Pa wasn't hurting Jenny none. Said she missed him and was tired of not having a man around the house."

Poor Carter. Killing his own daddy. And having a momma that didn't have a motherly bone in her body. What would become of Jenny, being raised by a woman like that?

Terrence stared at the marks on the wall again. Yeah, 476 days seemed like a long time, all right. But at least one day he'd get out. If Carter was convicted of murder, he'd be in the pen for the rest of his life. Terrence stared at the light coming through the small window near the ceiling. Light and darkness would trade places thousands and thousands of times for Carter. Then, he'd die. Terrence would go crazy if there was nothing more to look forward to than that.

"Why'd you make that mark on the wall so dark?" Carter's question startled Terrence back to the present.

"Man, you scared the shit outta me."

Carter laughed. "Yeah, you were a million miles away. So what's the deal with the mark?"

"It's been a year."

"A year since what? Since you came here?"

"Nah." Terrence hesitated.

Carter persisted. "Since what then?"

Terrence grinned. "You been hanging around me too long. Getting to be kind of a nag, aren't you?"

"Well?" Carter poked at him. "You gonna tell me what the dark mark means, or not?"

"It's been a year since I did what I did to land in this shit hole."

"And? Come on man, give it up. I told you what I did."

"I killed a man, too. Beat him up in a park."

"Why? What'd he do?"

"He didn't do nothing. I killed him 'cause he was Japanese."

Carter was quiet. Looked like he was trying to figure that one out.

"We'd just gotten a telegram telling us my daddy was dead. Japs killed him at Pearl Harbor. Somehow I figured killing a Japanese man would make me feel better."

Carter backed away. "Sorry, man." He pulled out a chair and flopped into it. His fingers began to drum on the table. "So your pa is gone, too."

"Yeah." Terrence sat up in his bunk and rubbed his head.

Carter stared at his drumming fingers.

"Now what are you thinking about?" Terrence leaped off his bunk. Was Carter thinking about Terrence killing a Japanese man? Thinking about his own daddy? Why was he so quiet?

"Breakfast!" called a guard from down the corridor. "Line up."

Terrence pulled on a shirt. "Okay, you been saved by breakfast this time. But I'll get back at you later."

"Yeah, yeah." Carter grinned as he shuffled to the cell door.

Terrence filed into the cafeteria behind Carter. Breakfast. He remembered the smell of Momma cooking bacon. Biscuits in the oven. Coffee perking on the counter. The memory made him hungry, but one look at the mush being served and he lost his appetite. Matter fact, eating that gruel they glopped into his bowl made him gag. The coffee—lukewarm and filled with grounds—didn't do much to help him wash it down.

"Hey, if it ain't Salt and Pepper," Peachie called from a table across the room.

That jerk lived for giving Terrence a hard time. Only thing he'd been able to do was avoid the mass of dumb, white lard whenever possible.

"Hey, Salt." Peachie pointed at Carter. "Yeah, you. Why don't you come over here and eat. Ain't you ready for a Pepper break?"

A gang followed Peachie's lead, laughing as they gestured for Carter to come over.

Carter stared hard at the mush in his bowl, like he thought if he stared hard enough it might turn into biscuits and gravy or something.

What did Carter think about the razzing the whites gave him for being in a cell with a black man? Some inmates acted like he'd caught some kind of disease from Terrence. Others had a weird kind of curiosity, creeping up to Carter to ask what it was like to be locked up with a nigger. One even asked if a colored boy pissed the same way. Man, oh man. There were some real dumb shits out there.

The mob at Peachie's table grew rowdy.

"Hey, Carter! You been sitting in the sun, or are you turning into a nigger?"

Hoots and snickers.

"Just don't forget you a white boy."

"Yeah. You ain't got no choice but to be in a cell with a nigger, but you ain't gotta hang around with him outside. Come on over here and sit with your own kind."

Carter put his spoon down and mumbled, "You ain't my kind."

Peachie stood so fast his chair fell. "What you say, boy?"

Terrence felt the skin on the back of his neck crawl. Adrenaline surged through his body. Made his fists clench. He kept his gaze low. "Ignore him, Carter. He's not worth it."

Carter glared at Peachie with steel blue eyes and lips so tight they looked like they might break if he spoke.

Peachie hustled toward them. His glare reminded Terrence of that kinda-crazy look he'd once seen in a rabid dog's eyes.

What would he do if Peachie caused them trouble? Get involved? Defend Carter? 'Course he would.

Where in the hell were the guards? He looked around the room and saw two standing by the door, watching the tension brewing like it was a ball game or something. Whispering to each other. Probably making a wager or something.

Peachie was standing right next to where they sat. Terrence didn't even have to look up to see. He could smell the white monster. Sweat. Cigarettes.

Carter and Peachie stared each other down, like cowboys at a shoot-out. Who would draw first? And why weren't those damn guards doing anything?

Peachie made the first move. "You gonna tell me what you said?"

"Don't think you really wanna know." Carter gritted his teeth.

Peachie leaned toward him. "Oh, yeah. I wanna know all right. And you're gonna tell me, boy."

Terrence wasn't sure what made him sicker—that big old tub-of-lard hairy belly that stuck out below Peachie's T-shirt or his god-awful smell.

Carter's glare was hard and cold, but Terrence was sure he saw doubt flicker in his eyes.

Don't say it, Carter.

"Okay, boys. Break it up!" A guard shouted as he maneuvered through dozens of gawking inmates. "Everybody sit down. You! Get back to your table." He poked Peachie with his club.

Peachie resisted at first, snarling at Carter. "This ain't over."

"Hey!" The guard poked again. "Let's go. Back to your cell!"

The sounds of the cafeteria—silverware clanking against dishes, the mumbling and shuffling of the inmates—grew quiet as the guards emptied the room.

What was going on in Carter's head? He sure wasn't saying nothing.

Another guard approached their table. "Back to the cell, you two." He mumbled under his breath, "Salt and Pepper," and snickered to himself.

Carter tossed his spoon into his bowl and rose.

"You didn't eat much," Terrence whispered. He tore a piece of bread and put it in his pocket.

"Yeah, right. Kinda lost my appetite," Carter said, and shuffled back to the cell.

The guard slammed the cell door shut. Its echo faded and another awkward silence followed.

Terrence opened his algebra book and pulled out a piece of paper. He read the word problem and thought about how to start the calculation. Read it again. And again. Then, he shut the book. No way was he going to be able to concentrate enough to figure out a word problem. First he had to figure out Carter.

"Hey, Carter?"

Carter's gaze didn't flinch from where he'd been staring. "What."

"What're you thinking about?"

"Don't wanna talk about it."

Archy skittered from under the bed.

Terrence smiled and took the piece of bread out of his pocket. He sprinkled crumbs on the floor. "Wanna meet Archy?" he asked.

"Who?"

Terrence leaned over and watched his pet roach attack the scattered crumbs. "Archy. Archy the Cockroach."

Carter sat up and watched at the floor where the shiny, brown bug feasted. "Cockroach? You crazy?" He took his shoe off.

"Hey!" Terrence shouted. "Don't even think about it!"

"It's a damn cockroach, you fool!"

As if he sensed danger, Archy skittered out of the cell.

"Man, if I'd known you'd act like that, I wouldn't have told you about him. You're not afraid of a cockroach, are you?"

Carter returned his shoe to his foot. "I ain't afraid of nothing. But it's a *cockroach.*"

"Hey man, desperate times call for desperate measures. He's my pet. My cell dog." An idea popped into Terrence's head and he grinned. "You ain't gonna judge Archy by what he *looks* like, are you? Why, you'd be no better than Peachie."

"Aw, come on. That's stretching it, Tee."

"No, it ain't. I'm guessing to Peachie, I'm no better than a cockroach. By his way of thinking, no nigger is. Bet you even thought that when they threw you in this cell with me. Probably wanted to smash me with your shoe, too. Right?" Terrence clasped his hands behind his head and tilted back in his chair. "I'm guessing I've graduated up a level, maybe two, now that you've got to know me a little." He watched for Carter's response.

"Maybe one level. Maybe."

"Well, me and Archy, we've gotten to know each other better, too. I bring him scraps from the cafeteria, and he comes to greet me every day. I figure we all do what we got to do to survive in this world. All any creature wants is to be understood. Accepted for what he is."

Carter flopped back down on his mattress and went back to staring at the ceiling. "Man, you're getting a little too philosophical for me."

"Nah. It's pretty simple, really. My daddy used to tell me to live and let live. For a long time, I didn't know what he meant by that. But then I watched the way he lived his life. Realized that even when someone did something that shoulda made him mad, he just went on with his business. Kinda like he knew fighting wouldn't do no good no how." He stared outside the cell. "You just lay there and chew on that for a while, Carter. And don't even think about putting that smelly shoe of yours anywhere near Archy."

Carter flipped over and faced the wall. "Tee?"

"Yeah."

"You wanna know what I was thinking before we went to eat?"

"Yeah, what?"

"I used to think there wasn't anything I'd ever envy about a colored's life. But . . ."

Terrence held his breath.

Carter sat up. " . . . I always knew I missed having a pa who acted like a real pa should." He glanced at Terrence, then stared at the floor.

"Sounds like your pa was a good man. You were lucky to have him for the time you did." He cleared his throat. "What I would've give to have a pa like that, a pa worth killing for."

CHAPTER 52

Nobu

FEBRUARY 14, 1943

The day Nobu had looked forward to—but now dreaded—had arrived. Valentine's Day. Until a week ago, he had anticipated showering Yuki with tokens of affection—chocolates he'd purchased in town. A haiku he'd written for her.

He glared at the gaudy, red, heart-shaped box, filled with an assortment of chocolates he had intended to give to her. A plastic cupid glued to the center of a mass of pleated lace taunted him. None of the arrows in his quiver were for Nobu.

He ripped the evil-looking cherub from the box and threw it on the floor, feeling only slight satisfaction when it broke in half. His heart raced and heat flashed on the back of his neck as he remembered Yuki's answer to his invitation to the dance.

"I'm sorry, Nobu-san," she'd said, her voice trembling. "I can't go with you."

Her words had been like a punch in the gut, but he'd replied softly. "Why? Have I done something wrong?"

She wouldn't even look at him. Like an impenetrable wall, silence hung between them, though when she finally spoke again, that wall hadn't protected him.

"I have feelings for someone else," she said. Then she ran away.

Fond memories of their time together mixed with confusion and rage, like a cyclone. He would explode if he didn't get out of the tiny apartment. He grabbed his journal from under his mattress, threw his curtain open, and stormed past Mama.

"Nobu? Where are you going?" she asked.

He shook his head. *Sorry, Mama. Can't answer your questions.* Grabbing his jacket, he hurried out, and slammed the door behind him.

At times like this, he felt like he was in a prison within a prison. Bad enough that he was living behind barbed wire. But to also be stuck in a small room with Mama and Sachi? Where he couldn't do anything without one of them asking, "What are you doing, Nobu?" It drove him mad.

He found a dry place to sit in front of the mess hall and leaned against the building. Tossing a few stones, he looked up and searched for a glimpse of sunshine through the clouds. Closing his eyes when he felt them burn, he wiped them with his sleeve and gritted his teeth. No way would he cry over a girl. He'd write instead.

February 14, 1943

I thought I'd be dancing with Yuki tonight. I couldn't wait to hold her as we swayed to the tunes of Sinatra. But when I asked her to the dance, she turned me down! Is there something wrong with me? I thought everything was going along great.

Then Sachi told me about that soldier, Collins. How he's been eyeing Yuki. Flirting with her. She said it seemed Yuki liked it. So that's it? Yuki has feelings for Collins? A Caucasian! Hakujin!

We spent so much time together in the last two months. Didn't she have a good time at the New Year's Eve Dance? Is there something about me she doesn't like? Maybe the way I kissed her at midnight?

No. It's all Collins's fault. If he hadn't flirted, teased—probably even offered her special privileges—she'd still be with me, and in my arms tonight.

The hakujins! It's not enough they stole our lives away from us. Now they steal our women!

I'd planned to give her chocolates. And the haiku I wrote for her:

Sunshine fills my heart.
'Tis not light from my window,
But thoughts of Yuki.

Dammit! It's been hard enough to be stuck behind this barbed wire with no control over my life. Now it's worse—like being trapped in a tiny fish bowl, always having to look at Yuki and Collins.

He heard two men talking and looked up from his journal.

A kid about Nobu's age spoke to an older man, maybe his father. "So you think they're going to start letting some of us out?" Hands in his pockets, he continued reading a bulletin posted on the outside of the mess hall.

"Who knows?" the older man replied, his gaze moving down the form.

"What's this?" asked the kid.

"What?"

"Have a look at number twenty-seven."

More block residents began to approach. They whispered first, but soon their grumbling turned louder, and they shook their heads. Some men stomped away, throwing their hands in the air. One woman grabbed her stomach and walked away alone.

Nobu had to see what all the fuss was about. He walked over, stood on his toes, and strained to see the bulletin, scanning it for the two questions he heard mumbled most often. Questions 27 and 28:

Question 27: Are you willing to serve in the Armed Forces of the United States on combat duty, wherever ordered? *What does that have to do with leave clearance?*

Question 28: Will you swear unqualified allegiance to the United States of America and faithfully defend the United States from any or all attack by foreign or domestic forces, and forswear any form of allegiance or obedience to the Japanese emperor, or any other foreign government, power or organization?

The words rose from the page and threw him a hard punch.

What the—? Hell, no! Why would I serve a country that rounded up its own citizens, shipped them off in trains, and corralled them behind barbed wire? And number twenty-eight? How could they ask me this? I'm an American citizen. I've never even been to Japan—know nothing of the Japanese emperor. Even so why should I swear unqualified allegiance to this country that has no allegiance to me?

He knew how he wanted to answer those questions: No. No. Hell, no! But how *should* he answer? What would be the consequences of *no-no*? What would Mama say? And what would Papa say if he were alive? Mama and Papa were *Issei*—first generation. Even after living and working in America for over two decades, they'd been denied citizenship by the American government, like every other *Issei*. If they answered "yes," forswore allegiance to the Japanese emperor, the *Issei* would be without a country. Yet, if they answered "no," they would be labeled "disloyal." How could *they* possibly answer Question 28?

What about Yuki? *Forget Yuki.* Why should he care how she would answer? Of course, she'd say anything to stay by the side of her soldier.

He could think of a hundred reasons to answer "no" to both questions. And only one reason to answer "yes." Fear. Fear of the consequences of answering "no."

Rage threatened to erupt. Fear rolled in tsunami waves, splashed over his anger, simmered it. But when the wave receded, it left boiling fury exposed.

He would not let fear drive him. When his time came to answer, he would answer "no" to both.

The gray sky tore with a rip of thunder, and a hard, cold rain began to fall as Nobu drifted back to his apartment. He pulled his jacket over his head and started to run. God, how he didn't want to see Mama now—didn't want to talk to anyone. All he wanted to do was spill his anger onto the pages of his journal.

He arrived at the stoop in front of their unit. Water dripped from the eaves above, but he didn't care, couldn't stand the thought of Sachi asking what he was writing about again. He removed his journal from his shirt and sat on the top step. Holding his jacket as shelter from the rain, he began to write.

To hell with them all. They stole Yuki, but they'll never steal my dignity. I will answer NO-NO! Let's see what they will do!

CHAPTER 53

Sachi

FEBRUARY 14, 1943

Sachi looked in the mirror as she brushed her long hair and pulled it up into a red ribbon. Valentine's Day! Next to Christmas, it was her favorite holiday, even if it wasn't quite the same in camp as it had been in California—not as much candy, no stores to shop for valentines.

Her teacher at the camp, Mrs. Yamamura, had tried to continue some of the same traditions as back home. Last week, she gave her students an hour at the end of the school day to cut out pieces of red construction paper and white lace to make cards for special people.

Sachi made them for Mama, Nobu, and Jubie. And though she hadn't told anybody, not even Jubie, she made a card for Papa, too. Nobody would understand. They'd all think she was silly, especially Mama. But sometimes she felt like Papa watched her—like he knew what she was doing. And if that were true, what would he think if she didn't make him a card?

The best part of getting ready for Valentine's Day had been the time spent with Jubie, decorating shoeboxes to hold all of the cards they couldn't wait to receive. She looked forward to receiving dozens and dozens like the year before, when she'd held her breath as she opened each envelope. She still remembered holding the last unopened card in her hand, hoping it was from her secret crush. She'd set it aside, unopened. It was two whole days before she could bear to open it, and she'd torn it in half when it wasn't from him.

But there was nobody in camp to have a crush on. She wasn't sure if that was good or bad, but it didn't matter. She'd been having fun on the sidelines, watching Nobu's crush on Yuki.

She stared at her reflection as she buttoned her blouse, thinking about the awful mood Nobu had been in the last few days. Something must have happened with Yuki. He didn't walk around with a goofy smile on his face anymore. No whistling happily like he had every other day since Thanksgiving. It had to have something to do with Private Collins, because almost every time she passed by the gate, he was talking to Yuki. The way being in love affected Nobu, and the way she felt last Valentine's Day when she didn't get a card from her secret crush, she decided right then and there: She'd never let herself fall in love.

So what should she do about Private Collins? Of all the soldiers, he was the nicest. She'd liked him since the day he told her Jubie had been looking for her at the gate. If he hadn't said anything, who knows? She and Jubie might have never met.

A thought tickled her. If Private Collins wasn't so old, maybe *he'd* be her secret crush. But that was silly. How could she have a crush on him if he was stealing Nobu's girl?

Secret crush? She scolded herself. He probably thought of her as just a little girl. She leaned in closer to the mirror and pinched her cheeks until they turned pink. She could look older, if only Mama would let her wear a little makeup. Like some blush. Or maybe lipstick. She rolled her eyes. No way.

At least she wasn't as naïve as Private Collins probably thought. Bet he didn't know she'd figured out what was going on between Yuki and him. And since he didn't know what she'd been able to figure out, he wouldn't understand why she was suddenly so cool.

She shook the troubling thoughts out of her head. She would worry about what to do with Private Collins when the time came. For now, she was too excited about the dance she and Jubie had planned later in the afternoon.

She thought it plenty unfair that she couldn't go to the Valentine's Day dance—too young, according to the posters. Silly rule. She could understand someone telling her she was too young to go on a date, but what would be the harm in going to the dance? She didn't plan to dance with a boy. All she wanted to do was watch the lovey-dovey couples.

Three days before, she had complained to Jubie about how angry she was that she didn't get to go to the dance. Wide-eyed, her friend had leapt off the couch, and talking so fast Sachi could hardly understand her, squealed, "We can have our own dance!"

Sachi leaped up, too, and they bounced around, too excited to contain themselves. Then she stopped and asked, "But where will we have it?"

"Why, right here in my living room. I just know Ma'll say it's okay."

With that detail taken care of, ideas flooded Sachi's head. "You can do the Japanese dance I taught you. And I'll bring a kimono for you to wear—"

"Hey, yeah! And you can show off the jitterbug I taught you. Ma has a full skirt you can swirl around in."

Sachi spun around, imagining the skirt flaring out.

"Hey," Jubie added. "Wanna invite your mama?"

The question had taken her by surprise. No way would Mama come over to Jubie's house. Of course, she couldn't say that—couldn't let Jubie know Mama still refused to mix with colored people and still didn't know Sachi was still friends with Jubie.

The fear of being discovered was like a big cloud that followed Sachi everywhere, and she could never completely enjoy Jubie's sunshine without being afraid that one day the big, dark cloud would break and rain all over.

"You just gonna stare at me with your eyes all a-bugging out?" Jubie waited, hands perched on her skinny hips. "You don't like my idea about inviting your mama?"

Think! Think of something to say.

"I . . . I don't think Mama will have time to come watch us dance. I . . . uh . . . I heard her tell Nobu she'd help him get ready for the dance in camp." She rolled her eyes. "You know those boys. They can't do anything for themselves."

Jubie tapped her foot and stared with doubtful eyes. "Hmm. Seem like Nobu would wanna get hisself ready. Anyways, my ma's gonna wanna see us dance. Think I'll invite Auntie Bess, too."

Sachi knew Jubie hadn't fallen for her excuse. But, at least she'd dropped the idea and hadn't brought it up again.

Sachi primped the red bow she'd tied in her hair one more time. Excited that it was almost time to leave for Jubie's house, she watched her reflection as she flipped her ponytail back and forth like the older girls did when they danced the jitterbug.

The apartment was finally empty, and Sachi's heart fluttered, like it always did when she was about to do something she knew she shouldn't do. Nobu had gone to fill out some paperwork at the mess hall, and Mama had finally left for the showers. She peeked out the window to make sure her mother had turned the corner, then kneeled next to the box that held Mama's kimono. Jubie had already tried wearing Sachi's kimono. It had been too short and came up so high on Jubie's skinny legs they both laughed until their sides ached. But this was a special day, and Sachi wanted her friend to look pretty when she danced for Mrs. Franklin and Auntie Bess.

She hesitated before removing the lid, and took a deep breath to chase away the tickle inside. She knew she shouldn't take Mama's kimono without asking. It was sneaky, yes, but there was no choice. Besides, what was the harm? She'd take care of it. Mama would never know.

The silk kimono was bright red and embroidered with a thousand white cranes. She unfolded it to check the length. Perfect. After carefully folding the kimono again, she tucked it into her satchel, and closed the box. Then, she grabbed her coat and rushed out the door.

Cold rain tingled on her cheeks. When she turned the corner toward the gate, the raindrops grew larger and slapped harder with the blowing wind. She raised her satchel over her head and ran toward the gate, but stopped suddenly when she saw Yuki talking to Private Collins again.

Only, this time she was crying. Sachi backed up behind the administration building and peered around the corner to watch.

Private Collins gave Yuki a handkerchief, and she wiped her eyes.

Why was she crying? Had Private Collins said something mean to her? If so, maybe Yuki would like Nobu better. But Sachi couldn't imagine the private ever being mean. Besides, Yuki didn't look angry with him.

Sachi watched, trying to figure them out.

Private Collins gave a quick glance around, then touched Yuki's cheek. He smiled and said something to her. She smiled back.

No, Yuki definitely was not angry with Private Collins.

He took her hand and kissed it. Yuki smiled and walked away.

A gasp escaped Sachi. The kiss, given so tenderly to Yuki, hurt Sachi like a kick in the stomach.

She stormed toward the gate, so mad she wanted to punch the private.

How could he?

Watching the private stare at Yuki as she walked away, Sachi grew angrier and angrier.

She interrupted the private's stare when she stomped closer, splashing water all around. His look of surprise made her wonder how she could feel angry and sad at the same time. She wanted to scream, yet tears burned her eyes.

"Hello, Sachi," he said, smiling.

She ignored him and signed out.

"I'm glad you're here. I have something for you." He handed a small white envelope to her. "It's a valentine."

She wasn't sure whether to gaze at him or glare at him. *A valentine?* Now what was she supposed to do? She wanted to open it, but she couldn't betray Nobu. No, Yuki had already done enough betraying for the two of them.

Her anger was so huge it drowned out the thrill of her first valentine of the day, and she gave Private Collins her most livid glare. It was all she could do not to snarl at him.

"What is it, Sachi? Aren't you going to open it?"

Shaking her head back and forth, she held the white envelope in front of him and tore it in half. "You stole my brother's girlfriend." She did snarl then, and shoved the torn valentine into her satchel.

She ran away, hoping the rain had hidden her tears.

When she arrived at Jubie's house, she wiped the rain and tears from her cheeks and knocked on the door.

Auntie Bess answered. "Well, hello there, sugar. Happy Valentine's Day."

"Hi, Auntie Bess." Sachi felt better just seeing her full-cheeked smile and hearing the happy laugh that greeted her. "I hope you and Mrs. Franklin are ready for some good dancing."

"Oh, yes. We so excited. Baked y'all some cookies, too."

Sachi inhaled the scent of cinnamon and vanilla. "Smells good!"

Mrs. Franklin smiled from the kitchen doorway and held a plate of cookies. "Take this back to Jubie's room with you," she said. "She waiting for you there."

Sachi picked up a cookie and took a bite. Turning to walk down the tiny hall, she called back. "Thank you, Mrs. Franklin." At Jubie's bedroom doorway, she announced, "I'm here! Your mama made us some cookies."

"I know," Jubie said, and rushed to her closet. "Looky here! Mama found this skirt for you to wear when you do your jitterbug." She held up a red skirt with a poofy white lace slip.

"Ooh! With that on, even *my* jitterbug will look good."

Jubie held it to Sachi's waist. "Might have to pin it to make it fit."

Sachi took her backpack off and put it on Jubie's bed. "I have something for you, too." Slowly, and with great drama, she pulled the red kimono out.

Jubie's eyes widened. "Lordy, lordy. Ain't that pretty!" She touched the red silk, then traced a white crane with her slender, dark fingers.

"It's my mama's," Sachi whispered. "So you'll need to be very careful with it."

"'Course I will. Can I put it on now?"

"Yes! I'll help you. I didn't bring the *obi*—that's the belt. There are too many pieces to a kimono. It would take us forever to put it all on properly. Today, we'll just tie it together with your belt."

Jubie slid the kimono on over her clothes, gently running her hands over the silk. "I ain't never touched nothing so soft before. So cool and smooth. I ain't never gonna wanna take it off." She pulled the belt from the loops of her blue jeans.

"I almost forgot," Sachi exclaimed, rummaging again through her satchel. "I made this for you." She pulled out a white envelope that said "Jubie" on the front. When she noticed half of the envelope from Private Collins was stuck to Jubie's card, her eyes widened, and she grabbed it and shoved it back in the satchel.

Jubie's gaze first followed Sachi's swift hand to the backpack, then to the card Sachi held for her. "For me?" She gently opened the envelope and smiled. "You made this? It's so pretty. I ain't never had no handmade valentine card before."

"You can put it in the valentines box you made."

Jubie frowned. "I don't have a card for you," she whispered, then quickly burst into a sly smile and opened her nightstand drawer. "But I do have this." She handed Sachi something wrapped in a cloth napkin.

Sachi carefully opened the red-stained napkin and found inside a heart-shaped cookie, decorated with red frosting. "Jubie! It's beautiful, and delicious, too, I'll bet."

"Yeah, it's good all right. I know 'cause I ate all the ones with mistakes. 'Bout five of 'em." She stuck out her tongue and held up her hands. "See? I got red all over me."

Sachi took a bite. "Mmm. Best valentine cookie I've ever had."

Jubie watched Sachi quietly. That was kind of unusual for Jubie—to be quiet.

"What?" Sachi asked.

"Mind if I ask you what was that piece of envelope you tried so hard to hide?"

It was a long story, and she didn't feel like explaining the whole thing. "It was nothing. Just a piece of garbage that was at the bottom of my pack."

Jubie rolled her eyes. "You a bad liar. But anyways, for some reason you don't wanna talk about it now." She picked up the red skirt. "Okay. Put this on. You just let me know when you ready to talk, hear?"

"I know." Sachi fluffed up the skirt and swirled around. "How do I look?"

Bunching up the waistline, Jubie replied, "Almost perfect." She called into the living room. "Ma, we need some help taking in the skirt now."

Mrs. Franklin and Auntie Bess appeared at the bedroom door.

"Ooh, don't you girls look pretty," Mrs. Franklin said.

Auntie Bess clapped her hands. "Sachi, what a fine-looking robe you brought for Jubie to wear."

Jubie extended her arms and slowly turned around. "It's a *kimono*, Auntie Bess. And it's Sachi's mama's."

Sachi felt her cheeks burn, and she wished Jubie hadn't told them that part.

"Mama, can you fix your skirt so it don't fall down when Sachi dances?"

"Sure can. I got me some safety pins in the living room. Come on."

Sachi followed Jubie who followed her mama. Auntie Bess brought up the end of the line, dancing and humming "In the Mood."

Mrs. Franklin held pins in her mouth as she cinched the waist tight. Using the last pin, she said, "That should keep it where it belongs." Then, she took a seat on the sofa next to Auntie Bess.

The girls giggled at each other.

Sachi whispered to Jubie. "You go first."

"You sure?"

"Your mama and Auntie Bess are too excited to wait."

"Well, okay then. You gonna sing for me, right?"

Sachi knew Jubie didn't have any music to play. But she didn't know *she'd* have to sing for Jubie's dance. And in front of Mrs. Franklin and Auntie Bess? She hated her voice. "Well, I don't know."

"Oh, come on." Jubie pleaded. "I can't dance without music."

Nervous as she was, she didn't want to be the cause of cancelling the dance. She huffed. "I guess."

Jubie took her starting pose and folded her hands in front of her. She looked down and closed her eyes. Jubie's skin was about as far away from white porcelain as the number one was from a thousand. Still, she reminded Sachi of the geisha dolls she left in California.

Sachi began to hum "*Sakura*"—the cherry blossom song. Her voice quivered with nerves. At least Mrs. Franklin and Auntie Bess didn't know what the song was supposed to sound like, and wouldn't know if she mispronounced some of the words. She took a deep breath. "*Sakura, sakura . . .*"

Jubie raised her arms, exposing the kimono's long, flowing sleeves. She tilted her head up, as if gazing at cherry blossoms on a tree. Mama's kimono must have cast a magic spell on Jubie's skinny, awkward frame, because she was prettier than Sachi had ever seen her.

Jubie swayed her arms back and forth, dipped and rose, then turned around.

Trying hard to make her tune match the beauty of Jubie's dance, Sachi continued to sing. "*Yayoi no sorawa.*"

Mrs. Franklin and Auntie Bess watched from the sofa. Their eyes glistened with tears.

Jubie turned slowly, holding one arm up, and sweeping the other behind her. She looked at Sachi with a twinkle in her eyes. When the song ended, she returned to her starting position and again, closed her eyes.

For a moment, the room was silent. Then, Auntie Bess cheered and clapped her hands.

Mrs. Franklin wiped a tear from her cheek. "Oh, baby. That was so pretty. So pretty."

Sachi clapped too. "You looked just like a geisha." She covered her mouth with her hand and giggled. "Well, almost."

Jubie ran her hands over the long, silk sleeves. "It musta been your mama's kimono. Dancing just felt right today, like magic. Your turn!"

Sachi wished she had gone first. There was no way her jitterbug would be as good as Jubie's dance.

"You ready?" Jubie asked. "I got my song all ready for you."

Sachi felt a little queasy. "I guess," she said, wondering why she had gone along with the silly idea.

But when Jubie began singing "Boogie Woogie Bugle Boy" something hit her like a bolt of lightning. Her feet took on minds of their own, and they scooted effortlessly over the floor. She swished her full skirt and wiggled her hips.

Mrs. Franklin and Auntie Bess clapped to the beat of the music as Jubie's voice filled the room.

"Them Andrews Sisters best watch out," Auntie Bess said.

Sachi smiled so big her cheeks hurt. She swung her hips and twirled her finger in the air. As she spun around, Jubie shuffled up next to her and pretended to blow a bugle.

As Jubie Lee danced next to Sachi, she watched the silk of the red kimono drift like a cloud around her friend. Red. So light it floated. Just like her heart.

Before she knew it, Jubie ended her song with giggles and Mrs. Franklin and Auntie Bess cheered from the sofa.

Jubie hugged her. "You a jitterbug girl."

Auntie Bess pulled Jubie and Sachi together into the biggest, tightest hug Sachi had ever known. "Oh, my sugars. I so proud of you." She smiled through tears that fell on her round cheeks. "If'n I didn't know better, I'd say Jubie got her some Japanese blood and Sachi got her some Negro blood pumping in them baby girl veins."

Every bit of worry Sachi had about borrowing Mama's kimono had been squeezed right out. All that remained was joy. She didn't care if she got in trouble, didn't care how loud Mama yelled at her.

They skipped back to the bedroom to change. Jubie took the kimono off and handed it to Sachi. "We sure was good, wasn't we, Sach?"

"Better than good."

Jubie stared at her, quiet for a minute.

"What is it?" Sachi asked. It wasn't like Jubie to be quiet.

Jubie smiled, kind of sly. "You ever heard of being blood sisters?"

"Blood sisters?"

"Yeah. You know what Auntie Bess said about me having Japanese blood and you having Negro blood?"

"Yeah."

"What if we really did mix our blood? I give you some my Negro blood, and you give me some of your Japanese?"

"What in the world are you talking about?"

Jubie pulled a pin from Sachi's skirt. "I'll prick my finger, then you prick yours. Then, we'll press our fingers together, let my blood into your body, and your blood into mine. 'Fore you know it, we'll be sisters."

Sachi had never heard of such a thing. In fact, it sounded a little creepy. Still, Jubie was closer to being a sister than anyone she'd ever known. She'd always wanted a sister. "Well, I've never heard of that. But it sounds like a neat idea. Kind of."

"You scared? We don't gotta do it if you don't wanna."

"Of course I'm not scared."

"Ready, then? I'll go first." Jubie poked her forefinger with the pin.

Sachi watched a dark red dot emerge.

"Your turn," Jubie said, giving Sachi the pin.

Sachi tried to steady her hand so she wouldn't look nervous. She wasn't afraid of mixing their blood so much as she was afraid of the prick of the pin.

"Want me to do it?" Jubie offered. "You can close your eyes."

"I guess so." She passed the pin to Jubie and squeezed her eyes shut until she felt a piercing pain at the tip of her finger. Her eyes flashed open as the sharp sensation shot halfway up her arm. She watched the tiny drop of blood appear and felt queasy again.

Jubie held up her finger. "Ready to be sisters?"

Sachi took a couple of deep breaths. "I'm ready."

Jubie's warm hand was soothing as she guided Sachi's finger to press against hers. "Now I have your blood and you have mine." She squeezed tighter. "And no matter what, we'll be sisters forever."

Goose bumps tickled through Sachi, and she wondered if it was Jubie's blood pumping through her.

I have a sister.

Mrs. Franklin knocked on the bedroom door. "Sachi, will you be staying for dinner?"

Dinner?

The Red Kimono

Was it that late already? "No, ma'am." She let go of Jubie's finger. "I'd better get home. Mama will be wondering where I am." She folded Mama's kimono and placed it in her satchel.

Jubie smiled. "Sure was fun today, wasn't it?"

"It was perfect."

"And now we're sisters. That's even better than being valentines, ain't it?"

Sachi nodded. "A million times better."

It was still raining when she walked out of Jubie's house. But she skipped through it, humming "Boogie Woogie Bugle Boy," remembering how Jubie—her sister—danced with her. Water soaked through her clothes and left them wet and cold against her skin.

The thought of Mama's anger over the kimono returned and worsened her chill. Raindrops left polka dot splashes in the puddles she tried to jump. Sometimes she missed, and icy water splashed onto her legs that only an hour before were warmed by the jitterbug. She hoped Mama wouldn't be too upset and quickened her pace. Where would she say she'd been all afternoon? Maybe passing out valentines with Keiko? Or studying her Japanese lessons in the classroom with Mrs. Yamamura? Mama definitely wouldn't believe that one.

As she approached the entrance gate to the camp, she remembered the valentine from Private Collins. What would she say to him? She squinted her eyes to focus through the foggy rain. As she drew closer, she felt relieved. A shift change. Private Collins had been replaced by Private Gould, who was all business. Nothing to worry about. She signed in and walked through the gate, holding her satchel over her head.

"Stay dry," he called.

She couldn't help wondering what Private Collins was doing now that he was off. What had he thought when she tore his valentine's card in half earlier in the day? Maybe it was a mean thing to do, but she'd been so angry when she saw him with Yuki.

Her wet clothes were cold and heavy on her skin, and she ran to get out of the rain. By the time she reached her apartment, her shoes squished with every slow, heavy step up to the door. Her mind swirled with answers to all the questions Mama might ask.

Then, Jubie's words whispered in her ear. *No matter what, we'll be sisters forever.*

She stared at her hand on the cold door knob and took a deep breath. She should have asked before borrowing Mama's kimono and was sorry she hadn't.

But she wasn't sorry she'd let Jubie wear it. That red kimono had been magic. How else could a colored girl and a Japanese girl end up as sisters?

Her heaviness began to lighten. She lifted her hand from the knob and stared at the finger Jubie had pricked, wondering if the smudge of blood that remained was hers or Jubie's. She smiled.

It didn't really matter.

She returned her hand to the knob, turned it, and opened the door.

Inside, it was not at all what she had expected. Mama and Nobu sat across from each other at the table. She closed the door softly behind her, but neither noticed that she had returned. The room was too quiet, filled with so much tension it felt smaller and darker than usual.

"You cannot do this, Nobu." Mama had a strange calm in her voice.

Sachi recognized the mask Mama wore to hide her anger. What did Nobu do to make her so mad? Usually Sachi was the focus of anything that irritated her mother.

Her brother didn't answer, only stared at his hands, folded in front of him.

She couldn't stand the quiet any longer. She would rather Mama be upset with her for getting home so late. She had to know what was going on. "Is everything okay?" she asked.

Mama and Nobu seemed surprised to see her standing there.

"Sorry I'm late, Mama." Maybe her apology would change the subject.

"Be quiet!" Mama scolded. "Can you not see that your brother and I are discussing something important? This does not involve you."

"Mama, stop," Nobu said, rising from his chair and walking over to Sachi. He moved a strand of wet hair off her face. "Better get out of those wet clothes. You can change in my room. Mama and I should be finished soon."

When she opened her drawer to get her pajamas, she found the valentine's cards she'd made for Mama and Nobu. She glanced back at the table, where they were staring at each other again. Should she give the cards to them? Would it make Mama even angrier? Or, might it lighten the mood? She didn't care. It was Valentine's Day. She had to do it—the cards wouldn't mean as much tomorrow.

She grabbed her pajamas and hid the cards beneath them. "I made these for you," she whispered. "Happy Valentine's Day." Her stomach aflutter, she was too uncertain, too anxious to wait for their response. She hurried into Nobu's room and pulled the curtain shut.

She heard one envelope tear open.

"Thanks, Sach. It's really nice," Nobu said.

Mama spoke next. "Nobu, I am waiting. How can you think of answering 'no' to both questions?"

What questions were they talking about? And why was Mama so upset about it? One thing was for sure. Her mother had more important things on her mind than a silly card. No sense waiting for her to open it. She tossed her satchel onto the bed, and threw herself next to it.

What was she supposed to do while Mama and Nobu discussed whatever it was they were discussing?

She opened the satchel. The kimono! How would she get it back into the box without Mama seeing? As she shoved it deeper inside, she felt the valentine Private Collins had given her. She took out one half, and felt for the other.

She pulled each half out of its torn half-envelope, and held them together like puzzle pieces. Her heart raced as she read the words inscribed in the red heart on the front of the card.

To my special Valentine . . .

CHAPTER 54

Nobu

MARCH 15, 1943

The silence had been long and lonely since the day Nobu received notice that he would be transferred back to California. All those who had answered "no" to Question 27 and Question 28 were being sent to a maximum-security segregation camp called Tule Lake. He had known there would be consequences for the way he had answered, but he had no idea he would be sent away, separated from his family.

He studied Mama from across the room, trying to determine her mood before approaching to sit next to her. Her rigid posture and expressionless face definitely read anger. But her attempt to wipe tears from her cheeks before they were discovered was futile. She couldn't mask her sadness.

Sachi sat on the edge of her bed, staring at her feet as she swung them back and forth. No mistaking her mood. Only sadness there.

The previous night, he had tossed and turned with alternating waves of guilt and determination; guilt that he wouldn't be at Rohwer to take care of Mama and Sachi, determination that he could not have answered the questions any other way.

When he'd received his transfer orders, Sachi had begun to sob and asked, "Can't you change your answers so you can stay with us?"

Her question broke his heart. "I'm sorry, Sach. They won't let me change them." But he also bit his lip. *I wouldn't change my answers even if I could.*

Sachi would understand one day. But Mama was a different story. He had no idea what to say to her, how to respond to her anger and grief. Her shame.

It didn't matter anymore. The silence was killing him. He had to say something.

"Mama, talk to me," he said, maneuvering toward where she sat.

Her gaze remained fixed on the blank wall across the room.

He pulled out the chair next to her and sat down. "What are you thinking?"

At last, she spoke, though she still stared at the wall. "How could you have answered as a disloyal?"

Disloyal. The word was a flashpoint. A trigger for a barrage of angry words. He stood up and pounded the table.

Sachi stopped swinging her legs and gasped.

Mama's eyes widened with surprise.

"*I* am not disloyal!" he yelled. "It is America that has been disloyal!"

Seeing Mama's eyes fill with tears, he sat again and took a deep breath.

Calm down. Is this how you want to spend your last hours with Mama and Sachi?

His voice softened. "Don't you see, Mama? How else could I answer? If I'd answered 'yes,' they might have sent me off to war. I'm sorry. I refuse to fight for a country that could do this to us."

Her eyes grew cold. "But they're sending you away anyway, are they not? You could have lied. At least you would not be called a disloyal. And you would not have brought dishonor to this family."

Lie? To keep from bringing dishonor to our family?

Mama's words hit like an unexpected blow. His throat clutched as his mind filled so swiftly with a mix of emotions that he couldn't gather his thoughts to respond. Anger. Hurt. Isolation. Regret. Pride. All fought for space in his head. Anything he said would be hurtful. He was silent as he rose from the chair.

Mama looked up. "Where are you going?"

"To pack," he replied and walked to his room.

His tiny space. Only a corner separated by a curtain. What would the camp at Tule Lake be like? He didn't care if it was larger, but more privacy would be nice. Maybe a window. Of course, it could be a jail cell for all he knew, the way they talked about the No-No Boys being disloyal.

A green canvas duffle bag lay open on his bed, its gape awaiting the stack of books, crumpled clothes, and pair of shoes that surrounded it. But Nobu didn't feel like packing. Instead, he found his journal and shoved everything else off the bed.

March 15, 1943

Part of me is happy to be getting away from here. I need some breathing space. This apartment is too small for the three of us, especially when Mama is angry. She's angry a lot these days. I guess I don't blame her. I think her anger comes from fear. Fear of what lies ahead for me, and fear of what lies ahead for her after I'm gone. First Taro left for Hawaii, then Papa was killed, and now I am leaving for Tule Lake. She will be left on her own to take care of Sachi.

I'm scared, too, but I can't show it, especially in front of Mama and Sachi. I have no idea what waits for me. As long as we comply with their rules, behave as people who accept this life they cast upon us, we are left to live our miserable lives behind barbed wire. But now that some of us have issued our protests by answering "no" to Questions 27 and 28, look how we are treated—shipped off to maximum security as disloyal. They're even talking about sending us back to Japan! I've never even been to Japan. Hell, I barely speak Japanese.

Scared? Yeah, I'm scared.

It's been weird between Kazu and me. He told me he couldn't answer "no," even though a part of him wanted to. Said he couldn't do that to his mother. I don't understand him, and I can tell by the look in his eyes, he doesn't understand me. How could he swear allegiance to a country that took his father away? No matter. Kazu will stay, maybe be sent off to war. I will go to Tule Lake, disgraced in my mother's eyes.

"Nobu?" Sachi's face appeared around his curtain, her eyes puffy and red.

He set his journal aside. "Come here," he said, extending his hand.

She sat next to him and buried her face on his shoulder.

"What is it, Sach?"

Her response came in sniffles and gurgles. She attempted to hide her tears, but he felt their wet warmth soak his shirt.

He nudged her again. "You want to talk about it?"

Finally, she whispered, "Please don't leave me here alone. Can't I come with you?"

The question startled him. Come with him? He hadn't thought of that. Would she be better off staying with Mama, or coming with him? It was a difficult question to answer. Too many unknowns about the camp in Tule Lake.

"Nobu? Did you hear me? Can I come with you?"

He took a deep breath, hoping the answer would come by the time he exhaled. "I would love for you to come with me . . ."

She perked up and smiled. "Really?"

"No, wait Sach. I was saying I'd love for you to come, *but* you can't."

She buried her head in his shoulder again.

"I have no idea what the new camp will be like. And Mama needs you here. Besides, you and Jubie have become such good friends, you don't want to leave her, do you?"

She straightened and looked at him, aghast. "Jubie?"

Stifling a laugh, he replied, "Yes, I know about you and Jubie. You're not very good at hiding things."

"Does Mama know?"

"I don't think so. I didn't tell her, anyway."

"Because if Mama ever found out and said I couldn't play with her again, I think I'd run away."

"Be careful then," he said.

The Red Kimono

There wasn't much more to say in the few minutes they had. Or, maybe there was too much to say. After a short silence, Nobu spoke. "I guess I'd better finish packing."

She started crying again and hugged him. "I'm going to miss you so much. What am I going to do when you're gone? Mama is so quiet, and when we do talk, it's like she's angry with me."

He tugged at her ponytail. "Be patient with her. She's been through a lot, and she bears the burden of what is to become of all of us when we leave camp." He tickled her ribs. "Okay. Let me have a few minutes to finish packing, then you can walk me to the gate."

She slumped and pouted, lingering at the edge of his bed.

He knew what would cheer her. "Hey, you know what?"

"What?" she replied, eyes brightening.

"There's one good thing about me leaving."

She deflated and rolled her eyes. "What?"

"You can have my room—a room of your own!"

She perked up. "Oh, boy—" she exclaimed, then slumped again. "But I'd still sleep with Mama if it meant having you here."

"I know, Sach. But try to look at the bright side. You've wanted your own room since we left Berkeley. Now come on." He gave her a shove. "I need to finish packing."

"Okay, okay," she mumbled and shuffled out of his room.

A few more lines to add in the day's entry, then he'd have to hurry.

I didn't realize it before now, but it's Sachi I'll miss most of all. Yeah, the squirt gets on my nerves, but it won't be the same not seeing that spark of mischief in her eyes. I see her growing up a little every day, forming a mind of her own. How will she have changed when I see her again? And who knows when that will be? I need from her what I will not have at Tule Lake, her resilience— an antidote to my callous shell that thickens every day.

So much in life we take for granted. Then, it's gone.

He tossed the journal into the canvas bag, then piled his other scattered belongings on top, and zipped it up. Taking a last look around his room—the blank walls, the bed he'd made neatly for Sachi, the curtain that had been his barrier from the outside world—he decided home was a relative place. He had hated his little curtained corner when they first arrived. But now that he faced the uncertainty of the camp in California, he felt like he was being ripped from home all over again.

CHAPTER 55

Terrence

MARCH 15, 1943

"Showers!" A guard called from the front of the corridor.

Terrence rubbed his forehead and scribbled out his umpteenth attempt at solving an algebra problem.

Carter waited at the cell door, scratching his belly. "You coming?"

"Nah. You go on. I need to get this homework done before Mr. Blake comes this afternoon."

"You mean I'm gonna have to smell your stink until tomorrow?"

Terrence grinned and shook his head. "You preaching to the choir, man. I don't think there's enough soap in this whole prison to wash away your white boy smell."

The guard unlocked the cell door and Carter joined the procession of inmates headed to the showers. "See ya," he said before the door slammed shut.

Terrence noticed the clean clothes Carter left on his bunk. "Hey, wait!" he called, but Carter was too far down the corridor.

He remembered how Momma always joked about having to remind him of something he'd forgotten. His homework, sack lunch, wallet. "Where's your mind at, son?" she'd ask. "Don't know what you gonna do without me one of these days."

His algebra book lay open in front of him, calling to him like a nag. He gazed at the eight circled problems and groaned. Homework! He studied the problem over again.

Think!

Pencil to paper, he jotted figures on scratch paper, determined to solve the problem. *Xs. Ys. As. Bs.* His paper was full of a jumble of letters and numbers that looked like a foreign language. Why'd he have to take algebra anyways? Lawyers didn't need to know algebra. Even Mr. Blake had told him he was afraid he wouldn't be much help with that fancy math. So why'd he have to study it?

"You'll need to know it to get into college," Mr. Blake had said.

College. Would he ever really go to college? It was hard to imagine such a thing from inside a jail cell.

"Fight!" The call swelled as it ripped down the corridor from the shower.

Several guards ran by, guns drawn. Their shrill whistles echoed everywhere.

Hoots and taunts came from the direction of the showers, and those that had stayed behind watched from their cells like caged animals he'd seen in the zoo. Their eyes wide with frenzied excitement, they screamed and chanted.

Terrence's heart beat wild, too. He stared at the clothes on Carter's bed. All that screaming, the guards rushing to the showers . . . he pushed chilling thoughts out of his head.

The noises from the inmates went back and forth between murmurs and shouts. First they'd listen for what was going on, then they'd whoop it up. The fight was like gasoline on an ember, and the fire was burning out of control.

A new wave of guards rushed in, the rapid clap of their boots on the floor like machine gun fire. They pounded their clubs on the bars with one hand, held guns in the other, as they tried to outshout the raucous inmates.

"Quiet!"

"Shut up—get over there in that corner!"

They didn't have to tell Terrence twice. He didn't want any trouble. Only thing he cared about was what was going on with Carter. Something ate at his gut and told him Peachie had started something. *Shit!* He should have gone to the showers, too.

He felt helpless and sat quiet on his bunk. But his mind went rabid with visions of Peachie and his gang beating on Carter. There had to be something he could do. He felt like he was going to puke.

He'd gotten to like Carter, but thinking about what was going on made him realize it was more than that. Carter had ignored Peachie's harassment. He must've started to figure it wasn't right to judge a man by the color of his skin.

And how did he thank Carter? By letting him go to the showers by himself.

The guards lined up at the center, looking ready for action. At the slightest goad of any inmate, a guard rushed the cell door to shut him up. Soon, the corridor quieted. Twenty minutes later, the noise from the brawl in the shower quieted too.

But it did nothing to quiet Terrence's mind—that wouldn't happen until Carter showed up again. Pounding his forehead with clenched fists, he cursed himself for thinking homework was more important. He made a dozen deals with God, if only Carter would come back to the cell okay.

Several inmates paraded by his cell, wrapped in towels and clutching their clothes. Water dripped off their bodies, leaving a trail behind. Surrounded by armed guards, some snickered at Terrence as they shuffled by. And he felt sick all over again.

More than an hour passed. Terrence couldn't wait any longer. He flagged one of the guards.

One guard approached, his hand clutching the club at his side. "What is it?"

"Where's Carter? Looks like everyone else is back in his cell."

"Why don't you mind your own business? When the warden thinks you need to know, you'll know."

Dumb shit asshole.

But he knew to keep his mouth shut, even with the hate he felt for the fucking-idiot guard, the fear he felt for Carter. It all boiled up inside and shot at the guard in an angry glare.

The guard banged his club on the bars. "Get back!"

Terrence backed away from the door. Desperation pounded inside. He had to get out. Had to know where Carter was. Had to figure out a way to settle down, before he did something he'd regret. But what? What could he do?

Maybe seeing Mr. Blake would help. Maybe he could even find out what was going on. He checked the clock.

Only one more hour. You can handle that.

Still, he had to figure out what to do with himself. Couldn't do homework. No way would he be able to concentrate. He climbed into his bunk and stared at Carter's bunk above him. He closed his eyes. Took a deep breath. *Calm down.* Another breath. *Be patient. Only an hour.* He inhaled again.

He imagined the sound of water. Fishing with Daddy. Sun felt warm on his back. Sometimes a breeze would whoosh by to cool him, and leaves would fall into the river and swirl around the red and white bobber. Terrence wasn't sure what he liked more: the easy quiet between him and Daddy, or the talking they'd do when it was just the two of them.

"Nothing like getting away from all them women," Daddy would say, chuckling. "Spending some time with my boy."

Sometimes he'd get bored after a while, sitting there watching the bobber do nothing and he'd complain. "Daddy, there's no fish here today. Let's go do something else."

Daddy would cast his line again. "Patience, Son. Nothing good ever comes too quick."

He'd huff a little, knowing there wasn't no way Daddy was gonna let him leave before they caught a fish. Then, all of a sudden that lazy bobber would plunge underwater, and Terrence would get all excited.

"Jerk it! Jerk your pole," Daddy would yell.

Then, Terrence would reel the line in, faster and faster, until there it was—a perch at the end of the line. No, there wasn't anything like holding up that fish for Daddy to see, especially if Daddy hadn't caught one yet.

Daddy would smile real big. "See? What'd I tell you? Patience. You gotta be patient."

He had the best smile.

A guard called from outside the cell. "Hey, you!"

The bellow ripped Terrence away from the fishing hole, away from Daddy, back to real life. He sat up and looked at the guard. "Yeah?"

"Your lawyer was just here to see you. Too bad all visitations were cancelled for the day. The skirmish in the showers and all. Told him to come back tomorrow."

Terrence slammed his head on the pillow and tried to bring Daddy back. Waited for his words to fill his head.

Patience, Son.

I'm trying, Daddy. I'm trying real hard.

CHAPTER 56

Sachi

APRIL 20, 1943

A big, black hole. That's what life felt like with Nobu gone. It was almost as bad as when Papa died. Sachi never thought much about having her brother around. He was just there. Though there were days she might not see him from the time she got up in the morning until time for her to go to bed at night, she knew he was there.

Now he was gone. Not there for her to talk to anymore. Not there to bother. Not there to spy on. All she had to look forward to were his letters, and they didn't come very often. Even when they did, someone had blacked out so much of what he wrote and it was hard to figure out what he was trying to tell them. Why would they do that? Mama called it censoring and said it was the government trying to keep things a secret.

Who were these people who decided what should be kept secret between a brother and sister?

Huddled in the corner of her bed, she examined the little curtained room that used to be Nobu's. She'd added some of her own touches. Two dolls sat on the nightstand—the one Mama and Papa had given her for Christmas and the one Kate had given her when they left California. A picture she'd drawn of her house in Berkeley hung over her bed. Now the room was hers.

With her own room, she didn't have to sleep with Mama anymore. And it didn't come a minute too soon, because Mama was even grouchier now. She didn't know why, but her mother had always had more patience with Nobu. She never realized before that he'd been like a buffer. Whenever he was around, Mama was on her best behavior. Now, with him gone, Mama had no reason to put on a happy face. Instead, her face always looked like she was sucking on a lemon.

So Sachi spent as much time as possible away from the barracks.

Mama didn't even ask where she'd been anymore. That was good, she supposed. At least now she didn't have to make up lies to hide being with Jubie. But sometimes she felt lonely and missed how her family had once been.

She opened her nightstand drawer and took out a notebook. Maybe writing to Nobu would make her miss him less.

April 20, 1943

Dear Nobu,

How are things at Tule Lake? I guess by now, you have settled in to your new apartment. I've been adding my own touches to your old room—

She ripped the page out, wadded it up, and threw it on the floor. That wasn't what she wanted to say at all. She already knew he'd settled in, as best as he could, anyway. And she knew he wasn't happy at Tule Lake. She could tell that from his letter, even with the blacked-out parts. What she really wanted to tell him was how much she missed him, about how miserable it was to be alone with Mama. She wanted to tell him about Yuki and Private Collins, about how they still talked to each other all the time, though they tried to keep it a secret. She often wondered if they might even get married someday, with that lovey-dovey look in their eyes when they stared at each other. But she couldn't say any of that to Nobu, didn't want to make him sadder.

So what was she supposed to write? Something—anything—but a silly letter that pretended everything was okay. Maybe she'd write about Jubie.

April 20, 1943

Dear Nobu,

Yesterday Jubie and I played by the creek. It was still very cold, but we decided we were ready for springtime, even if springtime wasn't ready for us. We started building a dam and thought maybe we could make a little swimming hole for when the weather gets hot and sticky like it did last summer. When we moved one big rock, a couple of weird-looking lobster-like creatures skittered away. Jubie called them crawdads. She said you could eat them, and that she'd ask her Auntie Bess to cook up a pot. But first, she said we'd have to catch enough of them. I don't know. They looked a little creepy. How am I supposed to help catch them if I don't want to touch them? And eating them? Yuck.

People around here eat some strange foods, Nobu. Of course, Jubie probably thinks what we eat is strange, too.

I told her once that sometimes we eat our rice with seaweed wrapped around it. She crinkled her nose and asked what seaweed was. I had to remind myself that she's never even seen the ocean, so she's probably never heard of seaweed. When I explained that it was like thick, long blades of grass that grow in the ocean, she crinkled her nose even more, then stuck out her tongue! That's okay, because that's how I felt about eating crawdads.

Anyway, we got a good start building the dam before our hands started to freeze. At least we blocked the water enough so that it began filling up our future swimming hole. Maybe you'll be back by summer and you can come swimming with us.

In case you're worried about Mama finding out that I'm still hanging around with Jubie, don't be. She doesn't even ask where I've been anymore.

Sachi put her pen down and shook out her hand. It was always hard to decide how to close her letters to Nobu. She wanted to tell him about the black hole and about how much she missed him. But she didn't want to make him homesick. On the other hand, she didn't want him to think she didn't miss him either. Sometimes, she missed him so much it hurt. But as he boarded the train for California, he hugged her and told her to be a "big girl." He was only trying to make her feel better, but she'd felt a little insulted when he said that. After all, she was almost eleven now, hardly a *little* girl.

That settled it. She'd be the "big girl" he told her to be and wouldn't let Nobu know how much she missed him. Not quite, anyway.

Mama and I miss you, but we're doing fine. It's always nice to get your letters, Nobu. So please write us as soon as you can.

Love from your sister,

Sachi

She folded the letter and stuffed it in an envelope. There was a certain excitement she felt when mailing a letter to her brother. As she walked out the door to mail it, she began to calculate in her mind. It would take about a week to get to Nobu. And she'd give him a week to write back, though she wished he'd write sooner. Another week for his letter to reach her at Rohwer. Three weeks.

That was forever.

CHAPTER 57

Terrence

MAY 2, 1943

Outcast. Nothing felt lonelier. 'Course the whites shunned Terrence, just like they always had. Every chance, Peachie gave him the evil eye and that stupid smirk, like he knew he was rubbing salt in the gash left from missing Carter. Then, there was the waiting. Waiting and wondering when Peachie would strike at him.

Worse than the whites shunning him was the blacks that didn't want anything to do with him either.

"Go on. Get outta here," they'd say, whenever Terrence tried to sit with them in the cafeteria.

"Yeah. You ain't nothing but a dark-skinned white boy."

He did pretty good ignoring all that. But then they'd snicker and say something like, "Sure is too bad about your boy, Carter."

It was all Terrence could do to get away before the hurt inside erupted so hot he knew he'd do something that'd get him in trouble.

Hell. What'd all those jerks expect? A white and a black thrown together in a cell. They all must've hoped Terrence and Carter would let the same hate that pits one color against another in that godforsaken place explode within the four walls of their tiny cell. Must've been a big disappointment, all right. Sure, it took a while for the two of them to tiptoe around their hate, but somehow they'd figured it all out. Even got to be friends.

But Carter was gone. Terrence never could get anyone to tell him exactly what happened. He could tell the guards got a kick out of teasing him with pieces of information about that day in the shower. But they never let on about the whole story.

Maybe it was best he didn't know everything. Might not be able to control his anger if he did. Didn't matter anyhow. Carter was gone, and there was nothing he could do to change that.

Outcast.

The only person he could talk to about it was Mr. Blake. He sure didn't want to worry Momma with his talk about what it was like to be an outsider on the inside of a prison. She worried enough about him already. But with Mr. Blake, even if there was nothing he could do about it, at least he listened. By the time his weekly visits rolled around, Terrence had plenty he needed to get off his chest.

It helped some when Mr. Blake would tell him he was doing real good on his studies. The best news came when he told Terrence maybe he could even get out early, with his good behavior and the way he was doing with his studies. He tried not to get his hopes up, but it was awful hard not to.

He ran his fingers over the 384 marks on the wall. Even if he didn't get released early, he'd passed the halfway point—346 days to go. Every time the thought of leaving early popped into his head, he'd push it back, and wouldn't allow himself to get his hopes up. April 12, 1944. That was the release date he'd keep waiting for. If he got out sooner, it'd just be icing on the cake.

He ought to be reading his social studies chapters, but in the lazy hours after lunch, he always got sleepy. Maybe he'd just close his eyes for a little bit.

There he was, on the side of that creek, fishing with Daddy again. The sky was blue, with wisps of clouds drifting by. After a while, those clouds turned to dark, monster billows and the water that had calmly trickled by began to rush.

"Beautiful day, ain't it, son?" Daddy asked, smiling.

"Well, it was, but it's looking a little stormy now," Terrence replied. "Think we should go in?"

"What you talking about, boy? Them skies are blue as I ever seen 'em."

Terrence looked up, confused. The sky was black.

Daddy grinned and watched his bobber. "Pickens are kinda slim today, ain't they?"

A rustling across the creek caught Terrence's attention, and he tried to make out two men. Nobu? What was he doing there? And was that Mr. Kimura standing next to him? Looked like they were fishing together. Terrence never knew Nobu liked to fish.

"Hey, Nobu!" he called.

Nobu and his father both looked up from watching their bobbers.

Mr. Kimura slipped into water that had begun to rage.

Nobu grabbed for him, but missed. "Papa!" He yelled and jumped in.

"Nobu, wait!" Terrence called. What could he do? How could he help? He cast his fishing line toward his friend. "Grab the line," he yelled.

He looked to his daddy for help, but Daddy just watched his lazy bobber. He sat with his back against a rock, head propped with one hand, seeming to enjoy sunshine.

But it had all turned dark for Terrence. Why couldn't Daddy see what was going on?

"Daddy!" he called.

His father closed his eyes. "I said, 'patience,' son. Them fish'll be biting soon enough."

Terrence yelled at Nobu again. "Did you get the line?"

Nobu held up his arm, showing he'd wrapped the line around his jacket. "Let some line out! I need to reach Papa!"

No, Terrence couldn't do that. He had to save Nobu. He struggled to reel him in, his pole bending like it was going to break.

"I said let the line out! Not in." Nobu was struggling to untangle his arm. "Let me go. Let me go. I have to save Papa."

The torrential waters carried Mr. Kimura down the river. Terrence saw panic in his eyes. He'd seen it before. That day in the park. The memory made Terrence sick to his stomach. And the sicker he felt, the faster he reeled Nobu to the shore.

As Nobu splashed toward where Terrence stood on the bank, the glare in his eyes fired off more memories of that day in the park. He stood on the muddy shore, tangled in fishing line and called after his father. "Papa! I'm sorry!" He struggled to free himself from the line, but it had turned to barbed wire, and the harder he fought it, the bloodier he became.

Mr. Kimura disappeared into the raging water.

A ravaged Nobu stood in front of Terrence. "Why? Why did you kill my father?"

Terrence's own voice woke him.

I'm sorry. I'm sorry.

He sat up on his bunk and rubbed his eyes, wet with tears.

"Hey, you!" A guard clanked on the cell door.

Terrence took his sleeve and wiped his eyes. "Yeah?"

"Got a surprise for you."

What now?

JAN MORRILL

He turned to the guard.

Carter?

It was Carter, all right. He had a patch over his eye and his sly smile was missing several teeth. But heck. It was the best smile Terrence had ever seen.

Carter limped into the cell and groaned as he lowered himself into a chair. "Miss me?"

Was he still dreaming? "What the—"

Carter snickered. "Hey, man. Put them eyes back in that black head of yours. You look like you seen a ghost."

"Holy shit!" Terrence leaped off of his bunk. He had the urge to hug Carter, but thought better of it. "You're white enough to be a damn ghost. A scary one, too." He pulled out a chair. "Where you been? What happened?"

The grin faded from Carter's face. "Been laid up in the infirmary."

Terrence crossed his arms and studied Carter's bruised face. "Looks like you got beat up pretty good."

Fear flashed in Carter's eyes—quick as lightning—before he rose from his chair and turned away. He clutched the cell door and kicked his foot against it, over and over.

That bad. Terrence took a deep breath. Yeah. He shoulda been with Carter that day. "Hey, we don't gotta talk about—"

"It was Peachie started it all."

"Always is." Terrence was walking on glass. Didn't want to say something that might shut his friend down.

Carter leaned his head on the bars. "Yeah. I was minding my own business, just trying to get out of that shower fast as I could. Before Peachie and his boys could hassle me."

Guilt punched Terrence again. "I shoulda been there."

"Damn right you shoulda been there."

His heart sank, until he saw Carter's dumb grin.

"Man, it wouldn't have done no good." Carter slid his tongue through the empty space where teeth had been and reminded Terrence of a snake. "You woulda just got beat up, too."

The sudden quiet felt like a monster, lurching, ready to eat up whatever else Carter had to say. He hesitated to ask what happened next.

"I'd just finished rinsing off, and started to grab my towel. But

Peachie grabbed it first. 'What'll you give me for it?' he asked. I told him to just forget it. Figured it'd be best to drip dry. So I started to leave the shower to get my clothes. He grabbed my arm and said, 'Guess you ain't so brave without your nigger here to protect you.'"

Terrence clenched his teeth. *Fucking asshole.*

Carter rubbed the back of his neck and slithered his tongue through his teeth again.

It was going to take some time to get used to Carter's new habit.

"Someone pushed me. I slipped," Carter continued. "Went down real hard. My head got kinda fuzzy. Man, all of a sudden, it was like I was raw meat set out in front of a pack of wild dogs. They started kicking, calling me all kinda names. I couldn't breathe, and every time a foot got my rib, it felt like I'd been stabbed."

Something sour burned in the back of Terrence's throat. The kicks. Like stabbing. His throat tightened and he couldn't breathe. Carter was lucky to be alive. If only Mr. Kimura had been that lucky. Blinking his eyes, he tried to shake the vision out of his head. He studied Carter's patch. "What happened to your eye?"

Carter touched the gray patch. "Someone stuck his foot in it. Don't know whose it was, but guess it don't matter. It got infected, and the doctor said it couldn't be saved. Anyway, I blacked out right after that. Not sure how much time passed before I woke up in a hospital bed."

"Bastards."

Carter smiled, and ran his tongue over his gums again. "So, anyways, bet you couldn't wait for me to get back."

"Get back? Man, I thought you were dead."

"Dead?" Carter's eyes widened.

"Yeah. That's what I figured when I couldn't get the guards to tell me anything, and all that time passed without knowing anything. Even Peachie and his gang think you're dead."

"They do?"

"Pretty sure."

"Man, there's gotta be something we can do with that." Carter lisped through a toothless grin.

The inmates lined up for dinner, and for once, Terrence couldn't wait to run into Peachie. With what he and Carter had planned, they'd scare the shit out of him. Maybe then he'd leave them alone.

Terrence shuffled into the cafeteria behind other inmates from the block. Carter hid behind Terrence like they'd planned.

Keeping an eye out for Peachie, Terrence sniffed the air. Smelled like they were having spaghetti. Not again. Probably made from last night's leftover meat loaf. They never cooked the noodles enough, and they sprinkled it with a smelly white powder they called cheese.

There he was. Peachie, strutting in through the door across the room, like he was king of the world. His gang followed behind like a posse.

Terrence reached back and tapped Carter. *Stay hidden.*

They waited until Peachie found a table. His boys pulled out chairs on either side, like Jesus and his disciples at The Last Supper.

Terrence sat catty-corner and watched him snarl.

Carter snuck up and stood behind Peachie, quiet and still.

Peachie glared at Terrence. "Who the hell do you think you are, boy?"

Terrence ignored him.

Peachie slammed his hand against the table. "You hear me? Ain't no place at this table for no nigger."

Terrence scratched his eyebrow. Another signal.

Carter removed his eye patch and blew on the back of Peachie's neck.

Peachie raised his shoulders and shuddered, then whipped around.

Carter met his gaze with his left eye bulging open. But where his right eye should have been was a gaping, mangled socket. He flashed his wide, toothless grin.

Terrence had to admit—Carter looked like a ghoul, all right.

Peachie gasped and leaped off of his chair, knocking it over. Backing away, he fell over it. "What're you doing here? I thought you were dead. They even sent me to solitary."

Carter didn't flinch, just glared at Peachie.

"What the hell's going on here?" Peachie cried.

His gang gawked, too, their knuckles white as they clutched their spoons.

Terrence slurped a spaghetti noodle. "Something wrong, Peachie?"

"It's . . . it's Carter. I thought he was dead," Peachie said, mouth and eyes gaping.

"He *is* dead, you big jerk."

"But, he's right there."

Terrence twirled pasta around his spoon. "I don't see anything."

Guards began to shove their way through the cafeteria. "What's going on here? Break it up," they yelled.

Terrence nodded his head at Carter. The final signal.

"Hey, you! Fatso!" Carter said to Peachie.

Terrence hadn't thought Peachie's eyes could bug out any more, but they did when he heard Carter speak.

"I *was* dead. And one of you killed me." He pointed at Peachie. "You!" Then, his glower and accusing finger pointed at the other boys. "Or was it you? Or you?" A wicked grin crossed his crazed-looking face. "I've come back for one reason and one reason only—to get the one that killed me." He grinned and slithered his tongue where his teeth had been. "Don't you know? When you come back from the dead, you got all kinda new powers."

Peachie turned even whiter than the white he'd been before. Terrence thought he'd bust with laughter, until the guards arrived to break up all the fun.

CHAPTER 58

Nobu

TULE LAKE, CALIFORNIA
JULY 31, 1943

July 31, 1943

Here I am in Tule Lake, California—Camp Disloyal. Like cattle, we're moved from place to place at the whim of the American government. Maximum security. No way could it ever come close to feeling like home. Especially without Mama and Sachi here.

I thought summers in Arkansas were unbearable. Hot and steamy. Mosquitoes and invisible bugs that made my body itch all the time. Snakes. And the endless buzzing of cicadas, night and day. But this place is hell on earth. Someone told me the camp was built on a lava bed. I can believe that, the way dust swirls and practically splashes up wherever I walk. The landscape is flat, except for a mound they call Abalone Hill, half a mountain that looks as though its top was blown off a million years ago. Worst of all is the heat that radiates off of everything, so dry it makes me thirsty just to look at it.

Tule Lake is an angry-looking place, full of people like me—who marked no-no and are now called "disloyal." Some have even applied for repatriation to Japan. The anger makes this place feel even hotter.

Funny, as much as Mama and Sachi got on my nerves sometimes, I never realized how they added a kind of softness to my life.

I have a roommate here. His name is Ichiro. He looks to be maybe five years older than me. He's sitting in the room with me now. Kind of quiet, but he's never still. His leg bounces up and down, like he's always got something on his mind. He's got a bandana tied around his head. It reminds me of the day I found Papa cutting down a tree in the backyard. I couldn't have been more than six or seven, and I thought it looked silly for a man to wear such a scarf, so I asked him why he was wearing it. In a gruff voice, he told me it was called a hachimaki, and it was worn by samurais. Then he laughed and said, "It will take the strength of a samurai to battle this tree." I'd forgotten about that day, until I saw Ichiro's hachimaki. My new roommate may be quiet on the outside, but with that hachimaki tied on his head, the look in his eyes tells me he has a lot to say.

I've got a lot to say, too. But not to a stranger.

I should write a letter to Sachi and Mama. But heck. What's the use? Who knows if I'll still be here by the time they receive it?

"So where are you from, anyway?" Ichiro's voice vibrated with the cadence of his jackhammer leg.

"Berkeley."

Ichiro rolled his eyes and adjusted his hachimaki. "No, I mean what camp did you come from?"

Besides the fact this guy appeared to be a smart-ass, Nobu wasn't in the mood to carry on a conversation. He scribbled another sentence into his journal, attempting to look occupied.

Ichiro's trying to strike up a conversation. Not interested though.

"Hey. What was your name again? No-no?"

Nobu put his pencil down and glared at Ichiro. "No-bu."

"Oh, yeah, that's right. So, I asked you a question, Nobu. Where did you come from?" Ichiro rocked back and forth in his chair.

"Rohwer."

"Where's Rohwer?"

"Arkansas."

"And before that?"

Nobu's heart beat as fast as Ichiro's damn jackhammer leg. This guy was getting on his nerves.

"And before that?" Ichiro asked again.

"Hey, what's the deal? Why are you being so nosy? I don't hear you telling me where you're from."

Ichiro shrugged. "All you have to do is ask. Before here, Topaz. Before Topaz, Tanforan. And before that, Sacramento."

"We were supposed to go to Tanforan, but when we got there they sent our bus on to Santa Anita." Nobu stared out the window. So they'd both lived in horse stalls.

"We? Who's we?"

Nobu had had enough and was not in the mood to talk about his family with this wisecracker. He shoved his journal into his pocket. "I'm going out for a while."

When he walked out the door, heat blasted him, followed by a gust of wind full of stinging dust. He tried to protect his eyes from the bright sun and gritty wind, but it did little good, so he turned around and walked backwards. A tumbleweed swiped his leg as it barreled past. He watched it skip down the row of barracks, the wind chasing behind it. He'd seen tumbleweeds in Westerns before, but never thought he'd see one in real life. They seemed more fitting for a science fiction movie than a Western; they were aliens skittering along the surface of a barren planet.

Turning the corner, he found a building that provided shelter from the wind and sun. From there he watched armed guards in the towers. Armed guards outside the barbed wire. Everywhere he turned, armed guards.

He leaned against the side of the building, then slid to the ground, and pulled at his shirtsleeve to wipe the grit from his face, out of his eyes. But his shirt was too full of dust and dirt. His eyes watered and he blinked them hard, until he could see well enough to continue writing in his journal.

I have no country.

That's what I realize here at Tule Lake. This place has a different feel than the other camps I've been in. At least in those places, they tried to tell us it was for our own good to be there. Here, they make no secret that this is a prison, a place to keep those they believe to be a threat to this country.

Thinking about it still takes my breath away. A threat to this country? All because I answered "no" to two questions? Did they expect us to be like whipped dogs, loyal to those who kick us? Not me!

Still, I wish nobody harm, though they think I do.

He heard shouting in the distance, a group of men calling something out in rhythm. But he couldn't make out what they were saying. The uproar grew louder, until finally, he could understand the words.

Wah shoi! Wah shoi! Heave ho! Heave ho!

The ground rumbled in a cadence. The noise grew louder. Just as he stood to see where the commotion came from, the group turned the corner. There must have been a hundred of them, marching like military men. All wore the same *hachimaki* that Ichiro had worn.

Wah shoi! Wah shoi!

The strange energy fed his curiosity and he decided to follow, staying far behind, hidden in shadows.

Marching through row after row of barracks, the formation grew as more men in *hachimakis* rushed out of their apartments, feeding an entity that grew larger, louder.

They stopped in a large area near the gate, each man like one cell in a huge organism.

Precise. Uniform. United.

Push-ups. Sit-ups. Jumping jacks.

All in unison, all the same.

Five straight lines of men. Two stood at the front to lead.

One was Ichiro.

Pairing up, they began a choreographed sequence of karate moves. Clench-fisted stances. Blocks. Kicks. All accompanied by strong, guttural cries.

A powerful dance.

Like the tumbleweed that whipped around Tule Lake, Nobu felt pushed toward these men, chased by the winds of injustice. What was it that drew him? Their shouts? Their cadence?

No. It was their cohesiveness. Their brotherhood.

CHAPTER 59

Terrence

AUGUST 7, 1943

Thirteen! Terrence couldn't believe his little sister was a teenager, and he felt kinda sad about the "little girl" time he'd missed. He drummed the table to clear his mind. This was supposed to be a happy day, with Momma bringing Patty and Missy for a birthday celebration later on. He'd been trying to think of something to give Patty, but pickings were kinda slim.

Archy the Cockroach skittered under the bunk. Maybe a new pet? Nah. She hated bugs. Besides, he'd miss having the little guy around. But maybe the book. He'd finished reading and correcting it and was sure Mr. Blake wouldn't mind if he passed it on to his sister. She'd get a kick outta knowing he'd found himself his own cockroach and named it Archy.

He'd have to make a card. But dang, he was no artist. Tearing a piece of paper from his notebook, he tried to think of something to draw. He pulled *archy and mehitabel* from the stack of books on the table. Mehitabel the Cat. Perfect. Patty loved cats. He'd draw Mehitabel dressed in the Cleopatra costume of her previous life.

"What're you drawing?" asked Carter.

"A cat. Today is Patty's birthday."

"How old is she?"

"Thirteen."

"A teenager, huh?" Carter's voice got quiet and he stared out at the corridor.

"How old's Jenny anyways?" Terrence asked.

"She's nine. Be ten next month."

He could tell by the distant look in Carter's eyes—sad and mad at the same time—he was probably thinking about his daddy doing things to Jenny.

Time to change the subject. He didn't want Carter dwelling on it and he for sure didn't wanna let it ruin Patty's birthday. "Man, this is one time I think I'm glad to be holed up in this place. Can you imagine having a teenage sister? All that time she'll be spending in the bathroom, trying to make herself pretty for all the boys?"

Carter flashed a toothless grin. "Yeah. Sometimes girls aren't much fun to be around. One minute, they're happy-go-lucky. Next minute, they're little witches."

Terrence had already seen some of that moodiness in Patty. Like that time she scowled all through dinner, then left the table crying when he took a carrot off her plate. Heck, she didn't even like carrots. He thought he was doing her a favor.

"Momma!" she had yelled, tearing away from the table. "Make him stop!" Then she stormed off to her room.

Momma just shook her head and smiled. "Don't pay her no mind, son. It's just she getting ready for the monthly curse. You best get ready for it, too."

He didn't know nothing about the monthly curse, but he'd seen enough to decide not to touch it with a ten-foot pole.

Grinning at Carter, he clasped his hands and stretched them over his head. "Like I said. I'm sure not gonna miss being around my sister during her crazy times." He drew Cleopatra eyes on Mehitabel the Cat and held it up for Carter to see. "Finished."

"Patty like cats?"

"Yeah. We got one at home named Clyde. But this here is Mehitabel. She's Archy's friend. I'm giving her my copy of archy and mehitabel for her birthday."

"Why don't you give her your pet cockroach, too?" Carter shuddered. "'Fraid I can't take the same liking to Archy as you."

When Terrence walked into the visitor area, he slowed his pace to study Patty. She looked all grown up, sitting next to Momma and Missy. Dressed all pretty in her birthday dress. How was it that turning thirteen could make her look so different, not like a little girl anymore? He kind of missed his little-girl sister. All of a sudden, she was gone.

But it wasn't just that she looked older. She had some kinda weird, dreamy look in her eyes, like she was in some faraway place. Had Momma seen it, too?

Momma turned in his direction and flashed a big smile that made her cheeks even rounder. It always gave him a happy feeling inside. He pulled out a chair. "Happy birthday, Sis."

Patty giggled, and for a second, she looked like the little girl he remembered.

"Got something for you." He flashed his gift, then hid it under his shirt again. "Gonna have to give it to the guard to bring around to you."

Patty's eyes got real big. "Really? What is it?"

Missy's eyes rolled, an unmistakable message. He shoulda brought something for her, too. "I got a big surprise for you next time, little Miss. But this time it's Patty's special day." He held up a finger—a motion to wait—and left his booth to give Patty's present to the guard.

When he returned, he found Patty whispering in Momma's ear. Though curious as all get out, he pretended not to see. They jolted back to their original positions when he sat again.

"The guard's bringing your present around," he said.

Patty nudged Momma.

"Son," Momma said, "Missy and me'll go after the guard bring your present. Patty say she wanna have some time alone with you." She frowned at Patty and shook her head. "Don't like cutting off my time with you, but it's her birthday and all."

Prison had sure enough changed things in the Harris family. There was a time when Patty didn't want anything to do with Terrence. Now she was asking to be alone with him.

The guard arrived on the visitors' side with the gift. Missy jumped out of her chair to see what it was, then grabbed for it.

Patty whined, "Hey, that's for me."

Some things hadn't changed.

Patty crinkled her nose. "Archy and Mehi . . . Mehi?"

"Archy and Mehitabel," he said. "Mr. Blake gave it to me."

She flipped through the pages, Missy gawking over her shoulder.

"I think you'll like Mehitabel. She used to be Cleopatra, you know. Me? I like Archy. Matter a fact . . ." He hesitated.

"What?" Patty and Missy asked at the same time.

Terrence leaned in. "Now, don't laugh, but I got a pet cockroach. Named him Archy."

Momma slapped her hands on the table. "Terrence! You got a pet roach?"

His sisters giggled.

"Hey, now. Don't knock it. It ain't—I mean it *isn't*—like I can have a dog or a cat for a pet. We make do with what we got around here. Anyways, Patty, that's one of my favorite books. I expect to see it taken care of real good when I get outta here."

Missy tried to pull the book closer.

"Careful now, Missy. Sis will read it to you. Right, Patty?"

"Yeah, I guess," she mumbled, then glanced at Momma with raised brows.

Momma clucked her tongue. "Guess me and Missy will leave you two alone now." She blew a kiss to Terrence. "See you next week, son. Take care yourself."

"Okay, bye, Momma. Bye, Missy." He watched Patty, waiting for her to say something.

She stared at her hands, folded on the table and bit the corner of her lip.

The silence seemed too long. "What's going on, Patty?"

"Terrence?" She bit her nails.

"Yeah?"

"You ever had a real bad crush on someone?"

He exhaled, relieved and tickled, and stifled a chuckle. An urge to tease struck him, but right now he had to be a good big brother. "Yeah. 'Course, it's usually the girls that have a crush on me." He winked.

"Well, actually, I think he—his name is William—William has a crush on me, too. Anyways, he keeps smiling at me from across the class-room." She twirled her ponytail around her finger and had that faraway look in her eyes again.

He tried to remember his first big crush. Maria. Man, she was pretty. Not as pretty as Patty though. Sure, that first crush had been a big deal, but he still didn't know why his sister needed to talk to him alone. Momma would've understood.

Sitting back in his chair, he waited, trying hard to be patient. *Girls!*

"Well . . ." She seemed to be avoiding looking at him.

He checked the clock on the wall. "Patty, I don't wanna rush you, but my time is almost up. You need to talk to me about something?"

"Terrence, now don't you get mad at me."

Uneasiness swiped at him. What was going on? "I ain't gonna get mad at you, but you best tell me quick." He glanced at the clock again.

She took a deep breath. "Well . . . what would you say if I told you . . . William is, well, he's white?"

CHAPTER 60

Sachi

AUGUST 18, 1943

Obon! The Buddhist custom was one of Sachi's favorite times of year. Strange that honoring the dead could be such fun. Three days of beautiful colors and yummy delights, when all the women would gather to prepare the Japanese food she had missed so much since being in camp. She giggled, listening to them whisper about secret stashes of special spices they'd carried from California. But her favorite part of the celebration was *bon-odori*, the dance.

Oh, the beautiful kimonos! The sight of silk pastels—yellow, pink, blue—floating and drifting with each dancer's movement. It made the hot, sticky summer air feel a little cooler.

Best of all, now that she was eleven, she truly felt a part of the ceremony as she danced with the women. There had been no *Obon* celebration at the Santa Anita Assembly Center the year before. Too many disrupted lives and nobody to organize the event. All the years before that, Sachi was just a little girl. She'd looked silly then, following the women in kimonos as they danced around the large circle. How clumsy she was in her dance, though she tried to copy their graceful motions. For Rohwer's *bon-odori*, she remembered all of her dance lessons and no longer felt awkward like before.

Nothing made her feel more grown up, more proud, than the look in her mother's eyes as she watched Sachi dance. When she caught Mama smiling, a little teary-eyed, Sachi decided all of the boring practices she'd complained about had been worth it. It was good that she had changed her mind about asking Jubie to celebrate *Obon* at the camp. If Jubie had come, it might have ruined everything.

Still, wishing Jubie could be there to dance with her and the other women was a dark cloud over the celebration. She imagined seeing Jubie move in the circle with them, while chastising herself for her slipup.

Jubie had become so good at Japanese dancing in the last few months that Sachi had the brilliant idea to invite her to *Obon*, not even thinking about how she'd explain it to Mama when Jubie showed up for the dance. She'd been so excited she simply blurted out the invitation. Brilliant idea? No. Brilliantly stupid? Yes.

For several weeks, Sachi worried about how to get herself out of the mess without hurting Jubie's feelings. Finally, she realized she didn't have to withdraw the invitation. She could change it instead, and decided to do it on a hot afternoon the week before, when Jubie walked Sachi back to camp. All the while, Sachi's stomach had tickled with nerves about Mama seeing them together.

"Hey, Jubie," she'd said, picking up a round stone from the side of the road. "Instead of coming to the camp to celebrate, what do you think about having our own *Obon* celebration?" They could honor the dead in private. Two friends—two sisters—honoring their dead fathers.

Sachi turned the stone in her hand and felt its warmth. "We could have a picnic and dance in the shade by the creek. It's going to be so crowded in camp, and all those people will make it feel even hotter."

But sometimes Jubie was too smart for her own good. Sachi could tell when she'd been "figgered out," as Jubie called it.

Her friend was silent as she walked next to Sachi, and that wasn't good. She was hardly ever quiet, and it was a sign that something was wrong. So, Sachi talked for both of them, speaking faster, like she always did when she got nervous.

"I'll bring some special Japanese food—it's so funny how the ladies in camp compete to see who can make the best rice rolls. We can have a picnic." She stopped for a second, only to breathe, then continued. "Then I'll show you some new dances and we can practice in the shade and maybe even take a little swim in the creek if we get too hot."

Jubie stopped walking and stared at her. She didn't have to say a single word for Sachi to know what she was thinking.

You think you hiding something from me, but you ain't.

Finally, Jubie spoke. "I ever tell you about Auntie Bess not allowing no phony faces around?"

"Phony face? No. What's that?"

"Auntie Bess say you wearing a phony face anytime you ain't being truthful about something. She catches me ever time. She say she got some secret way of knowing. I didn't believe she knew what she was talking about, but I do now, 'cause I's catching you with a phony face. What you hiding? Might as well spit it out, 'cause I'm gonna find out one way or the other."

Sachi's unease erupted in a giggle. "What makes you think I'm hiding something?"

"I just know it. It's coming out loud and clear as them jar flies making them buzzing noises ever where. Come on, you can tell me. What's wrong?"

Whatever Jubie thought Sachi was hiding, it couldn't be as hurtful as what it really was. How was she supposed to tell her best friend that her mother didn't like her, just because she was colored? But, she'd been "figgered out," and there was no sense trying to hide behind her phony face any longer.

She took a deep breath. "Jubie, you know it doesn't matter what anybody else thinks, you're my best friend, my sister. Right?"

Jubie opened her eyes a little wider. "Yeah."

"Well, my mother . . . she—" Sachi bit her lip.

"What is it? You can tell me. What's wrong with your mama?"

The alarm in Jubie's voice made Sachi's heart ache, but she forced herself to spit the words out. "She doesn't like us playing together."

Confusion and hurt flashed in Jubie's amber eyes. There were some things Jubie couldn't hide, either.

"I'm sorry." Sachi panicked and started talking fast all over again. "But she doesn't know you. And, she doesn't know I still see you, either. When I'm with you, she thinks I'm with my Japanese friends." She couldn't bear to see Jubie's reaction, but couldn't turn away, either.

"You been lying to your mama about us?"

She'd never looked at it as lying, but of course it was. Just because

Mama was being unreasonable didn't make what she was doing any less a lie. "I guess so," she said softly.

"Why your mama don't like me?"

Sachi pointed to the shade of a big tree at the side of the road. "Let's get out of the sun and I'll try to explain it to you." She shook her head as they crossed the road. How in the world would she explain this to Jubie? It was a conversation she'd hoped she'd never have to have. But, how could she think she'd avoid it either?

They sat down and leaned against the trunk. Above, the tree buzzed with cicadas.

Sachi picked up a stick and scratched the dirt. "Remember when I told you three boys killed my papa because he was Japanese?"

"Yeah."

"Well, what I never told you was . . . one of those boys was colored."

Jubie looked up. It was quiet again, except for the whispering sound of the wind in the leaves and the noise of the awful, ugly cicadas. Sachi usually hated the constant buzzing, but as she waited for Jubie to say something, she was glad it filled the uncomfortable silence.

Zzzzzz. Zzzzzz. Zzzzzz.

Sachi had to try to explain, fill the big quiet. "My mother holds Papa's murder against all colored people. That's why she doesn't want me to be friends with you." She leaned toward her friend to watch for an expression. Jubie wasn't saying anything to help Sachi figure her out.

Finally, Jubie spoke. "She hold it against white folks, too? After all, two of them boys was white."

Sachi had never looked at it that way. Why *did* Mama only hold it against Terrence? "I don't know. But I think she's wrong, Jubie. That's why I've been hiding our friendship. I know you no more had anything to do with my papa's death than I had anything to do with the bombing of Pearl Harbor. It doesn't make sense that some people—my mama included—hold the act of some against those who had nothing to do with it."

"No, but it do happen a lot. What we gonna do about it?" Jubie asked.

Sachi thought for a minute before realizing she had no real answer to Jubie's question. She stood up and dusted herself off, then smiled at her friend. "There may be nothing we can do about all those other people, but you and I can do something on our own. You know what we're going to do?"

At last the sparkle returned to Jubie's eyes. "No, what?"

"We're going to have our own celebration by the creek! That's what we're going to do. And no matter what all those other people think, we'll have a great time, even if you *are* colored and I *am* Japanese."

CHAPTER 61

Terrence

NOVEMBER 17, 1943

Terrence stared at Patty's letter. God, he couldn't wait to get out of that miserable cell. Helplessness overwhelmed him and settled heavy as the biscuits and gravy he'd had for breakfast.

Dear Terrence,

I got a problem, and I need you to tell me what I should do. You see, William and me had gotten to be friends—just friends, cause I know Momma doesn't think I'm old enough for anything else. I guess that was fine, at least for now, cause it was nice just talking with him.

Yeah, I said "it was nice." Because one day we were walking down the hall, minding our own business, when these bullies grabbed both of William's arms and pulled him outside. I followed cause I was scared what they might do to him.

Anyways, they started punching on him, calling him a nigger-lover. Other kids started coming up and watching, then they started calling him names, too. Poor William. He tried to fight back, but those bullies were a lot bigger.

No matter how hard I tried not to cry, I couldn't help it. And that just made things worse. They started teasing me, too, but that didn't hurt near as much as seeing what they were doing to William. He didn't deserve any of that.

I begged them to stop, even begged the kids watching to help me make them stop. But they just stood there. Some even laughed.

It's not fair, Terrence. I know how it feels to be called a nigger, but I'm guessing poor William never had to deal with being called names before.

Terrence stared at his clenched fist.

Now, he stays away from me. But I can tell by the look in his eyes, he feels bad about it. I guess I understand. What else can he do? Anyhow, it hasn't really helped much. Those boys still call him names.

I wish you were here, Terrence. What should I do?

Love,

Patty

How could she ask him that question when he was in jail for doing the very same thing those bullies did to William? What was he supposed to tell her?

He hung his head in his hands. What would Daddy have said? Nothing but a blank, dark space occupied his mind. Then, a memory from a night a long time ago began to creep in—when he'd overheard one of Momma and Daddy's conversations from their bedroom next to his.

Patty wasn't even born yet, so he couldn't have been more than four or five when he woke to the sound of muffled voices. He remembered thinking it was strange that they were talking in the middle of the night. He'd known he shouldn't be eavesdropping, but he pressed his ear to the wall anyway.

"John," Momma said, "what you gonna do about it?"

Daddy's deep voice rumbled on the wall. "Ain't gonna do nothing, Momma. Ain't nothing I *can* do that's gonna change anything no how."

Momma's tone got louder and she talked real fast. "But you didn't mess up that engine. You one of the best mechanics Allen's Garage ever had. You can't let Mr. Allen fire you for something you didn't do—just 'cause you the one who found it broke? You been a good employee for near five years now. You got to stand up for yourself."

Terrence remembered a long silence, when his ears rang with quiet. He'd pressed harder against the wall, straining to hear Daddy's reply.

"You think arguing with Mr. Allen's gonna get me my job back? 'Course not. Only make matters worse." Daddy paused. "You know what I am gonna do though?"

"What?"

"Ain't got no choice, Momma. Gotta get me a job. I'm gonna join the navy."

"John! You can't!"

"Momma, hush now or you wake Terrence. I done made up my mind, and there ain't nothing more to be said about it."

Terrence stared at the darkness that had taken him back to his boyhood bedroom. Thoughts flooded his head. Daddy might've never joined the navy if that old Allen hadn't fired him for something he didn't do. Which means he wouldn't have been at Pearl Harbor when it was attacked. And that means he wouldn't be dead. And if the Japs hadn't killed his Daddy, Terrence wouldn't have been looking to get back at one of them that day in the park. And he wouldn't be in this jail cell. If all that hadn't happened, he'd be home, right where he should be, helping Patty with her problem about William.

That all made him wonder if Daddy would do it like that all over again. Would he still ignore what Allen said? And would Daddy tell Patty to ignore what was happening to William? Would he leave things be to keep from stirring up any more trouble?

All Terrence could think was what might've happened if Daddy *had* gone back to talk some sense into Allen. Maybe the old guy had had a bad day when he'd fired Daddy. What if there'd been the smallest chance he could've got his job back?

Well . . . they sure as heck would've all been in a better place than they were now.

What would Carter think he should tell Patty? What if it happened to Jenny? Carter was deep into a book over on his bunk, but Terrence didn't care. He had to talk to someone.

"Hey, Carter."

Carter flipped a page.

"Got a minute?"

"Yeah, what is it?" He set the book down.

Terrence drew a deep breath. "What would you say to Jenny if she told you a Negro kid had a crush on her—"

Carter sprang up. "I'd tell her to stay away from him. Then I'd tell him to keep his dirty hands off her."

He might as well have punched Terrence in the gut. Unable to hold back a gasp, he glanced down at Patty's letter. Sure couldn't let Carter see the surprise in his eyes. No way would he let him know he'd hurt him.

Carter's book slapped to the floor. Bedsprings squeaked.

"Hey, sorry, Tee. I wasn't thinking." Carter whispered from near the cell door.

Terrence turned away.

"After what Pa did to Jenny, I can't think of her with anyone. Doesn't matter if he's a Negro or not. Not *anyone*."

Terrence huffed, still not ready to talk to this guy he thought he knew. But he couldn't hold his anger inside. "You mean to tell me it didn't have anything to do with the guy being a Negro?"

Silence.

Carter pulled out a chair and sat across from Terrence. "Okay, I won't deny that got me going. Mostly, it was just imagining some guy messing with Jenny again. Why'd you ask me that anyways?"

Terrence stared at Carter, still not sure if he wanted to talk to him.

"Come on, Tee. I said I was sorry. You know I don't got nothing against coloreds. But come on. There's a real world out there, with plenty other people who don't want to see a white girl with a colored kid. Why would I want Jenny going through all that? So, why'd you ask me that question?" He pointed to the letter on the table. "That from Patty?"

"Yeah." Feeling protective, Terrence folded the letter and put it in his pocket.

"What'd she have to say?"

Terrence rolled his eyes. No use fighting Carter off. "She said she and this white kid named William have a crush on each other. Said some bullies beat up on William. Called him a nigger lover."

"Guess I been called *that* a few times," Carter said, grinning.

Terrence smiled. All those times Peachie and his gang called Carter a nigger lover, just 'cause he shared a cell with a colored man. Heck, they almost killed Carter over it. No wonder it was a blow to hear Carter's response to his question. A hard blow that still smarted some.

"She wants me to tell her what to do," Terrence said. "What in the world am I supposed say?"

"Hmm. That's a tough one." Carter rubbed the back of his neck. "It's funny, you know. Behind these bars, we're kinda in a protected world of our own." He tore a piece of paper off a tablet and put it in his mouth, then chewed on it like gum. "We can sit here and talk about how it's okay for our sisters to have crushes on boys with skin different from theirs—after all, you and me get along just fine. But that ain't the real world, is it?"

"Guess not." Something about Carter's reaction still stuck in his craw. Until . . . he smiled at a realization that hit him. "You forgot I'm colored, didn't you?"

"Huh?"

"When you said what you said about what you'd do to a Negro kid who liked Jenny. You didn't think about me being colored when you said it. Right?"

Carter tapped his fingers on the table. "Maybe. Never really thought about it."

"'Course not! That's my point. If you'd thought about me being colored, you wouldn't have said what you said. I know you wouldn't have. So somehow, the color of our skin doesn't matter to us no more."

"Maybe. Why do you suppose that is?"

Terrence got up and walked over to Carter. "'Cause we're the same color," he said, poking Carter's chest, "right inside there."

"There you go getting all philosophical again, Tee."

"Maybe. But it's true."

"Yeah, but like I said, it ain't the real world. So what're you going to tell your sis?"

"I don't know. I'll think of something."

Carter smacked on his paper gum. "Might come as a surprise, but there's some things can't be fixed."

"You might be right." Terrence smiled. "Least not while I'm in here anyways." He stared at the markings on the wall near his bunk. Only 147 days to go. "But you know what? I got less than five months in this place."

"Yeah? Then what?"

Terrence tore a sheet of paper from the tablet. "Can't say right now. Mr. Blake's been trying to tell me to get a college education. Keeps giving me these articles on civil rights. But I don't know. It's not something I ever thought I could do. Then again, maybe he's right. Someone's gotta do something, 'cause it sure ain't gonna get better on its own."

"You're right about one thing," Carter said. "Nothing's gonna happen overnight. And for sure not in time to help Patty figure out what to do about William."

"No, but bad as she feels now, she's just a kid. She'll get over it." Terrence rubbed the sides of his forehead. "I feel bad about what William's going through, but I can't fix that problem from a jail cell. For now, maybe it'll help to remind Patty that I'll be outta here soon. Then we can figure something out together."

CHAPTER 62
Sachi

APRIL 12, 1944

It seemed like it had been raining forever. But at last, patches of blue appeared between gray clouds that drifted away from camp. Sometimes, sunlight cast shadows; but like ghosts, they disappeared when the monster gray clouds shoved the sun behind them again.

Sachi watched a line of people file through the gate. Their shadows disappeared, reappeared, then disappeared again. Each carried the few things that still existed in their lives. Suitcases. Boxes. Babies. For weeks, they'd been coming, transferred from the relocation center in Jerome, Arkansas.

Mama told her it was because Jerome was being closed and that eventually, all the internees would come to Rohwer. Sometimes she wondered if the government was just playing games—like chess—moving the internees around all the time. Why had the people from Jerome been transferred to Rohwer? Were they considered "disloyal" like Nobu and all the others who were sent to Tule Lake? She still couldn't believe so many had to be sent away, just because of how they answered two silly questions. Nobu was her brother. No way was he disloyal.

Hundreds of people had been arriving every day. Even with the rows of new barracks and the units vacated by the transferred occupants, she wondered if there would be room for everyone.

But Sachi didn't worry so much about that. All she cared about was who she might see come through the gate. She'd watched people reunited with family or friends, and whenever it happened, she got a little lump in her throat, seeing the laughter and tears of those brought together with loved ones.

Excitement and anticipation flitted all around, like a brightly colored butterfly. Would it light on Sachi, too? Would she find old friends? Maybe

Sam? Even if she weren't so lucky, maybe she and Jubie would meet new friends.

Jubie watched from outside the gate. Sachi waved at her, wondering why visitors were not allowed inside while the internees were arriving from Jerome. What difference did it make whether Jubie stood a few feet outside the gate, or inside next to her? Just one more dumb rule. Praise to Buddha that she'd learned Papa's philosophy. *Shikata ga nai.* We do what we must do.

Sachi and Jubie had worked out their own sign language to communicate. A smile and raised eyebrows expressed excitement, perhaps at the sight of a group of giggling girls—possibilities for new friends. The flash of an exaggerated frown and "thumbs down" showed disapproval, maybe of a scowling woman. Who would want her as a new resident in the camp?

A bunch of boys Nobu's age sauntered through the gate, joking around and punching each other. It was obvious they were showing off in front of the gaggle of girls who whispered to each other and tried to act like they didn't know the boys were watching.

Sachi signaled to Jubie, and pounded her heart in a mocking way. She laughed at the scene, but inside, it made her miss Nobu. She'd have to write to him about how love-struck the Jerome boys acted in front of the Rohwer girls. On second thought, that might not be a good idea. It would only remind him of Yuki.

Tired of watching new internees arrive, Sachi huffed. Her exaggerated yawn signaled Jubie: *I'm bored.*

Jubie nodded her head. *Me, too.* Then she pointed in the direction of town. *I'm going home. See you later.*

Sachi waved goodbye, yet felt a little perturbed. Now what was she supposed to do? Things would *really* be dull without Jubie.

Time for something new. She stared at the cast of characters trudging off the bus and through the gate. She could pretend they were characters in one of her books. But which book? *Pride and Prejudice*, of course! She was almost finished reading it, and kept imagining what the characters looked like, especially Elizabeth Bennett and Mr. Fitzwilliam Darcy. Fitzwilliam. She loved that name—perfect for an aloof and proud gentleman.

She watched one young woman walk around, staring at the camp, her new home. Very proper and pretty, too. She would make a good Elizabeth and she imagined her in a nineteenth century-era dress and imprinted her image in her mind for her next reading of the novel. Now, on to find a Mr. Darcy.

He had to be handsome, very proud. What about that one? Probably too young to be as regal as she imagined Mr. Darcy to be. There? No, he looks cocky, not proud.

Maybe the man walking through the gate. Handsome, and he had a proud stride, though with a bit of a limp. Something about him. He wasn't quite right for the role of Mr. Darcy, but she couldn't take her eyes off of him. He wore a hat that hid much of his face, until he turned slightly. She studied his profile. Maybe too old.

But . . .

Her pulse quickened and excitement surged through her, but only for the tiniest moment. Swift as a rushing river, sadness swept it away. That man looked just like Papa. The same long nose, unique among Japanese men. But the hat he wore was too big, and covered much of his head. Still, the likeness drew her like a magnet. So much like Papa from the side—same height, but thinner.

Would she ever stop seeing Papa everywhere? And now, even in the book she read?

Moving closer to get a better look, she hoped he would look as much like her father from the front, but feared he would not.

She tiptoed toward him, like a cat stalking a field mouse. One tiny step forward. Stop. Another measured step. Stop. She lingered in that moment of wondering, that magical split second of fantasy.

The similarity was overwhelming. Nothing else in the world mattered but the man she was approaching.

Another inch forward. Gravel beneath her feet crackled.

He turned around.

Her heart jolted. Her breath caught in her throat. She held it, afraid to breathe, lest she lose the moment.

His eyes—eyes that were surely Papa's—widened.

Every part of her wanted to lunge forward. To hug him and never let go. Every part, that is, except the awful, nagging memory that Papa was dead.

This man is a stranger.

And that look on his face, half caught between a cry and a scream. Did she startle him? Was he angry that she stared?

No. His eyes were kind. So much like Papa's, except . . .

Are those tears?

He opened his mouth as if he wanted to speak, but no words came.

Fear prickled over her body and she stepped back. Too much like Papa—a ghost come to haunt her.

He held his arms toward her.

Her face was hot. Her body was cold. She turned to run away.

He called her, his voice broken. "Sachiko? Please, do not run away. It's me. Papa."

Drawn to him again, she whispered, "Papa? No. My papa died."

How can this be?

He inched toward her, shaking his head slowly. "Died? No. I did not die. Why would you think—" He stopped and his eyes widened. "Sachi-chan. I did not die. They took me away while I was in the hospital. I could not find you."

She willed herself to remain still, to not run away. She stared at the barracks, the clouds in the sky, dust on her shoe. She smelled wet dirt, heard birds sing. All of it seemed real. But if it was a dream, she hoped never to wake.

The-Man-Who-Said-He-Was-Papa knelt down and hugged her, gently at first.

Still afraid, she shut her eyes and wished with all her heart for it to be true. Yet, she was unable to believe it. It was too much. Her heart beat so hard and fast she thought she might explode. She cried, as her words struggled against a flood of questions roaring in her mind.

But we received a telegram that said you had died. Why did they lie to us? Why couldn't you find us?

She wrapped her arms around his neck. The word, his name—Papa—lingered at the tip of her tongue. Something inside feared if she said it the dream would dissolve, like it had so many times before.

"Sachi-chan," he whispered. "It is me."

A tentative comfort began to wash over her, like feeling water from the camp showers finally turn from icy cold to warm.

Only Papa could make her feel that indescribable warmth. Only Papa.

He turned his cheek to her and tapped it. "Are you not forgetting something?" he asked, his eyes twinkling.

Joy and relief came at last. "Papa!" she cried, then gave him the kiss he always asked for. "It is you."

He picked her up and spun around. "Sachi-chan. I don't believe it," he cried as he put her down. "I do not believe it." He held her at arm's length and looked at her. "You've grown into a beautiful young, lady."

A young lady? Nobody had ever called her that before.

"Where's Mama? And Nobu and Taro?" he asked.

She needed her own answers and asked again as she pressed her face into his coat. "What happened, Papa? Why did they tell us you were dead? Why didn't you find us?"

"I do not know what happened. We will figure it out. But for now, please. Take me to Mama and Nobu and Taro." He clutched her hands in his, and she remembered all the times in the past when she had felt his strong hands hold hers.

"I will take you to Mama, but Nobu and Taro . . ."

"But what? Is everything all right with your brothers?"

"Papa, Nobu is in the Tule Lake camp."

"Tule Lake? Why would he be there?"

"They sent him there because of his answers on the loyalty questionnaire." She didn't want to tell Papa the rest.

His eyes widened. "You mean . . . he answered no-no?"

She found it odd, her sudden need to protect Nobu. Protect him from Papa? "He said he had to answer no-no. Because America was disloyal to him. To all of us."

Papa shook his head and clucked his tongue. "Nobu, Nobu," he whispered. "And Taro?"

"Taro joined the army. That was while you were still in the hospital. Mama told you, but I guess you didn't hear her."

Still shaking his head, he took Sachi's hand. "Please, take me to Mama now."

She had so much to tell Papa about all the things that had happened since she'd seen him. But walking next to his silence, she could not make her mouth speak, though her mind raced with memories of the last two years.

They stopped at the stoop to the apartment. Papa stared at the door and squeezed Sachi's hand.

"See the flowers I planted?" She pointed at daffodils that lined the edge of the porch. "I remembered what you told me when we used to plant in your garden. You said to tuck the bulbs into earth's blanket in the fall so they would sleep through the winter until they woke in the spring."

A quick glance, and he returned his gaze to the door. "I'm glad you remembered, Sachi-chan. They are lovely." He stepped up one stair and stopped. "Perhaps you should tell Mama that I am here. It would startle her if I just walked inside."

She grappled with the impossibility of his request. Wouldn't she also be startled at Sachi announcing Papa was waiting outside the door? She might even scold Sachi for lying. She hesitated. "But—"

The door flew open. "Sachiko!" Mama scolded. "Who are you talk—"

Papa looked up and removed his hat. "Sumiko-san."

The color went out of Mama's face. Grabbing the door, she stepped back, like she had seen a ghost.

Papa rushed up the stairs to help her.

Gazing up at him, she cried, "Michio?"

"Yes, it's me."

"But, how—?" Her gaze traveled from his face, then up and down his body.

He touched her arms with a tenderness in his eyes that Sachi had almost forgotten. Mama fell against him as he guided her through the door. "Let us go inside and sit down. We will talk."

Sachi stared at the door as it began to creep shut. Only fifteen minutes ago, Papa was still dead. Fear filled her again.

No. Please don't let it be a dream.

Once again, she struggled to use every sense to search for signs that she was awake and not dreaming. Inhaling, she caught the scent of supper cooking in the mess hall. *Roast beef?* If she was dreaming, she would smell Papa's chicken and dumplings. Her daffodils danced with the same cool breeze that brushed her skin. Bright, happy yellow.

Then she remembered what Jubie told her once: "Ain't nobody dreams in color, cause color don't matter in dreams."

Sachi tugged at her jumper. Purple. The daffodils. Yellow. Their stems. Green. The sky. Blue. Colors everywhere!

Papa opened the door. "Sachi-chan, are you coming inside?"

Smiling at the man standing in the open door—the man who really was Papa—she skipped up the steps.

CHAPTER 63

Terrence

APRIL 12, 1944

Release time was noon. Terrence could hardly stand waiting and paced back and forth at the cell door. He checked the clock in the corridor. Eleven o'clock.

Back and forth. Back and forth. How many paces until noon?

He figured Momma was counting the minutes too. She was probably already waiting outside. Last time she came to visit, she told him she could hardly believe it would be the last time she'd have to see Terrence from behind a window.

Remembering her tear-filled eyes made him smile. She'd tried to hide it, but he knew her too well.

"Son, next time we come, it's gonna be to take you home." She'd dug a hanky out of her purse and blew her nose in a funny, honking way that always made him chuckle. "And I be able to give you a good, long hug 'stead of just wishing I could."

He inhaled long and deep. The next two hours were going to seem longer than the 730 days he'd already waited.

"Hey, Tee," Carter called from his bunk, "you ready to get out of here or something? Settle down. You're making me nervous."

Much as he wanted out, he was gonna miss the white boy. He worried about leaving him alone there. Wondered how he'd do if he had to go to San Quentin when his trial was over.

The thought made Terrence queasy, even tempered his impatience to get out. What a waste, Carter being in prison the rest of his life. With what went on between his daddy and Jenny, maybe he'd get off with a lighter sentence. But he also knew life didn't always work out that way.

Memories of his 730 days flooded his mind. Arriving at the facility. Wondering how he'd survive two years in prison. The haunting nightmares of Mr. Kimura. The way the guards snickered when they threw

Carter in the cell with him. Peachie and his gang. He chuckled. And of course, the day Carter came back from the dead.

Yeah, it was Carter who'd made the whole thing bearable. Maybe Terrence had made it a little more bearable for Carter too. Now, he'd be gone, and he couldn't imagine being left like Carter was about to be left. Who would the guards throw in with Carter now? Another colored? One of Peachie's gang? A feeling of desperation penetrated him like a chill.

Less than an hour left. He had to say something to his cell mate. "Carter?"

"Yeah?"

What should he say? How could he put his thoughts into words without sounding like a wimp? "Can you believe it's almost time?"

"Yeah. The way you're pacing back and forth, I can believe it. Hell. What time you supposed to get outta here anyways?"

"Noon."

"Well, it's about damn time."

Terrence smiled. Carter wasn't gonna be no wimp, neither. "You right about that. Heck, I 'bout had enough of being stuck in this tiny cell with a white boy."

They were quiet for what seemed like a long time. Terrence flopped onto his bunk and stared at Carter's bunk above him. "Sure feel sorry for whoever's here after me, what with your snoring and all."

"Bet he won't whine about it as much. And I'm guessing for sure he won't have a cockroach for a pet. You got Archy packed with all your books and stuff you're taking?"

Archy. 'Course he couldn't take him. No way Momma would allow it. He'd kinda miss that cockroach. "Nah," he said, "I'll leave him for you. He doesn't need much care. Just sneak a few crumbs from the cafeteria every once in a while."

"Yeah, right. Like I'm gonna take care of your cockroach."

Quiet again.

Terrence ran his fingers over the marks on the wall, then dug his pencil out from under the mattress. One last mark. Seven hundred thirty.

"What do you think your momma's gonna cook for dinner tonight?" Carter asked.

Terrence's mouth watered with the thought. "Don't know, but I'm guessing pot roast. She knows it's my favorite. Whatever, it'll be better than the crap around this place."

"Hell, yeah. What I wouldn't give for a home-cooked meal. But that's *never* gonna happen."

Never. The word sent Terrence into a deep, dark hole and covered him with a heavy sadness. "Maybe I'll bring you something some time," he replied. But could he ever bring himself to return to that place? Much as he'd miss Carter, would he come to visit?

"Yeah, and my name's Franklin Roosevelt. You ain't never coming back here." Carter cleared his throat.

Terrence couldn't take the defeat in Carter's voice. A surge of resolution shot through his body and he sat up. "I'll be back. Just wait and see."

"What're you talking about?"

"What if those ideas Mr. Blake's been pushing on me come true? What if I finish my education? Get a law degree? Maybe someday I could file an appeal for you. Get you outta here. It'd take a while, but least I could get you outta here something short of forever."

"Come on, Tee. What if it came *true*? You mean like a *wish*? Man, you living in a fairy tale. There ain't no happy-ever-afters. Trust me. I know. I ain't never seen one yet."

"It ain't—isn't—just wishing, Carter. I'm gonna do it. Been sitting in this cell for 730 days, wondering what I was gonna do with my life. Everything's been pointing in one direction. All started with realizing how stupid I was when I went after Mr. Kimura for being Japanese— then all that wondering about how to make that right. Then, there was Peachie and his goons. That made me think about how many stupid people there are on the outside. I knew I had to do something to change it. And what about what Patty told me about what those bullies did to William? So, why couldn't I help you someday?"

"I don't want to spoil your dreams or nothing, Tee. But I'll believe it when I see it."

"'Suppose that's all I can ask." He walked over to check the clock again. Eleven fifty-five. They'd come for him in five minutes. He thought he might jump out of his pants with excitement. But he also felt like he was getting ready to be ripped apart.

He looked over at Carter's bunk. Still and quiet.

"It's about time," Terrence said.

"Yep."

He walked slowly toward Carter's top bunk. "You take care of yourself."

Carter stared at the ceiling. "Hey, you're the one going out into that mean world. *You* be careful. Just remember what I said. It ain't no fairy tale."

Terrence reached to shake his cell mate's hand. "Guess I'll see you around."

Carter extended his hand, but his gaze remained fixed on the ceiling. "Yep."

Terrence looked up at where Carter stared. Nothing but dull, gray stucco.

The guard's keys jingled at the door. "Time to go."

Time to go. Seven hundred thirty days.

Yet, he hesitated.

He took a last look at his cell mate—his friend—picked up his box of books and walked out.

The guard slammed the door. Hard metal against hard metal.

Carter spoke through the ringing echo it left. "Take care of yourself, Tee."

He stepped outside and took a deep breath. Blue sky, so blue. Wind rattled through the leaves in the trees just outside the yard.

And there. Beyond the gate. Momma, Patty, and Missy. And Mr. Blake.

Gravel crackled beneath his feet as his steps quickened, like his heartbeat.

Momma held out her arms.

He could see her quivering with anticipation.

Missy jumped up and down, clapping her hands. Patty watched quietly, her hands covering her mouth.

Mr. Blake beamed and wore a smile that reminded him of Daddy's.

A guard opened the gate and Terrence ran until he reached Momma's arms. She wrapped them around his body and squeezed. So warm. So soft.

Home.

CHAPTER 64
Sachi

APRIL 12, 1944

Sachi couldn't wait to understand how they had remained separated from Papa all this time. Maybe if she understood, she would finally believe it was all real, not a dream.

Seated at the table across from Papa, she glanced at the clock on the wall. One o'clock. It had been just after lunch when he stepped off the bus from Jerome. She watched him stare out the window.

The look in his eyes made him seem very far away as he spoke. "The night they took me away from the hospital, it's all very hazy, like a dream."

Mama wiped her eyes. "You were in a coma, Michio-san."

"Yes, but still, I could hear voices. From what I could gather, the men talking were with the FBI. They were whispering and I assumed it must be late in the night. When someone strapped me to a gurney, I wondered where they were taking me."

Sachi tried to make sense of facts that were laced between the words and tears of her parents' conversation.

Papa continued. "The next thing I knew, I woke up in an infirmary at the camp in Santa Fe, and they were calling me Ihara. I was still confused, didn't know what was going on, but I knew my name was not Ihara. I kept trying to tell them my name was Michio Kimura."

Mama gasped and put her hand over her mouth. "They called you Ihara? That was the name of the man in the bed next to you at the hospital." She shook her head as she continued. "When we received the telegram that you had . . . died . . . it must have been Ihara that died."

Ihara died and they thought he was Papa? How could that happen? Sachi felt relief and gratitude about the terrible mistake, but at the same time, she couldn't help feeling sad for the family who must still be wondering about their father. How were they going to feel when they found out he would never be coming home?

"Oh, dear," Papa said, hanging his head in his hands. "All this time you thought I was dead. All because of a paperwork error?"

Mama's eyes filled with tears. "And they couldn't bother to send us another telegram to let us know they'd made a mistake."

Papa turned away, and Sachi caught him wiping his eyes. "I later learned the Santa Fe camp was where they sent leaders in the Japanese community, because they thought we were alien enemies. I was in that make-shift hospital for months, drifting in and out of consciousness. The doctor told me I probably would not walk again. But a kind nurse worked with me every day. When I began to feel stronger, I was released into one of the barracks."

Sachi tried to hold back more tears as she listened. Strange, that a part of her was so angry she wanted to scold him for not trying harder to find them. Yet, another part of her wanted to protect him.

It wasn't his fault.

But why? Why couldn't he find them after all that time?

"We had a funeral for you, Papa. I remember staring at the picture of you that Mama placed at the altar. I wished that picture would come alive, and when it didn't, I wished I could wake from the terrible dream. Why didn't you write to us, try to find us?"

For a split second, anger flashed in his eyes. "I did try. You don't think—" He took a long, deep breath, then continued. "As I recovered in the hospital, I heard bits and pieces of information about what was happening on the outside—that Japanese families were beginning to be *relocated* to assembly centers and internment camps. First, I tried to write to you at home, but my letters were returned. Next, I learned that families from Berkeley and the Bay Area had been sent to an assembly center at the Tanforan Racetrack. I wrote to you there, shuddering at the thought of you living in horse stalls. Months later, those letters were also returned."

Mama shook her head, then stopped, her eyes widening. "When our bus arrived at Tanforan, we stopped only briefly. Our driver got off the bus, but told us to stay in our seats. We watched him talking to a uniformed man. Whatever that man said, it upset our driver. He was arguing and waving his hands in the air. He returned to the bus, then slammed the door. It frightened us. We did not know what was going on. All he would tell us was that we were going on to Santa Anita. They never told us why."

Papa glared at his clenched hand, slowly pounding the table. "I told the authorities I could not find you—that all of my letters had been returned. They never bothered to explain that some families had been sent to Santa Anita instead. How difficult could it have been to find that information? Did they not keep records?"

Wiping tears from her eyes, Mama replied, "How difficult would it have been to send us another telegram? They simply did not care. All those years apart because of paperwork errors." She was quiet for a moment. "Why did you not try to find us in the other camps?"

"Sumiko, I did try. You must remember that for most of the last two years, I was in a Justice Department camp—maximum security. It was very difficult to get information about *anything*." His eyes watered as he smiled at Mama. "But it is all in the past. There is nothing more to be done about it. We are together, and soon, Nobu and Taro will be with us, too. It is all that matters now."

The rough, dry hands he placed over Mama's reminded Sachi of the cracked leather of the big chair where Papa used to read to her. It seemed like only yesterday, yet it seemed a thousand years ago. All that time missed. And why? Because some army man decided their bus should go on to another camp? Or because lazy people sitting behind desks couldn't take the time to give Papa the information he needed? Such fleeting decisions had changed lives forever.

She remembered sitting on Papa's lap in that old leather chair. Listening to his voice rumble in his chest as he read each word. The scent of incense in his clothes.

Of course, it was wonderful—magical—that Papa had returned. But she could never return to those times. Everything was different. She had been nine years old then. Now, she was almost twelve.

And Papa was so different now. His hair, gray above his ears. He had scars below his eye, above his lip. And he walked with a limp. Would it—could it—ever be the same again?

He caught her staring, and she turned away, afraid he would read her mind and be hurt by her thoughts. But when he smiled at her, deep lines in his face crinkled and in the darkness of his eyes, she again saw the twinkle she had loved years ago.

CHAPTER 65

Sachi

MAY 2, 1944

The day had finally arrived. Mama and Papa's twenty-second wedding anniversary! Sachi concentrated hard on designing the card she would give to them later that afternoon. Beneath a large "22" she'd written on a piece of paper, she began to draw a bride and groom.

What a wonderful idea Papa had—that he and Mama should have a reuniting ceremony. There was nothing more romantic than a wedding, and best of all, Papa had asked Sachi to "officiate" by reading the words he'd written for the big event.

At first, Mama thought the idea was silly, but Papa kept after her.

One night, Sachi had peeked from behind her curtain and saw Papa sitting at the edge of the bed. Mama was lying down next to him.

"Sumiko," he whispered. "We've been apart for two and a half years. It is no surprise that we feel awkward together. Perhaps it would help to reaffirm our commitment."

Mama exhaled. "I thought you were dead, Michio-san, and now you are alive. A commitment is a commitment. I do not need a new ceremony. It will simply take some time to adjust."

"Perhaps *I* need a ceremony," he'd replied.

A few days later, he had announced that their anniversary would be the perfect opportunity to celebrate and told Mama that he'd even written some verses for the event.

Sachi had tried to control her excitement, but couldn't help trying to persuade Mama. Ever since Papa first brought up the idea, a wedding was all she could think about.

She pleaded. "It'll be fun, Mama. Besides, how many kids get to see their own parents' wedding? Please?"

Mama had clucked her tongue and shook her head at them. "Oh, all right. What can I say to two against one?"

Sachi stood and clapped her hands. "Yippee!"

She added the finishing touches to the bride's gown on her card. On the inside, she wrote, "Happy Wedding to the best parents ever."

Mama was shuffling around in a corner of the room.

"What are you doing?" Sachi asked.

"I thought I would wear my red kimono for the ceremony. The very one I wore when Papa and I married"—she turned and smiled at Sachi—"the first time."

The red kimono?

An image of Jubie dancing in Mama's red kimono flashed and her heart began to race.

Calm down. Mama will never know.

She stared at the card, afraid to watch her mother pull the kimono from the box.

Mama gasped. "Oh, no!"

Papa looked up from his book. "What is it?"

Sachi squeezed her eyes shut.

"My kimono," Mama cried. "It has water spots on it."

"What?" Papa rose from his chair and walked to the corner. He looked up at the ceiling. "Perhaps we have a leak."

The rain! Sachi remembered it was raining the day Jubie had worn the kimono. But they were inside for the dance. Then she remembered she'd held her satchel over her head as she ran home in the rain—the satchel that held Mama's kimono.

Please, let there be a leak in the roof.

"No, I do not see a leak," Papa said.

Her stomach sank and she wished she could sneak out without them noticing.

Mama pointed at the box. "It could not be a leak. There are no watermarks on the outside of the box."

They both looked at Sachi.

She wanted to smile—do anything to act normal, not guilty. But she was frozen.

Papa spoke first. "Sachi-chan?"

"Yes?"

"Do you know anything about this?"

"No. How should I know how it got water spots?"

Mama lunged toward her. "Sachiko! I can tell when you are lying to me! This was my wedding kimono. What did you do?"

She started to cry and hid the card she'd drawn under the table. She didn't know the red kimono she had "borrowed" was Mama's wedding kimono. "I didn't know, Mama."

"So, you do know what happened?" Papa asked.

Oops. "No. But I didn't know it was Mama's wedding kimono."

Mama began to cry and looked at Papa. "You see! You see what I have had to put up with while you have been gone? She is lying. I know she is lying. I have not taken it out of its box since we moved from California. She must know what happened to it." She glared at Sachi. "How could you?" she cried, then ran out the door.

Papa stared at Sachi and waited for her to speak.

"Papa, I don't—"

"Sachiko!" he interrupted. "I have never known you to tell me a lie. Are you lying now?"

There was no way she could continue to get away with it. "Yes, Papa. I'm sorry."

"Sorry for what, your lie or ruining Mama's kimono?"

"Both."

"How did this happen, and why would you lie to us?"

She'd never seen such anger in his eyes.

How could she possibly explain everything so that he would understand? There was no way. No way. All she could do was blurt everything out.

"Papa, I have a friend. Her name is Jubie. Mama told me I couldn't play with her anymore, because she's . . . she's colored and we thought a colored boy killed you. The day we met, I found out her father was killed, too. All because he was a Negro. Don't you see, Papa? That meant we both lost our fathers because of the color of their skin." She put her head on the table and started to cry again.

Papa pulled out a chair and sat.

She lifted her head and continued. As she spoke, anger began to grow inside her. "I couldn't believe Mama said I couldn't play with Jubie anymore. I thought she was just as hateful as the people who put us in these camps, just because we looked like the Japanese who attacked Pearl Harbor. How could she think *they* were wrong, but tell me I couldn't play with Jubie? Did she think that was okay?" She took a deep breath and waited for Papa to speak.

But he only stared at her.

"Well, Papa? What do you say to that? Isn't it true that Mama should not have judged Jubie for the color of her skin?"

His face hardly moved as he spoke. "You still have not told me what happened to the kimono."

Didn't he hear what she said?

"Sachiko? The kimono?"

"Well, the day I borrowed it, Jubie and I were having a dance with her ma and Auntie Bess. I'd been teaching Jubie Japanese dances, and she had taught me the jitterbug. I didn't see the harm in borrowing the kimono for Jubie. I was very careful and thought Mama would never find out. But it was raining that day, and it must have soaked through the satchel that held it. I'm sorry, Papa. I'm sorry. Please don't be mad at Jubie. It's my fault, not hers. That's why I lied. I was afraid both you and Mama would tell me I couldn't play with her anymore. But she's my sister, Papa."

"What?"

"Oh. I forgot that part. That day Jubie danced in Mama's kimono. We became blood sisters. We decided Mama's kimono was magic, because that's the only way a Negro girl and a Japanese girl could become sisters."

A smile appeared for a tiny moment on Papa's face, then he grew stern and folded his arms. "Sachiko, Sachiko. First, it is never okay to lie. Second, you should not have borrowed your mother's kimono. Just because she would never find out does not make it okay. You were wrong on two accounts, and we must figure out how you can make it up to Mama."

Somehow, she knew there was a third thing he wanted to say, but he was quiet.

He unfolded his arms, leaned toward her and smiled again. "Third, I must tell you I am proud that you did not judge Jubie by the color of her skin. You are right. She no more had anything to do with my 'death' than we had anything to do with the bombing of Pearl Harbor."

Sachi stood up and exclaimed, "That's exactly what I thought, Papa!"

"But—"

Sachi interrupted. "I know, I know. Mama's kimono. But what can I do to let her know I'm sorry?" she asked.

"*Shikata ga nai, Sachi-chan. Shikata ga nai.*"

CHAPTER 66

Nobu

AUGUST 8, 1945

August 8, 1945

This camp is an angry place. My brothers—those I march with—are full of rage. Many talk of going to Japan. Some are defiant, even to the armed guards. They find themselves in lockup as a result. I wouldn't believe it if I didn't see it with my own eyes—American soldiers throwing American citizens in the stockade. Their crime? Showing their frustration for the way they've been treated—for being relocated and relocated and relocated for no reason, except that they look like the enemy.

Sure, I'm angry, too. About being forced to leave our homes, being relocated. About the loyalty questionnaire, the way we were treated for our honesty. About the years lost with Papa. How could so much time pass, thinking he was dead? Yet, he was alive. In another camp.

I know where to draw the line about showing that anger. I'll keep it inside, at least for now. Anything to keep from being imprisoned within a prison.

Ichiro burst through the door, gasping. "Have you heard?" He bent over his knees, panting and shaking his head.

Nobu looked up from his journal. Alarmed at Ichiro's terror, he leaped out of the chair. "Heard what?"

His friend darted around the room like a caged animal. "They bombed Japan! The fucking Americans dropped an atomic bomb on Hiroshima!"

A burst of nausea churned in Nobu, yet somewhere deep inside he refused to believe it. "No way. What are you talking about?"

"It's true. I heard it on the radio when I was walking by the guard tower just now." Ichiro pulled at his hair. "They said the city has been destroyed. Destroyed!" His voice cracked. "Shit, Nobu. Do you know how many people that would be? Thousands and thousands."

Nobu fell into the chair again and buried his face in his hands. What kind of a bomb could destroy a city, kill that many people?

He listened to Ichiro hiss and knew it was his way of holding back tears. But others in the camp did not suffer in silence. The surrounding barracks began to fill with a morbid chorus of moans and cries.

Women screamed.

"No! My mother was there!"

"My sister!"

"Not my parents!"

What about *his* grandparents? *Obaasan* and *Ojiisan* lived in Hiroshima. He'd only met them once, when he was just a little boy. He didn't know them well, but they were his grandparents. Mama's mother and father. Did Mama know about it yet?

"Let's go," Ichiro said.

"Where?"

"I don't care. Anywhere. But I can't sit around here." Ichiro grabbed his *hachimaki* off of his bedpost and tied it around his head. Hatred glowed in his eyes. "I'm going out to find the guys."

"I want to finish an entry here. I'll catch up with you later."

Ichiro sneered and waved him off. "Suit yourself."

Nobu reviewed what he'd written. *Sure, I'm angry, too.* Then, let new questions spill onto the page. Questions that fueled his fury.

All those people, dead. Maybe even Obaasan and Ojiisan. What were they doing when it happened? Working in the garden? Having a cup of tea together? Poor Mama, having to wonder every day about where Taro is and what he is doing. Now, she must also wonder if her parents are alive or dead.

All these years I've wondered what kind of government could throw its own citizens behind barbed wire out of fear. Now, I wonder what kind of government would use such a weapon to destroy hundreds of thousands of innocent lives?

CHAPTER 67

Sachi

AUGUST 9, 1945

A giant bomb dropped
In a land far away, yet
Close enough to hurt.

Of course, Sachi knew what a bomb was. But Papa said the one that fell on Hiroshima was an atomic bomb. She had never heard that word before—atomic. He wouldn't tell her much, but she knew something very bad had happened. If only he understood; wondering was much worse than knowing.

So many things told Sachi this was something too terrible to talk about—at least to children. But she wasn't a child! She was almost twelve. When would they trust her to understand grown-up things?

She would never forget what happened the day before, when she returned to camp from Jubie's house. As soon as she walked through the gate, she heard women crying inside the barracks. Men were walking up and down the barracks' rows with strange, sad looks on their faces. Sometimes they stopped and whispered in small groups; other times, they shuffled along in a daze.

That day, she'd walked into their dark apartment and found Mama and Papa sitting across from each other at the table. The only light in the room came from a candle flickering between them. Incense burned next to it. She noticed Papa wore the very same grim expression he had worn the day he heard about Japan attacking Pearl Harbor.

Mama's *o-juzu* beads made clicking noises as she tousled them in her hands. Her eyes red and puffy, she shook her head and whimpered. "*Okaasan. Otosan.*" Mama. Papa.

"What's wrong?" Sachi asked.

Papa took her hand and walked with her to her room behind the curtain. They sat on the bed. "Sachi, something terrible has happened. But, do not be afraid. We will be fine," he said, patting her leg.

"What, Papa? What happened?"

"It appears the United States dropped a bomb on Hiroshima."

She shrugged her shoulders, confused. "But don't they drop bombs all the time in a war?"

"This was a bomb that does even more damage. An atomic bomb was dropped on Hiroshima, where your obaasan and ojiisan live."

Sachi gasped. No wonder Mama was so sad.

"Many people had family in Hiroshima. If it is true, it will be a very long time before we know who might have been hurt there."

She had heard the others talking. Papa was protecting her. It wasn't only injuries that worried everyone. Though they always whispered when children were around, she heard the whispers about a city the size of San Francisco being completely destroyed. They said that hundreds of thousands might have died.

She imagined San Francisco completely destroyed and suddenly understood the horror of the atomic bomb.

The whispers turned to talk of Japan's surrender. She didn't know a lot about war, but if the United States was at war with Japan, wouldn't surrender be a good thing? Then why were the women crying? And why did some of the men look so angry?

If the war was over, wouldn't everyone get to go home, at last?

That night, she tossed and turned, trying to block out the sound of Mama's crying. She couldn't imagine what it was like for Mama to have her parents living so far away and not know if they were hurt or okay. Dead or alive. She stared at the ceiling, wishing there was something she could say to make her mother feel better, to make her stop crying.

The night turned even darker when Mama said the most dreadful thing of all. "Michio-san, I must return to Japan."

CHAPTER 68

Sachi

NOVEMBER 2, 1945

Sachi pulled the pillow over her head and shut her eyes. Why did Mama and Papa have to argue all the time? That day Papa arrived from Jerome—the day she learned he was alive—she thought nothing in the world would ever be wrong again.

Didn't Mama feel the same way? She was always angry or crying, especially after she decided to return to Japan.

Poor Papa. Only a few months after returning, everyone is mad at him.

Mama cried. "But I do not want you and Sachi to stay in Arkansas!"

Pulling the pillow tighter around her ears, Sachi curled into a ball under the covers and wished her stomachache would go away.

Papa spoke softly. "Sumiko-san, listen to me. There is nothing left for us to return to in California. Besides, since you have decided you must return to Japan, what does it matter to you if we stay here or return to California?"

"When I return to Japan . . ." Mama's voice broke, " . . . if I find that my mother and father did not survive the bombing, I will come back to America. But I do not want to come back to Arkansas." She blew her nose.

Sachi wasn't sure what she hated more, the sound of Mama crying, or knowing poor Papa was only trying to do what he thought best.

"Sumiko. Do you understand we are still hated in California? I refuse to expose my family to that. Perhaps in a few years, when things have settled—"

Mama whined. "A few years?"

"Please, Sumiko. You will wake Sachiko."

The apartment quieted, except for Mama's occasional sniffling. Sachi threw back the covers and tiptoed to the curtain that separated her corner from Mama and Papa. She peeked through it into the splinter of light.

Her parents sat on the bed and stared at the floor, their faces droopy and sad.

"I have found a job," Papa said. "A few families have decided to stay and work on a plantation near Little Rock."

Mama's back straightened. Her eyes widened. "You are going to be farmer? But you're a banker. What do you know of farming?"

Even Sachi had a hard time picturing her father as a farmer. All her life he'd worked in a bank. She didn't like the thought of him working in the hot sun all day.

Papa raised his voice. "What do you think I did while I was at Jerome? Bank? No. I farmed. Plowed the ground. Planted seeds. Harvested crops." He glared at Mama. "What kind of job do you think I could get in California right now?"

She stared at him with a look in her eyes Sachi knew too well. Defeat. She'd felt it herself, when Nobu left for Tule Lake and told her she couldn't come with him.

"So there is nothing more to be said? Then, I am going to bed." Mama lay down and turned to face the wall.

Papa wiped his eyes. Running his hand through his hair, he shuffled toward Sachi's curtain.

Panic shot through her and she jumped back into bed and pulled the covers up, pretending to be asleep. But her heart beat so hard and loud she was sure Papa would hear it.

When he drew the curtain, light cast over her eyelids. The warmth of Papa's hand hovered before he touched her hair and brushed it out of her face. Her heart pounded even harder as she wondered if she should open her eyes.

No. What would she say?

"Sweet dreams, Sachi-chan," he whispered, then pulled the curtain shut and turned off the light.

In the big, dark silence, she closed her eyes. Tears burned.

Sweet dreams? How could they be?

CHAPTER 69

Nobu

NOVEMBER 10, 1945

"Here's your mail," Ichiro said, tossing a letter onto the table in front of Nobu.

As soon as Nobu saw it was from Papa, he tore it open. A year and a half since Papa had shown up alive in Rohwer, and still, he couldn't believe it. He hadn't seen Papa yet, though he wondered about him constantly. What did he look like? Had he changed in all the years since Nobu had seen him? Would Papa think Nobu had changed?

He unfolded the letter and devoured the words like a man so hungry he hardly takes time to taste the food placed in front of him.

Staying in Arkansas. He had to read it again. *Staying in Arkansas.* Surely that's not what Papa meant.

Worse, was reading what Papa said next. *Mama is returning to Japan.* How could that be? Why? And how could Papa let her do that?

I cannot stop her. She still has not heard from her parents and says she must return to Japan to find out what happened. I am torn. I do not want to let Mama go alone, yet I cannot go with her. I must stay for you, Sachi, and Taro. You are Americans. I cannot expect you to go to Japan.

He crumpled the letter and threw it across the room.

"What's up?" Ichiro asked.

"My mother is returning to Japan and my father has decided to stay in Arkansas. My family will be separated, even after we leave camp."

"Your mother is wise to return to Japan—"

"Hey! It's not for the same reason you're going. Her parents lived in Hiroshima. She hasn't heard from them since the bombing."

"As far as I'm concerned, the reason doesn't matter. There will be nothing for us here. But, why is your father staying in Arkansas of all places?"

Nobu's leg started bouncing up and down—a bad habit he'd picked up from Ichiro. He took a deep breath, trying to calm himself. "He doesn't believe the hatred toward the Japanese has changed in California. And he doesn't think he can get a job here." Unable to sit still, Nobu had to get up. He paced around the table, stooped to pick up the letter, then read it to Ichiro.

The owner of a cotton plantation near Little Rock has asked me to be his foreman. I have accepted his offer, Nobu. Sachi can attend school in Little Rock. I would like for you to come back and work with me. Perhaps when Taro returns, he will come, too. It has been far too long since you children have all been together.

Ichiro slapped Nobu's back. "Come to Japan with me then. Your mother would be happy to have you there."

The suggestion punched Nobu in the gut and the battle in his head began again. Japan? Maybe. What did he owe America, anyway? He was miserable and disappointed in his country. So why the reluctance to leave? He was born an American. It was all he knew. He was not Japanese, and knew so little of the country that attacked Pearl Harbor.

Maybe he only wanted to stay because he was afraid. He could barely admit to *himself* that he might be such a chicken shit he'd stay in a country he hated. How could he admit it to Ichiro?

So what about Arkansas? Papa? No. He couldn't bear the thought of returning to that place.

He walked to the window and watched dust swirl in the wind. "I'm staying in California. I'll start over here if I have to. There's nothing for me in Arkansas or Japan."

"Fine. Have it your way. I'm leaving for drills," Ichiro said, tying a *hachimaki* around his forehead. "You coming?"

"You go ahead. I need to reply to my father. I'll catch up with you later."

Ichiro grabbed his jacket off the chair. "Right. See you later," he said, then rushed out the door.

For several minutes, Nobu sat in the empty apartment. He had to reply to Papa, but didn't know what to say. He tore a sheet of paper from a notebook, wishing to empty his mind of thoughts that flooded it. There was so much he wanted to say, but he knew to temper his words.

He stared at the white void for several minutes before beginning to write.

November 10, 1945

Dear Papa,

I received your letter today. It still feels strange to hold something from you in my hand. Thinking you were dead for so long, sometimes I'm afraid I'll wake to find your return has all been a dream.

What next? Chewing on his pencil, he wondered if he should let Papa know how unhappy he was to read the plans he'd written about. Should he show respect and accept it? That didn't make sense if in the end, he planned to tell Papa he refused to join him there to become a farmer. He placed his pencil on the page again.

Papa, it surprised me that you and Mama have made separate plans. I understand that you are torn, but it's hard for me to believe Mama is returning to Japan and you have decided to stay in Arkansas. It never entered my mind that you, Mama, and Sachi would not return to California.

Struggling with how to tell Papa about his plans to stay in California, he walked to the window again and stared outside. His No-No brothers approached from the far end of the barrack row, again marching in formation. Their shouting pulsed through him.

Wah-shoi! Wah-shoi!

He called himself *koshinuke*—coward. Why couldn't he stand up to Papa for once?

Slamming into the chair again, he let anger pump courage through his hand, to his pencil and onto paper.

After I leave Tule Lake, I will stay in California. I had hoped to see you after my release, but there are only bad memories for me in Arkansas. I understand Mama wanting to return to Japan to find her parents, but I can't understand your decision to remain in Arkansas rather than return to California to fight for the life we had before the war.

Snatching the crumpled letter off the table, Nobu read Papa's closing words.

Mama is not happy with my decision to stay, and I suspect you will not be either, my son. But shikata ga nai. *It cannot be helped. I will do what I must do.*

Nobu bit his lip and pounded his fist on the table. He grabbed the pencil and continued his letter.

Papa, you may say shikata ga nai, but I believe everything in our lives can be helped. We can—we must—control our own destinies. Never again will I be carried by a stream that flows in a direction I do not choose to go. Instead, I will fight, swim upstream if I must. To hell with those in California who still hate us. Shikata ga nai? No. That is the coward's way.

Your son,

Nobu

Regret threatened to make him tear the letter to pieces. Perhaps he shouldn't have been so harsh. Papa was only doing what he believed to be best for his family.

Wah-shoi! Wah-shoi! The No-No Boys of Tule Lake marched past his doorway.

He scribbled Papa's address on the envelope, then grabbed his coat, and ran out the door, ready to join the formation.

Slamming the door behind him, he called, "Wait up! I'm coming."

CHAPTER 70

Sachi

NOVEMBER 14, 1945

"Sachiko, come here, please," Mama called from the living room.

Sachi rolled her eyes. What now? She closed the book she'd been reading and tossed it on the bed. "I'm coming." She huffed and threw aside the curtain that divided her room.

Her mother sat at the table, staring at the *o-juzu* beads she held in her hands. Everything about her—sad eyes framed by dark circles, drooped shoulders—told Sachi this was not a conversation she wanted to have.

"Yes?" Sachi replied and pulled out a chair.

Mama looked up from her beads and stared at her for a moment, then brought the hand that held the *o-juzu* to touch Sachi's cheek.

Mama's affection felt unfamiliar. Sachi had the urge to back away and to cry. She knew what Mama was going to say. She was going to tell Sachi about going to Japan. What if she insisted Sachi go with her? Fear surged as she thought of a thousand excuses not to go. How could she tell Mama she didn't want to—wouldn't go with her? She wanted to stay in Arkansas with Papa.

But how could she not want to be with her own mother?

"This is a very small apartment," Mama said. "The only wall separating your room from this one is a thin curtain. So perhaps you already know what I am going to tell you." She ran her hand over Sachi's hair. "It may be difficult for you to hear this, Sachi-chan, but I think you are old enough to understand these things now."

Old enough? Words she had longed to hear. She smiled, and the tear she had fought fell down her cheek.

Mama wiped it away. "Do you disagree?"

"No, I *want* to know. I'm old enough to understand, whatever it is." She felt a little afraid. But wondering about something was worse than knowing the truth.

"Good." Mama twisted the beads in her hands.

The room was quiet. Sachi listened for sounds to fill the uncomfortable silence: wind rattling the window panes; muffled sounds from the family next door. She waited for Mama's next words. She didn't want to stare, afraid it might make Mama too nervous to continue, so she scanned the room for something else to look at. Papa's slippers under the bed. His folded newspaper on the nightstand.

"You never met my parents, your *ojiisan* and *obaasan*. You have only seen pictures and letters from them. I am very sorry about that. Especially now."

Trying to settle the leg that refused to hold still, Sachi shifted and sat on it. "I'm sorry, Mama. I heard people talking about the bombings in Hiroshima and Nagasaki." She looked down at her lap, wanting so terribly to touch Mama's hand, but not able to bring herself to do it. "I'm sorry you don't know how they are." She looked up and smiled. "But sometimes, no news is good news, right?"

Mama smiled slightly, but her eyes watered. "Perhaps. But I think wondering is worse than knowing what really happened."

Sachi couldn't believe it. Without hesitation, she touched her mother's hand. "I just thought that very thing."

"Then, you will understand that I must return to Japan to find out."

Sachi cringed and sat back in her chair, waiting for the words she dreaded.

Please don't ask me to come with you.

Mama covered her face with her hands. When she finally placed them on her lap, her eyes were red. She spoke quickly. "I have missed my mother and father for so many years, Sachi-chan. I love your papa. He has been a good husband and a good father. But as a very young woman, I was not ready to leave Japan. I have tried to adjust to America all of these years, but it is not my home." She put her hand in her pocket and pulled a photograph out. "I carry this with me always," she said, holding it for Sachi to see.

Sachi couldn't believe the girl she saw standing between two adults. "Is that you with your parents? You look just like me."

"Yes. When this photograph was taken, I was sixteen—only four years older than you are—and already promised to your papa in marriage."

She tried to imagine Mama and Papa choosing who she would marry. She didn't know what to say, except to ask, "How did you feel about that?"

"In the years of my courtship with Papa, I kept hoping my parents would change their minds. When the time came to meet your father, I did not want to move to America. To leave all of my friends. To leave Inaba-san—" Mama stopped abruptly and covered her mouth. She rose from her chair and hurried to the window.

"Who was Inaba-san?"

"Nothing. Nobody. I am only trying to explain to you that I had a life in Japan. I did not want to leave."

Sachi stared at the picture. *Obaasan* reminded her of Mama. Watching her mother as she stared out the window, Sachi wondered if she would look like her someday.

Mama spoke again, her voice trembling. "I am sorry I forced you to learn Japanese. To learn to play the *o-koto*. To dance Japanese dances." She wiped tears from her face before turning to Sachi. "Can you understand that it was my way of holding on to Japan?"

Sachi remembered all the times she didn't want to practice, how she thought her mother was mean for making her do it. How angry she felt all those times she wanted to do something else instead. But, she had to admit—at least it was better than her parents telling her who she had to marry.

Mama returned to the chair and clutched its back. Sachi could hardly stand the imploring look in her eyes, and she searched her heart for words of comfort, words other than, "I will go with you."

The fear of what would come from Mama's mouth bound Sachi's heart. She wobbled back and forth on the uneven legs of the chair.

"When we thought Papa died, I missed my home even more. I cannot tell you how much I wanted to be with my parents, to run away from all of the hatred Americans hold toward the Japanese. Every night, I dreamed of going home."

All those nights her mother lay weeping, was it for Papa? Or, was it for Japan, perhaps even someone named . . . Inaba-san? Queasiness rolled in her stomach.

Mama sat again. "Then, when they put us in these camps where we were forced to live like prisoners behind barbed wire, I longed for Japan even more. I could not talk to anybody about it. I was too afraid of being called a traitor. Yet, I felt angry. Why should missing my home make me disloyal to America?" She stared at Sachi, as if waiting for an answer.

"I don't know. Sometimes, I'm homesick, too. But then, I tell myself home is wherever my family is." Her heart stopped. *So stupid to say that!* She'd given Mama the perfect opening to ask her to come to Japan.

Mama straightened with a deep breath.

Sachi felt sick. Her throat tightened, prepared to give Mama an answer she wouldn't want to hear. Thoughts of losing Papa again—of leaving Jubie—spun in her head.

The *o-juzu* beads clicked faster as Mama moved them through her fingers. "Sachi-chan."

Why wouldn't Mama look at her? Sachi's heart pounded harder. Would Mama *force* her to go to Japan? Where was Papa? She needed his help.

Mama stopped twisting her beads, then whispered, "I am so sorry . . . I must leave you behind."

Feeling the look of relief on her face, Sachi was happy Mama wouldn't look at her. She forced a solemn face, not wanting to let her mother see her relief.

"I have already spoken to Papa about it, and of course, he wants you to stay with him. Do you understand that I cannot take you with me? Do you see that I have no idea what the conditions in Japan will be like?"

"Yes, Mama."

JAN MORRILL

"But most of all, Sachi-chan, I know that taking you from America would be as hard for you as it was for me to leave Japan. This is your home. You are an American."

Joy. Sadness. Love. Pride. Longing. How could all of these feelings be mixed up together? She felt she might explode with the fullness of it. No longer afraid, she leaped up to hug Mama.

Mama held her, and Sachi breathed in the scent of cedar in her mother's clothes, tasted salt in the tears still on her cheek. Mama pulled her closer—so close Sachi could hear the rapid flutter of Mama's heart begin to calm.

Then Sachi felt it, too. *Gaman*. Endurance. Resolve. No matter what the future held, everything was going to be okay.

CHAPTER 71

Sachi

NOVEMBER 19, 1945

A porcelain mask
Once broken, but now removed
My true face revealed

Sachi found it strange, even upsetting. Why did she hesitate to get on the bus that would take her and Papa to Little Rock? It wasn't like they were being taken to a place unknown, like when they left California. This time, they would not be imprisoned behind barbed wire or made to live in tar paper barracks. Papa had shown her pictures of where they would live on the plantation where he had found work. It was so much nicer than the tiny spaces she'd lived in for the last four years. And she'd finally have her own bedroom again.

No more barbed wire fences. No more guards with guns. No more having to sign out when she left camp. They were free. Why then, didn't she feel happy?

She stood by the gate, watching the men, women, and children of the camp file out, carrying suitcases and boxes. Some would be boarding the train that waited down the road. Soon, Mama would be one of the passengers on that train. She would take the long ride back to California, but it would be only the first part of her journey. Next, she would take a ship back to Japan.

She felt sad, imagining Mama alone as she searched for her parents. And even with the frustration she felt toward Mama at times, it was hard for Sachi to imagine life without her.

A bus engine started up and rumbled. Only a few Japanese would board the buses, to be taken to places not so far away, yet a world away.

Strange that there were more tears than smiles.

A cold wind blew. It howled through the rows of barracks, like the last breath of a camp that had once been alive with Japanese. A hat tumbled back inside the gate. A man turned and paused, as if deciding to chase it, but instead, walked to the train.

Mama and Papa faced each other and whispered quietly. Sachi couldn't hear what they were saying, but she could read every little sentiment their eyes expressed to each other.

I am sorry to be leaving you. Please take care of yourself. Take care of our children.

I will miss you.

You will stay in my heart.

She wanted to be near Mama, too, and her throat tightened. What would it be like not to see her every day? Remembering how Mama had changed when Papa wasn't around, she wondered if Papa might change without Mama.

Shaking off the thoughts that made her sad, she walked to the fence post where she had been stacking rocks the day she'd first talked to Jubie. It seemed like another life. A life when Papa was dead. A life when she thought she had to look the same as everyone else to fit it. A life before she knew a Japanese girl and a colored girl could be sisters.

Then, she smiled. No matter what happened in the weeks and months to come, her new life was a better life.

Where was Jubie, anyway? She promised to be there before the buses left, so Sachi wasn't too worried. Still, a tiny fear nagged at her. What if something held Jubie up and kept them from saying goodbye?

Stones that had fallen lay scattered around the fence. She knelt to gather several and began to stack them again.

Breathe.

But what if Jubie doesn't come in time?

She stacked another.

Stay calm.

Then another.

"Hi, Sach," Jubie whispered.

Her hushed greeting made Sachi's stomach tickle. It wasn't like Jubie to be quiet. But she pushed her sadness away and smiled. "I was beginning to think you weren't going to make it."

"I had to get something." Jubie held up a paper sack with a bow tied around it. "This is for you."

Sachi's eyes widened with excitement as Jubie gave her the bag. But within seconds, her excitement faded. She had nothing for Jubie.

"Go on! Open it!"

But I don't have anything for you. The words tried to barge through Sachi's lips, but she held them back, struggling to think of something to give to her sister. "Thanks, Jubie," she said and removed the bow, then opened the bag.

Tears burned in Sachi's eyes as she smiled and pulled Mrs. Franklin's red poofy skirt from the bag.

Jubie smiled, too. "You like it?"

"I love it! But, it's your ma's."

"She say nobody do the jitterbug in that skirt the way you do it. So she say I could give it to you. 'Sides, that's the skirt you wore the day we became sisters."

Sachi grabbed her sister and squeezed tight. "I love it, Jubie. I love you," she whispered.

What can I give her?

At last, she knew. "I have something for you, too! Wait here," she said, before turning to run to her suitcase.

She grabbed the doll that rested against it, then hurried back to Jubie.

"Sachi-chan, wait!" called Mama.

She rolled her eyes and turned back. "Yes?"

"I see that Jubie gave you that red skirt." She opened her suitcase. "I would like for you to give this to Jubie . . . from me," she said.

The red kimono?

"Mama? Really?"

Mama held the neatly folded kimono toward Sachi. "So you and Jubie will always have its magic."

She couldn't believe it and didn't know if she was happier because it meant her mother forgave her, or because she accepted Jubie. She bowed to her mother as she accepted the kimono. "Thank you, Mama." Then, swelling with joy, she wrapped her arms around her mother. "It's the best gift ever!" she said.

Papa checked his watch. "Sachi-chan, you will need to hurry. It is almost time to get on the bus."

"Okay, Papa. I'll just be a minute."

A minute. Then, she would have to say goodbye.

She hid the kimono behind her as she approached Jubie.

"Whatcha got?" Jubie asked and tried to peek.

Sachi drew the kimono from behind her with great drama. "This is for you. It's from Mama and me."

Thrill spread over Jubie's face like a sunrise, from her wide eyes to her bright smile. "Oh, my Lord!" She ran her hand over the red, splotched silk. "Your mama's kimono!"

"Mama said it's so we could keep our magic."

Jubie stared at her, quiet and still. This time, Sachi didn't mind her quiet. She knew what Jubie was thinking without a single word.

Your mama accepts me.

"Sachi-chan," Papa called. "We must go now."

Her heart sank. "I guess I have to get on the bus." There were still a thousand things left to say, yet doing so would release a flood of tears. A good, long hug would have to do.

"It's okay," Jubie whispered. "You go on and cry. I be crying, too." She drew away from Sachi and looked her in the eyes. "But you know what? Like I keep telling you. We be sisters forever. Especially with this kimono!" She smiled that crooked smile Sachi would always remember. "I'll write you ever day. And guess what? Ma told me we'd find a way to come up and visit you sometime real soon. It ain't so far away. Least it ain't California."

The stones lying on the ground around them blurred through Sachi's tears. She knelt and picked one up. "Remember when we first met, I told you what Papa said about stacking rocks? That it was a good way to take my mind off things that bother me?"

"Yeah."

"Want to help me put this one on top? Maybe we won't feel so sad."

"Sure. I'll help." She knelt beside her and placed her hand on Sachi's. Together they let the rock hover.

A deep breath.

They let it touch the stone below it.

Another deep breath.

And together, they gently let go.

THE END

SUGGESTED READING AND RESOURCES

Non-fiction

Inada, Lawon Fusao, ed. *Only What We Could Carry: The Japanese American Internment Experience*. Berkeley: Heyday Books, 2000.

Rohwer Outpost (Rohwer Internment Camp, Arkansas). 1942–1945.

Takei, George. *To the Stars: The Autobiography of George Takei, Star Trek's Mr. Sulu*. New York: Simon and Schuster, 1994.

Tunnel, Michael O., and George W. Chilcoat. *The Children of Topaz: The Story of a Japanese-American Internment Camp*. New York: Holiday House, 1996.

Uchida, Yoshiko. *Desert Exile: The Uprooting of a Japanese-American Family*. Seattle: University of Washington Press, 1982.

Fiction

Dallas, Sandra. *Tallgrass*. New York: St. Martin's Press, 2007.

Guterson, David. *Snow Falling on Cedars*. New York: Harcourt Brace & Company, 1994.

Houston, Jeanne Wakatsuki, and James D. Houston. *Farewell to Manzanar*. Boston: Houghton Mifflin Company, 1973.

Schiffer, Vivienne. *Camp Nine*, Fayetteville: The University of Arkansas Press, 2011.

Documentary

Time of Fear, directed by Sue Williams. Perf. George Takei. (PBS Home Video, 2005), DVD.

Websites

The Butler Center for Arkansas Studies, www.butlercenter.org/news/rohwer-collection.html.

Densho: The Japanese American Legacy Project, www.densho.org.

Heart Mountain Wyoming Foundation, www.heartmountain.org.

The Japanese American National Museum, www.janm.org.

JAN MORRILL was born and (mostly) raised in California. Her mother, a Buddhist Japanese American, was an internee during World War II. Her father, a Southern Baptist redhead of Irish descent, retired from the Air Force. Many of her stories reflect memories of growing up in a multicultural, multi-religious, multi-political environment. An artist as well as a writer, Jan is currently working on the sequel to *The Red Kimono*. Visit her at www.janmorrill.com.